MW01146009

THE HOME FOR
WAYWARD CLOCKS

A Novel By
Kathie Giorgio

MINT HILL BOOKS
MAIN STREET RAG PUBLISHING COMPANY
CHARLOTTE, NORTH CAROLINA

Copyright © 2011, Kathie Giorgio

Cover image: Watercolor and ink drawing by Christopher T. Werkman
Cover photographed by Ron Wimmer of Ron Wimmer Photography
Author image by Ron Wimmer of Ron Wimmer Photography

Acknowledgments:

These chapters appeared in different form in the following magazines:

Jabberwock Review: "A Brief Battle"
Karamu: "Matching"
Lady Jane Miscellany: "A Brief Battle"
Oyez Review: "Seconds"
The Pedestal: "Ticking"
Thema: "What Counts"

"Marriage in Orange" was previously published in the Main Street Rag short fiction anthology, *A La Carte: Short Stories That Stir The Foodie In All Of Us.*

Library of Congress Control Number: 2010933347

ISBN: 978-1-59948-255-2

Produced in the United States of America

Mint Hill Books
Main Street Rag Publishing Company
PO Box 690100
Charlotte, NC 28227-7001
www.MainStreetRag.com

This novel is dedicated to, of course, the usual group of suspects: husband Michael, kids Christopher, Andy, Katie and Olivia. If I was a player on Wheel of Fortune, I would have to gush, "I have a tremendous husband and four wonderful children!" But I would actually be telling the truth.

It's also dedicated to the students and faculty and friends of my studio, AllWriters' Workplace & Workshop. Your continued faith and belief in me, as a writer and as an instructor, keeps me going.

A special hug to student and best bud, Christopher Werkman, the artist who created the beautiful cover. You painted from my words, and James came to life.

And thank you to Main Street Rag Publishing Company for giving me this opportunity.

Lots of love and gratitude to everyone. Thank you.

Contents

PROLOGUE:

TICKING

The baby was crying again and Helena paced the floor. The thing just never shut up, never left her alone. It didn't matter if she gave him breast or bottle, picked him up or put him down, played a music box or left him in silence, he cried and cried and cried. She knew he slept sometimes, she knew it. She watched him. But even then, even when he breathed deep in sleep and his eyelids fluttered above flushed cheeks, she still heard his piercing voice shriek on, flying into all her corners and curves of silence.

Now she turned away, leaving the baby alone again in his room. She called her husband at work. "He won't stop," she said immediately after his hello. "I'm going to kill him, I swear I'm going to kill him." Then she slammed the phone down.

Returning to the nursery, she stared down at the baby, his eyes squeezed shut, his mouth a dark echoing oval. A cave, she thought. His mouth is a cave and I'm going to fall in and be lost forever. He wants to swallow me whole. "Shut up!" she shouted.

The baby gasped and stopped, closing his mouth and opening his eyes. He looked at her, he looked straight at her, and then he raised his arms and wailed again.

"Please, please," she said. "Please, please. Just be quiet for a little while, just ten minutes, just five." She rocked his cradle, back and forth, fast then slow, but he screamed just the same. He waved his arms and finally, she snatched him up and squeezed him tightly. He quivered and curled against her, pressing his hot damp face into her neck. She felt his heat spread like a river through her body and her own skin began to moisten.

Carrying him, she paced around the room. "Please, please," she said over and over. "Please, please." She felt his body relax and after a while, she tugged him away from her neck to see if he was sleeping.

He wasn't. He stared at her, not blinking.

Quickly, she put him back in his cradle. The corners of his mouth turned up and he seemed to smile. For that moment and that moment alone, she felt her lips reflex and she smiled back at him.

Then she stepped away and immediately, he began to cry again. It started out low, but it built up quickly and soon his voice took solid shape, stuffing itself through doorways, crashing against windows, layering itself on the floor like wave after wave of briny thick water. His hands and feet beat furiously at the bars of the cradle and his head whipped from the left to the right.

"Stop it!" she screamed. Running back across the room, tearing through his voice, she put her face against his. "Stop it! Stop it! Stop it!" Then she took his blanket, his stuffed bear, the little gift pillow with his birth date and weight and length embroidered on it and stacked them all up on his face. If enough was there, it would muffle his cries. Then she flew out of the nursery to the living room and sat on the couch. She covered her ears with her hands and she rocked.

She remembered the pregnancy, the rolling contortion of her body, the pressure of those horrible first and last kicks. Her husband crowed with delight, but she cried at the way her stomach heaved, the way her skin molded around the baby's knee or elbow or head. She knew that he writhed and howled inside her, his mouth perpetually wide, sounds thrashing through fluid, disturbing her sleep, disturbing her thoughts. She dreamed of babies with voices like foghorns, factory whistles and firetruck sirens. She woke to find her belly surging, toppling her in the bed. Then came the labor and the pain that left her hearing only her own voice, bent out of shape from screaming. The pain promised more to come and it did, a wet, blotchy baby against her chest, blood smeared on his face and her breasts, and he opened his mouth and screeched.

Now a shadow passed by and Helena felt a breeze on her cheek. Looking up, she saw her husband's back as he ran into the nursery. She took her hands from her ears and realized it was quiet. She held her breath. Then, as big wails flooded the room, she curled herself into a ball. Her husband appeared in the doorway, holding the baby. "He was turning blue!" he yelled and the baby bawled louder. "You could've killed him!"

"I said I was going to," she whispered, but she turned away, her fingers shaking. She heard her husband go back to the nursery, and then there was his off-tune tenor as he changed the baby's diaper.

"Oh, where have you been, Jamie boy, Jamie boy," he sang. "Oh, where have you been, charming James?"

That soft voice, that used to sing to her. That called her Helena baby, Helena sweetheart, come to bed, Helena girl. Come to bed. And she did and he kept calling her back and then she grew large and soon there was no more quiet, no more silence. Only noise and more noise.

"Jamie crack corn and I don't care," her husband sang. The baby was quiet, except for the hiccups.

Yet she could still hear him screaming. It was there behind her husband's soft croon, in the hollow echo of the baby's wet belches. Helena surged to her feet and ran from the house.

She bathed in the moonlight. She shivered just a little, but the soft silver kept her warm, a light blanket of silence. There was no noise on top of the hill. She didn't even hear any birds. Down below, lights sparked like fire in her house and her husband's shadow moved from window to window. There was a dark curve on his shoulder and she knew it was the baby.

Alone on the hill, she shuddered.

The house fell dark. Then the porch light blinked on and the front door opened and she could see her husband, looking out, looking for her. She sat still in the moonlight, hiding in the gleam, knowing the silver light would mask her white-blonde hair, her pale skin.

"Helena!" he called. "Helena baby, come home! C'mon, darlin'! I'm sorry, I know you didn't mean it! It was an accident!"

She sat still. Soon, he went inside. The porch light died.

Watching the moonlight, Helena waited until her eyes wanted to close and the grass grew wet against her thighs. Then she went down the hill and thought about hiding in the root cellar, hiding in the dark and the damp where nobody ever went. Never going inside her house again. Never touching that hot, clammy head again. Never hearing that voice. But her husband returned to the front door. "Helena baby," he said. "It's late, sweetheart. Come to bed."

So she did. Their lovemaking was silent and tender, but she was braced, feeling the baby in the next room, knowing he was waiting, knowing he would bust in just when she was at fever pitch.

And he did, his voice ripping her husband away from her skin like a rent piece of cloth. He ran naked to the nursery and began to sing.

"Oh, baby love, my baby love..."

She crawled under the damp sheets and cried.

The next day was the same. And the next. The baby cried and she picked him up. He cried and she put him down. She left him in his room for hours and he keened while she sat on the floor in the corner of the kitchen. She rocked, banging the back of her head against the cabinet. She stopped eating and drinking and there was no sleep, even when her husband took over in the middle of the night. That voice ricocheted around the house and inside her head.

On a mid-morning when she stood in a nightshirt she'd worn for a week, never finding a moment to take it off, never finding a moment for a shower, the baby lifted his head from her neck and bellowed right in her ear. The sound severed her spine and she went limp, slumping to the floor. But her arms remained stiff. She held the baby straight out, he flailed between her fingers. And then she began to shake him.

She saw the top of his hair, the bottom of his chin, a flash of white forehead and throat. He kept crying, but the sound became rubbery, then flimsy, going faint and loud with each thrust forward, pull back. And then he stopped altogether.

She held him still and for a moment, they both trembled. Then he tucked his head, drew his legs up, and curled into a ball around her hands. She rolled him on the floor, then smacked her forehead against her knees and cried.

When she was spent, there was one solid minute of silence. She raised her head, basked in it, and felt her shoulders relax. She felt hungry, but she was too tired to get up.

Then the baby uncurled and began to scream. Stretching out his arm, he batted her leg, his fingers wide and extended. She covered her ears and ran out of the house. But his barrage followed her.

Helena had to do something. Outside, she tripped over the root cellar doors and while she rubbed her toes, she remembered wanting to hide down there, in the dark and the damp and the quiet.

The dark, the damp, the quiet.

The quiet.

She straightened. Returning to the house, she stepped lightly over the crying baby and went to rummage in the pantry. She found the cardboard box her husband brought home last week, filled with groceries from the store. Going to the nursery, she took the blanket from the cradle and tossed it into the box. In the kitchen, the baby's sobs softened to a whimper and she stopped for a moment, trying to think what it reminded her of.

She snapped her fingers. A puppy. He sounded just like the puppy her little brother got when he was seven. And she remembered what her brother tried to keep the puppy quiet, to keep him company. It reminds him of his mother's heartbeat, her brother said. It hadn't worked, but maybe it would now. Maybe it would here.

She hated that puppy. It cried all night, keeping the whole family up. Her brother cried too, when it died. When she killed it. When she wrung its soft neck. She never told anybody, but she helped her brother bury it out behind the house, marking the grave with a lopsided cross he made himself out of wooden clothespins.

Going into the bedroom, she dug into the back of the closet until she found a wind-up alarm clock, a gift from her mother that she never used. It always ticked too loudly, shredding the blanket of dark silence that always lulled her to sleep.. She threw it in the box, then went out to the kitchen to collect the baby.

When he saw her, he screamed, holding his hands out to her. She picked him up by the collar of his sleeper, dangling him like it was the scruff of his neck. She dropped him in the box, then carried everything outside.

By the root cellar double doors, she had to put it all down. The doors needed both hands for opening, tugging them up and then laying them to the side. The sunlight fell in on cement steps. Going down, she smelled the damp and felt the dark close in. Like a womb, she thought. He'll be fine down here.

She set the box in a far corner, then arranged the baby on his back. His shriek went up to a strident pitch and his hands turned into little fists, beating at the air. She covered him with the blanket, then wound the alarm clock and placed it by his head. The ticking sounded loud and hollow and the baby paused for just a second, held his breath, looked at the clock, then began to cry again.

She shrugged, walking away and closing the double doors. It didn't matter if the clock worked or not; she wouldn't hear him anymore. She would sleep for a few hours, then go down to feed him. She slid a heavy branch through the door latches, telling herself it was to keep someone from breaking in, when she knew it was so he wouldn't break out. He couldn't, she knew that, not yet. But babies grow; she wasn't sure how fast.

In the house, the sun suddenly seemed brighter. She made herself a ham and cheese sandwich and sat down at the table, eating with her eyes closed. She drank a whole glass of cold milk. Then she went into the living room where the sun flowed through a window, splashing a big square patch on the floor. She smiled and curled into the warmth like a cat. In a moment, she was asleep.

When her husband came home, Helena met him at the door. Putting the bawling baby into his arms, she said, "Do something with him. I'm going out for a while."

As she moved past, her husband touched her shoulder. "Are you okay?" he asked. "You didn't call all day."

"I'm fine," she said. She flinched when the baby cried louder.

Her husband kissed the back of the baby's neck. "I told you it would get better. I told you you could do it."

Helena shrugged and smiled and her husband smiled back. She knew they could both be happy again. All afternoon, she planned as she sat in the sun and read, sat in the sun and ate, sat in the sun and let the blessed silence soak into her skin. The baby was locked up tight and he had his clock so she knew he was all right. When she went to feed him, she brought along a rolled-up newspaper. While it didn't stop him from screaming, it made her feel better. Like she was doing something, teaching him something. Teaching him to obey. She would replace the newspaper tomorrow with a wooden brush. And then, as the baby grew, there could be a belt, a choke collar, a leash, a cage.

He would behave. He would be quiet. She looked at him now, crying in his father's arms. He wouldn't get away with that. Not tomorrow. The thought of another day in the silent sun made her smile.

Then she waved goodbye and slipped away, light as air, the baby's cries hanging in a black cloud behind her.

CHAPTER ONE:

JAMES

And so you are born and your mother treats you like a dog. A runt, a whelp, a cur. Imagine being two years old and the collar around your neck feels as natural as your diaper. More natural, in some ways, and in some ways, more comfortable. Your mother often forgets to change your diaper. The soft puppy collar around your neck doesn't hurt until she hooks you to the leash, drags you down the cement steps to the root cellar. Then it does hurt. Even when you run, you can't keep up with her, and the steps are still hard for you to navigate. But as the collar digs in and your breathing constricts, you know it will end as soon as she drops you in the box, locks you in the cage. Then you can lie in the dark and listen to the clock tick, play with the little bell on your collar. The soft sounds are as smooth and soothing as a mother's voice is meant to be.

Imagine.

Imagine being five years old and sent off to school for the first time because, your mother tells you, she has no choice and so you must go. You climb onto the school bus that day and you don't know what to do, and so the driver leads you to a seat and pushes you into it. Surrounded by all the noise of happy raucous children fresh from a summer of lake swimming and playing in the park, you look out the window, try to catch a last glimpse of your mother. But she is inside already, the door closed, and you know she's found a favorite sunny patch and has curled up to sleep.

At school, you touch the tender skin of your neck, free to the air, no collar there, it's hanging on a hook in the root cellar, waiting for your return. You squint in the bright light of the kindergarten room and watch the children. Everything about them is foreign. They run from toy to toy, learning station to learning station, and you wonder what they are doing. There are blocks and magnetic letters and puzzles and big sheets of paper next to buckets of crayons. But you don't know what any of these things are for. You head for the safety of a dim corner, out of the sun, and find a small clock toy, a toy that you can wind and it ticks and tocks and plays a little tune and it feels familiar, so you sit facing the corner, turn your back to all the others, to all the shrieks and laughter and rough and tumble, and you wind the clock, over and over, and rock to its rhythm.

Imagine not knowing how to play.

Imagine the release from a leather collar making it more difficult to breathe, rather than easier. Imagine not understanding, not recognizing, freedom. How could you recognize what you'd never known? It's like trying to find a word in the dictionary when you don't know how to spell it.

By the end of that first day of school, you know you are very, very different. And everyone else, the teacher, the children, seem to recognize that too, and they step carefully around you, and nobody asks you to play. You sit alone and you hold your clock and you watch the world go by. A world that seems more wonderful and vibrant by the minute. Yet you just don't know how to join in. And nobody seems to know how to show you.

Imagine.

James didn't have to imagine. He knew. At five years old, what was unimaginable to everyone else was commonplace to James. As common as making a peanut butter sandwich or flipping a pillow to the cool side in the middle of the night. And while James lived every day with the unimaginable, with root cellars and collars and tethers and belts, his own imagination began to stretch to impossible contortions. As he sat with his back to a world he longed to be in, he looked into a clock face and listened to the ticking with his whole heart. At home, down deep in the root cellar, he turned his face in the dark toward the alarm clock and the deep and sonorous tick told him stories and made him smile. He listened to the clocks and he believed they listened to him. He talked to them, telling them about his day, telling them about the strange world that he just didn't understand, and they talked back and surrounded him with a worn and comfortable quilt of familiarity. At school, the toy clock's tick was an invitation to play. At home, the alarm clock's tock was his after school milk and cookies. To James, they were enough. Because he just didn't know any better.

Imagine.

On this day, a mid-morning in mid-September, sixty-eight years after that first day of kindergarten, James knew immediately that he'd made a mistake. He always told himself to never turn his back, to never turn away from the security monitor when outsiders were in his house, but he did anyway, and as soon as he did, it proved fatal. There was a pile of keys that needed to be sorted by clock type and as he reached for them, just for a second, for barely a breath, a crash echoed throughout the house. He didn't even have to look back at the monitor to see where it came from; he knew. As soon as the sound reached his ears, it slid straight down to his heart and he heard that clock calling. Crying for rescue.

James flew from his chair and down the hallway, up the stairs to the third floor, to the middle room on the right. The last place where he saw the tourists, a gray-haired man holding hands with his soft-spoken wife, both of them followed by their sullen teenage son. When James saw that boy, hunched behind his parents as they paid the admission, James knew he was trouble. Hair down to his shoulders, pockmarked face, jeans black and big enough to stuff dozens of clocks down the legs. James wondered if there was any way he could convince the husband and wife to leave the boy outside, that he'd be happier playing his Gameboy or GameCube or GameThis or GameThat, whatever it was that he held clenched in his dirty hands. Could James do that and still seem hospitable, still welcome this couple into his home and museum, the Home for Wayward Clocks? Still pay their admission and help him to support himself, support his clocks, support the whole town? The only way to keep those clocks ticking was money and the only way to make money was to keep those clocks ticking. In the end, James chose polite silence and watched this family walk to the first room, the living room, and then he hurried to the control center to study them on the security camera. He felt all the clocks stiffen in every room, on every floor. They sensed danger as well.

Closing his eyes, James silently apologized to the clocks and he promised to keep up a stern vigil. But when those keys were just out of his reach, he turned. And he heard every clock in that place that trusted him call his name just before the crash. The victim's voice was the loudest of all.

James recognized that voice and as he entered the room, he already knew who it was, but praying, he said out loud, "Please, please don't let it be the Anniversary Waltzer. Please." The parents moved away and the boy slunk to the other side of the room. There was the four-hundred day clock, the one that sang the Anniversary Waltz every hour, the one whose four crystal-cut balls at the base of the pendulum threw rainbows around that room every day at noon, when the sun fell in just right. Its glass dome was shattered, one hand was bent, the other spoked upwards through the broken shards on the floor. One of the four crystals was missing, but from the purple and pink and green flashes James saw in the mess of dome glass, glass that doesn't throw colors, he knew where the crystal went. In pieces everywhere. "Oh, no," he said and knelt carefully, trying to assess, to determine damage and the possibility of repair. He listened closely for a heartbeat.

"I'm sorry," the father said. "My son bumped against it. Of course we'll pay for it."

"Bumped into it?" James shot a glare at the boy who sneered, then looked away.

"Yes, bumped it," the mother said. "Brian, come over here and apologize to the man." She held out her hand, held out her hand to a boy who must have been sixteen years old at least, and she smiled.

The boy's head snapped upright and he pushed his hair away from his face. His eyes went wide and when he stepped forward, James witnessed a moment of gentleness, the quick brushing of a mother's fingers with her son's, and James' breath caught and his heart paused and he wondered if he'd been wrong.

But still, there was a broken clock, a possibly dead clock, and James seethed. Carefully, he picked the base out of the pile and set the clock upright. Its pendulum tried to spin, but it was out of balance with the missing ball. It was like watching a dog with two broken legs try to run.

"I'm sorry," the boy said quietly.

The mother stooped down. "Really, he didn't mean it. What can we pay you for the clock?" She touched James' shoulder and he froze, feeling the warmth in her fingertips. But he knew how quickly that could change. All she had to do was raise her hand, close her fingers. He shrugged her away.

"This was a four-hundred day clock," James said. Seeing their confused faces, he conceded and fell into the layman's language. "An anniversary clock." James remembered buying the clock at an estate sale, the seller's sad face as he packed it in a box. "It celebrated," James said, "a marriage." In the garage that day, the seller's face was sodden with love, with sorrow. He said he gave his wife the clock on their tenth anniversary, but his wife left before their twenty-third. The seller said he couldn't stand to look at the clock anymore.

James couldn't imagine. It wasn't the clock's fault.

The father cleared his throat.

James sighed and stood, lifting what was left of the clock. "It was worth four hundred and fifty dollars," he said. "I don't know if it can be fixed."

The wife gasped, the son snorted, but the father and James stood and looked each other in the eye. With the clock's body warm in James' hands, he didn't flinch. Then the father got out his checkbook. They left immediately, the boy's baritone whine hushed as they went through the hallway to the door.

Setting the clock carefully on a table, James extricated the missing hand from the pile of glass. The pendulum kept trying to work, staggering forward and back, and that cheered him; it meant the movement was mostly intact. It was likely that only a few of the tiny pieces would have to be replaced, pieces knocked loose by the fall. The hard part would be finding a new crystal ball for the pendulum. It was extremely difficult to come up with an exact match, but a match was necessary or James was afraid the clock's internal equilibrium could be gone forever. It would be like giving someone the wrong type of blood.

He went for a broom and dustpan and his burial supplies. After carefully sweeping up the remains, the parts so broken, they could never be used in this clock or transplanted into another, James put them onto a piece of royal blue crushed velvet. Pulling the corners together, he tied it shut with a piece of fine leather, making it into a small velvet pouch. A fitting casket for clock parts that served their time well.

James carried the pouch and the clock to his basement workshop. The pouch would be buried later in the graveyard behind the house. He bedded the clock on a piece of lambs wool and tucked the folds into the pendulum, gently convincing the clock to stop its struggles. It needed to rest during the repair. The first step was to try and find a match to the ball; if there was a match among all the stored clock parts in the basement, then James could move on to checking and adjusting the movement.

James went to a closet and started looking through boxes of skeleton parts. Three boxes alone held all sizes and shapes of pendulum ornaments. Sighing, he stacked one box on another to take back to the control center at the front of the house. He would know the match when he saw it. He knew exactly what to search for. When it came to clocks, James knew it all. And what he didn't know, he imagined.

In the tiny town of What Cheer, Iowa, James was called the Clock-Keeper; he was the keeper of the clocks. They graced his life, blessed him with their time and chime, told him of their past, looked into his future. As he walked up the stairs and back through the house that day, James marveled at his family of timepieces, all huddled safely under his roof. Mantel clocks and wall clocks, grandfathers and grandmothers. Cuckoos, cathedrals and old-fashioned alarm clocks. So many were unwanted; he found them in Goodwills and St. Vincent's, rummage sales and flea markets, in the middle of garbage piles or just perched precariously on the curb of a street. James picked them up, paid for them if necessary and lovingly tucked them under his jacket where he felt them settle in against his skin, sigh in relief. If they didn't work, he tried to fix them, opening their bodies, carefully repairing and oiling parts or replacing them completely from the boxes of skeletons. There were so many that couldn't be fixed; they looked intact, but when he worked his way inside, there was just a mess. Parts so twisted, they were unrecognizable, or parts so old and dead, he could only replace them if he found the clock's identical twin.

James never threw a clock away, even if it couldn't be fixed. After harvesting the useful parts from the clock's heart and lungs and intestines, he buried the rest in the graveyard. Then he found a spot for the outer shell, the body and face, in the middle of a batch of working clocks. James imagined that the dead felt better around the living. And he felt better for them.

As James walked toward the control room, the chimes began to go off. It was eleven o'clock and the clocks were settled now, relaxed, with only James in the house. If he listened carefully, he could distinguish all of the voices, determine which clock each was, where it sat in what room. He noted the absence of the anniversary clock's waltz and he felt a jolt of sadness. But the others raised their voices and James knew the songs would go on for ten minutes or more. Key-wound and weight-wound clocks tended to not be very accurate; they were affected by the weather and by the environment around them. James struggled to provide a stable home, he struggled to imagine what a stable home was, but changes were always just under the surface.

In the control room, James looked up at the clock he hung there, a solid wall clock shaped like a sunburst. Its rays leapt out in gold and silver, extending nearly three feet from the face. This clock had no voice, it was meant to be silent, and he always glanced up at it and at other silent clocks as the others chattered. Looking into their quiet faces, James felt the clocks receive his affectionate acknowledgment and so they continued on their steady tick.

He looked at clocks first thing in the morning, last thing at night. They told him where to be, what to do, who he was. How could he not be faithful to something he looked up to so many times a day and searched for in the middle of the night when he woke up disoriented and disturbed from his dreams? Their ticking resonated through to his own heartbeat, their chime rushed in his blood.

James took a quick check of the security monitors. The front door was closed, but unlocked, and the porch was empty. In each of the rooms, the sounds began to die away as the clocks settled in to wait for their next performance. For some, that was the quarter hour. For others, there were thirty or sixty minutes of rest. And the silent ones made use of this quiet time to send their ticks out louder than the others, making sure they could be heard, that they were an active part of the family.

James began to sift through the boxes of pendulum ornaments, sending bright crystal balls and diamonds and hexagons in a shiny rain through his fingers. There were figures too, horses and dancers and cherubs and sealed-together hearts. He set aside the balls to compare their heft and clarity and to find the one that would be a perfect match for the waltzer.

For James, the clocks were companions. Friends that would never leave. Family that gave darkness a body, a shape, a sound to listen to when there was nothing else. Without them, the darkness would have the stillness, the hopelessness of a grave, a root cellar hidden behind a house, the dirt pulled over his head, no way out, and he would forget to breathe. But the clocks told James to breathe, to always move on to the next inhale, the next step. The clocks talked to James in a way no one else ever did. They had the softest voices he ever heard. He didn't duck when they spoke.

Soon, he had eighty-four cut crystal balls balanced on the desktop. He closed the boxes, placed them on the floor, and then stepped back and studied the balls as the light fell in from the window and set them on fire. Like a song played low on a radio for company, James heard the quarter-hour being chimed. He glanced at his watch; it was indeed eleven-fifteen. Watching the secondhand for a moment, James thought he detected a hesitation. Did he wind the watch this morning? He couldn't remember, though he also couldn't imagine forgetting. Carefully, he took the tiny stem between his thumb and forefinger and gave a gentle twist. It was tight. Fully wound.

Nothing in the museum that told time had a battery in it. The new clocks, the modern ones charged by a battery, were efficient, but they didn't touch James' heart. There was no contact, no touch, not like with the others, the wind-every-8-days, 14-days, 31-days variety. Those modern clocks were even equipped with light sensors to turn off their sounds during the night; clocks were not meant to be silent at any time, but especially not at night. It was the middle of the night when James heard them the clearest, when he snuggled deeper, alone in his bed, while the old grandfather down the hall somberly chimed three and then was echoed by all the others, floor by floor. The comfort of those sounds came to James in his sleep and he sighed and smiled and rolled over for the next set of dreams.

Quickly, he began to eliminate the crystal balls. Too large, too small, too bright, not enough color. He held them until his hand was full, weighted like a boy with marbles, and then he gently returned them to the boxes. The balls narrowed down, forty left, thirty, twenty, ten. And then three. These he balanced one by one on his palm, then rolled them through his fingers, checking all angles, looking at them in the sun and in the dark when he cupped his hands around them. One ball began to stand out more than the others and James felt a weight lift from his shoulders. The missing piece was here. The waltzer would live again.

All the living clocks would outlast James; their hearts would keep beating after his stopped, as long as there was someone to wind them, to touch them and nudge them forward. James hoped even the dead clocks would live on, that there would always be somebody to take care of them, to treat them as if they were alive and still functional.

James imagined that time was coming; he knew he needed to train another clock-keeper. And he didn't know where to begin. There were so many that needed care and so many strangers out there that just couldn't be trusted. That would sneer and bump into clocks the moment a back was turned. As soon as a mistake was made.

As James walked back to the workroom, the chosen crystal ball in his pocket and the others in their stacked cartons in his arms, he heard his heartbeat echo the clocks' welcome and he felt himself connect in a way he couldn't with anything or anybody else. It was as if their hands and arms moved around him as they moved around their numbers. It was like being held in a timeless embrace.

The day passed as usual, James watching for visitors, taking care of himself and the clocks, working on the waltzer. He worked through the afternoon and after supper, stopping only when his eyes began to water and blur so badly, he could no longer concentrate. He apologized to the clock, telling it he wished he was younger, just ten years would have given him the ability and energy to stay up all night until it worked. But as the clock rested silently on the lambs' wool, James could see its age and knew it understood his. It needed to sleep and so did he. The clocks understood him when he was young, and now he was old, alongside of them, and they still understood. He went up to the third floor, changed into pajamas, then sat on the edge of his bed.

On the bedside table was another four-hundred day clock, his mother's anniversary clock. James' father gave it to his mother on their first wedding anniversary. James remembered his mother winding it every November twelfth, the only day that the clock needed to be wound. That's why anniversary clocks were given that name; they were given as gifts for celebrations and only needed to be wound once a year on that important day, a way to commemorate the event. After a time, when his mother no longer cared to remember her marriage, James wound the clock, and he wound it still, on November twelfth. Only he remembered the union that brought him to life.

James' mother's clock originally sat in a place of honor, the middle of her big multi-mirrored dressing table. The pendulum was a party of four couples dancing, spinning around and around, to the left, then to the right, every fifteen seconds, and as a little boy, James grew dizzy watching them and their reflections. His mother's dressing table was a glittering ballroom. The dancers almost always looked happy and the young James wanted them to stay that way. He concentrated on them especially hard during moments when his mother's voice rose to a shrill yowl, his father's desperate hum an underlying accompaniment to the dancers' feet and his mother's lament.

As his parents' voices grew and twisted, the dancers twirled faster, their ankles flexing on top of cruelly pointed toes. The women's gloved hands on the men's shoulders crept toward their throats. Once, when his mother's voice reached a new crescendo, James lifted the clock's glass dome to stop the dancers from hurting each other. He wanted them to go back to the flash of their feet, the heat of their embrace. It was James that got hurt though; his mother said she didn't like animals playing with her things. It didn't matter that James wasn't playing at all. It didn't matter that he wasn't an animal, not outside of her imagination...he knew he was a little boy.

And later, when his father was gone and James was thirteen and his mother melted into a sleeping cat on the floor, even the clock didn't matter to her. It sat, unwound and unwatched, unadmired on her dressing table. James took the clock, stole it away, and set it on his own desk. He missed the mirrored reflection, but once he wound the clock, the dancers spun away while he did his homework. The ticking soothed him and he missed it the most on those days and nights when his mother locked him in the root cellar. He wanted the clock to be happy; it needed someone to pay attention. Once the clock was used to his room, out of the limelight of the sparkling ballroom, but the center of James' attention, the pendulum moved a little more slowly, a little more smoothly, and the dancers relaxed from an anxious jitterbug to a waltz. His mother never mentioned the clock's disappearance, though James imagined she knew where it was.

Sixty years later, seated on the edge of his bed, James watched the clock and admired the same dancers as they followed the same path, day after day after day, to the left, to the right, to the left again, still every fifteen seconds, and their joints were as smooth as when he was thirteen or ten or six or four. That clock never broke, James made sure of that, and he kept it behind the closed door of his bedroom, out of the public's eye. The clock sang and danced through his father's disappearance and death and then his mother's, and James' own journey from the root cellar to the Home for Wayward Clocks. When James wound that clock every November twelfth, he thought of his father, the soft voice, the gentle hand, telling an eight-year old boy that he'd be back soon, to take care, I love you. And James thought of his mother, during her beautiful moments, when she was curled on the floor, asleep, her blonde hair awash in rainbow sunlight refracted through the front window. James thanked them for the only thing they ever gave him, this life, this path of time and ticking and tucked-away memories.

James watched the clock every night and when he was eased into sleep, he spun with the dancers, slipping from one woman to the next, hand to hand, chest to breast, danced to oblivion where time finally stopped.

Oh, if only.

In the Home for Wayward Clocks, James imagined he was never alone; he was never in silence. There was such comfort in that.

CHAPTER TWO:

MARRIAGE IN ORANGE
The Waltzer's Story

Patty knew that Ben would interrupt her. She could count his footsteps from the time the lawnmower stopped to when the back door swung open, banging as it always did against the refrigerator. The metallic bang, the heavy thump of Ben's grass-stained sneakers hitting the floor would cause her to pause in her rhythm, her ritual of following whatever came next on her list, her organization that allowed her to get everything done the way it should be. And at the right price, even when she was being extravagant.

He smacked the back door just as she spilled her two grocery bags of Halloween-special orange Oreos over the counter. She didn't acknowledge him, she just turned her back, feeling the cold breeze from the yard stroke the most vulnerable exposed skin on her inclined neck. She began to organize her Oreos into their departments; two packages for the cupboard, left of the sink, top shelf, because the first would go swiftly, and twenty-two more packages for the freezer. These Oreos had to stay fresh for the duration, for the year until Halloween came around again and orange Oreos replaced the traditional white crème on the shelves. The orange Oreos were the best the year offered, better than the garish red Christmas variety, the green for St. Patrick's Day, the fresh-washed spring-sky blue for Easter.

Behind her, she heard Ben sigh and she swore she felt the hungry heat of his breath, drawn from the stale base of his lungs, replace the cold on her neck. "Patty," he said. "They're all the same. They all taste the same."

"No, they don't." Her response was automatic, delivered in a flat, I-don't-care-what-you-think voice. As automatic as waking up every morning beside Ben, kissing him goodbye with her eyes closed, the kiss gone by so fast, she never even tasted his lips. She stopped for a second and stared at her piles of packages. What did Ben taste like?

He started toward the living room, toward the right side of the sofa that reclined and let him stare at the ceiling, his hands folded on his chest as if he was in an overstuffed naugahyde casket, and he didn't say anything else. It wasn't worth it, she knew. They had this argument every year and there was never a winner. Though Patty always bought all the orange Oreos she wanted. She supposed there was some victory in that.

When she heard the neat squeak-chunk of the recliner popping free, she nearly called to him, to ask him if his Saturday chores were done, just for something to say. But she stopped herself. Of course they were. They always were. Nothing was more important to Ben than mowing the lawn in October, making sure that when the snow finally came, the grass beneath was short and crisp, allowing frosty moisture through to the hidden dark soil below. But she did wait to see if his thoughts would turn to this particular day, if he would give voice to what she knew was circled in red on the calendar.

Their twenty-third anniversary.

She put a pot of coffee on. Orange Oreos were especially good with a cup of good, hot, fresh coffee. While the coffee dripped steadily, filling the kitchen with its rich scent of French vanilla, she carried the twenty-two packages to their basement freezer. The cookies were on sale that week, a buy-two-get-one-free deal, plus she had an entire year's worth of Oreo coupons saved up. Between those and the special, she'd only spent a few dollars. Well, nine. That, she figured, would make the cookies taste even better. Though if necessary, she would have paid full price.

As she closed the freezer, she heard the anniversary clock go off upstairs. It played *The Anniversary Waltz* and she waited for and heard the deep grumble of Ben's hum. He always sang along with it. Always. And always off-key. She always asked him not to and he never listened.

She remembered when he used to listen. She thought he couldn't help it, his ears stuck out so, like sweet danish beneath the burr of a buzz-cut. She remembered the first time she told him about the orange Oreos. She was a freshman in college, he was a junior, and she was in hot-steamed giggle over being in love with an older man, an older man who paid her every attention. They were in the campus grocery store when she squealed over the Oreos and he laughed with her and joined her on the walk home, ripping open the package and stuffing the cookies in his mouth, in hers, their teeth changing to the color of cartoon pumpkins. She wished for a cup of coffee then, but because he was with her, she ate them without and enjoyed every bite.

She went upstairs now, to fill her special mug, thick glass, a melancholy yet warm amber that always reminded her of autumn, her favorite season, even in the heat of a heavy July midnight.

On campus that first orange night, she met Ben after hours in his dorm room and when he pulled back his beaten-up bedspread, she saw an entire twin-sized mattress full of orange Oreos. He made love to her there, her bare body crushing the cookies, sending the crème in smears up her thighs and across her back and she thought for a moment, her eyes closed, that it was a waste of perfectly good Oreos, why couldn't he have chosen the plain variety? But when he began to lick the crumbs off her, and the crumbs were everywhere, in every crevice and fold and rise, she began to think differently. The orange creme spread on his erect penis made it look like a squash and at times, they laughed so hard, they had to stop their lovemaking. There just wasn't breath for it.

After pouring herself an amber mug of coffee, she brought one of the unopened packages of cookies over to the table. She opened it, relishing the whoosh of released air, the chocolate and crème entering the kitchen with a force that made her mouth water. She stacked five of the cookies there, just to the right of her cup, admiring the tower of black-orange-black-orange, neat and straight without a single lean.

She wondered if he would remember. She wondered why she did.

Twenty-three years. So it wasn't the big two-five. But still. October first had no other meaning for her now. Once, it was the more official start of fall, despite what the calendar said. It was the month when the leaves not only turned, they fell, and the clocks had to be set backwards. The nights were buried in black, speckled with stars that suddenly hung loosely from the sky, the morning air so sharp, it felt like it would shatter when she opened the front door to get the newspaper. And for twenty-three years, October first marked the day she changed her life. The day she swore in front of a whole church full of friends and family and God Himself that she would love this man forever. They served orange Oreos at the reception.

Patty listened to the hum of the television and she looked at the stack of Oreos. She wondered when the charm changed to annoyance.

Ben brought orange Oreos to her in the hospital after the births of their three children. Two of them, born in late October and early November, made it easy. But the youngest was born in early April, the season for sky-blue Oreos. Ben had shaved the crème of plain Oreos, played with food coloring until he got something close to orange (by his estimation; to Patty, it looked like a very painful yellow), then put the crème back between the cookies. Oreos for Christmas, tucked-away Oreos for Valentine's Day (offered as a repeat in the bedsheets during the first five years of their marriage), frozen Oreos on her birthday in July. It was Ben that gave her the idea to buy a multitude of packages and freeze enough for the year.

It was when the stockpile began to appear in the freezer every October that the Oreo gifts stopped. And then one October, about ten years ago, Ben stood and watched her organize her cookies and he said, "They all taste the same, you know." She'd been speechless. The next year, she offered her feeble, "No, they don't." And that's where they left it. But then other things happened.

She began to wear nightgowns to bed. So Ben began to sleep in boxers and T-shirts. They argued about money. When they went out to dinner, it was usually with the kids, but if it wasn't, they talked about the kids, then stared at their plates. He began going out for drinks and ball games with the guys from work, guys she only knew by name, never by face. She started working out at the Y and she swapped stories with the other sweaty women. They ate salads after class, except once a month, they went out for burgers and fries and shakes and onion rings so big, they could have been dog collars. And she began telling these women things she never told Ben.

Now, she looked at the Oreos. Her coffee was cold. The weight of her elbows on the table, growing heavier with her thoughts, brought the tower to a slight lean. And she wasn't hungry at all.

Carefully, she lowered the tower, spread it out into a straight line like a hard chocolate centipede, and then she put the cookies back into the package. She rolled it shut and clipped it with a clothespin.

The anniversary clock was just going off when she went into the living room. It began to chime *The Anniversary Waltz* and she saw Ben's foot, high up on the couch recliner, begin to tap, a pointless swaying in the air, a conductor's baton clothed in brown argyle. A-one-two-three. And he started to hum.

Patty crossed to the clock and lifted the dome. With one finger, she stopped the pendulum and the song stopped between the two and three. Ben's hum hung in the air for a moment more, then guttered down into his chest.

"Hey," he said.

"I hate when you sing," she said. She stood there, facing the newly dead clock, unable to move forward without the rhythm of time, its voice struck numb in its throat. She decided that when Ben left the room, she would start the clock, let it finish its song, then stop it again. And then it would go out to the storage shelf in the garage. She heard the clunk of the couch's recliner handle, then the swoosh as the footrest slid back to its hidden place in the couch's base. A creak and a muffled pop of a knee joint told her that Ben was leaning forward.

"You used to love it when I sang," he said.

She remembered hearing him. Singing the three-toned "Na-bis-co" as they hurried down the street with their first shared package of cookies. His voice nestled in her ear as they danced at their wedding. Commercial jingles as he tried to divert her during labors. Humming along with whatever was on the radio as he made love to her.

That humming disappeared when the lovemaking grew shorter, then shorter still, until there were no words, no sighs, no laughter, just restrained grunts. And finally, silence.

"I don't like it anymore," she said to the clock.

He stood, she heard his quick exhalation. "And orange Oreos taste just the same, Patty," he said and he left the room.

She hoped, to pack. If not, she would.

Nudging the clock, she set it in motion and it resumed singing. From the bedroom, she thought she heard Ben's low, guarded hum. Then she stopped the clock and brought it to the garage. She set it on the shelf, then pushed it toward the back, to protect it from unforeseen falls.

After returning to the kitchen, Patty stuck her mug in the microwave and unclipped the package, sending that orange Oreo scent into the air. To blend with the coffee, her thoughts, the new silence. She was surprised to find herself afraid; she wondered if Oreos could change too.

CHAPTER THREE:

JAMES

nd so learning is difficult for you. Imagine not knowing the alphabet, not knowing there even is such a thing. Imagine recognizing the sound of numbers, but only as warnings that thrust from your mother's mouth as she counts backwards. "You have five seconds to get to the root cellar, young man! Five…four… three…" You never hear the two, one; by then you are running, tumbling down the steps into the darkness, because if you get there before she finishes the countdown, you usually escape a beating and only have to tolerate the twin thunderclaps of the root cellar doors being shut, and the scrape of a tree branch as it's pushed through the latch. Being alone in the dark is scary, but not as bad as being alone while the welts on your skin burn so badly, you can't imagine why they don't glow in the dark. Why they don't throw up huge red beams of pain, bringing a firestorm to the underground damp of the root cellar.

School pulls you, lures you away with the promise of pleasure and brightness and sound from the awful familiarity of home. You try so hard. You watch the others, you listen to your teacher, and you begin to make headway. By the end of kindergarten, you not only know your letters, but you are reading. And it is something you love to do. The weekly class trip to the school library is a treasure and you always carry home your carefully chosen book gripped tightly in both your hands. But sometimes, you don't get to read it. Sometimes, if you accidentally sound out a word that you don't recognize and your voice shatters the silence into shreds of consonants and vowels, your mother tears the book away from you, tosses it across the room, and down to the root cellar you go. Sometimes for days.

You take to quickly reading your library book on the bus ride home. If you get to read it again, and again, it's a gift and so, so delicious.

Imagine.

Imagine doing all your homework silently. Imagine doing everything silently. You have to be invisible. But you try, because it is the only way to be, and you want to please your beautiful mother, even as you fail, and fail, and fail again.

Leaving kindergarten behind, you also have to leave behind the toy clock, but you harvest relationships with two others. The alarm clock in the root cellar, which you can wind all by yourself now, and your mother's anniversary clock, visited on secret forays to her room while your mother sleeps on in the sun. The alarm clock becomes your brother, your best friend, and the anniversary clock grows into a friendly older woman who could have been your mother. Who you wish was your mother. In your mind, the clocks' pendulums ripen into hearts and their voices express the deepest desires in their souls. In your soul. The clocks speak for you and to you and with them there, you imagine that your life is crowded with company. With love and concern and want and need. A developing history of picnics and county fairs, good-natured arguments and late-night whispered conversations. Family. A family so different from just you and your mother.

Imagine.

James could. Clocks provided warmth and warmth was what James needed. Clocks never used their hands and voices to hurt, and their bodies, round and square and rectangular and solid, never coiled like a cat on the floor. James could give them all the solace and comfort he learned to crave. The comfort and warmth he saw all around him as the kids whispered secrets and laughed and pushed each other on swings at recess. As they held each other's hands and danced in dizzy circles around each other and around Maypoles and Ring-Around-The-Rosie. As they dashed past him after school to waiting mothers' arms and embraces. James watched closely then, tried to imagine what it would be like to have slender arms encircle him, rosy lips plant a kiss on his cheek. He dreamed of his mother's hair falling around his face and shoulders like a bright blonde cloak.

Instead, he embraced the steady ticking of a clock. And the clocks embraced him. They were always there. They were always with him, even in the dark. Even when he hurt. Especially when he hurt.

Imagine.

After breakfast the next day, James checked his schedule to see who needed winding. There were quite a few and so he set about collecting the necessary keys from the old card catalog cabinet. The card catalog itself was a find, sold when What Cheer's library went to a computer system instead of the old drawers full of cards. They sold off the cabinets, and the day of the sale, James made sure he was there early. Sure enough, they pulled one from way in the back; it was a beautiful thing, easily from the early nineteenth century. So he bought it and kept it in the control room, using it to store individual identification index cards and all the different keys for the clocks. Each clock was given a number when it moved into the museum. That number went on a card, along with where James bought the clock and when, and the clock's location in the house. If there was a key, that was stored there too.

That day's keys jangling from a ring attached to his belt loop, James traveled through all three floors of the house, stopping in several rooms. Nine o'clock came and went and he paid attention as the clocks chorused their glory. In the morning, the clocks' chiming always reminded James of being in a church. There was a reverence as their voices raised in rooms filled with the early sun.

When the winding was finished, James looked out the front door. There were no cars parked on the street and nobody strolled on the sidewalk. He propped the door open, an invitation to tourists, but set the alarm so that anyone crossing over the threshold would be announced with the sound of a doorbell. Westminster chimes, of course. He could hear this down in his workshop and he wanted to get to work on the broken four-hundred day clock, the waltzer. All that was left was to set the new crystal and balance the movement, and then the clock would breathe again.

As James got to work, he remembered the estate sale where he bought the clock a few years ago. The man had it on a back shelf of the garage, almost hidden away, but James found it, as he found all abandoned clocks. It was lovely, just old enough to avoid the battery, and its version of "The Anniversary Waltz" was full-throated and pensive. James admired the way the four beveled crystals on the pendulum caught the sunlight.

There was no price tag, so he turned to the man. "How much for this clock?" he asked. He knew there was the possibility it wasn't for sale, but in such instances, he always asked. Sometimes it only took that request to get someone to sell.

The man took the clock from James and held it for a moment. He opened his mouth and closed it and James stepped back, giving him room to make his decision. James never tricked anyone out of their clock; if the clock was loved, it was best left alone. But here, as it was shoved on a back shelf in a cold garage, James imagined that the clock didn't feel loved and he wanted to make it warm. He knew that asking for its price would either earn him the clock or the clock an honored place back in its home. But then the man said, "Twenty-three dollars."

That was an odd price and amazingly low. James thought about offering more, just to be fair, but the man's face, stiff with stoicism and yet with just a softening of sadness around the eyebrows and the mouth, made James reach quietly for his wallet. "I'm happy to pay it," James said.

The man glanced at James, then looked away. "It's silly, I suppose," he said. "It's how long we were married. Twenty-three years."

James liked him for that, for translating those years into the clock's worth, though James wondered why the years stopped, why the marriage was referred to in the past tense. Was the wife dead or just gone? It didn't feel right to ask, so James quietly handed over the money and helped to pack the clock upright in a box. "It doesn't need to stop running," James said when the man reached out to stop the pendulum. "Let's just pack paper around the dome and it should be fine. I don't live far from here."

James took over the clock's packing, though the man kept his hands perched on the edge of the box. James felt the warmth of his touch, and maybe the missing wife's too, dissipate from the clock's brass base. He quickly said, "It's a great day for an estate sale. Lovely weather," to get the man's mind off the memory being packed gently with paper.

The man nodded and turned away. "She left. Two days after our anniversary."

James froze and despite his ministrations, the clock stopped running. The man's shoulders were set, braced really, a straight line from the left to the right. But James saw a muscle quiver at the base of his neck. As the man trembled, James lifted the dome and pushed the crystal balls. The clock hesitated, but then swung back into motion. The man's neck muscle smoothed and his shoulders relaxed and James resumed packing the box.

"I'm sorry," James said. Those two words didn't seem like much, but what else was there to say? James knew that cruelty couldn't be soothed by words. Actions, whether leaving a husband or striking a child, left nothing but silence. James held the box against his chest.

"I bought her that clock for our tenth anniversary. I have the key taped to its base. Be sure to wind it on October first."

He looked so forlorn that James held the box out. "Are you sure you want to sell it? It's not big, it could fit anywhere...and it might help you. To remember." James felt the clock inside hold its breath. "The good parts, anyway."

"No," the man said. "I can't forget. Not the good or the bad. That's the problem." He crossed his arms. James hesitated a moment more, but the man closed his eyes. "Please take it," he said.

And now this clock was broken and resting quietly on James' workbench. James felt like he hadn't taken care of it, not when someone was able to slip by and bring it harm. For a moment, James felt that seller, the deserted husband, standing behind him, watching him balance the crystal balls, trying to revive the clock, and he could see the accusation in his eyes. No clock deserved to fall, to go from secure to insecure, to hit the ground and feel the life knocked out of it. This clock still struggled to live, its three-balled limp quickly turned into a full and rolling sweep. James shoved the sad man out of his sight, out of his room, and watched the pendulum twirl, testing how long he would be able to detect the new crystal. It was a very close match, the same size, the same weight, but the clarity was just a little different. It wasn't as old as the others and so the light that shot through was clear, not yellowed. After a couple dozen turns though, it became harder to pick out and James imagined the youth of that crystal ball spreading to the rest of the clock. It needed weight and balance…yet a shot of youth didn't hurt either.

The pendulum paused longer than it should before it switched directions and so James opened the back, tightened and oiled the parts, set things to rights. He closed the door and nudged the pendulum again, then watched as the balls spun without a hitch, without a hesitation. That left only the matter of the glass dome replacement. This clock was a standard size and so that wasn't a problem; James just fetched a spare from the skeleton closet and then covered the clock in safety and security. He felt the clock sigh then, echoing James' own breath, felt the clock relax back into its life like a butterfly visiting its cocoon.

He carried it back to its customary place. Setting it firmly on the table, James made sure that all four legs were balanced, it was centered, not near any edges, and he promised it safety. He told it there was no need for fear and he asked for forgiveness. James failed once; it would never happen again. The clock's breath quickly blended in with the others, its tick quiet and smooth. James wondered if it ever thought about the twenty-three year old marriage it represented. He wondered if it missed the man or his wife.

It wasn't hard for James to imagine missing someone who hurt you so much. No matter what other people said. No matter if it didn't make sense.

The top of the hour arrived and the clock, like the others, began to sing. James sat down and listened, hearing its voice above all the rest. The sound of its chime, a gentle ring, soft in timbre, deep in echo, offered James forgiveness. The volume grew, the voice deepened; this clock knew it alone had James' attention. It sang for that wife, sad and cruel enough to leave, and it sang for that husband, wise enough to give her a beautiful clock for their anniversary, yet left ultimately alone. And it sang for the clock-keeper, in celebration of the sanctuary James provided.

It wasn't alone. No one in that house was ever alone. James made sure of that.

When the clock's song was over, when the choir fell silent again, James reached into his back pocket and pulled out his wallet. There was the father's check for four hundred and fifty dollars. Yet the clock was fine. James fixed it without any outlay. The clock was worth a little bit less now, with the not-quite-matching pendulum ornament. James held a four-hundred dollar profit.

He looked at the address on the check. The family was from Georgia. James thought about tucking the check into an envelope, sending it with a note of apology to that peaches and sunshine state, thick with accents like molasses.

But then he thought of the look on that boy's face. And the touch of the mother's hand, her voice soft as she said her son's name. That family already had so much. So much that James couldn't begin to imagine. And yet he still wanted it so badly, this unimaginable thing, that touch, that voice, that look; his fingers clenched into a fist, crumpling the check.

Carefully, James smoothed it, then returned it to his wallet. That much money could go a long way in fixing the broken or saving the lost and abandoned. That much money could keep this house running. And James too.

At least that was something.

A trip to the bank was in order.

Living in What Cheer, Iowa, the only time a car was needed was to get out. James could walk the length of the town in just fifteen minutes or so. He laughed when they put in the drive-through at the bank and he made a habit of walking through it. No one cared.

James pretty much did whatever he wanted, since he saved the sorry little town. Even though he never intended to.

So he set off for the bank. The check was warm in his pocket and he whistled, planning ahead for the weekend, a trip out of town to a flea market thirty miles away. He hoped for good weather, for sun breathing warmth down his neck as he wandered from booth to booth, hands in pockets, glancing around and under and over tables for clocks. Some sellers knew James from past experience and they would have clocks waiting for him, hidden away in their vans and trucks, so that he would have the first opportunity to buy. While James appreciated this, he really liked dealing with new sellers. The ones that didn't know him, and didn't know clocks, and so he could buy them for a few bucks and a song.

Heading down the street, James glanced at all the markers pointing out the town's attractions. The signs were everywhere, at every corner, little white arrows pointing this way and that as if people passing through wouldn't just naturally run across these places because there was nowhere else to go. The Home For Wayward Clocks, this way. The gift shop, that way. Lodging, a small Victorian house transformed into a bed and breakfast, just across the street from the museum. A restaurant. All tourist necessities were available in What Cheer now. The town finally looked like its name, inquisitive, eager to help, to serve and entertain. Eager to survive, really. A few years before, the town was covered in a shade of drab. Nothing here but corn and unemployment, cows and depression. And a man who lived alone in a house full of clocks.

Nobody liked James then. All they knew about him really was that he moved to What Cheer when he was a young man, lived in an apartment above the gas station, and worked for years as the night time janitor at the public schools. He didn't like to spend much money; the cashiers hated to see him coming because they knew he would have a fistful of coupons that would all have to be tallied off the final bill. He bought clocks though and it became a common thing to see young James, middle-aged James, and now old James walking down the street, holding a clock or two. He saved enough money to buy the run-down Victorian, run down like the rest of the town, and then he fixed it up and filled it to the eaves with clocks.

Now, even with What Cheer thriving, the townsfolk still didn't like him. He didn't talk much and what little he said usually wasn't very nice. But because he didn't talk, they didn't know his past, they didn't know what he survived; they couldn't imagine what made him into a grumpy and strange old man who collected clocks. But they did know that he managed to save their butts when the town was going through a bad economic depression.

At that time, What Cheer wasn't the only thing shaded in drab and depressed. James was too. Being a janitor wasn't much, but it felt like a lot when James was laid off. It was okay for a while, he looked for work, but then the food started running out. There was electricity to pay for. Telephone. The telephone was the first thing to go. He kept looking for jobs on an empty stomach and with nothing to put in the telephone box on the applications. But everyone else was looking too and those lucky enough to be working weren't hiring.

One night, James sat in the middle of his living room, staring at his bank book. There wasn't much left. The only thing he had worth selling was the clocks and as he looked around at them all, he knew he would die first. And his entire ticking family would die with him. He thought about taking a box of matches and setting himself on fire, letting the flame spread to the others, and in the end, the ashes would all be blended. No James, no clocks, no heart nor pendulums nor faces nor arms, just a single pile of gray, the house an extension of the clock burial ground in the back yard.

James decided the electricity could go. He wondered how long he could make the money last, buying only bread and peanut butter. Soon there would be no money for gas to drive to job interviews. The only places to look would be within walking distance, within What Cheer itself. Where there was nothing.

James slept that night in the living room, his hands clenched around his bank book.

The following day, he drove to the next town on his last quarter tank of gas to see if any jobs had opened up. On the freeway, he passed billboard after billboard, most blank, some sporting a bright red sign that said, "Your business advertised here! Thousands of viewers each day!" The roads were full of strangers passing through Iowa as fast as they could. There was just nothing to see except Iowans starving in the middle of all that corn.

Those red letters stayed in James' eyes after he drove past, stayed there like stamps on his corneas. They flashed neon. *Your business advertised here!* He thought of his house, of all his clocks, the way people looked at him strangely when he passed them on the street.

Maybe there *was* something to see in Iowa.

So James came up with the idea for the Home for Wayward Clocks. He took what little money he had left and rented a billboard, and then he went to the hardware store and bought an OPEN sign. He propped his door and waited.

It was a horrible hard decision, to let strangers into his home, walking on his stairs and carpeting and hallways. Breathing his air. Tourists bent and peered and commented on all the members of James' family. He felt like he no longer tended to the clocks; the clocks now tended to him as they drew in tourists and passers-by hungry for a break from the endlessness of Iowa. The strangers brought their wallets with them. And with their wallets came the renewed ringing of the telephone, the steady burning of electric lights and the humming of the refrigerator, keeping everything fresh and cold and good. James fixed the clocks, the clocks fed James, and his ingenuity and fortune spread to others.

The lady across the street created the bed and breakfast, the Time To Sleep Inn. The restaurant in town, a little lunch counter, became the Tick-Tock Quick-Stop Restaurant, open twenty-four hours a day. A clock tower was built, a wrought iron and brick modern affair with Westminster chimes that went off every fifteen minutes and could be heard throughout the town. It stood next to the official "Welcome to What Cheer, Iowa, Home of the Home for Wayward Clocks" sign. The clock tower was usually off by about twelve minutes, something which brought James no end of frustration. A gift clock shop opened up, It's About Time, selling clocks as souvenirs since James refused. The only thing James sold at the Home, other than admission and repair services, was postcards. He had some especially made, featuring the Home For Wayward Clocks sign in front of the house and shots of the various rooms. The gift shop only kept modern clocks in stock, all batteries, all electric. The owners agreed not to offer any repair services, as that was James' area. A lot of their clocks came back to him.

The mayor gave James the key to the city. But James hadn't planned on saving What Cheer, he planned only on saving his clocks and himself.

Everyone knew that if James ever decided to move, if he packed up all the clocks and took the Home away, the town would lose its edge and sink back into that gray time when there were no tourists, there was no money. So wherever James went, there were smiles and handshakes and his back was slapped until it stung, and then the people turned and rolled their eyes behind his back. James was offered free meals at the restaurant, but he refused and they insisted and eventually settled for having Saturday night specials delivered to his door. Coupons were slid to him like contraband in the grocery store. Only the kids remained the same, generation after generation, laughing at James and making crude remarks whenever he passed. The kids didn't care that he saved the town. They only wanted to get out.

On weekends, a steady stream of visitors waited in line to get in to the Home. Weekdays were quieter. The town bustled on weekends, breathed easier and rested during the week, a familiar pattern in tourist areas like Las Vegas and Niagara Falls and the Grand Canyon. And What Cheer, Iowa. James blocked certain rooms off, like his bedroom and bathroom, his workroom in the basement. But the rest of the house was wide open, the clocks ticking in wary welcome. They understood, they knew there was no other way except to let people in. With some of his profits, James bought the security system and built the control center so that he could see into all the rooms at once, making sure that no one got hurt, no one got taken. But the only way the security system worked was to make sure he was alert. All the time. James thought of the waltzer and he shuddered. He had to take better care.

Coming to the bank, James strolled up to the drive-through lane. Even though he knew it was coming, he still jumped when the voice squawked at him through the speaker. "Hello, James, what can I do for you today?"

"Just cashing a check, Sophie," he said. He was relieved that it was his favorite teller. There were so many young ones, with flouncy blonde hair and long red nails, and James never knew what to say to them. Sophie was safe. Her brown hair was tucked behind her ears and she always smiled and just said what had to be said.

The money came back out through the tube and James counted it just to make sure, even though Sophie never made mistakes. "Thanks," he said.

"Don't spend it all in one place," she said.

James would. There was a flea market. Clocks were waiting.

On the way back home, he stopped at the small graveyard behind the Catholic church. Many visitors who came to the Home also stopped there. There seemed to be a connection between a fascination with clocks and a fascination with death, and James just couldn't understand it. He spent most of his life trying to avoid death, and here, people sought it out. Folks stood over the graves, pondering how each person died, what each person saw. Just the way they stood in front of the clocks in the museum, each with a placard like a headstone, and they marveled over the history those clocks must have ticked through. The dust of ancestors settled on the movements, the bones fallen to ash in the graves.

For a while, after the clock boom, James wondered if the church would hang out a shingle too, advertising the graves, charging admission. Time To Die Cemetery, the sign would say. A person standing in a ticket booth shaped like a crypt would collect five dollars a head. But thankfully, the church never put out a sign. The priest was willing to let tourists have picnics there, among the gravestones. They ate chicken from the Tick Tock Quick Stop, the smell of fried batter mixing with fresh dirt and old flowers wilted in pots.

On this day, the graveyard was empty and James nearly stepped in, making it as far as the grass on the other side of the gates. He thought about reading the names, the dates, doing the math in his head for fun so he could figure the age of the body under the stone. But he didn't. The clocks beckoned. James just didn't like people much, alive or dead.

But he did glance around quickly before turning away. Once, a woman brought him a clock that she said she found on her husband's fresh-dug grave. It turned out to be a clock James fixed once before, for someone else. He couldn't go by a graveyard now without taking a quick look. In case someone was there he knew. In case a stranger was there. The graveyard struck James as the worst place to abandon a clock, even worse than the side of the road or on a pile of garbage. This was the place of the dead where no one was ever heard from again.

It was a mantel clock that the woman found and brought James and so he thought about mantel clocks as he walked home. Those clocks were designed to truly sit on a mantel, right above a fireplace. The original clocks were extremely heavy, made from marble or brass, and once a mantel clock was hefted above a fireplace, it was intended to stay there. The clocks were thought of as permanent home furnishings, like a couch or armoire; their heaviness guaranteed them a lifetime on one mantel. But lifetimes change and so the clocks moved anyway and many sat in various rooms in the museum.

Over the years, mantel clocks became lighter, carved from wood, rich mahogany or classic oak. They began sitting on more than mantels. They squatted on shelves, on bedside tables and desks. James had two fireplaces and on those mantels were ten of the original brass and marble clocks; five on each. He dusted and cleaned them where they sat; only once a year did he pick them up and move them. Their heaviness always made him ache the next day, an ache of purpose and accomplishment and a job well done.

Returning home, James walked through the rooms and checked on the clocks, even though the winding was done for the day. James never knew when a problem might show up, when a clock would inexplicably fall ill, even if it was just ticking away a few hours, a few minutes, before. Mantel clocks were still on his mind and so he paid special attention to them. James imagined that sometimes a certain clock sent out distress signals when there was a problem somewhere, and those signals reached him, infiltrated his brain waves and started him thinking about that certain genre of clock. So he wondered now if there was a problem somewhere with a mantel clock that led him to think of them on a day when everyone was already tended. He started out in the living room, at the first mantel full of heavy originals. Stopping before each one, he listened for pauses, for catches in the breath and the rhythm.

He laid his hands on each of the clocks as he went by, patting their backs, stroking their hands. Some of the hands were old and ornate, requiring a delicate touch so they wouldn't lose any more of their gold or their flexibility. Other hands, though younger, were stubborn and resistant, alerting James to the need for a drop of oil to encourage them on their journey around the face. When the clocks chimed, he stopped and stood in place, his eyes closed, his head tilted.

Whether the clocks sang a song or simply doled out the hours, their voices reached him and he opened his heart and listened. Like he used to listen to his mother, before her heart closed forever, closed like a fist against his face. James felt like a Christian receiving Jesus; it was his responsibility to listen to the clocks. They chose him to hear their souls.

James thought of that graveyard as he moved again through the rooms, pausing, listening, touching. The graveyard made him think of his own death and he worried about who would tend to the clocks when he was gone. The town council promised James the Home would be well taken care of; they'd find somebody, if only he left the Home to them, to their direction. It was good to know that the museum's doors wouldn't close when James' eyes did for the final time, but there needed to be somebody special there. He or she needed to be more than a caretaker, a supervisor, someone who opened the door in the morning and locked it at night, from the outside.

James felt that the key to the town of What Cheer should have meant something. The promise that the Home for Wayward Clocks would remain open when he was gone should have made him feel safe, should have made him feel that the clocks were safe, in good hands. But the council just couldn't imagine the need to have someone live there, in the museum, to be with the clocks through the day and into the night.

James knew the need. The clocks did too. He felt their gratitude as he tended to them. But it was more than tending. You just don't leave your family alone and unprotected at night.

James found the graveyard clock in the exact center of the fireplace mantel on the second floor. He thought of it sitting on a grave late at night in the dark, the fresh dirt pulling at its legs. Did it worry about being buried? About being pulled under, trapped away from the light and the air? James imagined that it did, and he knew how it felt to be held in the cold underground. Did it think its voice would never be heard again, its heart stilled with the crumbling of the grave, a dead hand wrapped around the pendulum? Around the clock's heart? James deliberately kept this clock in the center of the mantel, where it could feel the warmth from the noonday sun falling in the windows, where it could draw in the heat from a late-night fire, the flames flickering in playful shadows on the wall.

James wanted this for all his clocks. To feel warm and safe and secure. And to know that someone was always close by. To know that the closing of a door, the click of a lock, didn't seal in loneliness forever.

CHAPTER FOUR:

HELD FAST

The Graveyard Clock's Story

I didn't even notice his name at first. I read the obituaries for years and learned to block out those capital-lettered names until I found what I needed to know:

Were they my age?

What did they die of?

When I found someone younger, I felt lucky and thought, There but for the grace of God goes me. When it was someone older, I thought it was his or her time and I hoped and prayed that I made it even longer. Even longer than the ones that said one-hundred and two. But when there was someone my age, I had to read what killed them. It was usually the cancer and then I wondered if it was after me too. Only then did I look at the name. I would sound it out, compare it to my own, add up syllables, vowels, consonants, and feel relieved when our names didn't match up. I could always find some way that we were different. And then I felt I would have at least one more day to live. To wait.

So at first, the name whipped by, a blur of block letters. I saw my age so I read the cause. Prostate cancer. And I let out a breath because that's one thing that can't get me. Us women seem to have an overabundance of spaces and places that fall victim to the cancer, so I'm always glad when I find a kind that has no choice but to leave me alone. But then I looked at the name.

And I thought, It can't be. And then I thought, Oh, no. Because it was Jerry. And Jerry wasn't ever supposed to die.

For a while, I just stared at his name, printed so fine, like a title in bold black. His proper name always did have a high class ring to it: Gerald R. Endicott. It was that "cott" that did it. There's just something almighty about it. But he was always Jerry to me.

I scanned the rest of the obituary. He was survived by his wife and three sons and five grandchildren. And me, I wanted to add. He was survived by me, though I never in my life wanted to live on this world without him someplace on it.

And suddenly, it was like that world hollowed out. Like all the insides just fell away, leaving only the sky and ocean blue shells with the crusts of green and yellow land. I was scattered like the dirt of the world; there was suddenly no possibility of Jerry to fill me.

I wandered into the living room and sat on the couch. I wondered if I should go to the funeral, if I could say goodbye. I hadn't seen Jerry face to face in over fifty years; no one at his funeral would know me.

Fifty years. Yet every day, Jerry walked with me to my mailbox, he drove with me across town to the hardware store or the dress shop. He told me what to buy, what tool to use, what looked good. When I sat down to eat my supper, he sat across from me and made me laugh with tales from his workday. And at night, I always slept on the left side of the bed, leaving the right side for him.

On my mantel was the old clock Jerry and I found when we were sixteen. We were wandering through the graveyard, figuring on finding a hidden shady spot to fool around, when we found this clock on someone's grave.

"That's really weird," I said and I squatted down to give it a closer look. The clock wasn't working; one of its hands hung loose while the other seemed soldered on the number four.

Jerry knelt next to me. "Pretty though," he said, even though it wasn't. "Like you." Then he lifted the thing up. It was so heavy, it made him grunt. "I'm going to give it to you, to show you that I'm yours for all time."

He carried it to the far back corner of the graveyard, then set it under a tree. It was there and then that I let him do all the things he ever wanted to do. He was mine for all time and I was so grateful and in love that there didn't seem to be any reason to say no anymore. Afterward, we lay in the grass, his entire body pressed against my bare back, his arm around my middle and his hand between my breasts and over my heart. And I reached out and held the loose hand on the clock. I wanted to thank it. The time it brought me sealed the deal with Jerry. He was mine for all time. He thought I was beautiful.

We brought the clock to my home, taking turns carrying it and sometimes each holding an end and carrying it together. Then Jerry kept my mama busy talking in the kitchen while I stumbled with it up the stairs and hid it on the floor of my closet, under a jumble of clean clothes I always forgot to hang up.

My mama found it, of course. I told her we got it at the junkyard and she told me to get rid of it. I said no, because Jerry said it was pretty like me. She shook her head, but she let me keep it then. She understood about me and Jerry. She always said a girl like me was lucky to get a guy like him. The day he left for college, she cried. I didn't. I knew he'd be back, even if she said he wouldn't. The clock sealed the deal; he was mine for all time.

That clock sat on my bedroom dresser the four years Jerry was away and I stayed home and worked at the Super Mart. And it came with me when I moved into my own place above the store. I kept the clock, even though I hadn't heard from Jerry much in most of those four years. I kept it because I had to prepare a place for him and me and the clock held our time together. I brought it with me to the few other places I lived and it's been on this mantel since I bought the house when I turned thirty-five. I was tired of waiting on Jerry to buy us a house so I decided just to make the decision for him. Only widow women and divorcees and old maids owned homes, I thought, but I told myself I wasn't one of those, I was just waiting on Jerry, and I went out and bought one anyway.

I knew what happened to him. I saw his graduation announcement in the paper and I attended the ceremony, way in the back row. He got a job a state away and eventually, I followed him there and got a job too, head cashier in the grocery store. I hoped I would bump into him, that he would come through my line and I would smile and he'd remember to come home. I about died when I read his wedding announcement. I thought about going, like I did to his graduation, but I just couldn't. I'd have to go home and my mama would be there and she would give me that look that told me she'd been right all along. I knew

I should give up then, like my mama said, but I never did. I figured he was smart enough to realize he made a mistake. And I figured his wife could always die. Women get the cancer everywhere. Like my mama.

His house was about two miles away from mine. He had his three boys and sometimes, I drove by on a Sunday afternoon, just to see them playing football in the front yard. I decided they were my sons by association. I wondered what would happen to them now.

The clock on the mantel chimed and I blinked away my dry-docked tears. That clock was beautiful now, completely different than when we found it. Years ago, before I followed Jerry to the next state, I brought it to a clock shop and museum. The guy there lived with clocks the way old women live with cats and I figured if anyone could fix it, he could. And he did. When I got it back, it was shiny and ticking and both hands clung to the right numbers. The biggest surprise was the chime; it rang four times an hour, Westminster, the clock guy said, and the sound was deep and sad, like it remembered the graveyard. It cost me my whole paycheck to have it fixed, but it was worth it; the clock ran perfectly after that. All I had to do was wind it every other week. Sometimes I forgot, but I noticed right away when that sound went missing. At night when I sat on my couch, I closed my eyes and pretended the clock's voice was Jerry's, telling me how pretty I was and how he was mine for all time.

And now, the clock was the only voice Jerry had left.

Looking at that clock, I felt sorta mad. I waited over fifty years for that man. He wasn't supposed to die first, his wife was! Why, with all her secret organs and innards, didn't she get the cancer? Maybe he didn't eat right, maybe he didn't exercise. It got him. It just got him. And now he wouldn't ever be coming home and resting on the right side of the bed.

It felt like when he went to college and never wrote to me, even though he promised he would. That last night before he left, we lay together on the back seat of his car and he told me he'd write every day and call every weekend and come home whenever he could. He said it and I let him have me so many times because I wanted him to get his fill of me so he wouldn't get hungry in school.

Maybe I shouldn't have given him his fill. Free milk, my mama said. Maybe if I'd waited, he'd be waiting now, instead of me.

And then I got even madder. For four years, I wrote to him, but he never wrote back. I called him, but he was never there. I called his folks, trying to find out when he'd be home, but they said he was too busy at school. Too busy to come home at Thanksgiving? Too busy to come home at Christmas? For four years? My mama laughed.

I gave him his fill. He said I was pretty and he was mine for all time.

And then I got the maddest I've ever been in my whole life. I went up to that clock and I wanted to make it stop ticking and making its noise and talking to me the way Jerry did. But I didn't know how; I just wound the clock a couple days before. There was no way to unwind it, no battery to pull out, no cord to yank from the wall. It wasn't that kind of clock. So I hauled the thing forward and it tried to hold fast onto my mantel, digging big claw marks in the wood. I yanked it around, pointed the beautiful face away from me, and opened its back compartment. There were all sorts of moving parts there, a small round pendulum and little wheels and springs that went back and forth, and I grabbed each and every one. I pulled them out and I threw them around the room until there were no more moving parts and then I pulled out what was left. I heard the tings and pings as metal hit my walls, my lamps, my floor, but the one sound I listened for finally gasped and disappeared. The clock stopped ticking.

Panting, I shoved it back on the mantel, pressing its face against the brick of my chimney. I heard the scratch as the glass hit the rough surface. It wasn't beautiful anymore, this clock. It wasn't even pretty, like Jerry said it was when he gave it to me. It was a wreck.

I was wrecked. Jerry was wrecked forever.

Going back to my couch, I swept away all the clock parts and then I sank into the cushions. I looked at the clock shell and I shook. I was mad and sad at the same time and I wanted so much to cry, but my chest was clenched up and nothing would come out.

I kept looking at the clock until the dry heaves stopped. And I knew it wasn't enough to tear it apart. It just wasn't enough. I got up and on hands and knees that were suddenly old and creaky, I began to search for all the scattered clock parts.

Istayed hidden behind our tree and watched as Jerry's casket was lowered into the ground. Jerry returned to our home state for burial, wanting to be planted next to his mama and daddy, and my mama, though she was four rows over, and I returned with him, carrying the clock in a rolling suitcase on the plane. Security took forever. The clock was too heavy to carry for an old lady like me, an old lady getting older every day, every minute. There was just no need to be young anymore.

I saw the wife and I knew she would be next, as wrinkled and crinkled up as she was. She must have been crying, the way her shoulders moved and a hankie kept going up to her big nose, but no sound reached me. I thought maybe she had the cancer of the voice-box and couldn't talk anymore. I gave up smoking thirty years ago so I'd never lose my voice.

I watched while they buried him and I watched while the diggers filled his hole up with dirt. Then I watched nothing, just the empty air around his stone, until it was too dark to see.

The clock and I rolled together over the dead people until I got to Jerry's new grave. The clock pinged and rattled with every bump; I had found all those ripped-out pieces and stuffed them back inside.

Carefully, remembering to lift with my knees, I put the clock in front of Jerry's stone. The clock sat on a grave just like so many years ago. This time, though, it sunk into fresh dirt. When Jerry and I found it, it was on bright green grass.

"I'm giving you back this clock, Jerry," I said to the dirt. "I can't believe I kept it all these years. But you gave it to me and you said it proved that you were mine for all time, so I thought it was a promise. I couldn't throw away a promise."

His stone was so stark. There was just his name and the dates of birth and death. No inscription, no fond remembrance. It made me sad, but at the same time, I had to push down a need to kick it.

"You were supposed to come back, Jerry. You promised. And I kept waiting...there were no other men. Not once." And there weren't. I never dated. No one else ever asked. No one else ever loved me.

And Jerry didn't either. With a rush, I knew that as certainly as I used to know he'd come back. He never loved me at all. My knees went shaky and weak and I went down into the dirt.

"The clock is ugly!" I hollered. "You said it was pretty like me, but it wasn't! It was ugly!" I sobbed. "Like me!" I scooped up handfuls of dirt and threw it at the stone. It fell in clumps on the clock. I knew if I dug far enough, I could get to the coffin, pull it open, and smack Jerry across the face. Because that's what he deserved; one of those loud, neck-snapping slaps you see on television that leave red marks on pale cheeks.

But digging through six feet of dirt just wasn't in me. I stopped after a few inches and staggered to my feet. "You can have the clock, Jerry," I whispered. "It kept me company for all these years. Now I don't want your company anymore." But I knew I was lying. I knew that if Jerry suddenly plunged through the dirt, offered me his arm and said, "Let's go home, Elizabeth," I'd link up with him in a minute. I knew if I could, I'd be the dirt that rested around his coffin. I knew I was dirt.

My mama was right. She always said she was right, and she was. Free milk just doesn't make anyone buy a cow.

As I turned to walk away, I knocked right into a woman. I let out a yelp and nearly went backwards. Looking closer, I recognized the wrinkled crinkled big-nose from the funeral. Jerry's wife. As dark as it was, it was hard to see her expression. But she wasn't crying, I saw that much. She just stared at me, so I stuck my toe in her husband's dirt and said nothing.

Then she said, "Are you Elizabeth?"

And I startled. Only Jerry called me Elizabeth; he said it suited me. He said it was regal and...beautiful. I was always plain Betty to everyone else. I looked over my shoulder at the clock. Its face glowed. Then I nodded.

"I thought so. Jerry talked about you all the time." She moved forward and looked down at the stone. "I don't know why I'm here, exactly. I couldn't sleep. I kept thinking...I kept thinking he might be cold. I even put a blanket in my car." She laughed. "And you...you brought him a clock?"

"He talked about me?" I stepped sideways, off Jerry's dirt, and steadied myself on my rolling suitcase.

She grimaced. "All the time. It was Elizabeth this and Elizabeth that. It was like competing with a ghost I could never see." She moved next to me and touched my sleeve. "I always pictured you as younger."

I stuck my chin out. "I was younger, when he met me."

She stared, then shook her head. Reaching down, she touched the clock. "Why the clock? Why a broken old clock?"

I looked down at it and it didn't look so broken anymore. In this dark light, it was beautiful again and when I listened hard, I could hear its tick. I knew in the middle of the night, its chime would ring out and Jerry would hear it and I would hear it back at home as I sat listening on my couch. "I wanted to give it to him," I said. "So...so he would know that he's still mine for all time." Then I grabbed my suitcase and left, running as fast as I could over the graves.

"Hey!" I heard her call. "Hey, take your clock! I don't want it here!" I smiled when I heard her grunt and mutter, "Damn, this thing is heavy."

I knew she wouldn't be able to move it. It would hold fast to Jerry's dirt, just as it held fast to my mantel for so long. It was Jerry's clock now and Jerry's time to wait. When I met him in heaven, he would have the clock in his arms.

And then he would have me. He was mine for all time. And I would be beautiful again.

CHAPTER FIVE:

JAMES

And so school teaches you a lot more than about letters and numbers. Through your reading, imagine learning that mothers make beef stew and gingerbread houses, they remember to turn on nightlights that slice the dark into brightness, they comb unruly hair and help with homework. Dick and Jane's mother always wears dresses. Their mother plays. Their mother smiles.

You look up from your reading at your own mother and you are confused. How else can you feel, in your world where childhood memories involve a parade of collars, a small red one with a buckle and a bell, a blue one with dancing white bones, black leather with bright silver teeth. A choker. Imagine hearing your mother's voice, sliding from a soft to a shrill yowl, her hand snatching the leash that holds you, her child, and jerking you off your feet and skidding your bare bottom across the dirt floor of the root cellar. Imagine spankings with a rolled-up newspaper, a hairbrush, a belt. You are called an animal by the woman who, the books tell you, is supposed to love you from your first bubbly kick inside of her skin until you stand next to her to catch her last breath. You are supposed to love her forever. She is supposed to love you.

Imagine.

You listen carefully to the conversations your classmates have in the lunchroom. There are some sad tales, tears shared when a child complains of a raised voice, or a spanking with an open palm, or being sent to a room for the rest of the night. These punished children speak of hating their mothers then, they say it out loud, with clogged and wet voices, "Oh, I hate her! I hate her! She is so mean!"

Imagine hating your mother. You think of your spankings, with belts and wooden hairbrushes, that go on until your skin is ruptured and red. You think of her shriek, of the damp and dark of the root cellar, the days spent there. The nights. You think of sitting on your bed in your room, your arms crossed, your feet not even swinging, and how you control your breath to make the littlest inhale, the littlest exhale, and you try and you try and you try to be quiet, and yet somehow, she manages to even hear you think and so you are in her way again. You've always thought of yourself as a very naughty boy, even though you're never quite sure what it is that you do.

At the cafeteria table, you blink.

Yet there are other times too. Times when your mother is asleep, curled in the warm bath of sunshine, and her hair is spread on the floor, and her face is smooth and thoughtless. The sun pinks her cheeks and she is so beautiful.

And sometimes she remembers to make meals. She mostly remembers to buy food. Sometimes she sits right next to you at the table and she looks at you. She looks at you and you know from the steadiness of her eyes that she's actually seeing you. And sometimes, rarely, she even smiles.

No. You don't hate your mother.

Imagine.

In the stories you read, it's the stepmothers who are evil, who do mean things, and you consider that for a while. Maybe your mother is really your stepmother, and your real mother died at your birth and no one has ever told you about her. Your father never mentioned anything like that before he disappeared. He always referred to your mother as your mother. But maybe?

Yet your hair is the same shade of blonde, and has that gentle wave in it that gets snarled if it's not brushed enough. And your eyes are as blue as hers.

You know she is your mother. You know this in the deepest way. She is your mother. You belong to her.

And so you listen to the conversations, read your books, and wonder what it is that makes you so different. Why do other mothers reach out, draw children in with a hug, while your mother's arm flares back, then connects with your cheek in a dizzying smack? Why do other mothers insist that their children go out for fresh air while yours is content to have you strain for the thin slat of sunshine coming between two bolted wooden doors? What have you done?

What have you done?

Imagine.

James never understood what he did, not exactly. Sometimes, he thought his mother was so angry just because he breathed. Just because he'd been born. And as he sat through days and nights, either collared and leashed to the root cellar wall or locked in a dog kennel, sometimes with a bowl of water, sometimes not, sometimes with a bowl of whatever stale snack was in the pantry, sometimes not, the alarm clock ticking near his ear, the tiny baby blanket barely draped over his shoulders or resting on his knees, James often wished he'd never been born at all.

The graveyard clock was a sad clock and James knew it. Sadness was in its voice, in the slowness of its tick. He kept its black enameled cast iron body so shiny, it reflected the flames in the fireplace, licks of orange and yellow splintering the solid black. But even that glow couldn't cheer this clock up. James felt its sorrow when he wound it every other week, in the catch in the gears that just couldn't be repaired.

James repaired this clock twice, lifted it from death and returned it to the light of day. The first time, years ago, a woman brought the clock to him. She said it hadn't worked in all the time she had it, that she'd just let it sit silently on her dresser. James couldn't imagine walking past a muted clock for years and never once attempting to resurrect it. When he fixed it, he felt like he performed open heart surgery. More than that; he imagined he gave that clock back its soul. He found all original parts in his skeleton boxes and in antique shops all around Iowa and Wisconsin. When that clock chimed for the first time in decades, James sat back and applauded. He applauded the clock as much as himself. James fixed it; but it remembered its voice and heart and it used them well.

When the woman picked up her clock and heard the voice for the first time, a flush went around her cheeks and up to her eyebrows. When the chime stopped, she whispered her thanks, whispered as if her own voice wasn't worthy next to the sound of that song. James watched the way she touched the clock; first with the tips of her fingers, then sliding her whole palm over its body. She loved that clock and for that moment, James loved her too and forgave her ignorance.

But several years later, the clock came back when another woman found it in the graveyard. She held the clock like it was the ugliest thing on earth. She dumped it on him, dumped it like an abandoned baby or a box of unwanted puppies. When James caught it, cradled it against his chest, all its parts jangled inside. There wasn't one working part left out of all that he'd so painstakingly replaced and repaired in its body; even the hands hung loose and broken. But it was the dirt that was unforgivable. There was loose dirt pushed up through the clock's skin, through its legs and through cracks into its insides.

No clock deserved that. No clock deserved this abuse. Nothing and no one belonged in the dirt. James knew what that was like; he understood the darkness and the smell of heavy dankness pressing down until it seemed that there was no air at all. The first thing he did was take the clock down to his shop and shine a light upon it. A warm and big light that illuminated the clock's skin and the sadness in its face. And then James started to clean.

Most of the parts were tucked away inside, but they needed to be individually washed and straightened and oiled. It took James months to restore it. It was like putting an entire life back together, piece by piece.

The original woman, that whispering woman, showed up at James' door a couple months after he finally fixed the clock. She told him some story about losing the clock and asked if there were any others like it. She said she missed the clock's voice. James told her no, straight out and flat, and then he shut the door in her face. He forgave her once. But he never made a mistake twice.

From the other side of his door, James listened as the whispering woman cried. The clock knew and grew sadder still, but James couldn't let it go. Not in good conscience. Not to her, definitely not to her. She didn't deserve that clock. And it didn't deserve her.

Standing by it now, listening to the hesitation in its tick, thinking about the graveyard, James tried to let it know that everything was okay. It was safe.

All James' clocks were safe.

James had to go out again that day, but he waited awhile, catching his breath, building his nerve. He could only handle people a little at a time and dealing with Sophie and with his memories of the two mantel clock women were enough for one morning. But there were things he needed at the grocery store and so he steeled himself with lunch before heading back out. He told himself, like he told himself every day, afternoons were a dead time in a grocery store. Most people do their shopping in the morning or on their way home from work. He wouldn't have to talk much, maybe not at all, he might just be able to buy the necessities, pay with cash and a quick smile, and then go. Bolstering his spirits, James grabbed his little cart and took off for the store.

For a while, James tried doing the grocery shopping just once a week. He thought it would lessen the stress of having to be out in public, facing the long aisles of too much food and too many bodies pushing around carts, if it wasn't on a daily basis. But only going once a week extended his time actually inside the grocery store. Instead of dashing in and dashing out, laden only with whatever he ran out of that day, he had to push a full-sized store cart and fill it and stand in line behind everyone else who had too many items for the express lane. It was too much. Facing it once a day for only fifteen or so minutes at a time was hard, but manageable; a necessary moment of discomfort.

Trying to fit in with the theme after the town's revitalization, the grocery store renamed itself the Shop Around The Clock. It used to be Marv's 24-Hour Shopper. James' picture was in a frame at the entry. In it, he held a ridiculously huge pair of scissors, preparing to cut the ribbon for the grand re-opening, the grocery store newly repainted and decorated with psychedelic neon wall clocks. The owner spent weeks creating cassette tapes of songs that mentioned clocks or time. Rock Around The Clock, of course. Time In A Bottle. If I Could Turn Back Time. Clock of the Heart. These songs played continuously, but from the looks on the shoppers' faces, they never listened so it was an exercise in futility. Other than that, the grocery store was the same. Still just Marv's 24-Hour Shopper under the glitz and forced glamour. Same food, same prices. Even with James' picture at the front, the cashiers still asked for James' identification when he wrote a check. Though they smiled at him now. So he used cash; cash was faster. Another reason for going every day and keeping the order small.

As James moved through the store, checking his list against each aisle's index of ingredients, he peeked around every corner. If he saw someone he knew, he ducked back and moved on to another item on the list. Avoiding acquaintances saved him the head nods, the smiles, the passing of inane conversation. It also kept James' heart from accelerating from already-in-overdrive to panic. Sometimes, when an item was halfway down an aisle, someone would come around the far corner as he dashed for the middle. Then it was a race; could he get the item, toss it into his little rolling cart, and escape before he and the person met? Sometimes, they called his name and then he was stuck. If he tried not to hear them, they only yelled louder.

On this day, James thought he was safe. He had his toilet paper, bread, day-old doughnuts, and chicken breasts for dinner, along with some fresh corn on the cob and a half-gallon of low-fat milk. There was only the country-meadow air freshener to grab and then he could be out the door. He spun on his heels and headed to the top of Aisle Seven, intending to move quickly past the endcaps to

Aisle Twelve and then head for the express lane. But as he shot past Aisle Nine, he heard the mayor's voice. There was no mistaking or ignoring the mayor's voice; he had a politician's command and he demanded an audience.

"James!" he called. "James, how are you?"

The question James always found impossible to answer. What did people really want to know? Did they want to know the state of his health or his mind? Did they just want him to say, "Oh, fine, fine," and then shut up while they loaded their litanies on him, their problems and preachings, the latest town gossip? Did they even hear themselves ask the question, let alone listen for an answer? James faced the mayor and decided just to duck his head and smile.

"Good, good," the mayor said, patting James' shoulder. James stepped quickly backwards, just far enough to be out of reach, so the mayor's fingers stroked the air. "Listen, I have a favor to ask you."

James locked his knees and waited.

"The wife, she went to this antique mall in Davenport the other day. And she had to come home with this cuckoo clock. Loves it, she says, says it caught on her skirt as she walked by and she looked down and saw how it had a hold of her and so she bought it." He shook his head and laughed.

James wondered why the cuckoo clock chose the mayor's wife. She was a wisp of a thing with breasts. She shook his hand at the ceremony where he received the key to the city and he found himself briefly wanting to squeeze more than her fingers. An urge James didn't have often, but those breasts were irrepressible. James tucked away a smile as he wondered if the cuckoo bird was in heat.

"Anyway, it doesn't run quite right and she's heartbroken. It cuckoos the hour on the half and the half on the hour. Makes it hellishly hard to tell time."

Misplaced hands, James thought. Someone at some time moved the hands backwards instead of forwards and messed up the clock's mind. "Simple fix," he said out loud.

The mayor beamed. "Oh, I'm glad to hear it. I'll have someone bring it around, if that's all right with you."

James nodded.

"Thank you, James. Good talking to you!" He stepped closer before James could adjust and clapped him on the back. James gasped and didn't breathe again until the mayor disappeared down Aisle Ten. Why, James wondered, didn't the mayor just send someone around for groceries, why did food deserve a personal touch, but the clock would be delivered by a stranger? Quickly, James collected his air freshener and moved through the checkout.

Outside again, he stopped for a moment in the shade of the building and wiped his face with a handkerchief. His heart slowed and he waited for the sweat to cool and evaporate from his skin, and then he headed down the sidewalk. The town's clock tower chimed one-thirty, so he knew it was only eighteen minutes past the hour. For a moment, he pictured the clock tower as a huge cuckoo clock. Big enough to require an ostrich as the cuckoo. Without thinking, James laughed out loud. Slapping his hand over his mouth, he glanced around, but no one else was out, no one to demand an explanation for his sudden bray, no one to seek any explanation at all. That allowed him to smile during the trip home.

All cuckoo clocks made James smile. Cuckoos were spread throughout the Home, at least one on every wall in every room, to lighten the mood, lift the spirit. When a cuckoo bird flew out of its door, its window, its chimney, or in one case, a cat's mouth, James had to smile and he felt the rest of the clocks brighten. No matter how rich or formal the tone, a cuckoo bird's chirp always sounded ridiculous. They were like a bride wearing sneakers. Whenever James heard laughter coming from the visitors, he knew what he'd see even before he looked in the room or checked the security monitor; a crowd gathered around a performing cuckoo.

James had them all, from miniature to gigantic, with faces as big as a grandfather clock's or as small as a quarter. Some played tinny music, others just cuckooed, all had moving parts, from the traditional bird to waterwheels to dancers twirling in lederhosen around an overweight oom-pah band, tiny red faces blowing into a tuba, a horn and a clarinet.

Franz Anton Ketterer invented the cuckoo. It was always very hard for James to imagine that someone had to invent each individual kind of clock, but especially the cuckoo clock. What kind of mind thought up a little bird barreling out of a small door and coo-cooing the hour?

James often wished that he could invent a clock. A special clock, one that would be named after him. But while he could see the clock in his mind, he could never build it into existence. He sketched his idea once, trying to see through his dreams into what was left of his soul, into whatever it was that made that pendulum swing in his own body, but he didn't get very far. He wanted to create a statue clock of a mother, leaning down to a boy. She was looking at her wrist watch, silver and slim and bright, which James pictured as a working clock. Her boy gazed upwards, his arm outstretched, bearing his own tiny golden watch, also a working clock. She was teaching him to tell time, to divide up his life into hours and minutes and seconds and set him on a path of days and nights that fell as evenly as a heartbeat. James wanted both of those clocks to have an internal pendulum, but those pendulums would swing in perfect synchrony, in rhythm and motion with each other. Two hearts beating as individual, but also completely dependent upon each other. If one ran fast, so would the other. If one stopped, then both were silenced. But James never figured out how to make it work.

For a moment, James stopped on the street, clenched his hands around the handle of his little cart, and stared at the sidewalk. Thinking of that clock, the one that only existed in his mind, in his imagination, always set him into disarray, and he had to focus hard to bring his body back into balance. He shoved that woman and her little boy as far back in his mind as he could reach. James knew that clock would never tick, never chime. There was no living model. He just couldn't imagine.

CHAPTER SIX:

A LADY'S HAIR
The Cuckoo Clock Story

Ty hated it when his mother plucked her beard. She always did it at the kitchen table, sitting at his father's place under the old cuckoo clock. She set up a makeup mirror and turned the little round lights on bright. At ten years old, Ty knew makeup mirrors were supposed to be for makeup; he never knew women had beards to pluck until his mother announced what she did from time to time, at the table. The worst part was when she waited until he had his head buried in the fridge and then she yelled, "Oh, wow, Ty! Look at this one! I musta missed it before!" When he looked over, she straightened out a long curly hair, holding it between her two hands the way a fisherman holds a prize catch. The really long ones usually came from her neck.

He always stuck his head back in the fridge and held it there, hoping the cold air would freeze the image of his mother, tweezers to her chin, and he could smash her with a hammer into little tiny ice shards. The beard-plucking was gross and it made his stomach feel funny. He hated her when she did that and hated her worse when she made him a part of it.

He hated his name too. Ty. Short for Tyler, which wasn't so bad, except no one ever called him that. At school, he was dubbed Tynee, NeckTy, Tyed-Up-In-Knots. He hated those, but at least he could

Kathie Giorgio

figure them out, but then a new name showed up when a bigger boy grinned and said to a girl bent over the water fountain, "Hey, Amber, wanna tie one on?" The girl blushed almost as red as Ty himself. He didn't know what the boy meant, but everyone else howled and started calling him Ty-One-On. Amber smiled at him before he ran away.

Girls seemed to like his name, like the way they could drawl, "Hiiii, Tyyyy," as he went by. He never answered, but when he tried to scowl, he felt his face automatically lift in a grin. So the girls wouldn't stop. They "Hi, Tyed" him wherever he went and he couldn't stop them and he blushed and grinned. Like a dork, he told himself. Like a fucking dork, using the new word that was too dangerous to say aloud. He used it silently and often, trying to take the gloss off it, make it an ordinary word that slid naturally into his vocabulary. Fucking cereal, fucking toothpaste. Fucking hot dog. Fucking cuckoo clock, fucking makeup mirror. He admired how it sounded, low and sharp, within the walls of his brain. He thought it would sound better shouted out loud, echoing down the halls at school, ricocheting against the gun metal lockers.

Ty looked at the girls and wondered if they plucked beards as soft and downy as the hair on his arm. He wondered why men shaved and women plucked. He knew his own father shaved, though he never watched. His father spent a lot of time in the bathroom with the door closed. There was always a disposable razor stuck in the toothbrush holder. The razor had a plastic handle and varied in color from blue to black to a blue/black combination. His mother kept a pink razor in the shower and Ty knew she used it on her arms and legs. Why tweezers on her face and a razor on her limbs? Ty imagined how dangerous shaving was, how easy it could be to cut your own throat. He touched his father's razor once or twice, ran his fingers over the blade and was stunned by so much blood at so little hurt. He could die without knowing it.

The day he became Ty-One-On, Ty pulled his best friend Barry over to their favorite rock by the side of the street. The big rock looked like a baked potato and Ty's mother said that whoever owned that house deliberately stuck the rock there as an oddity. Ty just thought it was cool and he and Barry liked to sit on it and watch the cars go by. "Did you hear what that guy called me today?" Ty asked. "Ty-One-On."

Barry nodded.

"So what does Ty-One-On mean?" Ty scuffed his shoe against the potato's skin.

"Damned if I know," Barry said. He looked at Ty and grinned, then licked his lips over the swear word. "Damned if I know."

Ty laughed and smacked his hands against his thighs. "Well, damned if I know either!"

They smiled and sat next to each other, bumping their shoulders together.

"Fuck," Ty said softly, bravely, trying it out.

Barry's eyes widened, then he frowned and brought his big front teeth to his lower lip. "Fuck," he said too, drawing out every letter.

Ty jumped down and walked away, dragging his backpack on the ground. Barry followed. "Does your mom have a makeup mirror?" Ty asked.

"A mirror where she puts on makeup?" Barry asked. "Yeah, she's got one. Doesn't call it that though. It's in her room and it's like a table, and there's lots of lights in a big circle. She calls it a vanity. You know, you've seen it."

Ty had. It was pretty, in a way, when the lights glowed bright and reflected off the oval mirror. It looked like a movie star. "My mom sits at the kitchen table with hers. It's little...she keeps it under the sink in the bathroom." They were getting close to home, so Ty put his backpack over his shoulders again. His mom yelled if she caught him dragging it. "Does your mom have..." He motioned in the air, bringing his thumb and forefinger together and apart. "Tweezers?"

Barry nodded. "Yeah, she pulls out her eyebrows with them."

Ty stopped, fingering the dark short hairs that he knew arched above his eyes. "Her eyebrows?"

"Yeah. She makes them real thin." Barry grinned. "It's weird."

"Yeah." They got to the intersection where Barry had to go right and Ty left. "Barry, does your mom pull out a beard?"

Barry laughed. "Women don't have beards!"

Ty touched his own chin. No hair yet. "My mom does. She plucks out her beard, she says. I saw her and everything."

Now Barry stopped and his mouth dropped open. "Oh. My. God," he said, each word a sentence all its own.

That's what Ty was afraid of, that reaction. That was exactly it. "Not your mom?" he asked one more time, hoping maybe Barry was lying, maybe he'd break down and tell the truth.

"No." Barry shook his head. "No, Ty, not ever."

Ty sighed and slouched. His backpack fell to the ground. "Great," he said. "My mom's a freak."

Barry nodded.

"Fuck," Ty said. "A fucking freak."

The next time Ty found his mother in front of her makeup mirror, he didn't dive into the fridge. He stood by the table and watched. His mother pulled her face this way and that, putting the tweezers to her skin and yanking out hairs that Ty could barely see. The underside of her chin became blotchy with red. Finally, she put the tweezers down and looked at him. "Is there something you need?" she asked.

"Why do you do that?" He pointed to the mirror, the tweezers, her face.

"Pluck my beard, you mean?" She shrugged. "To get rid of the hair. See?" She picked up his hand, put his palm under her chin. It felt smooth and the red spots weren't even warm. "Like a baby's behind," she said and smiled.

"But why do you have a beard? You're a girl." Ty took his hand back.

She laughed. "Well, yeah, I am, but when girls get older, sometimes they get hair where they don't want it. And then it has to be pulled out if they still want to look like a lady."

"Like eyebrows?"

"Yeah, some ladies do their eyebrows. I like mine the way they are."

"So…" He reached out and touched the tweezers. They were cold and the edges looked sharp. "All old ladies have beards?"

"Yep." She nodded and turned off her mirror. "It's a fact of life." Then she stopped and blinked. "Though I'm not old."

Liar! he wanted to yell. Not Barry's mom! It's just eyebrows for Barry's mom! But he turned and walked away without saying a word, until he got to the kitchen entryway. The cuckoo clock went off, the bird flickering in and out like a bizarre snake tongue, and, thinking he wouldn't be heard over the raucous chirping, Ty muttered, "Fucking freak."

"Ty-ler!" His mother was at his side in a second, shaking his shoulder. "Did you just say what I think you said?"

He thought he said it soft.

She dragged him to the sink. "Don't you ever talk like that!" She looked all around the counter and in the cabinets. Then she grabbed the plastic bottle of dish soap and pointed it at him like a gun. "Open your mouth!" she demanded.

Ty didn't know what to do, so he stuck out his tongue, then sucked it back in like the cuckoo bird. In, out, in, out, and his mother snatched and pounced and then she finally caught it between her fingers. She squirted the soap all over until he gagged. "Now rinse your mouth out and go to your room until supper! No video games!"

Ty spat and spat, but the taste just wouldn't go away. His mouth kept foaming, the bubbles going up the back of his throat and out his nose where they popped and got into his eyes. It was funny, in a way, but he couldn't hold back the tears and he cried in earnest as he swirled cup after cup of water around in his mouth. Then he ran to his room and slammed the door.

All because his mother was a freak. All because of a beard. "Damn," he said softly into his pillow. "Shit. Fuck." But in the walls of his brain, he screamed the words as loud as he could.

The next day, Barry was absent from school so Ty had to walk home by himself. He wandered down the couple blocks and paused for a moment by the baked potato rock. He wondered if Barry told the truth when they talked about beards; maybe he just didn't want to admit his mother plucked too. Though he told that bit about the eyebrows. Ty's mom's eyebrows were bushy and full, prone to collapsing into a vicious V over her nose.

Ty was just about to make his left turn when he heard a soft, "Pssst!" He looked around. Amy Sue Dander waved at him, her head poking out of a bush at the edge of her yard. "Ty!" she whispered. "C'mere!" She ducked back inside, then popped out again and Ty smiled, thinking she was like the cuckoo bird at home. In, out, in, out.

He carefully spread the leaves and followed her. The bush was all hollowed out, like a cave, within the spindly branches. He dropped his backpack and breathed out in appreciation. "Wow, Amy Sue, this is cool! Did you make this?"

She shook her head. "Hi, Ty," she said, her voice low. "I just found it this way. It's my favorite private place."

He sat down on the ground, noticing the way the branches spread clear to the grass so nobody could see their feet from the outside.

Amy Sue smiled at him. She waggled her eyebrows, which he noticed were blonde, like her curls, though a little darker. "So you wanna see something really cool?"

"Sure. What?"

Amy Sue's smile spread wider and her hands reached for her waist. "I'll show you mine if you show me yours," she said, her voice suddenly full and throaty.

"Show you my—" Ty's tongue caught on the roof of his mouth as in one swift motion, Amy Sue pulled down her jeans and underpants. They bunched around her ankles and then she pulled her shirt up high, almost to her chin.

She was so smooth, pink and smooth all over. He felt his eyes move of their own accord from her chin to below her belly button. Between her legs, there were two fat rolls of skin, joined in the middle by a crease. He found himself being pulled there, up on his hands and knees, and he crawled over to her and stared at her crotch, just a few inches away from his nose.

She wiggled a bit. "See?" she said. "Now I've shown you mine, you have to show me yours. It's a game Barry showed me."

Barry! He never said anything about this! Ty stood up unsteadily. "Show you my…?" he said and reached for his belt buckle. She nodded vigorously. Pulling at his belt and button and zipper, Ty allowed his pants to fall to his ankles, just like Amy Sue's.

"Oh, look!" Amy Sue squealed. "It's pointing right at me, just like Barry's did!"

Ty looked down and sure enough, his penis was up and pointing directly at Amy Sue. He felt different too and he just didn't know what to say. They stood there for a while, looking each other up and down. Mostly down. Amy Sue's cheeks turned red and Ty felt his own face grow warm.

Abruptly, he reached down and pulled up his pants. Amy Sue did too. The sounds of snaps and zippers seemed impossibly loud. Ty put on his backpack. Then he followed Amy Sue out, crawling under the bush.

Standing on the sidewalk, Ty stared at Amy Sue. She smiled and looked away. Then he touched her chin. It was smooth, as smooth as the rest of her. "Amy Sue, do you ever use a tweezers on your chin?"

She frowned. "A tweezers? Why?"

He shrugged. "I don't know. Just asking."

"My mom does sometimes. I don't. Maybe later though. It might be a lady thing."

Ty closed his eyes and kissed her cheek. He felt like he had to, it was right, like it was a law. Amy Sue shrieked, then ran toward her house. "Bye, Ty!" she yelled over her shoulder.

Ty walked slowly the rest of the way home, thinking about beards and tweezers and bushes and soft pink folds of skin. And about Amy Sue's voice as she popped her head out of the bush like a cuckoo bird, saying, "Hi, Ty!" His name didn't seem so bad now.

He got home just as the cuckoo clock chirped four, so he knew he was late. But the sound of the shower told him that his mother would never know. Throwing his backpack into a corner, he helped himself to some cookies and milk. He thought of his mother, sitting at the table the day before, her hands pulling and stretching the skin beneath her chin. He thought of her eyebrows and Amy Sue's and

Barry's mother's. And he thought of Amy Sue and the smooth fat place between her legs.

He wondered.

Quickly, he moved to the bathroom. He heard the water, heard his mother singing. Slowly, he opened the door. Her silhouette shimmered behind the shower curtain, her arms upraised, fingers scrubbing her head. She was washing her hair. He started taking showers by himself when he was six, but he could still remember how it felt to have her wash his hair while he sat in the warm water of the bathtub. Her fingers were strong and rough, yet he still leaned into her hands. It never felt as good with his own.

He pulled back the curtain just enough to see with one eye. His mother's eyes were closed against the shampoo and her face was raised as she sang. He took a deep breath and he looked.

No smooth fat skin. Just a wet dark triangle of hair.

He backed away and shut the door. Her song never stopped so he knew he wasn't caught. Going back to the kitchen, he sat down and tried to puzzle it all out.

Amy Sue's skin was smooth; his mother's, hairy. His mother and Barry's plucked some hairs and left others alone. He thought about what Amy Sue said, about how her mother used tweezers and how maybe she would too, someday. A lady thing. And he thought of his father's razor in the toothbrush holder in the bathroom.

It was all beginning to make sense, in a cuckoo sort of way. Logic dodged in, out, in, out. Women plucked, men shaved. Not all women plucked the same places. Smooth skin could grow hair on both men and women. Some kept it, some didn't. Men grew beards, kept them or shaved them off. Women grew beards, but always plucked them. It was a lady thing. It was weird, but it seemed to work.

His mother walked into the kitchen, a towel still wrapped around her head. "Hi, honey," she said. "I didn't hear you come in. Did you get your own snack?"

Ty nodded. "Mom, I'm sorry."

She stopped by his chair. "For what?"

He lowered his eyes. "For what I said yesterday."

She squeezed his shoulder. "Oh, that. That kind of stuff happens sometimes, sweetheart. It's okay."

Maybe, Ty thought, looking up at the cuckoo clock, maybe swearing's a man thing.

Barry was still sick the next day and Ty stalked the playground, looking for Amy Sue. A strange feeling tugged the right corner of his mouth; he felt a new expression on his face, a sort of sideways smile. When he saw her on the swingset with her best friend Judy, his breath caught. Then he went up to her. "Hey, Amy Sue," he said.

Amy Sue stopped swinging. "Hi, Ty," she said softly as Judy giggled.

He leaned toward her, the corner of his mouth turning up in that new way. "Amy Sue," he said slowly, remembering the boy's words a few days before. "Wanna Ty-One-On? Wanna Ty-One-On with me?" He looked in her face, then dropped his gaze down, down to her lap. He still didn't know what those words meant, but they sounded the way he felt yesterday and he laughed when Amy Sue squealed and jumped off the swing, running away with Judy.

Spinning around, he threw his arms wide and he looked straight up, up as far as he could, into the sky. "Fuck!" he bellowed. The word roared out of his throat and it felt so good, so good, that he didn't care who heard. He didn't care at all.

It was just too good. It was a man thing.

CHAPTER SEVEN:

JAMES

A nd so what about fathers? In your books, fathers usually wear suits and go off to work every morning, just like your father did, though he didn't wear a suit. The Papa Bear in Goldilocks and the Three Bears was gruff, always growling out orders. Your father wasn't like that. He was quiet. He didn't say much. When he did talk, it was always in a soft tone meant to soothe, meant to comfort, meant to lull your mother back into peace. The father in Dick and Jane wore suits and went to work, but he wore casual pants and mowed the lawn on weekends, like your father. The Dick and Jane dad smoked a pipe, while yours smoked a cigar.

While your father was still around, there was always a supper to eat, breakfast in the morning, a bag lunch packed for you in the refrigerator. At night, after supper, you and he would sit silently in the living room, your father smoking a cigar, you breathing it in. Your mother was in her bedroom, at her vanity, looking at her reflection, or she was gone, out the door, and you and your father never knew if she was coming back. But still, you were silent. Just in case.

Until your father disappeared one foggy morning, your mother put you in the root cellar for only a few hours after each school day. She always remembered to let you up before your father came home, and he would find you in your room, doing homework, and he patted your head and asked for your help with supper. He cooked, you set the table.

Your mother slept or stared in the living room, under a soft blanket that your father placed there when he got home.

When your mother had one of her fits, what you decided were temper tantrums, your father just sat, made patting motions with his hands, and whispered to her. Their voices made an odd sort of harmony.

But he never did anything.

Imagine.

You are eight years old when he wakes you in the early morning. When he places both of his hands on either side of your face and whispers that he's leaving, he's going to find a new place for the two of you, and he will be back for you. "I know what goes on, son," he says. You try to protest, but he leaves anyway, off into the grainy gray of a foggy morning, and you are now with your mother alone. All you can do is hang on with your whole life to his words, that he will be back for you. Hang on as the days lead to weeks and to years.

Yet those other words are there too, just under the surface of your skin, and they poke you, growing sharper as you get older. *I know what goes on, son.* You think of the evenings spent in the living room, your father smoking his cigar. Sitting still. Whispering.

Those words flame red. Like the burning end of a cigar. Like the welts on your body.

Imagine a father who knows not doing anything. Imagine him just leaving. How could he never come back? With your father gone, the root cellar bursts wide open, sucks you in, slams the doors closed. Your mother no longer bothers to hide, because there is no one to hide from. There is no longer the relief of a father coming home, calling your name, patting your head. There is only your mother and your mother and your mother.

Imagine.

James watched as his mind colored his father as a protector, then a journeying hero, then nothing at all. Someone who sat and did nothing was nothing, James decided. A coward. A well-meaning coward, but a coward.

I know what goes on, son.

How could anybody know and not do anything? How could he know and sit and smoke his cigar and pat his son's head?

Imagine.

The next day, on his way to fetch the morning paper, James stopped when he heard the painful bleat of a cuckoo. Glancing into the living room, James saw a plain yellow cuckoo bird, smacking its head against the door of its clock as it announced the time. It was seven o'clock and seven times that bird banged its head. James winced and touched his own forehead in sympathy.

He tried so hard to fix that clock, but he just couldn't find the right bird. One day, a woman brought the cuckoo, a woman who looked thrown together in sweat pants and a sweater, one purple, one orange, and an urgent look on her face that let James know she got up that morning and came straight to the Home. The clock was tucked under her arm like an already-read newspaper and she set it directly in his hands.

"The bird's gone," she said simply.

James opened the little hatch and sure enough, there was only a perch and what was left of the missing bird's feet.

"When it goes off now, the perch knocks on the door from the inside, making this awful cracking sound, and there's still a cuckoo, even though there's no bird. It's like a haunted cuckoo house," the woman said.

James nodded. "The bird doesn't actually make the noise. It's just part of the mechanism. The voice is inside the clock."

"I never knew that!" She shrugged. "I thought the cuckoo bird... you know."

You thought the cuckoo bird was alive, James said to himself. Individually alive, as if the clock was just a house around it and only the bird made it work. Everyone thought that. But the cuckoo bird was just a part of the cuckoo clock, a part of the whole. Like your tongue or your eye or your knee. A part of your mechanism.

She followed James down to his workshop where he set the clock gently on the bench and began rummaging around the skeleton boxes for perchless cuckoo birds. "So what happened to this clock?" James asked. "Where's the bird? It would be best if we could put the original back."

"I don't know." She sighed and put her hands on her hips. "My son went nuts the other night. He had a date with a girl and you know how boys get before a date." She waggled her eyebrows.

James didn't date until after he was an adult and then he only dated one woman, Diana, whom he met at the beginning of the town's rejuvenation. He remembered the first time they went out, just for lemonade and hot dogs at the park. He wasn't ever sure what made him go with Diana that day, a woman whose name he didn't know yet, a stranger in town. She just looked at him and didn't look away. James kept glancing up from his place in line at the hot dog stand and there she was, her eyes flat on his. The Home had been open for only about a month at that time and it was still a rare treat for James to eat out. It felt like a celebration, being able to afford a hot dog and fries and now a girl was looking at him too. He checked his fly, made sure it was closed. He reached the vendor first, but she stepped beside him and said, "He'll order for the both of us." So he swallowed and splurged and ordered four Chicago-style dogs and cheese-covered fries and two large lemonades and then he followed her to a bench under a tree.

That morning with the cuckoo woman in his basement, as he dug through boxes of homeless cuckoo birds, James remembered the flutter-heart feeling and sweaty palms as Diana's hips swayed in front of him, her hair curling like beckoning fingers. "You know how boys get before a date," the cuckoo bird woman said and James put her words and his memory together and thought, Oh, that.

"Then, right before it was time for him to pick her up, she calls him. And she ditches him. Says she got a better offer. A better offer!" The woman paced around the room, looking on the shelves and into corners. "There is no better offer than my boy, my Ty."

"Your boy, Mai tai?" James said.

She nodded and her eyes went out of focus. "Ty. Tyler. He's mine, my Ty. I named him after my first boyfriend, in the fourth grade, imagine! Tyler Ostman." She blinked. "Anyway, he gets mad and he slams the phone down just as my cuckoo goes off. So he turns and grabs the bird, rips it off its perch, and throws it through the window." She stopped and touched James' window, as if checking to make sure it was in one piece. "I mean, through the window, a little bird like that! There's glass everywhere, inside and out. Then he locks himself in his room and doesn't come out for the rest of the weekend. Though he ate the food I left on a tray." She stopped and smiled.

James looked at the clock. Other than the missing bird, there wasn't a scratch on it. It seemed well-maintained. "Did the clock land on something soft?"

She looked at him, her eyes sort of glazed. "What?"

"When he ripped the bird out, the clock must have fallen off the wall from the force. What did it land on?"

"Oh." She waved a hand. "It didn't fall. My husband had it up there on an anchor. He anchors everything, even our crucifix. That clock wasn't going anywhere. It was a real bitch to get it down."

Every bird James found was either too small or too big. He scooped them up, admired the colors, red and blue and yellow, and the realistic ones too, their feathers a mottled brown. "And you never found the cuckoo?"

"Nope, and I looked everywhere. It disappeared in the snow. I even shoveled." She leaned briefly against the window and for a moment, James saw the tired slope of her shoulders, the sag in her face.

James wondered what it must be like to raise a boy. Especially a boy who gets hurt by girls. Especially a boy who takes it out on a poor cuckoo bird. James wondered if it was harder to raise a boy like that than a boy who rarely talked, who stayed quiet and out of the way, even when he wasn't put in an out-of-the-way place. He thought of Ty locked away in his room, his own choice, and he wondered what Ty did that kept his mother from grabbing him and throwing him down the root cellar. James shook his head and looked at the clock again and tried to get the picture out of his mind of a shivering cold-blue cuckoo bird trapped in snow in the middle of a suburban lawn. Thrown there by a boy whose mother still brought him dinner on a tray and worried if he ate. "Well, if I can find the right size bird, I should be able to fix it for you," James said. "Or maybe the real bird will show up with the thaw."

She straightened. "Actually, I don't want the clock back. I just thought, well, you like clocks. Maybe you could fix it and find a home for it."

"You don't want it?" Under his hands, James felt the clock gasp.

"No. It would just remind my boy about this girl. He feels just awful. I don't like it when he feels bad." She smiled directly at James then and he saw it. Her love for her son was plain, in the rise of her cheeks, the squint of her eyes. It was right there.

Just not on the right face and not for the right person and many, many years too late.

James patted the clock. "I'll take care of it," he said and Ty's mother left.

This particular clock's bird remained extinct. James went to antique malls and flea markets, estate sales and rummages, and even to other clock shops to look through their skeleton boxes. He brought home entire flocks of bright little wooden birds. But none of them fit just right.

James finally chose a bird that was just a little too big. Too small, and the clock's door wouldn't open. It needed the momentum of the beak to flip it outward. The chosen bird, a plain but glorious yellow, willingly threw himself at the door and thwacked it the correct number of times. But the noise was painful to hear and it always reminded James of a boy and his mother and a bird thrown through a window.

That morning, when the bird stopped thwacking, James patted the clock gently and then continued to the front door. On his porch, he found a girl reading his newspaper. She sat on the top step and looked at James openly; no sign of guilt at being caught.

James recognized her right away. She was part of a gaggle of teens that hung around downtown until all hours of the night. Sometimes they were there during the day as well, ducking behind buildings if someone from the schools or a police officer drove by. James always crossed the street to avoid them. Unfortunately, avoidance wasn't enough to keep from hearing their jibes and seeing their sneers. Their laughter always followed him home.

There was one taunt in particular. They liked to yell, "Clock-keeper! Clock-keeper! Too bad you're not a cock-keeper!" And then they laughed that laugh.

James never knew just what that was supposed to mean. Were they saying he wasn't a man, that he didn't have a penis? Once, James heard one of them say, "Or maybe he is a cock-keeper. Maybe he keeps lots of cocks." And then it seemed like they thought he was homosexual. But it never made sense to him, and he never understood the gusto and hilarity behind the shouted verse.

Their laughter invaded James' sleep sometimes, the taunting tone of it, echoing back to all the laughter he ever heard. That sound, that clear-as-a-bell you'll-never-fit-in sound.

Bad enough to hear it in the streets. Worse still to hear it at night, in voices that he could never forget.

So now James stared at this girl and she looked back at him. Then she smiled, showing the most even set of square teeth he ever saw. Folding the paper neatly, she handed it to him. "I like the comics," she said. "My folks don't get the paper."

"Well, from now on, go buy your own," James said and turned to walk in the house. All he wanted was his newspaper and a cup of coffee. He liked the comics too. *Mary Worth* was his favorite. But then something glinted on the girl's lap. James looked a little closer, the thought coming unbidden that maybe she had a knife. Maybe she was going to rob him. He knew from reading the front page that teenagers were like that.

But it was a clock. From the way the sun reflected on it, James knew it was either brass or brass-plated. He tucked the newspaper under his arm and waited.

The girl looked at her lap. "My alarm clock broke," she said slowly. She fell silent, then she just lifted it toward him. Its face was steel gray and mute. He began to reach out, to pick it up.

But then the clock-keeper cock-keeper rhyme came into his head again and he pulled his hands back like they'd been burned. "I guess you'll have to get a new one," he said and turned to leave. From the open front door, he could smell the coffee. He had day-old crullers too, just sitting there at his place at the table, waiting.

"But I don't want a new clock." There was real misery in her voice, enough to make James stop. "Can't you fix it? You're the clock-keeper."

"That's what you tell me, every time I walk into town," he said, not turning. He waited, and then he heard her sigh. It wasn't an exasperated sound, it was softer. She sounded sad. But she also sounded trapped.

"I'm real sorry," she said.

James wanted to tell her that this went beyond sorry. He wanted to tell her that sorry wasn't enough. And he wanted to just walk away, to leave her with her broken clock. But before he could speak, she started talking again. Her voice was just above a whisper and it felt like she was telling James a secret.

"This clock's gotten me up pretty much every day of my life. My mom says someone gave it to me on the day I was born, but she doesn't remember who." She stopped for a second, then her voice dropped even lower. "I don't think my mom even remembers me sometimes." James looked back at her as she picked the clock up, then held it out again, its legs balanced neatly on her two palms. "Anyway, the last two mornings, it didn't go off. I...well, I miss it."

James nodded and picked up the clock. It was a Baby Ben, a tiny version of the classic round-faced wind-up alarm clock. The alarm clock that was James' first friend, that shared the space with him inside a cardboard box in the root cellar, was a larger version, a Big Ben. James knew he would miss it if it ever stopped. The Ben line had a loud clanging alarm that used to wake up millions every day, before clock radios began zapping people to consciousness with rock music.

He held the girl's little clock to his ear and heard its steady ticking. The hands were on the correct time. "It's just the alarm that won't work?"

The girl nodded.

"And it's always worked before. For how long? Fourteen years? Fifteen?"

She smiled, but just barely. "I'm fifteen," she said. "Sixteen in December."

James thought again about turning her down. About handing the clock back and going inside without another word. This girl needed him to fix her clock and he didn't care for her at all. But the clock was heavy in his hands and it needed him too and he did care about that. It wouldn't be happy unless it was doing its job, even if its job was to wake this girl up in time to skip out of school. "Walk around back," James said. "That's where the entrance is to the repair shop." He saw fear in her face as he carried the clock inside and closed the door. The clock's tick seemed to slow for a second, but then it picked up again.

James looked longingly for a moment at his breakfast and he took a deep sniff of the coffee. It would all have to wait. Food and drink weren't allowed in his workshop where crumbs could gum up a mechanism and a spill could be disastrous. He shook his head at the little clock as they headed down the stairs. "You could do better, you know," James said. "You could do so much better. She'll probably just throw you through a window someday. Teenagers do that. If something makes them mad."

James' basement was exposed to the back yard, so there was an outdoor entrance. The girl was already standing there, her face pressed against the window. James waved at her, then unlocked the door. She practically fell in.

"I thought —" she said breathlessly. "I thought —"

"That I was going to steal your clock?" James set it carefully on the worktable.

"Yeah. 'Cause you were mad."

He shook his head. "I don't steal clocks. Not ever. I buy them, they're given to me, but not one clock in this house is stolen." Except for his mother's anniversary clock. He did take that from her dressing table. But his mother knew about it and never took it back, so James figured it didn't really count. His mother was dead anyway.

"There's lots of clocks here, huh?" She pulled up a stool, sat close to James. Close to her clock.

He glanced at her. "There's a few. You've never been in here?" He knew she never set foot in here as a teen, but he thought maybe, as a little girl, her parents came for a tour.

"Nope. My folks say it's like living in Paris and never seeing the Eiffel Tower. You never see the neat stuff in your own town."

James liked having the Home compared to the Eiffel Tower. He flipped the clock over on its face and pried open the back. The girl leaned closer, looking over his elbow. "You said it's just the alarm that's not working, right?"

She nodded. Her shoulders were tense, hunched up close to her ears.

James saw the problem right away. Two springs were broken, keeping the timing mechanism from figuring out the correct time to make the clock go off. Confused, the little clock just decided to stay silent. It was like it had a couple broken blood vessels in its brain and couldn't think quite right. That could be fixed. Just had to reconnect the arteries. "So, do you have a name?" James asked as he went in search of some replacement springs.

"Cooley," she said.

He stopped to look at her. "I never heard that name before."

She shrugged. "It's a nickname, I guess, but that's what everyone calls me. 'Cause I'm so cool, you know?"

James found the right size springs and he placed them carefully next to the clock. Springs had a habit of jumping away and getting lost so he kept his eyes trained on them. "Everyone meaning your parents? Or everyone meaning that group of kids?"

He was amazed to see her blush, just a little. It was like she controlled it. It started at her neck, turning the skin a tomato color, and then it got to her chin. But before it spread to her cheeks, it was like she fought it down. "My friends."

"What do your parents call you?" James pried the two broken springs out, then worked to set in the new ones. Cooley leaned forward and took the broken springs. She glanced at James quickly and he pretended to not see as she tucked them slyly in her jeans pocket, the motion pulling the too-baggy denim dangerously low over her hips.

"Nothing really. My mother calls me all sorts of names. My dad doesn't say much at all." She laughed, but there was no happiness in her voice. It was that tone, the one James heard when the kids laughed on the street. It made him flinch and his fingers stumbled. This girl put him on edge.

Her laughter guttered suddenly to a stop. "Is my clock almost done?"

James snapped the back on and twisted the alarm-set knob until the clock sang out in a rich cow bell, its vibrations tingling his fingers. Cooley sat straight up and gasped, a smile on her face brighter than a flashlight piercing the dark. She held out both hands for her clock and James gave it to her, feeling like a saint handing out a miracle. Cooley suddenly looked like a little girl, the delight on her face plain and clear under the black make-up. She shut off the alarm and then hugged the little clock to her chest. "Thank you!"

"You're welcome." James tidied up a bit, making sure the workbench would be ready for whatever clock showed up next.

"So how much do I owe you?" Cooley reached into her pocket again. James thought about the two broken springs in there, original parts from her clock. He wondered what she would do with them. Bury them in her back yard?

"It was just a couple springs," he said. "No charge."

"Really?" She smiled again. "Cool."

But then James thought about it. He thought about how he had her here, away from her friends, her clock held tightly in her hands. A clock repaired by the clock-keeper. "Except for two things," he said quickly.

She froze, her knuckles whitening. "What?"

He held up one finger. "First. The next time I walk by you and your friends downtown, you'll tell them to shut up and never use that clock-keeper rhyme again."

She looked at the floor. "I said I was sorry," she muttered.

He held up another finger and pointed the V at her. "Second, if you ever decide to get rid of that little clock, you won't throw it through a window. You'll bring it here."

Her eyes came flying back up to meet his. "Why would I throw it through a window?"

He shook his head. "You'd be amazed. I bet you never thought you'd skip school and answer to Cooley either."

She looked away again, tucked the clock into her coat. "Okay. Thanks."

James turned toward the outside door, preparing to show her out, but then he changed his mind and headed up the stairs. If she went out the front, he could watch her walk away. There wouldn't be any time for foolishness in his back yard, near the clock cemetery.

"Where are you going?" she called.

"I'm showing you out a different way. Come on."

She followed him up the stairs, but once they were in the hallway, she walked beside him. He saw her looking from side to side, taking in all the clocks, her upper teeth busily working her lower lip. "Bet it gets noisy in here," she said.

"My visitors say it does. I don't think of it as noise."

Cooley smiled and James suddenly felt like they were sharing secrets again. "My alarm clock doesn't sound noisy to me either," she said. "My friends have radio and CD alarm clocks and they wake up to music, but this clock sounds like music to me. Sometimes I hear it in my dream and it just fits right in. Then I'll say, oh, wait, that's my alarm, and wake myself up." She shook her head. "I even heard it the last two mornings when it didn't go off."

"The Ben clocks work really hard to wake people up. It's their job."

She looked at him.

"That's the kind of clock you have. A Baby Ben. I have a Big Ben. Same kind, only larger." He wondered how she never noticed the words Baby Ben written in scroll under the twelve.

"I thought Big Ben was that huge clock in London."

"It is. The alarm clock line was named after it." James really wanted to see Big Ben, the original. A long time ago, he bought an old LP record of sound effects at a rummage sale, just because one of the sounds was Big Ben. He played it over and over again, picturing himself standing at the giant clock's base as it chimed the middle of the day or the dead of night. James wanted to be there, to see it, touch it, feel the reverberation deep in his stomach. But he could never leave the Home, his clocks, his family, for that long.

Cooley stopped in front of a dwarf tall clock, squatting by an archway. The clock was only four feet tall and Cooley, at least a foot taller, bent down to look into its face. "This is a really short grandfather clock." She reached out to touch the mahogany, but James blocked her hand.

"It's not a grandfather clock." He touched the wood himself, reassuring the clock that it wasn't about to be hurt. "A grandfather clock is actually called a tall clock or a longcase clock. This is a dwarf tall clock, more commonly called the grandmother clock. And it's actually quite tall for the type; they range in size from two to five feet. This one was made by a man in Massachusetts, James Wilder, in 1823."

Cooley's smile prettied her face. James wondered what color her hair really was, beneath the purple-red dye job. "Grandmother clock. I like that. It does look sort of grandmotherly, like it could give a hug."

This time, when she reached out to touch, James didn't stop her. Her fingers graced the case, following the whorls of pattern in the wood. He noticed her fingernails were all painted black, except for her middle finger on the right hand. That nail was still a tender baby pink, a pre-adolescent pink, a pink that came before the polished color.

That little nail softened him, until he realized what that bare nail would be used for. What it in fact had been used for, on one of his last walks downtown. He could see the other fingers furled over, fisted, except for that one naked nail, pointing straight up.

Clock-keeper, clock-keeper, too bad you're not a cock-keeper!

James turned abruptly. "It's time for you to go. I need to have my breakfast before visiting hours."

"Oh, yeah," she said behind him. "That coffee smells really good."

There may have been a request for an invitation in her voice. James wasn't sure. But he didn't care. He didn't trust her, didn't know when the smile would turn into a sneer, when her whisper would turn harsh and mocking. Women could change so quickly, like his mother, like Diana, and Cooley, though young, was almost a woman. It was time to get her out of there. Her clock was fixed.

Although she walked quickly, James made sure to stay in front of her. He didn't want her next to him, walking the way he imagined a friend would. When he reached the door, he opened it and waited.

She stood there uncertainly, patting her jacket where the Baby Ben hid. "Well...thank you," she said.

James looked away.

"Your name is James, isn't it?"

"Yes," he said. "It's James."

"My name is really Amy Sue. Not Cooley, though that's what I'm called. Amy Sue Dander."

James struggled to connect the two, the sweet name with the purple-haired taunter. He couldn't. "I think you look more like a Cooley." Her face fell and he wished for a moment that he hadn't spoken aloud. But no matter, she would never be back anyway. He wondered if she really could be an Amy Sue. But then he shut the door firmly behind her. It wasn't worth thinking about. Amy Sue or Cooley, she was dangerous.

Remembering his newspaper, James tracked it down, finally finding it on the kitchen table. He must have set it there on the way down to the workshop. After pouring his coffee, he sat down and turned to the comics. The page was creased, probably by that single pink nail. He sighed and tried to ignore it.

CHAPTER EIGHT:

A BRIEF BATTLE
The Grandmother Clock's Story

The day Audrey's special scratch'n'sniff cherry-scented hot pink thong panty snapped as she tucked it into place was the day she realized she was heading over that proverbial hill. Her friends talked about it all the time; you hit forty and it's all downhill from there, they said. Audrey felt like she spent all her life struggling uphill and she wasn't about to head down yet; if anything, she was going to level out. But the sting of the snap caused her to rub her rear and curse.

She stood in front of her opened dresser drawer and lifted out pair after pair of thong undies. She was suddenly afraid to put any of them on. This hurts, she thought, one hand still patting her backside. This really hurts.

Finally, she just pulled on her slacks over her bare skin. She reasoned that it wasn't that different from a thong; her buns were basically always bare anyway. But she didn't count on all the chafing in her unprotected crotch. By mid-morning, she was wiggling in her seat.

"I have to go shopping during lunch," she said to her office friend, DeAnne. "I need some new unmentionables."

DeAnne laughed. "Have fun at Frederick's then," she said.

Audrey never hid her underwear preferences. She was proud of the electric colors, the animal prints, the leather and the silk. Up above, she was even prouder of the underwire and pump, the feather-boaed number with straps of bright yellow feathers (to wear with strapless gowns…the yellow feathers fluttering over black velvet was to die for) and especially the nipple cut-outs which lifted her high, but gave her that natural naked look. Freddy's was indeed high on her shopping list.

But now, she looked at DeAnne and considered. DeAnne always looked nice. Her clothes were simple, but sharp, smooth with no pantyline. DeAnne still went out on Friday and Saturday nights and came in Monday, looking like she lived it up over the weekend. And Audrey knew from the last office birthday party that DeAnne was forty-six years old.

Audrey wondered if DeAnne wore thongs. Maybe there was a trick to keeping sagged behinds from snapping the material. "Hey," Audrey said. "Hey, DeAnne? Do you mind if I ask you a personal question?"

"Guess not," she said.

"What kind of unmentionables do you wear?"

Both women looked down the hallway outside their cubicle. No one was in sight. It was just before lunch and most everyone was out. DeAnne leaned way over and whispered in Audrey's ear anyway. "Lace bikinis mostly. Sometimes a silk thong."

"Lace?" Audrey always rejected lace as being too demure. "Doesn't that itch?"

"Only if I think about it," DeAnne said and instantly scratched. "But mostly, it makes me feel pretty."

"And the thong has never…snapped? Broken?"

DeAnne shook her head. "I'm not that far gone, Aud."

Audrey looked back at her screen. Apparently, she was.

That far gone.

She waited a few minutes, letting DeAnne bustle out to lunch first. Audrey wanted to leave last, in case DeAnne asked to come with. Not this time. Audrey wasn't going to Freddy's. She was sneaking to the Foundation Emporium, a store that specialized in unmentionables for all ages, but especially, as they liked to say in their ads, The Mature Woman. Audrey never thought of herself as mature, equating maturity with bland. Now she wondered if she should think of herself as old.

Moving slowly, Audrey left the office. She knew what she was going to have to buy. She wore them the first seventeen years of her life, when her mother did all the shopping.

Plain white cotton briefs.

The same as her mother wore her entire life. Audrey could still hear the satisfied snap of the waistband as her mother dressed every day. She used to snap the band on Audrey's too, when Audrey was still little enough to need help dressing. Back then, when she was four and five, six and seven, even up to ten, Audrey kind of liked the white briefs. They matched the plain white undershirts she wore that had a little silk bow right in the center of her chest. After her bath on hot summer nights, her mother let her run around in just her underwear and it seemed to Audrey the most elatedly free feeling in the world.

Until she got older and comfort was no longer an important consideration. With the arrival of breasts when she was twelve, Audrey wanted something wild, naughty, outlandish…as a teen, she wanted Wow. At sixteen, she dreamed about wearing sweet blouses with ribbons at the throat, matching skirts down to her ankles, all the rage then. But underneath, peekaboo unmentionables in chocolate brown, cinnamon red, cool mint green. The underneath unmentionable life was who she really was and Audrey wanted so much to be unwrapped and have someone discover edible undies and a push-up bra, discover Audrey, beneath the softspoken, shyly-dressed exterior.

While shopping with her mother, the teenaged Audrey pointed out all the gorgeous unmentionables, soft things in silk, rough things in leather, but her mother shook her head and dragged her to the plain white cotton brief section. Instead of white undershirts, she wore plain white bras with a pink rose nestled in her new cleavage.

Until she was seventeen. At seventeen, she graduated from high school, got a job, moved out, and carefully budgeted her paychecks to cover rent, food, electric, phone and unmentionables. Lots and lots of unmentionables for lots and lots of boys, and unwrapping and unwrapping and unwrapping. Audrey felt discovered.

Until now, at forty, when she felt found out. Her body betrayed her, insisting on no more exotic unmentionables, just plain white cotton briefs.

Outside of the Foundation Emporium, Audrey hesitated and stopped in the vestibule to put on a pair of dark glasses. She heard a deep ticking and when she looked up, an odd sort of clock looked back. It was only about four feet tall, too short to be a grandfather clock, but too tall to sit on a table. It was long and straight and its face was crackled with age, but someone took it upon himself to decorate it for the store. Painted on its body was a stiff white one-piece foundation garment, what looked like a combination bra, girdle, and garter belt. The poor clock looked restrained and ridiculous and Audrey knew she was going to look ridiculous too. Ridiculous and plain and old, old, old. If plain white cotton briefs were back in her life, girdles and longline bras couldn't be too far away.

Going inside, she made herself look straight ahead. She marched past rows of bright colors, trying not to see them out of the corners of her eyes, and she didn't stop until she reached the back of the store. There in a blinding blizzard were the plain white cotton briefs. Next to them were the plain white bras with the single rosebud in the middle. Audrey dug into a pile, a snowbank of warm cotton in a center aisle bin, her fingers recoiling despite the soft fabric, and she looked only for her size, coming up with seven sets. Clutching them, she could already feel the stranglehold of the elastic band. The underclothes were marked down, of course. As Audrey headed toward the cash register, she felt marked down.

She wanted her pile of plain all tucked quickly away in a brown paper bag, out of sight. And then she realized the clerk was male.

Male! In a women's foundation store! In Freddy's, it worked, the leer added to the shopping experience, but here…Audrey wished the brown paper bag could go over her head as well.

"Ah," the clerk said. "I see you've found…everything."

Audrey nodded, mute.

The clerk fingered the unmentionables. "Well…" he said and stopped. Then he leaned close to her, his silk tie draping a bright splash of purple on the brown counter. He whispered, "Are you sure you want these? We have so much more to offer. Are you sure you don't want some more time to shop?"

Audrey blushed. "Oh," she said. "I…" and she turned to look. She immediately saw a fantastic candy apple red crushed velvet thong with matching push-up bra, both trimmed in the richest of black.

Thong. That name twanged in Audrey's ears and her bottom burned. "No, thank you," she said quickly. "These are fine."

The clerk sighed and shook his head, but he wrapped her unbearable unmentionables in tissue and tucked them into a bag. It wasn't brown and paper, but a pretty pink, a plastic bag with handles. She thanked him and practically sprinted her getaway. The pathetic clock in the vestibule seemed to reach for her with arms covered with wrinkles and dangling skin as Audrey whipped through and out the revolving door. The clock gonged after her, its voice trembly and melancholy, calling her back. Back to the land of white, of no color, no sparkle, no Wow.

At the office, Audrey slipped into the ladies' lounge and put on her new things. They nestled comfortably around her waist, her thighs, under her breasts. The extra-wide straps didn't even cut into her shoulders. She sighed for a moment and let herself relax, but then she looked down. Plain white. Plain white covering her most exotic parts. No longer exotic, she thought. Get ready for a plain white life.

In her apartment that night, Audrey prowled from room to room. She wore only her bra and briefs and she tried to recapture that feeling of freedom, of airiness and innocence. But it just wasn't there. She snapped the waistband and she heard her mother. She looked in the mirror and she saw her mother.

Oh, no, she thought. Oh, no.

She cried and put all of her old unmentionables into three paper bags. Then she pulled on her robe, silk at least and an iridescent coral, and carried the bags to their final resting place: the dumpster behind her apartment complex.

She slept in the nude that night, the worn unmentionables on the floor next to the hamper, victims of a wild and angry throw, and a new set folded and waiting on the dresser.

But in the morning, she just couldn't force herself to put them on. "This is ridiculous!" she said out loud. "They're all I have to wear!" But every time she lifted a leg and approached the brief, her skin crawled and her knee locked. Finally, she just dressed over bare skin again and threw the plain white cotton briefs and rosebudded bras into the pink plastic bag with handles. She carefully smoothed out the worn set, folded it neatly, buried it at the bottom. She still had the receipt.

DeAnne was already at the office when Audrey showed up, clumsily trying to hide the bag under her coat. But it was no use; yesterday, she got back before DeAnne and managed to slip the bag into her file cabinet until it was time to go home. Now, DeAnne was eagle-eyed and she frankly stared at the pretty pink plastic bag when it dropped from under Audrey's coat to the floor.

"Not Frederick's?" DeAnne said.

"Oh, DeAnne," Audrey moaned. "Just don't ask."

DeAnne wisely obeyed. But once, when Audrey came back from getting a cup of coffee, heavy on the sugar just for today, she found DeAnne peering inside the pink plastic bag. "DeAnne!" she cried.

DeAnne quickly stepped away. "Oh, Audrey," she said. "I'm so sorry." She looked back at the bag. "I'm so sorry."

Audrey slumped into her chair and drank thick coffee until lunch.

Audrey ducked into the Foundation Emporium, giving the girdled grandmother clock a wide berth as she went by. It chortled the quarter hour and the passing of time and Audrey barely resisted the urge to flip it the finger. She looked around the store and found the same male clerk at his post beside the cash register. Today, his tie was orange. He smiled at her and she liked the way his smile looked, poised over the orange tie, a shocking stripe in the middle of his crisp white shirt. She quickly shoved the pink pretty bag back across the counter to him.

"I need to return these," she said. "I never wore them."

He looked down at the bag, tweaked it, then looked up at her. "We don't take returns, but how about an exchange? I'm sure we could find something you'll like."

Audrey took in again the candy apple red crushed velvet thong. She stepped toward it, touched it, relished the cat's-tongue bristle of the material between her fingers. But then she turned away and held her hands out to the clerk. "But I can't..." she said. "I can't wear those...anymore."

"The thong?" He smiled, then gave her a slow wink. It was the slowest wink she ever saw, nothing like the flash-fast blur of skin and eyelashes she encountered at the coffee bars, the sushi bars, the video store checkout. With this man, she had time to see the thick black lashes lower and linger, then lift like a stage curtain. "We have so much, so much more. Look." He waved behind her, a gesture as grand and gentle as a conductor's at the start of a great symphony.

She looked and she saw briefs. Briefs and bras, everywhere, paired and separate, folded and splayed. But not plain white cotton. There was silk and lace, leather and satin. A jungle of animal prints ran across a felt green table, electric oranges and reds and blues vibrated from headless mannequin torsos. In a shadowed back corner, there was even a small section of scratch'n'sniffs and nipple-cutouts.

"Oh!" Audrey breathed.

The man tucked the pretty pink plastic bag under his counter. "Go shop," he said. "Take your time. Then we'll tally up."

Audrey went through the racks and the tables and she surrendered. She gave in to the briefs and the bras that were to support her breasts and buns, not squeeze or separate, uplift or enlarge them. But she felt that the flag of surrender wasn't white at all, and it certainly wasn't cotton. It was leopard print in neon purple and it was satin.

As she paid her bill, happily giving over the extra amount, the clerk asked her what she was doing that night. Audrey swallowed and looked up.

He played with the end of his tie. "I thought maybe dinner and a movie."

Audrey thought again of the rising curtain wink, the soft wave of his arm as he introduced her to a new but familiar type of unmentionable. "Okay," she said. "And we can have a drink at my place after, if you'd like."

"Well…maybe," he said. "Maybe on our second date. There's no need to rush." He straightened his tie, tucking the tip into his waistband.

Audrey trembled. Then they agreed to meet after work. Heading through the vestibule, the grandmother clock began to moo. Audrey told her to shut up. She told her mother to shut up. She told every commercial and ad that whispered *demure* and *simple* and *quiet* to women reaching a certain age to shut up. To wake up and smell the scratch'n'sniffs.

Audrey couldn't wait to pull on her new unmentionables. She debated over which set, trying to decide on texture, color, and material. But she knew they would all be good.

As for Samuel, for that was the clerk's name and Audrey thought what a fine silky-soft name it was, he was right about no need to rush. These new briefs and bras called for a slower unwrapping; not even an unwrapping, but an unveiling. A soft, supportive, sensual unveiling.

With just the right amount of Wow.

CHAPTER NINE:

JAMES

And so you're never quite easy around people. It's hard to trust them, believe them, see them as benign. And it's about more than your mother, isn't it? It's about more than a woman who treats you as a bad, bad dog. Treats you in such a way that if you were a dog, the humane society would surely object and step in, removing you from the home, sending your mother to jail.

If you were a dog. But you aren't. Where is the humane society for children?

What about all these people around you while you are growing up, the teachers, the principals, the counselors and the kids? Those who look at your face and never see a smile, who never see your blue eyes because they are always cast to the floor, who don't seem to notice the slumped posture, the long sleeves hiding bruises, the turtlenecks even in May to hide collar burns? How can the teachers not notice the extended absences from school, days on end when your mother forgets you down in the root cellar? When you return, you always mumble the same excuse. "Flu." For five days? Four times during the course of one semester?

They all don't seem to notice. Or they all look away.

Imagine.

And you look at them from under your downcast eyes and you seethe. You can't talk, you don't dare speak, because somehow she would know and the collar would tighten and the doors would bolt and you'd never see the light of day again.

How can they not see your hurt? Sometimes, you give out the smallest of whimpers. You "carelessly" leave a sleeve rolled up, or stretch your turtleneck collar to scratch a nonexistent itch, and the colors are there, the marks, the dents, the artistry of abuse, and yet somehow, no one ever admits to seeing. Realizing. Widening their eyes to reality and then sweeping in to save you. It's what you imagine.

It never happens.

And so it was amazing that James got through school at all. But he did. Because even though he was always alone, it was different than being isolated in the root cellar. It was an escape. There was noise and light and movement. And even as he walked on the periphery of human existence, he needed them. Other people. He needed them all.

And so James seethed. Because sometimes people could hurt without doing anything at all.

In the evening, up to his elbows in dish-washing water, James stopped for a moment to listen to the dwarf tall clock Cooley touched that morning. That clock had a wonderful alto voice; he always pictured her as an opera star, standing in the spotlight, her eyes closed as if she almost couldn't bear the richness of her own talent. She warbled off the full four parts of a Westminster chime; it was the top of the hour, eight o'clock. Then she fell silent and James shut his own eyes, picturing her on the stage, mahogany skin gleaming, slipping down into the most regal of curtsies.

When James found the grandmother clock, he was in Des Moines, planning to attend a weekend flea market. He got there on Friday night after closing down the Home for the weekend, an apologetic note taped to the door. The town council was forever after him to get someone to fill in when he was gone, but he just couldn't do it. The thought of someone else tending these clocks, even for a weekend, was unbearable. As long as James was around, only James would be the clock-keeper.

With the flea market event not opening until morning, he wandered around downtown Des Moines. A lot of stores were already closed; it was after nine o'clock. But one store's lights rolled onto the sidewalk like lava and he walked toward it to see what was happening.

It was a store closeout. Everywhere, signs shouted, "Everything Must Go! We Won't Go Home Until The Last Thing Sells!" Inside, James saw women digging through bins, pulling things off racks. Lacy things, tiny things; those things he saw only on and off Diana and didn't understand them even then, when they were on a living, breathing woman. James blushed, stepped back and looked up. The store's marquee read, "Foundation Emporium."

The only open store in town and there was nothing that he wanted. James started to turn away when he heard the chimes. An alto, huskily feminine voice sang the third part of the Westminster chime; it was three-quarters past the hour. Shoulders hunched, James quietly slunk into the store and looked around. He felt horribly out of place, but other than a few stares and raised eyebrows, the women ignored him. James closed his eyes and listened closely. Gradually, coming through the canned music, he heard the steady tick. Tilting his head and turning his body, he opened his eyes when the rhythm came through loud and clear.

The clock was set aside, tucked into a back corner of the room. At first, James could only see her face and it was extraordinary, the copper filigree faded but still beautiful. The hands were deeply black, making James wonder if they were replacements, and they brushed smoothly past gracefully curved roman numerals.

It wasn't until he pushed aside the rack that he saw what they did to her. Her longcase, a rich reddish mahogany, was painted over into some kind of lady's garment. She was stripped to her underwear. James wanted to throw his coat over her.

"That clock was the store's mascot," a clerk said as he hurried by, trailing a new tape for his cash register.

"But is she for sale?" James asked.

The clerk dipped his head in a nod, then bolted for his counter where women waited in line, ten deep. From there, he called to James over his shoulder as he began running underwear through his scanner. "It's a neat clock. The store's original owner painted her into a Lacy Lady BodyEnhancer Bra/Girdle Combination, by Francois. We featured the clock in our ads when the store first opened…Support For The Passing of Time, it said." The woman waiting to pay rolled her eyes.

James found a price tag taped to the back of the clock. Six-hundred dollars. Then he carefully opened the longcase door, splitting the sides of the girdle, and looked inside. On a lower corner, there was the signature: James Wilder, 1823. This clock was worth at least five times its asking price. These underwear hawkers had no idea what they were doing. And after what they did to the body of that clock, defiling her, flaunting her, giving her a body she neither had nor wanted, James was going to take full advantage of their ignorance.

But he would have saved her even if she wasn't a Wilder. She needed help; she'd been hurt.

James pulled off the price tag and carried it up to the cash register. Counting heads, he saw that he would have a while to wait; he was now thirteenth in line. The woman in front of him turned.

"What would you want a clock like that for?" she said. "If they don't sell it, maybe they'll burn it, and then it'll never have to look like that again."

James cringed at the thought of that clock falling away to ashes. And he was surprised at the faces of the other women, turning in line to look at him. "The clock will be fine," he said. "I'll give it a good home."

The twelfth woman squinted. "You're going to keep it in your bedroom, aren't you?" she said. The other women murmured.

James opened his mouth, ready to snap back, wanting to remind these women that they were all in line with armfuls of the same type of garment the clock wore. How did that make them any better? But something in the twelfth woman's face caught him, stole his words away. While her expression was angry, her face was flushed with prettiness. She reminded James of his mother, who was always beautiful, but especially so when she was in high rage. James remembered admiring her, even as she raised her arm to strike or drew a collar tight around his neck. It was so hard to be angry at a beautiful woman. Yet this twelfth woman was softer, there were lines around her eyes and mouth, silky as the burnished hair that fell to her shoulders. In her arms, she held a pile of those underthings, brightly colored and, he remembered from Diana, impossibly soft to the touch. The other women clutched their underclothes or let them dangle from fingers and wrists and elbows. But this woman, this twelfth woman, hugged hers. Even as she was angry, she hugged.

"I'm going to refinish the clock," James said quietly. "I'm going to restore her. She will be beautiful."

The twelfth woman looked at him and then her mouth lifted, just a bit, deepening the small lines. James wanted to trace them with his finger. "As beautiful as she used to be?" she asked.

"More beautiful than ever."

She smiled full then. "Thank you," she said and turned to wait in line.

Of all the clocks James brought home from Des Moines that weekend, that dwarf tall clock was his treasure. It took weeks of careful stripping and staining, but eventually, she stood in the living room, gloriously shining and singing. James often wished that the twelfth woman would find the Home, come see what he did to this clock, hear her in all her glory.

That night, the clock just finished singing when James was startled by a rapping on the window above the sink. Leaning against the glass was the owner of What Cheer's gift clock shop, It's About Time. Not knowing exactly what to do, James opened the window. "Neal? What are you doing out there?"

"Hi, James." Neal stepped back and smiled, tipping his sweat-stained baseball cap. "I rang your doorbell several times, but you didn't answer. I was heading around back to see if you were in the repair shop when I saw you here at the sink. Didn't you hear the bell?"

The doorbell. James remembered hearing the dwarf tall clock's Westminster chimes and a myriad of other songs and bells. He must have gotten lost for a moment. "I guess I didn't. Go back to the front door, I'll let you in."

Drying his hands on the way, James wondered what Neal could want. James didn't get visitors often; at least, not visitors he knew. The tourists came and went, but the people in town remained just the people in town. Not friends. Just folks that James lived alongside.

Neal was waiting by the time James opened the door. They shook hands and James led Neal into the living room. He looked around and whistled. "I always forget what this place looks like inside," he said. "You make my little gift shop look...look..."

"Fake?" James asked. "Cheap?"

Neal glanced quickly at James. "My clocks are fine. People like them."

James shrugged. Whenever they talked, which wasn't often, James commented on Neal's merchandise. It's About Time carried battery-powered clocks and most were ceramic, little statues of angels and dogs and lighthouses. Some were those miniature brass clocks that ran on a watch battery. There wasn't a single clock in Neal's store that had to be wound. James had heard complaints about it too, from tourists who came back to the Home after going to It's About Time. They wanted clocks like James', they said, and he wouldn't sell his and Neal sold junk. James always sent them to antique stores and flea markets. Flea markets were like an animal shelter for clocks, he told them. Go find the unwanted and you'll get yourself a treasure.

They settled down, Neal on the couch, James in his recliner. The clocks huddled around, their ticking soothing James' nerves, but Neal became jumpy.

"I don't know how you can stand it, James," he said. "It's so noisy in here."

Neal's clocks were voiceless. "So what can I do for you, Neal?"

He leaned forward, laced his fingers and dangled his hands between his knees. "Well, I came from a town council meeting. I volunteered to come ask you a favor."

James sat back and put his feet up, figuring it would probably be another request to find a fill-in. "What is it?"

"The clock tower stopped working this morning. Well, right

before noon. The hands look to be just about joined. We thought maybe you could fix it, save the town a few bucks."

Several of the clocks went off, indicating the quarter-hour, and James sat for a moment and thought. He'd heard the clock tower earlier that morning, James remembered tilting his head toward the sound just as he poured his second cup of coffee, around ten. He couldn't recall hearing it since and wondered why he didn't notice the gap. "I've never looked at a clock that large before," James said when the clocks fell silent. "I don't know if I'll be able to do anything."

"Oh, c'mon, James," Neal said. He waved his hands. "Look around. How many of these have you fixed? How different could the clock tower be, other than bigger?"

What Cheer's clock tower wasn't huge; it only rose about forty feet up. Its black iron scrollwork rolled between four creamy brick legs. The clock's four-sided face itself was plain. Just flat white with black numbers. It made James angry when he first saw it. This was a clock that was supposed to represent the Home and the rest of the entire town, inviting visitors to come visit and enjoy. It should have been beautiful, maybe an unusual silver face with alabaster roman numerals, or an aristocratic crackled oval face, transplanted from an older forgotten clock. But the town went cheap and just hauled that plain face up the pretty tower. James refused to attend the ribbon-cutting ceremony, even though he was asked to cut the ribbon with those huge shiny gold scissors passed over from Shop Around The Clock's grand reopening. At home that day, James heard the high school band play a brassy fanfare, followed by the clock's first chime. It was five minutes past noon. His own clocks laughed, a jolly ticking of pendulums echoing around the Home; the clock tower was already slow.

It was left that way because it was so hard to adjust. When the tower was built, nobody thought to put in a staircase. For half the year, when Daylight Savings Time kicked into effect, the clock was a whole hour off. It was shameful.

"How do you figure I can get up there to fix it?" James asked.

Neal shrugged. "The council talked about that. The fire department could help out. Use one of their ladder trucks or something."

That made sense, though James didn't much relish climbing a ladder forty feet into the air. For a moment, he pictured himself riding the ladder up, the truck shooting him like a cannonball as he hung onto the rungs. James shuddered. This was the fire department; wouldn't they have to keep him safe? "All right then. I'll give it a shot." If this worked, James thought, he would be able to go up the clock once a month or so to adjust the hands to the correct time. He couldn't fix the town's cheapness, but he could try to make What Cheer look accurate and respectful.

Neal rubbed his hands together and stood up. "That's great, James. We appreciate it. In the morning, I'll have my wife run over and watch this place for you while you work on the tower."

"No," James said quickly. Neal's wife was a vacant woman who spent most of her days shuffling around the gift shop in her worn-out furry bedroom slippers. She carried a lavender feather duster and when she finished dusting the entire shop, she turned around and started over again. "I'll just close up for a bit in the morning."

"Oh, for Christ's sake, James." Neal pulled off his baseball cap and ran his fingers through his hair. James could see why he wore that cap; the hair he had left was stringy and thin, a sort of nondescript corn color. "Give it a break. Ione won't hurt anything. It's just for one morning."

James shook his head. A worn-out fuzzy-slippered woman armed with a duster could do more harm than Neal had the brains to imagine. "No offense to Ione, Neal," James said. "But nope." He looked over Neal's shoulder at an old office wall clock, one that told time long before battery power took over. Its electric cord made a thin brown stripe down the wall. "Look," James said. "I'll go over after closing time. Six o'clock. That gives me several hours of daylight to work." It would also give him one heck of a long workday.

Neal seemed satisfied, but he still groused. "You've gotta get off your high horse, James," he said. "You're getting up there, you know? Long in the tooth. You've got to find a helper for around here."

James stood up sharply. "If I'm getting up there, then maybe I shouldn't be climbing around a clock tower," he said. "Us old folks break our hips easily, you know." He waited for a moment, then narrowed his eyes. Neal always wanted to get into the Home; of all the people on the town board, he was the most vocal about James getting a replacement. James pictured Neal here and his wife, scattering their ceramic thoughtless clocks among the others, their faces sporting pricetags. And then he imagined some of his own clocks as well, with pricetags dangling from their pendulums. Neal always said, "Gotta move the merchandise." He could move a lot more merchandise with a house the size of the Home. Getting Ione here, even for just one morning, could be the first step in a long complicated take-over plan, because it would take complication to get James out. He leaned forward. Better to nip this in the bud now. "You're not getting in here, Neal. You and your wife are not getting your hands on my clocks." James felt the clocks brace themselves. They knew if there was going to be a fight, James had to be the winner.

Neal stared, then snorted and shook his head. "You are something, James," he said. "I don't know what, but you're something. Every time I think you're finally going over the deep end, I wonder how I could ever tell." He shouldered past James and headed for the front door.

James kept his back turned. "Call the fire department," he said. "Have them there at six-fifteen sharp."

"Six-fifteen, sure," Neal said and then there was the slam of the door. James sighed and sat back down in his recliner, putting the footrest up, waiting for the ticking to settle down again. From around the house, the sounds of clocks striking the three-quarter hour floated past like a warm shower. James felt his shoulders relaxing; his neck popped. His pulse, which sped up during the exchange with Neal, slowed down and he filled his lungs with air, let it out. The clocks sighed as well.

James focused again on the office wall clock. It was a plain thing, white face with black border, black also on the numbers marching around the rim. The second hand moved forward with a jerky audible thud. That was the reason James bought this clock; it reminded him of all those years of classroom clocks, high above the teacher's head, the sound of that sticky second hand reassuring the students that time was passing and they would soon be set free. But for James, being on his own after the school bell rang wasn't much; he spent most of his time at his desk in his bedroom. Or long uncounted hours down in the root cellar, when his mother locked the doors. Those classroom clocks led James through all twelve years of school, pushing him forward, dangling time in front of his nose like a carrot, except that carrot always led away from the bright and noisy classroom to the silence of his bedroom, the sting of his mother's voice and hand, the dampness and dark of the root cellar.

Those clocks appeared in doctors' offices too, and dentists', any place where most people wanted time to go faster. The move up, move up, move up sound, the step by step that the second hand took around that face, got people through the tough moments by letting them know that time goes on and on and on and before long, they'd be out of one situation and into another. It never promised that the next situation would be any better; only that the current one would soon be in the past.

So when James found this clock at a foreclosure sale, he bought it. A free clinic in Oskaloosa shut down and everything inside was sold. James went to that sale because he never knew what he might find in odd places, and what he found in Oskaloosa was this reminder. Every day when tourists invaded his house, he heard the steady thudding of this clock's second hand, telling him that before long, it would be evening and he'd be alone with his family again. Not having to share them with anybody. When people like Neal came by, or Cooley, the clock told him that they wouldn't be around forever; they'd leave him alone eventually.

Lately though, as he watched it, as he sat there even that night, it reminded him of something else too. Of Neal saying to get off his high horse and find a helper. A clock's time goes on and on and on. James' time wouldn't.

There wasn't anybody he could tell how scared that made him. There were just the clocks and they tried to steady him with their ticking and chiming. But he imagined they were just as scared as he was.

"Over the deep end," Neal said. "Getting up there."

On nights like that, the forward-tick of the old office clock felt like it was leading James right to that deep end. And the water threatened to close over his head. Sometimes, he wanted time to just stop. It was odd to think that time stopping could save James and his clocks, but that's exactly where his imagination took him. If he could stop time, he and the clocks could stay in that house forever and nobody could ever hurt them again.

He got up and crossed the room to the office clock. Trailing his fingers down its cord, James found the plug and pulled. Immediately, the second hand stopped moving and the missing sound filled up the room like a whirlpool.

For a moment, James was light-headed with relief. The forward march stopped, the deep end fell shallow, the getting-up-there became level. But then his heart began to swirl, like it was caught up in the whirlpool too, like the clock, and it ran around in circles, trying to find itself again. James tried to listen to the other clocks, the dwarf tall clock, the cuckoo clock with the too-big bird, the graveyard mantel clock, all the others. Their pendulums swung and spun and dipped around him. But his heart tumbled, it plunged to his stomach, then surged to his forehead, and he clutched first his chest and then his hair. He tried to catch his breath, to yell, but he couldn't.

Falling to his knees, James found the office clock plug and stuck it back into its socket. The second hand started up again, there was a hum as the clock's workings lurched into motion and then the familiar thud filled the empty whirling hole in the room. James rested his head against the wall and he breathed, in and out, in and out, until he felt his heart rest, settle in his chest, fall into a pattern with that old office clock. The office clock, the classroom clock, the doctor and dentist clock. The get-through-the-bad-times clock.

When he stopped trembling, when his heart felt strong and steady again, James crossed the room and sank into his recliner. He closed his eyes and listened as everywhere, in every room, in every corner, his family started calling out the nine o'clock hour. He heard the sounds and they lifted him, cradled him in the air, and he felt rocked and soothed. Time was going forward again, moving just the way it always did, before him and during his whole life. And after too, forever after, but he decided not to think about that. Not now.

James was caught up and carried away.

CHAPTER TEN:

SECONDS
The Office Clock's Story

Y ou look at the clock through the pink nubbled frame of your
bare toes. Your feet hang in midair, held up by silver stirrups,
and you think wildly for a moment of the Lone Ranger and
you want to yell for Tonto. But then you focus again on the clock,
its second hand. It thuds and lurches, spelling out time in movement
and sound, and as you watch it, you think of time passing, all the
little seconds left behind. Time should be sweeping, you think, the
second hand soaring around the clock face in an eternally graceful
arc. But for you, this clock. This lurching forward second by second,
little baby steps.

You reach under the paper gown and touch your stomach. It's
still flat and you're grateful for that, that there's no evidence of growth
from the inside. But in your head, you can't help it, you picture a
midget, small as a quarter, a cockroach, a kidney bean clinging to
your insides. Your womb. You never really thought about having a
womb before now. Until it became inhabited. Invaded? Lived in.

No womb at this inn, you think, and you try to laugh. Help,
Tonto, you say to your toes.

Legs cramping, you wonder what's taking the doctor so long.
The clock tells you it's already been ten minutes. Ten minutes since
you surrendered yourself to that room, pulled off your clothes, folded

them neatly on a chair and climbed astride the table. There is paper everywhere, beneath you on the table and over your body in a gown. You think of a mummy and change your plea to Help, Igor, which makes no sense, but you laugh inwardly anyway. The stirrups were already up when you mounted the table, so you obediently stuck your feet into them. Ten minutes ago.

It should be all over by now. The nurse said it would only take seconds.

Your hand rests gently on your stomach and you think again of that midget, clinging to your insides. That's impossible, of course, it should only look like a kidney bean. And you hate kidney beans.

It would be impossible. You tell yourself this again and again. It would be a reminder, a forever reminder, of something you so want to forget. What if it had his ears? Those eggplant ears that stuck out at such odd angles, the only feature you really know of him, the only thing you could focus on as you tried to look past him to the sky.

You see it all again and you close your eyes, trying to shut it out, but it's still there in the darkness, especially in the darkness. So you look at the clock, but the clock face is the curve of the sky, the lurching second hand his rhythm, the only sound the same sound your body made as it slapped the grass. The numbers count the times he drove himself in and in and in again until you thought you were nothing but motion, nothing but an ever-deepening pit.

Help, Tonto, a whisper between damp leaves and grass, a plea thrown past his ears into the blackness of the sky, staring down with so many dead pinpricks of light, the light that wouldn't shine around you. The light and the dark. You wished for a moon.

Your toes, trying to run, twitch in the stirrups and you twist your head sideways, trying to find something else to look at. But there's only the instruments, silver-cold, on the tray next to the table. You fight an impulse to throw out your arm, knock over the tray, send it all clattering to the floor. Bring the doctor, bring the nurse. Bring them all running.

Sighing, you look up at the ceiling. Your hand rests gently on your stomach. The clock's thudding fills your ears. Seconds keep lurching by.

It would be impossible. It would be a reminder. You would never forget. Never.

As if you can forget now. As if it's not always there, in your dreams at night, your thoughts wide awake, in between the bites of a sandwich, in the shirts you fold, in the pounding of your fingers against the keyboard. How can there be a reminder if you'll never forget anyway?

You look at the clock. It's been twenty minutes.

It only takes seconds.

Help, Tonto.

Your hand rests gently on your stomach.

The silver instruments glint and wait. In the stirrups, your feet fall asleep. A million bugs crawl up your legs. There were bugs in the grass where you fell. Where he knocked you down. You remember a mosquito landing on the inner curve of his ear. You reached up and wiped it away, leaving a tomato smear. He didn't notice. In and in and in again.

Your hand rests gently on your stomach. The fingers of your other hand slowly roll in, until you make a fist. Your sleeping toes curl, making little foot fists. You want to kick something.

Then you sigh and force yourself to relax, force yourself to fake it, loosen your fingers and toes, listen to time lurching forward. Your knees fall further apart. It only takes seconds.

Twenty-five minutes.

When the door opens seconds later, you turn your head and see the smiling nurse, the scowling doctor. The nurse takes your hand, leaving your stomach cold and bare under the paper. The doctor seats himself between your knees.

"This is the speculum," he says and you feel one of the silver instruments slip inside. In and in and in again.

It only takes seconds.

You squeeze your eyes tight and hear the clock lurching. Everything becomes black, everything, the eggplant ears, the dead pinpricks of light, the air and the sound and the grass. It's all gone. And then you yell.

No!

Your knees slam together.

The nurse cries out, but you rip your hand away and sit halfway up. Get it out, get it out! you scream. The doctor doesn't look at you, but quickly removes the speculum. You feel your body close up again. Close up tight and safe.

The doctor and the nurse leave. They said something, but you couldn't hear, your ears filled with the thudding of your heart and the lurch of seconds passing. Trembling, you remove your feet from the stirrups, one by one, and let your legs dangle down. You sit up and shred off the paper gown, tearing the ties and not caring.

Looking down at your naked body, you wonder if the ache will ever go away. There was bruising inside and out. Inside. In and in and in again.

But oh, so deep in, you see that midget kidney bean, still clinging to your insides. Its fingers and toes curved into fists.

Getting off the table, you dress slowly, moving as if the bruises are still there, still fresh, still purple and green and yellow. You take one more glance at the clock, at the second hand lurching around its circle, and then you leave. You get to the door by counting the black and white floor tiles, ten, eleven, twelve, and you don't say anything to the nurse, the doctor, standing in the hallway.

When you step outside, the air and light hit you full in the face. You blink, squint, then walk away, resisting the urge to look over your shoulder.

You think of the office clock and you wonder at how things can change. It only takes seconds.

You lurch forward, your hand resting gently on your stomach.

CHAPTER ELEVEN:

JAMES

A nd so you stumble through the days and the nights and the months and the years and there are so many days that mean nothing to you. The first Sunday in May. The third Sunday in June. Your own birthday, which you only know by the date listed on your report cards, and that allows you to calculate your age. Every December for the first few years of school, you listen closely as your teacher reads stories to the class about a fat red man named Santa and you are amazed at the idea of a stranger bringing you toys, but it never happens anyway. The only trees are outside and they hold leaves, not ornaments. You learn quickly that your mother doesn't know school breaks from school days and so you slide out of the house every morning, no matter what. Better to wander around the woods, better to take the long hike into town and then take it back, than to do something that attracts her attention and sends you to the root cellar.

Imagine a life without holidays and birthdays and events. Imagine showing up to kindergarten and throughout grade school on Valentine's Day, without a baggie of red and pink and purple cards for your classmates, and imagine how red your face burns when your teacher forces the other kids to give you the valentines with your name printed, then written in cursive on little envelopes, even though you have nothing for them. Imagine how that burn goes deeper when the teacher follows you out of the classroom, insisting you keep the stuffed shoebox that you decorated yourself, created from a box that she gave you because you never have one from home to bring. Shoes from thrift stores don't come in boxes.

One year, you try to make valentines for your classmates out of things around the house, but there is never much around the house. You slip aluminum foil out of the kitchen, scotch tape, and you use crayons that you sneak home from school. But your mother hears the crinkle of the foil, the scritch as the tape leaves its dispenser, and she sees the mess in your room, sparkle-silver and red waxy streaks and crooked hearts with sad loopy arrows. You spend Valentine's Day down the root cellar that year. When you return to school, the teacher still sends you home with your shoebox full of reluctant and unreciprocated valentines. She says she saved them for you special.

In fifth grade, you dare to ask your mother, as you sit at the supper table with a bowl of cereal that you fix yourself because she is pacing the house again, living room to kitchen to bedroom to bathroom, a sure sign that there will be no meal, "What is this Valentine's Day stuff anyway? All those hearts and I love yous. Where'd that come from? Why do they do that?"

She pauses and actually stares at you for a moment, her eyes suddenly sparkling instead of glassy. "Your daddy loved me," she says, clear, her voice a charm. "He gave me candy every year, in a big red heart." And then she walks on.

Your memory of your father is slipping away by this time, into the fog, just as he disappeared into the fog. He left three years earlier. He left you with her.

Imagine.

I know what happens, son.

And suddenly, you fling your cereal bowl across the table, and it shoots off the end and against the cabinet and makes a glorious mess, dripping down the scratched wood onto the floor. The bowl shatters and you know how it feels. When your mother grabs you by the collar, your shirt collar this time, and hauls you down the root cellar, to the belt, the chain, and the cold dirt floor, you don't care.

You don't care because red hearts and cupids and curlicue I love you's are fucking stupid.

Imagine a rage that thick.

James didn't have to. He felt it roil silently under his skin every day, and he swore it forged its own veins that ran parallel to his blood. Veins that formed a river. With all his might, he willed this parallel river to remain under his skin and to never, ever erupt in spatters as thick as cereal thrown suddenly against a cabinet.

In the morning, James followed his schedule as usual. Checking the calendar, he wrote a list of clocks to be wound that day, and then began moving through the house.

It was a Tuesday, which was usually the slowest day for tourists. The busiest weekday was Friday, James figured because these were people on three or four day weekends. James just unlocked the front door at opening time and settled down for a break with a second cup of coffee when he heard the welcome bell ring. Sighing, he put down his mug and went forward to greet. It was another family.

"Hi!" the father said. He had his arm wrapped around the mother and his hand held a little girl, about four years old. "We're just passing through, but we saw your billboard and thought we'd stop. We never heard of a clock museum before."

"Welcome to the Home for Wayward Clocks," James said. He automatically smiled at the mother and daughter. The little girl hid behind her father's legs. James collected their money and instructed them to walk freely around the house and look-but-don't-touch and ask-if-you-have-any-questions, but to please-stay-away-from-closed-doors. On his way back to the control center, he stopped for a moment by the waltzer, the newly repaired four-hundred day clock. Whispering, James told it and the others that everything was okay. There was a child in their midst again, but this was a little one, not even close to the surly black-clad teen that attacked the other day. He promised that he would watch the cameras and be vigilant. Then he went back to his post.

The tour seemed to be progressing as usual. The parents exclaimed over the clocks and stopped several times to wait for a particular one to go off. The little girl got over her shyness and began to wander around, but the mother seemed to always have a hand or a sharp word at the ready. Children really weren't often a problem and they were usually the most excited over the clocks. But their quick movements made James nervous. Children jumped around and danced during the chimes, swinging their arms and doing odd can-can kicks. They shrieked and laughed and then the chimes seemed to get a little more raucous. James couldn't decide if the wild chiming was due to fear of being broken or to sheer joy of being excitedly appreciated. Joy and fear both caused a clamoring in James' body and he just didn't know how to interpret the clocks when they were in a wild mood.

On that day, James saw the incident begin to happen. The parents stood under a birdcage clock, staring up at the face and waiting to hear the bird sing. The little girl moved off to the side and watched a blinking-eye clock, Felix the Cat. "Mama, lookit da kitty!" she called and the mother nodded and said, "Isn't that cute?" But she never took her eyes from the bottom of the birdcage. That was the first warning and James scooted forward on his chair. An ignored child was a dangerous child. The little girl seemed fascinated, but she didn't move from her place. The black and white cat's tail was a pendulum, swinging back and forth beneath the body of the clock, and as the pendulum moved, so did the eyes, left, right, left, right, in direct opposition to the tail. There was a Cheshire grin on Felix's face and the little girl laughed and swayed below him, as if she was a pendulum herself. James sat back again and tried to relax as he watched her. She was a miniature of her mother, both of them craning their necks to admire a clock, their arms crossed in front of their chests in anticipation.

Then the little girl looked over at her parents and the set of her eyebrows made James lean forward again. Second warning. Something was up. He could always see the gears working in kids' heads, but most of the time, the ideas stayed there and the children just smiled and imagined and went on their way. James knew what a powerful tool imagination was, how it was often satisfying in itself to pretend, and so he waited, watching for the little mischievous smile to indicate the plan was over, carried out only in a daydream.

Her parents still stood, waiting for the birdcage. The little girl looked quickly around the room and then went to grab a small footstool tucked in a corner. James used it to wind the higher clocks. Before she even placed it under the grinning cat, he knew what she was going to do. He shot out of his seat and ran up the stairs. The family was in the back east bedroom.

He wasn't even halfway down the hallway when he heard the crash, followed by the mother's cry and the little girl's shriek. When James flew into the room, he found the mother kneeling next to the little girl who held Felix's disembodied tail. The rest of the clock was in pieces on the floor. The father was halfway to them, his head still turned toward the birdcage clock. The bird, along with the other clocks in the room, was shouting, calling for James, calling for help. Telling him he failed, a clock was hurt, it was hurt!

Not again, James thought, not again. He snatched the tail out of the girl's hands. "What did you do?" he yelled. He had to yell, to be heard over the clocks. The girl fell into tears and the mother hugged her close. James watched her arms tighten and for a moment, his mind stumbled, trying to imagine the embrace, but then he remembered the scene in the monitor, the little girl's sly glance at her parents before she turned to the cat clock, and anger seethed just under his skin.

"It was an accident," the mother said. "She didn't mean to—"

"The hell she didn't!" James pointed at the footstool. "I watched through my monitors. She deliberately dragged that footstool over to climb up and grab this clock."

"I just wanted to touch his tail!" the girl sobbed.

"You watched?" the father said, joining the group.

"I have a security system." James nodded toward the camera hovering near the ceiling in a back corner. He lowered his voice now that the chiming was done, but he felt the clocks huddling close, holding their breath, waiting to see what he would do. James knew what they were thinking. He'd failed twice. Twice. Wasn't he capable of doing his job anymore? He felt sobs rising from his core, echoing the little girl's, but he choked them back. Not in front of the customers. Not in front of people. "I saw her look at you, then go

get the footstool. She knew what she was up to. And this clock is…"
He bent over the cat, its eyes still, staring straight up. "Dead." He
scooped it up, tried to reattach the tail so at least the body would be
whole. "Dead, unless I can fix it." The tail wouldn't reconnect; there
was something wrong with the pendulum wire.

The father picked the little girl up, cuddled her under his chin.
"It's okay, Sheila," he said, and for a moment, James was struck dumb,
looking at the two of them so close that way. The mother stood up
too, put her hand on the little girl's back. James stared at her fingers,
so pink and soft against the girl's dark blue sweatshirt. So pink and
soft. He pictured this mother, cupping the little girl's chin in those
fingers, bringing her lips down, kissing her cheek, all as she tucked
her into bed. A nightly routine. An every-night routine. Her fingers
moved, stroking the little girl's back, and James wanted to reach out
and grab that hand, place it on his own back or under his own chin,
offer his own cheek. Oh, to feel that.

Then the father said, "You should have told us this place is
inappropriate for children. It's not hands-on."

James blinked. Hands-on? He forced himself to look away from
the mother's fingers to study the destroyed clock, his Felix. "I told
you that you were to look, not touch."

"This is a child, children touch," the father said and he started to
walk away. The mother moved with him, in sync, her touch on the
girl unbroken. Sheila looked at James over her father's shoulder. Tears
rolled down both cheeks, but she looked at James. And smiled.

"Children can be controlled," James said sharply, then instantly
clenched his fists. Another part of the clock snapped. James
remembered hearing those words. He remembered being told not
to touch, not to play, not to make a mess, not to leave his room,
not to sass. His mother said that. *Children can be controlled.* She
said it through bared teeth. James remembered her hand and he
shuddered.

The father stopped and turned around. The mother swiveled with
him. James was glad to see the girl's back again. He didn't like her
face, that smile and those tears, letting him know she had everything
and he had nothing. "We'd like our money back," the father said.

The mother looked up at him. She was proud of him; James could tell by the tilt of her head, the set of her shoulders.

"No." He said it as forcefully as he could, even as sweat dripped down the inside of his shirt and his knees trembled. He held out the battered clock. "It will take all you paid, plus more, to fix this." His voice died, though he willed it to go on, to tell the man how much this clock would cost to fix, how much to replace, as he had the last father. But seeing them there, the two of them, mom and dad, wrapped around that child, took his tongue away. He couldn't risk speaking, it would lead to tears, and his mother said tears were to be smacked away. It took everything he had to say this much in their presence. So silently, he just held out the cat clock, the bruised body in one hand, the amputated tail in the other.

The father started to say something, but the mother shook her head. She made a sound like, "Shhh." The little girl lifted her head, twisted in her father's arms. The smile was still there, faint so the parents couldn't see it. The father sighed. "Christ, keep the money," he said. "It's just a stupid plastic cat clock."

They all pivoted and left, walking as a unit. James stood there, looking at Felix, trying to keep the tears down, trying not to think of his mother's hands, trying to swallow her words back down to a place so deep within himself, they would never emerge from his mouth again. As the family's footsteps echoed, as they reached the landing by the stairs, James heard the mother's soft voice, followed by the little girl's strident whine. And then the father.

"You know better than to touch things that aren't yours!"

A smack. A smack and a wail. Then the flurry of footsteps down the stairs.

She got hers. That was another thing James' mother used to say. The words came flying back up unbidden and James was powerless to push them back down. He was horrified. *You'll get yours.* Her hand drawn back like a pitcher ready to throw a fastball. James sat down on the closest chair and rested Felix on his lap. She got hers, that little girl. But his own cheek stung and he placed his fingers against his face and stroked.

James waited until the door chimed as it opened and slammed. Then he went to the control room, checked the monitors to make sure that no one walked in as the family walked out, and then went down the basement to the workroom.

He placed Felix on the bench. Taking inventory, he made his prognosis. Felix would run again, if he had the parts. Pieces of the broken body would have to be glued, which ruined the clock's value, but he would run again and that was all that mattered. Clocks didn't care if they had to limp along. Just so they lived.

One by one, James examined all of Felix's broken parts, then dove into the skeleton boxes and found replacements. Lining them up, broken to whole, side by side on a soft towel, James made sure all were present and accounted for. All the whole parts had to be washed, prepared for the transplant. The broken would be placed on a piece of velvet and buried. The delicate wire that held the pendulum and attached it to the clock's workings was stretched straight; it couldn't be used again. One more search in the boxes and a new wire was found, the slim triangle at the bottom ready to grip Felix's tail.

James stood there for a moment and eyeballed everything, connecting one piece to another in his mind. And he came up short. Again, he went over it, then one more time. There was definitely a gear missing. James looked inside Felix's body to make sure it wasn't rolling around loose, but he was empty. The missing gear was small, but important; all gears are important because they're interdependent, but at least it was only one.

James returned to the back east bedroom. The gear couldn't have gotten far. Its roundness would enable it to roll, so he got down on his hands and knees and crawled, trying to put his face as close to the carpet as possible.

And then he remembered Cooley, scooping up those two tiny old springs from her Baby Ben and tucking them into her pocket. The little girl wanted a part too, Felix's tail, but maybe she kept his gear. Maybe she took it.

James kept crawling, pushing back the anger that threatened to erupt out of his blood. A piece of one of his clocks in a stranger's pocket. He tried to control his breathing, blinked away the new set of tears that threatened to spill, tears of anger and frustration this time. But then he found it, threaded into a tiny pulled string in the carpet. Relief poured over him in a cold sweat and he cupped the gear in his hand and returned to the basement.

The clock was all there. Felix just had to be put back together. A feline Humpty Dumpty.

What could be replaced would be replaced. What was split would be glued. James sighed and lowered his head. It would be a full morning, gluing the clock, waiting for it to dry. The afternoon would be spent putting the movement back together and attaching the pendulum wire and gear. And then he'd have to hang Felix carefully on the wall, maybe a little higher this time. Out of the reach of little girls. Then the clock tower climb at six.

For the moment, even as James held the glue and the broken pieces of plastic in his hands, all he could see was the mother's pink fingers. James knew, just looking at them, just remembering them, that those fingers were warm. Warm and soft, maybe just the slightest bit moist.

But not cold. No, not cold at all.

At six o'clock, James locked the front door of the Home. Lorraine, the lady who ran the bed and breakfast, Time To Sleep Inn, across the street was out on her porch, shaking out some rugs. She flapped one in James' direction. "Hi, James!" she called.

He nodded and started walking. It would take about ten minutes to reach the clock tower. He carried a metal toolbox filled with his most often used tools and he took great pleasure in the banging sound as it hit against his thigh, the rattle as the tools shifted inside. It was a good sound, a going-to-work sound. It reminded James of the old metal lunchbox he used to carry to work when he was a janitor. The thermos inside always made a pleasant busy rolling-around sound. It always mashed the sandwiches, but he kept it anyway. The lunchbox made him feel good, like he was doing something important. Now, the toolbox made him feel the same way and his steps grew long and purposeful.

Downtown was quiet, which was typical for a Tuesday evening. Neal's and Ione's gift shop, It's About Time, was closed up tight, but James stopped and looked in the window. Battery-powered clocks ticked away, their faces blank and dumb. When clocks didn't run themselves, they didn't have anything to do but sit there. That's what these clocks did...they just sat on the bright green crushed velvet material Neal bought on overstock at the fabric store. James could see the shelves and counters, lined with more and more of the vacant clocks. One whole showcase carried the brass miniatures. Once, Neal showed James a replica of a grandfather clock. It was beautiful, James couldn't deny that. Its brass was finely etched and the detail of the clock's sun and moon movement above the face was perfect. But the plain white watchface and the battery-thin tick ruined it. It was pretty, but it had no personality. Neal offered to give it to James, to display at the Home alongside a business card for the gift shop, but James said no.

After looking quickly around, James waved at the window clocks anyway, just to give them something to think about, and then he moved on down the street. The restaurant, the Tick-Tock Quick-Stop, was next and the owner, Eugene, stood by the open doorway, drying his hands on a greasy towel.

"Hey, James," he said. "Heard you're fixin' the clock tower."

James stopped and propped one of his feet on the step. "Well, I'm going to try. I've never worked with anything this big before." James liked Gene. Saturday nights, he sent one of the teenage waiters to the Home, carrying the day's special. James always found it a treat to eat something he didn't cook and Gene knew James didn't like What Cheer crowds.

Gene nodded. "You'll be able to do it," he said. "You're like a heart surgeon. You fix tickers." He grinned and James laughed quickly behind his hand. "After you're done, why doncha come back here and have some dinner? It's Tuesday meatloaf. Comes with mashed potatoes and beef gravy, a biscuit, and for you, even a slab of Molly's fresh-baked peach pie and a cup of coffee, on the house."

When Gene sent over the Saturday supper, he always included some of his wife's pie and James knew it was the best in the world.

There was something about the crust, so sweet and crispy, it was a treat by itself. One Sunday, when James bumped into Gene at the Shop Around The Clock, James admitted how much he admired the pie crust and the next Saturday, Molly sent a surprise and a note. "James," it said, "heard you thought my crust was capital-T tasty. So I made extra dough and made you crust-bites, brushed with butter and sugar. Hope you like them." James ate every one, even before he ate his proper dinner, and he tucked away the note in a drawer in his kitchen. James never talked directly to Molly, face to face, but he saw her around town and that note made James feel like he knew her. He knew she had to be as sweet as her pies.

Now, James looked past Gene into the restaurant. It was crowded with folks, lots of the town's regulars and the town's families. If the clock tower took at least an hour, and it would probably take more, the crowd would thin before James returned. Crowds didn't bother James normally; he was used to pushing upstream against folks in flea markets. But here, it was different. Here, it was a crowd that would talk to him. "I don't know," James said to Gene. "We'll see what time it is when I'm done."

Gene looked into the restaurant, then back at James. "I'd give you a special table around back," he said. "It's real private. I reserve it for lovers...those folks usually want to be alone." He smirked and winked. "I'll give it an hour, then keep the table open for you."

James breathed deeply. He'd never eaten at the only restaurant in What Cheer, not once in his whole entire time there. He never even ate in restaurants when he was out on the road at flea markets and estate sales, preferring to call out for pizza or room service. But the idea of sitting at a table other than his own, sitting by himself while conversation buzzed around but not at him, eating a good meal, maybe even talking some with Gene and Molly, pulled him in. "Okay," he said. "If the back table's available, I'll take it."

They shook on it and Gene's hand was warm and meaty. Then James moved on to the clock tower.

He was dismayed when he saw all the people. He'd imagined it as just being himself, the fire truck, and the clock tower. He didn't even consider the firemen, somehow thinking that the truck was going to operate itself. But Neal and Ione were there, Ione's feet actually clad in bright white sneakers instead of her fuzzy slippers. It was like she bought those shoes special just to watch James fix the clock. Several of the guys from the fire department stood by the truck, and in a back corner, James saw Cooley's band of teenagers. They swung on a low black chain, looped between posts, that kept the clock tower corralled in a square. James hated that chain. As if the clock tower was going to get up and walk away. As if a single strand of chain would keep away vandals. Cooley was there, James recognized her reddish-purple hair. She was smoking a cigarette.

James stumbled for just a minute, the toolbox clanging loudly against his leg, but then he forced his shoulders back and his spine straight and he marched toward the fire truck. The clock tower needed him and he couldn't walk away now.

Neal met him. "Hey, James," he said. "Got the cherry picker. Thought it would be safer than a ladder truck."

"Why are there so many people here?" James asked. "All I really needed was someone to operate the truck." He wondered if the firemen could clear the area, let him work in peace.

"Well, Ione and I wanted to watch. We thought maybe we'd take you out to dinner at the diner afterwards, to say thank you."

The vision of the back table disappeared. Unless James could convince them to sit there; he thought maybe he could take that. He'd only have to talk to Neal; Ione never said a word. She smiled though, and waved.

Laughter roiled the air and James looked over at the teens. They were bent over, guffawing, but Cooley was a bit separate from them. She raised her cigarette and James thought it might be a wave, but he wasn't sure and he didn't respond. He thought of the price he put on fixing her clock, the promise taken from her to make the kids stop saying the clock-keeper rhyme, and he wondered if she'd hold to it. He wondered if he could take the clock back from her if she didn't. If he would even try.

Then Mark, one of the fire guys, shook James' hand. "Thought I'd give you a lift, James," he said and smiled. He demonstrated how to stand in the big cup, how to operate the little door so James could step out onto the deck at the top of the clock tower. Neal, Mark and James walked away a bit and looked up.

"See there?" Mark said, pointing at one of the brick legs. "At the top? There's an entry there. That's what leads to the insides of the clock."

What didn't look far up before looked far up now. The entryway seemed tiny. "I can fit through that?" James asked.

Mark nodded. "Sure. It's a regular door. Doorknob and everything. Just looks small from down here." He handed James a key. "It's locked, just an extra precaution to keep out vandals. Use this and you'll get right in." Then he fiddled with a large square flashlight, turning it on before handing it over. The light hit Mark's face and he shut his eyes and turned away. "It might be dark in there, use this. You ready?"

James gripped the toolbox tighter. "Let's do it." Climbing into the cup, James decided to keep looking up, not down. Mark patted the cup, then patted James. "This truck is great, James, you'll be fine," he said. "It's the star of our fleet, our newest one. We call her Cherry."

James liked old things, but being in a new fire truck made him feel safer. The thing lurched into motion and he rose into the air. James focused on that door, watching it grow bigger and bigger.

Then he heard it. "Clock keeper, clock keeper…" and "Look! Up in the sky! It's a bird, it's a plane, it's…Super Clock Keeper!" followed by more of that laughter. That laughter that James hated, that he heard all his life. He looked down and saw the teens, falling over themselves and pointing up. James couldn't tell if Cooley was laughing or not. "Liar!" he yelled. "You liar, Cooley!" He got dizzy looking down and he dropped the toolbox to grab hold of the edges of the cup. The noise of metal hitting metal rang out and the lift came to a grinding stop.

"You okay, James?" Mark yelled. "What was that noise?" His voice seemed small and came from so far down. James wanted to see Mark, see his eyes in his upraised face, but was afraid to look. The cup might tip.

James took a deep breath. "It's okay, I just dropped my toolbox. Keep going." The lift resumed. There was some movement from down below that James caught out of the corner of his eye. He tried to look without tilting his head. Neal headed over to the teens. In a moment, they all left, except for Cooley. She shook her head and planted herself on the ground. Neal stayed by her. James put his concentration back on the task at hand and he watched as the cup leveled out next to the entry, bumping gently against the bricks.

Carefully, James unlocked the door and then stepped inside. The tower felt solid, stronger than Cherry, safer. James felt the big clock's shoulders curl around him, protecting him. It knew James was there to help. The sunlight only brightened a small area and he was glad for the flashlight. He lit it and looked around.

It was like James shrunk and stepped into a clock on his workbench. Everything was familiar, but so giant. He moved around, shining the light this way and that. There was scaffolding everywhere, James could move with ease. He thought again about asking the town council to let him in there for regular maintenance. The clock face was plain, but the movement, the heart, was grand. Stopped as it was, James could admire every cog, every gear, as it slid into place, prepared to move. He wanted to be a part of it, to make this clock what it could be, a fine timepiece, not running late or ahead, but letting everyone know exactly what time it was, where they should be, how far along in their day.

James heard a tight hum. The clock was straining to run, but it was stuck somewhere. He moved around in a square, seeing everything lodged tight, but not finding the cause. Then the flashlight lit up a mess of twigs and white and black bird splatter stark against the cream of the brick. A nest, shaped oddly like a round-bottomed cup, was wedged in between two of the gears. James wondered how it got in here. He didn't see any birds now, just the scraggly nest, chewed in the gear's teeth. Moving closer, he looked inside. Five black and white speckled eggs. Barn swallows. He wondered if the parents would find the nest if it was moved outside.

Carefully, James put the flashlight and the toolbox down, making sure they were away from any edges, clear of falling. Then he grabbed the nest with both hands and tried to gently tug it free. The dried grass and twigs dug into his fingers, but James kept at it and it seemed to be coming loose.

Then it ripped. To James' horror, it ripped right in half and the nest crumbled and the five little eggs fell. He tried to catch them and one bounced on his fingers, slid against his palm and he felt a splash of warmth. But when he closed his fingers, there was only air and his own skin. The eggs flew through the scaffolding and on down, turning end over end…and James saw them hit the ground.

That's when he realized there was no floor. The scaffolding wrapped around the clock's insides. There was a roof overhead to keep out the rain. But there was nothing solid below. Just the bright green of grass and some gold where the sun was blocked by the tower.

Free of debris, the clock began to work, the hum shifting loose and deep, its gears connecting and rolling forward. James grabbed on to the scaffolding, trying to get his balance, to look around again at the familiar, and not down at the mess of black and white egg shells and what he knew must be splattered baby birds. He looked at the gears and wondered how to reset the time. It wouldn't be right anymore. Not that it ever was.

And that's when he remembered the time the clock stopped. A notch before noon. James made a scramble for the door, but then the clock began to chime.

The sound was everywhere. It was solid, pressing down, forcing James flat out on his stomach on the scaffolding. He put his hands over his ears, his ears that were already stunned, and he tried to yell, but he couldn't hear his own voice. The sound was burying him, the notes began to blend one into the other, and James didn't know if the clock bellowed the Westminster or if it was on the time, the sound was just a physical thing, holding him down, his face pushed to the scaffold and he looked at the smashed birds and the sound pressed into his ears and his body and over his eyes until he closed them. Until he closed them and everything swirled into a tidal wave of noise. James fell into the wave and kept falling, his arms and legs outstretched, and his mouth open, his voice ringing with the time, and he chimed and chimed and chimed.

CHAPTER TWELVE:

WHAT COUNTS
The Cat Clock's Story

As I wrapped the cat clock in tissue, I wished for nine lives. Then I decided that was selfish, so I cut back. Nine lives were a luxury. One was poverty. Three lives…three lives would be perfect. One for me with my normal children. One for me with Leatrice. And one for me with me. Just me. Not torn between four with the biggest chunk going to one. Or torn between five, if I was to count myself. And it was time, I thought, to count myself. In my head, I assigned everyone their number.

One, Leatrice, always Leatrice, my special girl, now twenty-four years old.

Two, Annie, my little girl, twenty-eight.

Three, Christopher, my man of the house, thirty.

Four, Leonard, my husband. Ex-husband, although it was never official.

And last, me.

I thought about the middle three, no longer around to be counted anymore. Because they thought they didn't count.

Leonard left when Leatrice was three. He said he couldn't handle it anymore, he was sorry. Off he went to Arizona, sending rubber cacti for Christopher and Annie, rubber checks for me and nothing at all for Leatrice. I always found a few spare dollars for little toys for her, telling her they were from Daddy. She tossed them across the room and went on playing with the toilet paper rolls, the paper towel rolls, empty tissue boxes.

Christopher and Annie each left when they were eighteen, off to attend the University of Arizona and to stay with their father, they said because he gave them attention. His cacti counted as attention. Christopher left without a word, but Annie looked sad and said, "Mama, we understand. She's a lot of work. But sometimes, it makes us wish we were a lot of work too."

So then there were just two to count. First, Leatrice, always Leatrice. And now, finally, me, about to send my last child, my forever child, to a residential facility.

Then there would be just me. I would be number one. But my heart would be broken in two.

I just closed the packing box when Leatrice lumbered into the kitchen. She was still in her flannel nightshirt, her favorite, red plaid with torn-out underarms. When I came back this afternoon, it would be the first thing I threw away. I couldn't send it with her; what would they think of a tattered nightshirt? For a minute though, as I stood there, watching her stretch, seeing the underarm holes lengthen and narrow, flashes of her flabby skin peeking through, I thought how lifeless the nightshirt was going to be that night, when I got back. How it was filled out now, with her, with all her parts and curves and messes and sudden sweetness. And I wondered if tonight, after all the lights were out, after I was supposed to be in bed, asleep, for the first time in twenty-four years without the constant hum of the baby monitor on my dresser, the constant drone of Leatrice's congested pug-nosed snoring, I would get up, pull the nightshirt out of the garbage and place it, carefully, next to me.

"Mama?" Leatrice said. "Key Cat?"

"Your kitty cat's safe in this box," I told her. "You can hang it up in your new room this afternoon. Someone will help you." I wondered who. Leatrice just stared at me, her mouth hanging slack, then she wandered away. I listened to her steps, tracking her as she returned to her room. "Mama?" she said, staring, I knew, at the empty spot above her light switch. "Key Cat?"

"Time for a bath, Leatrice." I went into the bathroom and began to run the water. Alerted by the sound, Leatrice appeared in the doorway, her arms upraised for me to take off her nightshirt. As I exposed her bare body, womanly, tubby, rounded and rolled, I saw that I should probably shave her before she left. Then I shook my head. Leatrice hated being shaved. I wanted this last morning to be peaceful. In the cool air, her nipples matured and swelled, round pink buttons that looked ripened to bursting.

I helped her into the tub, pushing her heavy body down into a squat, then a sit. She squealed the way she always did when the hot water hit her bottom and then she began to splash and kick. I never expected motherhood to include bathing a grown woman.

It used to be easy. In the tub, she was almost an ordinary child, splashing with her hands and feet, laughing, getting soapsuds in her eyes and nose. I pretended during those times that she was normal, that one day she would be just like her big brother and big sister.

It was hard to pretend when the little girl had fully-developed breasts and lacy brown pubic hair and legs so long, she couldn't sit Indian style in the tub anymore.

I sank to my knees and began to wash. She was oblivious, as always, just moving her busy hands up and away while I soaped. "Leatrice," I told her. "You're going to your new home today. Remember? A home with lots of kids like you." And a new mama, I wanted to say. A new mama to take care of you, who doesn't run out of energy by early afternoon. But I couldn't choke out the words.

Leatrice ignored me and continued to play. I sat back, letting her vigorous splashes rinse her body. I remembered once, right before Leonard left, him squatting on the floor in front of Leatrice. "Look at her, sweetheart," he said. "She's just a lump. She looks like a potato."

"What do you want to do then, cook her?" I asked. "She's your daughter. Same as Annie."

"She's not the same as Annie," he growled, poking Leatrice in the stomach. "Don't you ever say so. Don't you ever insult Annie that way."

I got between them, between his poking finger and my special girl. She didn't even look up at him. Nor at me, to be fair. And I always tried to be fair.

Christopher and Annie were the same way. When I placed Leatrice in their little circle, telling them to play with their sister awhile, they looked at each other and then just handed Leatrice a pile of newspapers, a hairbrush, an old envelope. Whatever was handy. When I glared at them, Christopher said, "Mama, she just *sits* there. It's not like she's going to play Scrabble with us. She doesn't even know the alphabet."

Now, I looked at Leatrice, suddenly sitting still in the water. She had that blank look on her face again. Her bath was over. "C'mon, sweetheart," I said, taking her arm and pulling her to her feet. "We have to get dressed. We're going bye-byes."

"Bye-byes!" she shouted and stumped off naked down the hallway. I followed after her. I used to close the curtains, attempt to hide her adult body from passersby, but I didn't bother anymore. It was too hard living in the dark. Even Leatrice needed sunshine.

"Mama?" Leatrice called from her room. "Key Cat?"

I didn't answer. I was just too tired to explain it away.

On the way home, I kept glancing at the empty passenger seat. I didn't know how long it was since I last drove in the car alone.

At the residential facility, a nice cheerful rehabbed Victorian home with knocked-out walls and so many windows, I only barely noticed the bars and alarms, I explained to Mary, the housemother, the new mama, about the cat clock. "I bought it when I was pregnant with her," I said. "Her whole nursery was done up in kitty cats." White crib, comforter with rainbow kitties grinning and winking. Stuffed kitty cats in every corner. A special pink sleeping kitty I called Boo-Cat sitting in the crib. Leatrice never took to it and I had it now on my own bed. Kitty curtains, kitty wallpaper border. "I found the clock in an antique mall. It's supposed to be Felix the Cat, remember Felix?" Mary, her eyes fixed on Leatrice as she wandered around the living room, nodded. Leatrice didn't touch anything, just walked from corner to corner. Good girl, I thought. "It's hung in her room ever since. Every morning, she says hello to Key Cat and every night, she says goodbye." I thought of her saying goodbye to Key Cat that night, without me there to echo, "Goodbye, Key Cat, goodbye, Leatrice." I never could get her to say goodnight.

Mary shifted her glance to me. "Key Cat? I thought it was Felix."

I nodded. "It is. But Key Cat is Leatrice's word for kitty cat." The kitty curtains and wallpaper border were still in Leatrice's room, a little worse for wear. Her bed was a twin size now, with a purple bedspread covered with black and white cats. I liked the rainbow kitties better.

I wondered what I would do with it now, that kitty cat room.

Then I left my daughter. I left her behind. I kissed her on the cheek as she sat on the bed in her new room with Mary next to her, holding her hand. Leatrice just stared when I said goodbye. Though when I walked out the door, I thought I heard her say, "Mama?" followed by Mary's soft, "Shhh."

I said goodbye to Leatrice, goodbye for a month because Mary said I shouldn't visit until a month passed. She said it would help Leatrice adjust if she was on her own. She's not *on her own*, I wanted to say. She's *alone*. There's a difference. But I nodded, kissed my daughter goodbye, a hard and long kiss, enough to last us both for a month, and walked out the door, thinking I heard her say, "Mama?"

But the kiss ran out. The next morning, after I tucked Leatrice's red plaid nightshirt under my pillow, I nearly drove back to bring Leatrice home. My day wasn't right, not without her walking into the kitchen, babbling over her cereal, splashing in her bath. I didn't know what to do. I sat at the table and drank a whole cup of coffee, straight through. It didn't even get cold. Then I reached for my keys and was almost out the door when Christopher called out of the blue. My Christopher. A voice I hadn't heard in almost twelve years. "Hello, Mama," he said. "I know what you did, Annie told me. And I wanted to tell you you did the right thing."

I couldn't catch my breath. I wanted to talk to him, to tell him it wasn't right, but all I could make was gagging noises into the phone.

"Mama? Mama, it's all right. Really. She's being taken care of. Annie told me the name of the place and I checked it out. It's one of the best. She'll be fine."

I began to cry, but I nodded. I wasn't sure if I was crying over leaving Leatrice behind or getting Christopher back.

"Mama, I thought we'd come out this weekend. Me, Barbara and Jimmy."

First the daughter-in-law and then the grandson I never met. Because Christopher didn't want them to meet Leatrice and I wouldn't meet them without her. "Oh," I said. "Oh, Christopher…" I wanted to ask if he'd actually gone to Leatrice's new home. If he'd seen her. Or if he just talked to someone about the place, about Mary. I told myself that even if he just talked to someone, it was worth counting. I told myself to breathe deep, to slow my heart down, to sit and hold on to the edge of the table with my free hand.

"We'll be there Friday night, okay? And leave Sunday, after supper . See you then." He paused a moment. "Love you, Mama," he said quickly, and hung up.

And suddenly, there was something to do. I walked down the hallway to Leatrice's room. I could sleep in there Friday and Saturday night, I decided. Christopher and Barbara could have my room, Jimmy could have Christopher's. When the phone rang again, I ran to it. It was Annie.

"How'd it go, Mama?"

I poured myself another cup of coffee and sat down and told her all about it. As I talked, my body braced, ready to run at a crash, a whimper, a startled, "Mama!" But the interruption never came.

I hung up the phone and sat there, thinking. I wasn't supposed to feel this way. My baby girl was in a residential facility for the rest of her life. I didn't want to put her there. I should be crying. I should be in my car, heading for her rescue.

And I did feel it. My arms trembled, my hands became fists, and for a moment, I beat the table, making my empty coffee cup bounce up and down and finally topple over the edge and crash on the floor. But then, it was done. I shoved the whole mess of my life away. Sweeping up my cup, I threw away the pieces, saying, "That's that. It's over." And it was. I gathered all my cleaning supplies together and went to the kitty cat room. I had a lot to do before Friday.

All weekend long, Leatrice's name was never mentioned. I played with my three-year old grandson, just played and played, tickling his ribs, whispering in his ear, reading him stories. Annie came along and at night, I sat at the kitchen table with her and with Christopher while Barbara got Jimmy ready for bed. I found out how Christopher loved his job, but felt like he never made enough money. Annie told me about John, her new boyfriend, how he treated her right and she thought she might marry him. Jimmy's upper left center tooth came in really crooked, Christopher said, but the dentist showed them how to apply pressure to it, and it finished out straight. Annie tried dying her hair red, but it looked, she said, like lipstick and felt like fingernail polish. I laughed and smiled and talked and nodded. Every now and then, I touched them, their hands, their cheeks, their hair.

I wondered silently about Leatrice, about what she was doing in her new home. I nearly brought her name up, but stopped when I saw my kids' faces, so open, so clear, like they were six and four again. That night, in the kitty cat room, I pictured Leatrice, sitting on the floor in a corner of the kitchen, playing with her toilet paper rolls, while I talked with Christopher and Annie. But I couldn't get the picture to come in clear.

There were no more kitty cats. The walls in this room were yellow now, a crayon yellow, the yellow of a child's sun. I bought yellow and white checked curtains on special at Shop-Ko and hung them at the window. The comforter on the bed was white with yellow tulips splashed all over it. Christopher and Annie helped me pick it out when they brought me on Saturday afternoon to a furniture store, to choose a new queen-sized bed. They insisted I be the first to sleep on it, in this brand new guest room. It was a spring room, a sunshine room, and I tried to be happy in it. But I thought I saw traces of rainbow kitties in the corners.

As they left Sunday night, Annie looked over her shoulder and said, "Oh. Dad said to say hello."

I swallowed and leaned forward into her words. I didn't know what to say. "Oh," I said finally. "Tell him I said hello back." Then nothing else came. It seemed like enough.

Almost three weeks after I moved Leatrice out, I woke up one morning with sun lighting up my bedroom. I looked at my clock; it was ten, half the morning gone already. I was always up at six o'clock, always, for twenty-four years.

I stared at the ceiling, felt the sun hitting my bed, warming my skin, my bones, making me melt into my sheets.

There was no hurry, no catching-up to do. I pulled on my bathrobe and went into the kitchen, planning on reading the paper with my first and second cups of hot coffee.

The package arrived five days before I was due to visit Leatrice. I ripped it open and found Felix the Cat, staring up at me with one eye and one empty socket. The note said, "I don't know if this can be repaired. However, I think it's best that Leatrice not have it here. It seems to make her angry. Perhaps it would be a good idea if you waited another couple weeks before coming to visit. Mary."

I stared at that disfigured cat. I could hear Leatrice's voice as she bellowed goodbye to the clock, to me. I heard her voice often, all my life, during the day and in my dreams. I held that poor cat and remembered the first day I called the residential facility, pleading for a tour. Leatrice was bellowing then, "No! Mama! No! Mama!" behind the closed door of the bathroom.

She played on the kitchen floor that morning, got into my cupboards where she knew she wasn't supposed to go, and dumped flour and sugar all over herself. All over her big grown body. I hauled her into the bathroom for a second bath, a bath she didn't want. We struggled, but I got her stripped and into the tub. I bent down to scoop up her clothes, throw them in the hall and out of the way, when she grabbed me by the shoulders and pulled me into the tub with her. My head went under and my face pressed against the drain. My arms were straightjacketed by my sides and she hit my back and I could only breathe water. Then she paused for a moment and I heaved with my back and neck, heaved like a great whale, so hard my muscles pulled and ached for days after. I ran out of the bathroom and shut the door, because Leatrice never learned how to use a doorknob.

She could die in there, I knew. But I could too.

Dripping wet, my daughter's voice echoing in my ears, I made that phone call. Now I looked down at that battered cat and I heard Christopher say again, "Mama, it's all right. She's being taken care of."

But it was me. I was being taken care of.

I looked through the box, but I couldn't find the cat's missing eye. Looking closer, I saw that the eyes were all one part, going back and forth in the cat's head. The eyepiece was broken in half, the missing eye apparently shattered. I stroked the kitty for a moment, wishing I could fix it, then headed down to the sunshine room. Right above the light switch, in its accustomed spot, I hung the cat again. It didn't work anymore, it just sat there, looking out at the room with its one good eye, a smile still on its face.

A reminder, I thought. A reminder that Leatrice once lived here. A reminder to Christopher and Annie that they had a sister. A reminder to me that I had a special girl.

And a reminder that it was all right. We were all being taken care of. It was the right thing.

I thought of my coveted three lives and looked at the clock and realized I already lived two and was now starting on the third. There was the life before Leatrice and the life with Leatrice. Now, it was time for the life despite Leatrice.

I touched the cat's tail, set it to swinging, but the empty eye socket spooked me so much, I had to stop it. I thought about planning my day.

My day.

First, I would call Mary, make sure Leatrice was okay, and arrange my visit for two weeks from now. Then maybe I'd call Leonard. "Hello back," I would say.

Or maybe I would call Christopher's house and talk to Jimmy, hear his laughter sing over the phone line. Or I could call Annie and invite her for the weekend, a special mother and daughter time. We could snuggle together in my room and she could whisper secrets about John.

Or maybe I would take a walk around the duck pond at the park, Leatrice's favorite place, then come back here and take a nap in the sunshine room. Just because I could.

It was all up to me.

CHAPTER THIRTEEN:

JAMES

And so you grow. Outwardly. Your arms and legs shoot out at embarrassing lengths and hang from your pants and your sleeves. Pink skin, almost white, kept hidden from the sun except for brief glimpses during school recesses, should be a beacon of trouble to those around you. But you tug your sleeves down as best you can, sit with your legs crossed at the ankles, pull your socks up as high as they will go. From time to time, your mother blinks and awakes from whatever world she prowls in and goes out to the local thrift stores to buy you new clothes. Overnight, you go from jeans and shirts that are much too small to much too big, hanging in puddles over your shoes, rolling up in thick bracelets on your wrists. And the clothes are always old.

A few kids along the way try to befriend you. The girl in fourth grade, the one with the big teeth and bigger glasses, who asks you day after day to play ball on the playground as you sit huddled in a shadow of the building. You tell her no with a shake of your head, no and no and no, and she keeps saying why and you keep saying no without saying a word. After two weeks, she becomes angry and throws the ball at you repeatedly, bouncing it off your nose, your forehead, your chin. You nestle your head on your knees and then she bounces the ball off your skull, each time harder, each time accompanied by a louder shriek. Kids gather around and take turns. And then you go inside and sit down at your math lesson, trying to see with eyes blurred with tears of anger or sadness, you can't tell which. After that, you sit alone.

Until the sixth grade and an albino boy sits next to you at lunch. Every day. He doesn't say a word. He offers you cookies. On the fifth day, you accept one, homemade chocolate chip, and it is like gold in your mouth. Melting gold. He takes you behind the building at recess and shares a cigarette and you have to run to the bathroom and throw up. Soon after, you are down the root cellar for three days and a weekend, and when you return to school, the albino boy is gone. You never know where. You never know how to ask.

A girl in high school smiles at you. You turn away and don't look back, but you hold that smile behind your closed eyes for days and nights. She begins keeping you company in the dark of the root cellar, her smile an imagined guidepost, and the ticking of the alarm clock becomes her heartbeat. You hold the clock against your chest so you can feel the rhythm as you think of what it would be like to touch her. What it would be like to be touched.

Imagine.

Because that's all James could do. He felt that the walls of the root cellar followed him wherever he went, keeping him from reaching out, keeping others from reaching in. But keeping him safe too. Because if no one touched, then no one hurt.

James opened his eyes and saw a face. It hovered above him and he saw long hair and brown eyes and he said, "Mama?" He felt his lips move together, touching gently twice for each M, but he heard no sound. The face shook side to side and James closed his eyes. Don't be so stupid, he said to himself. Mama wouldn't be here. And her eyes were blue.

When he opened his eyes again, the face wasn't there. James moved his arms and legs, shifted his body, and he felt the comfort of his sheets and blanket. Then he looked up and the face was there again.

Of course it wasn't Mama. It was too young. James saw the smile, the freckles on the nose, the upswept eyebrows and he gasped. "Diana?" He hadn't spoken that name in years, yet it rolled off his tongue as if he said it every day. But he couldn't hear it, couldn't hear the three subtle syllables of the name that couldn't be said aloud without making him ache. "Diana?"

She shook her head again and then James' vision cleared. He saw the purple-red hair, the nose ring. It was Cooley.

Cooley was in his bedroom.

He thrashed, trying to untuck the blankets, get out of bed, get her the hell out of his house. He was electrified with the need to tally, make sure everyone was there, that she hadn't touched or taken anything. But then there were arms, more arms than Cooley's, pushing him back into the bed. He looked around, saw Ione holding down one of his arms, Neal the other. Ione pursed her lips and shook her head, like she was shushing James, and Neal patted his shoulder.

"What's going on!" James yelled and he could feel the force of his words leaving his throat, flying into the room. But he couldn't hear them. It was like he hadn't said a thing.

Cooley reappeared, holding a notebook and a pen. She held them up in the air, displaying them, and then she began to write. Eventually, she handed James the notebook.

"James," the note said. "U had an accident. The clock went off while U were up there. U were 2 close 2 the sound and UR ears R hurt. U can't hear right now."

James remembered. He remembered the chime blending into just one enormous sound and he remembered the dead baby birds and all that pressure, pressure on his ears, pushing him into the scaffolding. But not hear?

He struggled again. He managed to get past Ione and Neal and staggered around, staring at the clocks, seeing the pendulums sway. But there was nothing, he couldn't hear a single tick. He looked at the clocks' hands and they were all on the quarter hour, but there were no chimes. Touching a clock, an old cathedral clock, he felt the vibration. The clock was talking, and James couldn't hear it.

No ticking. No ticking. A searing pain choked his chest and he clasped both hands over his heart, trying to find the rhythm. It was there, steady, but fast. James looked at the clock, watched the pendulum, tried to even out his beat.

Someone touched his arm and James turned and saw Ione. She patted him and smiled, then slowly formed her lips. Oh-kay, he was able to make out. Everything will be okay. James shook his head and looked back at the clock, then he let himself be led to bed.

James looked down as he was tucked in. He was in pajamas. Grabbing the blanket, he pulled it up to his neck. Neal smiled and reached for the notebook.

"It's OK," his note read. "Dr. Owen was here. It was he and I that got you undressed and into bed."

James sighed and tried to relax. He started to write his own note, but then stopped. His voice worked, he reasoned, only his ears didn't. "Is this permanent?" he asked. "Do my sounds make sense? I can't hear myself speak!"

Neal nodded. Then he wrote, "We don't know. Dr. said to wait a few days and if it's not better, there's a specialist in Des Moines. You're loud."

Cooley came back into the room, carrying Felix the Cat. "Be careful!" James shouted and he knew he must have made sense, because her fingers tightened.

She brought the clock to the bedside and James took it quickly, balancing it gently in the nest of his lap. He worked so hard to fix that clock; he didn't need her undoing everything. He checked it over as she scribbled in the notebook. Don't worry, James told the clock, I won't let any more girls touch you. He checked the pendulum, the glued spots. The clock was fine.

When James looked up, they all stared at him, Cooley over the top of the notebook. James realized he must have spoken aloud. He looked away.

Cooley handed over her note. "I found it on UR workbench," she said. "I can hang it back up 4 U. Same room as the dwarf tall clock?"

James wanted to yell at her, to tell her to stop writing in strange codes. He wanted to tell her to go away, for them all to go away, to just leave him alone. He snatched the pen from her hand. In big letters, he wrote, "STAY OUT OF MY WORKROOM! STAY OUT OF ALL MY ROOMS!" Then he wrote and underlined, "GET OUT!"

She must have been reading over the top of the notebook because before he was done with the exclamation point, she was gone. James put the notebook aside and then carefully lay the cat clock on the bedside table. He would hang it himself, as soon as he and the clocks were alone.

Ione came over and took the notebook. James watched her, amazed. This woman never said anything and here she scribbled away like Shakespeare. She handed him the page.

"You shouldn't of yelled at Amy Sue," she said. "She was only trying two help. She's been hear the hole time."

An illiterate Shakespeare. The woman couldn't spell. James looked at her note again, read it through while substituting corrections. Have, to, here, whole. The whole time. He glanced at the clocks again. It was ten-forty, over four hours since he went up that clock tower. Four hours since he'd heard anything. He listened carefully as he sucked air deep into his lungs, then let it out in what he knew should be a whoosh. But he couldn't even hear himself breathe. Sighing, James wrote, "I'd like to go to sleep now. Thank you."

Neal and Ione said something to each other. Then Neal took over the pen. "Why are you writing everything? You can talk. Do you want anything? Are you hungry?"

James shook his head and then wrote, "It's just easier this way. It's too hard to talk when I can't hear my own voice." Neal and Ione fussed around the room a little bit, then walked away, turning out the light as they went. James waited for a few minutes, until he was sure they were out the door, and then he got up and put the light back on. He went downstairs, wanting to make sure the doors were locked.

The Home was completely silent and James was chilled without the cloak of ticks and chimes to cover him. He touched clocks as he went by, but he couldn't hear their soft hellos. "Damn!" he yelled.

"Damn!" But there was nothing. Again, he clutched his chest, felt his heart, and then sank down onto the bottom step.

Closing his eyes, feeling that beating beneath his skin, he brought his lips together in rhythm with it. "Bum-bum," he said. "Bum-bum. Bum-bum." James tried to hear it, somewhere deep inside of himself, but it just wasn't there. Trembling, he went back upstairs to his room and picked up Felix. Then he went down the hall to the back east bedroom. Cooley was wrong. Felix didn't belong in the same room as the dwarf tall clock.

The spot on the wall looked empty without Felix. James set him down on a chair and went in search of a hammer. When he came back, he stood on the footstool and raised Felix's nail by a good foot. No child would be able to reach him here. No girl would ever touch him again.

Hanging him securely, James set the tail to wagging and watched the eyes start moving left and right, left and right. There was no sound, but the cat grinned with the same familiar smile James returned for years.

He remembered when the cat clock first arrived. It was in the middle of a summer day, a Saturday filled with tourists. James stood by the front door, getting a breather from answering questions, when a young man approached. He held the cat clock.

"Excuse me," he said. "Would you like this? I've looked throughout your home and I don't see another one like it."

James took the cat and looked it over. The face was missing a few numbers and its eyepiece was broken in half. Only one eye looked out through the sockets. "It's in pretty sad shape," James said.

"Oh, I know." The man reached out as if to stroke one of the cat's ears, but then he stopped and put his hand in his pocket. "Anyway, I know they can be quite valuable. I thought this might be a good place for it."

James looked at him quickly. Someone who knew the monetary value of a clock could be hard to bargain with. "How much do you want for it? It would need a lot of work."

"I don't want anything." The man rubbed his hair, making it stand up like a rooster's comb. "My mother died recently. This was hers and I…well, I just couldn't throw it out." He did touch the clock then, with one finger, right on the tip of its nose.

The clock suddenly felt cold in James' hands. The remaining eye looked up and despite the smile, the cat looked sad.

"Well, thank you for offering it to me." James shook the man's hand. "I'll take really good care of it."

"You think you can fix it?" he asked.

In James' mind, he was already fixing the clock, using a set of eyes he had down in the skeleton boxes. Once, when an old clock shop in Cedar Rapids closed, he picked up some Felix parts. He didn't own a Felix clock, not until this man arrived, but it never hurt to be ready. "Oh, yes," James said. "I'm sure I can."

This sparked a sudden smile and then the man ran down the stairs to his car.

Now James watched the clock with two good eyes run smoothly, but without a sound. "I wish I could hear you," he said to Felix. "I wish I could hear you tick, so I could know that I fixed you up just fine." The tail continued to wag steadily, so James figured everything must be in place again.

He left the room and went back downstairs. Without sound, he felt like he was in a new house, following a new path. He had to look at the clocks to recognize the room, to orient himself in the Home. He stopped by the dwarf tall clock. Her hands were just before eleven o'clock and her presence was warm and solid. Carefully, James knelt down and placed his cheek against her longcase. He waited and soon he felt it, that vibration that shook through the clock's body as she sang. Pressing in closer, James tried to pull that vibration into his head, through the passages to his eardrum. But nothing broke through. The clock sang just for him and he couldn't hear a single note.

Pulling away, James took his pajama sleeve and polished the oily spot from the clock's case, the spot left there by his own skin. He didn't want his own body to ruin the patina.

Standing and putting his fingers on the light switch, James remembered Cooley's words on the notebook paper. She asked if the cat clock hung in the same room as the dwarf tall clock.

She said dwarf tall clock. Not grandmother. James blinked. The words were still on the notebook paper upstairs. He could check and make sure she really used the right term.

Hitting the light, the darkness fell all around. James waited for his eyes to adjust. He always believed he could find his way around the Home blindfolded, just by following and recognizing all the different ticks and chimes. Now, he didn't know if he could find his own room in the dark.

"Goodnight, friends," James said out loud, hoping the clocks heard. Wishing he could hear his own voice.

In his sleep, James could still hear. He burrowed in deeper, listening to the ticking, the chimes, all the wonderful noise echoing throughout the Home. Everything was dark and it didn't matter that he couldn't see; he could hear. The ticking seemed continuous, all those clocks moving at different speeds, but then they began to stop. One by one, James heard clocks drop off and he scrambled to catch up with them, to find them again. The sounds grew fainter and fainter and then there was just one clock, one simple rhythm, tick-tock, tick-tock, and he tried to catch it, he tried to press his ear to it, he felt himself growing thinner and thinner, fainter and fainter with the beat. "Mama!" he yelled. "Mama!" And then the sound left him alone, he couldn't find it, no matter how he turned his head, and his heart slowed and stopped. And he died.

James woke up, the side of his face pressed into the pillow, his cheeks damp and his pajamas soaked with sweat. Turning on the light, he looked at the clocks, trying to hear through his sight, trying to imagine the sound as their pendulums moved back and forth and round and round. He had to hear! Staggering around the room, James stopped in front of one clock and then another, pressing his ears to their bodies, but nothing came through.

Falling to his knees by the bedside table, James looked at his mother's anniversary clock. The dancing couples spun around and around, going forward, moving back, every fifteen seconds, and he tried to hear the soft ticking that followed him all his life, the ticking he used to listen to while his mother and his father fought, while she screamed and he whispered, until he left for good and then she left and came back, left and came back. James took the glass dome off the clock, exposing the dancers to air, and they seemed to twirl faster, and he asked them, out loud, he begged them, "Please be noisy! Please stomp your feet! Let me hear you!"

And they looked at James and twirled, but there was still no sound. He saw the gilded hands meet on the three, it was three-fifteen in the morning, and he pressed his ear to the clock's base where he knew the music mechanism lay hidden, and he listened for the quarter-hour chime, the first part of the four-part Westminster, short and sweet, and there was nothing. The cold golden base vibrated against his skin, but there just was no sound. No sound at all.

James lunged to his feet and tripped over the blanket, hanging loose off the bed, and the glass dome flew from his hands and smashed on the floor. James saw the shards and pieces, the millions of sparkly-sharp shards and pieces, and he wanted to cry out, "Mama, I'm sorry!" because he knew she'd be angry, he wasn't supposed to play with her things, and he knew the belt would be coming, and the leash, the cage, the root cellar, and he had to hide the glass pieces, hide them before she came, even though she wouldn't be coming, he knew that, she was dead, but suddenly, it seemed as if she was right around the corner, leash in hand. The leash he hadn't seen in years, but felt every day, tugs here and there, just the way an amputee feels his missing leg. Scooping up the pieces of glass in his hands, he felt himself cry out, felt his chest constrict and his throat tighten, when his fingers and palms were sliced, and he dropped everything back to the floor, saw the glass explode even smaller, but he heard nothing.

James had to hear. He needed that steady rhythm, everything was going haywire, he had to hear! He ran through the broken glass and down the stairs into the kitchen. Digging through the silverware drawer, James picked a long, slim knife, one he thought would slip through the passages in his ears and pop whatever was there, lance whatever was swollen, and allow the sounds in. Standing straight, he put the knife point to his right ear and felt it, shiny-sharp, against his skin.

And he saw it. His reflection was in the kitchen window, he stood there with his hair straight up and a knife to his head, and he shuddered. He shuddered until he folded in half and dropped the knife to the floor.

It was insanity. It was insanity and James knew it and he didn't know who to call. There was no one to call. There was no one. And even if there was, he would never hear them.

There was blood everywhere. Dripping from his hands and his bare feet. There was a red trail across the kitchen floor and James knew it led all the way back up to his bedroom. A wave of nausea hit and he straightened and vomited into the kitchen sink. He felt the heaves, felt his body convulse and bend, felt even his bleeding toes curl, and yet he couldn't hear a sound. And James knew there were terrible, awful sounds coming from his stomach, through his throat, out his mouth.

Everything was such a mess and James couldn't keep it like that. Peace had to be restored, everything needed to be in its place. Clean and shiny. He rinsed his mouth and got out the bucket and sponge and a cleanser. Getting down on his knees, James plunged his hands into the soapy water. The cleanser bit deep into the gashes and he thought he felt his skin peel back. But he gritted his teeth and set to scrubbing. This had to be cleaned up before anyone saw it. Before Mama saw it. Anything was better than the root cellar.

James made it as far as the bottom of the stairs. It was so hard to scrub the carpeting. Looking back, he saw that his bleeding feet were leaving a new path where he washed the old one away. His hands were burning. It was hopeless.

Dropping the sponge into the bucket, James crawled into the living room. After turning on the light, he climbed into his recliner. At least he could see the pendulums from there. He could watch the rhythm. Trying to quiet his body, James focused as hard as he could. He stared and stared, trying to sleep with his eyes open, and after awhile, he was able to see the clocks behind his closed eyelids. He could see them and he was able to sleep.

D r. Owen and Neal broke the door down the next morning. James didn't hear it, he was still asleep in the recliner. He woke up to find them shaking him, Neal wide-eyed and flushed, Dr. Owen checking James' pulse. The door lay on the floor, completely off its hinges.

James could see their mouths moving, it looked like Neal was yelling, but James shook his head and tried to get up. That's when he saw his hands, raw and shredded from the night before. Dr. Owen pushed James back into the chair while Neal disappeared. He came back with the notebook. Quickly, he wrote something and handed it to James.

"What happened? The door was locked and we looked in the window and saw blood so we broke our way in."

James cleared his throat and tried his voice. "I broke a dome from one of my anniversary clocks. I cut myself trying to clean it up."

Dr. Owen said something and Neal scribbled. "Why are your hands so red?"

"I tried to wash the floors." James indicated the hallway, the last place he saw the rags and bucket. Neal looked around the corner, nodded and said something.

Dr. Owen pulled James to his feet. James followed both the doctor and Neal upstairs, picking their way around the glass, and then he sat on the bed. The room was a mess. Dr. Owen went into the bathroom and began running a bath while Neal stood there, his hand on James' shoulder. Then Dr. Owen took over the notebook.

"Go soak," he wrote. "Use lots of soap. When you come out, I need to look at your hands and feet, make sure there aren't still glass slivers. Then I'll bandage you up. I want to look at your ears too."

James sighed and went into the bathroom. He couldn't deny that his hands and feet hurt. They burned. And he needed Dr. Owen to look at his ears. There was nothing to do but obey. James shut the bathroom door, undressed, and sat in the tub.

The warm water seemed to help. He kept his hands and feet submerged as much as possible. He tried to relax, but he kept wondering what they were doing out there. He didn't want them to touch anything.

James washed his hair as best he could in a tub; he really preferred showers. Standing, he decided to turn on the shower to rinse off, so he shut the curtain. The warm water hitting his back and shoulders felt wonderful. Then there was a draft and when James turned, Neal was there, his eyes hard. James yelped and quickly covered himself. "What are you doing?" he asked. "Can't you let me just take a shower?"

Neal's eyes dropped to James' hands, then he nodded and backed away. James watched through the curtain, making sure Neal left the bathroom completely. Then he looked down at his own hands, trying to see what Neal saw, what he was looking for. It took a moment, but as James thought about last night, about how things must look, he was able to put it together.

They thought he tried to kill himself. The knife in the kitchen, the blood, the marks on his body, particularly his hands. Too close to the wrists? Then James looked at his feet and sighed. Did they really think he was the kind of person who would attempt suicide by slicing his feet and palms, rather than his wrists?

James began to laugh, but then he stopped. If they thought he was nuts, giggling in the shower wouldn't help.

When he got out, there was a fresh set of pajamas waiting on the lowered toilet lid. Someone must have come in again; James never heard the door.

And they must have looked through his drawers for the pajamas. James shook while he got dressed. He decided to get rid of everybody and then change into regular clothes. There were things that needed doing and he wasn't about to stay in his pajamas.

The bedroom was completely straightened. The glass was gone, the carpet soft and clean, and the dancers from his mother's anniversary clock still twirled, though they were exposed in the air. Ione was there now and she motioned to the bed. It had fresh sheets and was turned down, waiting. James grunted and climbed in. Anything to make them go away.

Before he could pull the covers up, the doctor sat down and took James' feet in his hands. He held up a bottle and a tube, the labels turned toward James so he could read them. Alcohol and an antibiotic ointment. James winced; it was going to hurt. And it did. The doctor prodded at James' feet for what seemed like hours. Then he smoothed on the ointment and wrapped both feet up in bandages. James wondered if he'd be able to get his shoes on. Then the doctor repeated the whole thing with James' hands. With all the bandages, James' fingers were barely able to move.

Next came the ears. James held still, even stopped breathing. He hoped the scope the doctor poked inside would somehow burst the bubble that was between James and hearing. He thought he heard a scraping, but it was so far away, he wasn't sure if he really heard it or if he only felt it. Finally, Dr. Owen fluffed the pillow, placed it between James and the headboard and pushed James back. He covered James, carefully tucking in the blankets. Then he grabbed the notebook. It seemed like he wrote forever. Dr. Owen was always long in talking. He said he wanted to get the most out of his education and so he showed it off all he could. James wasn't surprised when he wrote as much as he talked.

"James," he started. The entry in the notebook looked like a business letter, complete with paragraphs. "You really made a mess out of your feet and hands. It looks like you're clean of glass shards and I've covered you in ointment to prevent infection. I'll be back tomorrow to change the bandages. Your eardrums are both still very red and swollen. It's not surprising that you can't hear. I want to give it a couple days before I send you to a specialist. This might clear up on its own. I'm writing you a prescription for an anti-inflammatory and an antibiotic. It's too early to tell if there's any permanent damage to the inner ear. It looks like both your eardrums burst. I'll drop the prescriptions off at the pharmacy and Tom will send someone around with them later."

More people in the Home. More that James couldn't hear. How could he keep watch over the clocks if he couldn't hear all these invaders moving in and out and around? James pictured them, touching the clocks, poking the pendulums, moving the hands out of sync, even backwards, and parts rained to the floor. James would never catch up, he'd never get it all sorted out. His heart began to race and he clutched both his ears and rocked in the bed.

Someone patted his wet hair and James looked up. It was Ione and she again made that shape with her mouth: Oh-kay. But James shook his head hard. To his horror, he fell into tears in front of them all.

Dr. Owen and Neal gaped, but Ione grabbed him. She wrapped him tight and held him to her chest and began to sway. James cried until he thought he was dry, every pore, every tissue dehydrated and shriveled and dead. And then he felt it. He pressed his head harder into her chest.

Ione must have been humming. James could feel the vibration through her skin. And there was a beat against his cheek. A ticking so strong and steady, she could have been one of the clocks.

Bum-bum. Bum-bum.

James closed his eyes and sank into the rhythm. His tears dried into her blouse. Then, tenderly and carefully, she set James back against his pillow.

For a second, James scrambled, trying to get close to her again. But her lips puckered, Shhh, and he stopped. She smiled. "Thank you," James said. She nodded.

Dr. Owen waved goodbye. Neal said something to his wife, then nodded at James. He took up the notebook. "I'm going back to the shop," he wrote. "Ione will stay. Molly will be here with your lunch."

As soon as James read that last word, he felt his stomach rumble. The last time he ate was at lunch yesterday. He looked up at Ione who laughed. She took the notebook.

"I'm sure you haven't had brekfast," she said. "I'll go see what I can russle up."

Breakfast, James said silently, and rustle. "There are doughnuts in the cabinet. They're yesterday's day-olds, from the bakery. And there's coffee too."

She wrinkled her nose. Then she and Neal left and James was alone.

Really alone.

He looked around at all his clocks and for the first time, he felt friendless among them. They all talked to each other, curved in a circle that didn't include James. He couldn't hear them and they stared at him with blank faces. They held themselves back and all that was left was this awful hollow silence. No ticking. No rhythm. Nothing to keep James company. Nothing to keep James steady.

A flash of gold caught his attention and he looked at the bedside table. The dancers whirled away there, to the left, to the right, then to the left again. It was nine o'clock, the top of the hour, and no one, not even this sad clock that belonged to James' mother, said anything to him. This clock knew James better than anyone else and it couldn't reach him.

James hesitated, then firmly put his bandaged hand into the center of the pendulum. The clock stopped.

Closing his eyes, James thought about stopping other clocks. Felix, the cat he just fixed. The dwarf tall clock in the living room. The steady forward-moving plain-faced office clock.

James thought about stopping them all.

They couldn't talk to anyone but him. They wouldn't.

Someone touched his shoulder and James opened his eyes. Ione stood there with a tray. Behind her, Cooley carried two mugs of coffee. James sat up and Ione nestled the tray over his knees. He looked at it, wondered where it came from. He didn't own any such thing, breakfast in bed was ridiculous. Cooley placed one mug in front of James, then handed the other to Ione. She smiled at James, pointed to the tray, then patted her chest.

Cooley brought it over.

The food smelled really good and his stomach growled again. Scrambled eggs, bacon, two pieces of toast spread with butter and jelly. James knew he didn't have any bacon in the house and the eggs were probably outdated. "Where did all of this come from?" he asked out loud.

Ione pointed her mug at Cooley, who shrugged. She grabbed the notebook. "Mr. Simmons gave me all this stuff," she wrote.

Gene and Molly too. James thought about resisting. About telling Ione and Cooley to go away, throwing the food across the room, going downstairs and getting his usual day-old doughnut. But it just smelled too damn good. And some odd internal voice told James that maybe if he ate well, ate healthy, his ears would get better faster. He needed his ears to get better.

While James ate, Ione and Cooley talked. James saw their mouths moving, saw their shoulders shake in laughter. His fork fell a few times, slipping through his bandaged fingers, and they looked over, concern on their faces. But he wasn't about to let himself be fed. Then Cooley took the notebook again. "Sum clocks stopped. Do U want me 2 wind them?"

James froze and the food he just ate threatened to come back up. His heart slid, fell off rhythm, then began to jump over hurdles. James knew it was just that some clocks were due to be wound, he knew it, but somehow, it felt like he killed those clocks with his thoughts. He only thought about stopping them and they stopped.

James squeezed his eyes shut. He had to wind the clocks. He was the clock-keeper, not a clock-killer.

Ione patted his arm and he looked at her, startled. "Oh-kay," her lips formed. James thought for a moment of the rhythm of her heart against his cheek. He imagined it now, steady as if a clock tapped him gently with its pendulum, and he slowed that pendulum down until his heart met it, beat for beat. When James felt settled again, he pushed the tray away. "I have to wind those clocks," he said. "There are others that will be due too."

Then he stared at his hands. At his fingers, stiff in the bandages.

Ione took the notebook. "Let Amy Sue help you," she said. "She helps me out every weekand at the store. She's very carful with the clocks, never broke a won. Let her help."

Weekend, careful, one. James put the notebook in his lap and wished for a red pen. His mother's anniversary clock sat unmoving beside him, still exposed, still unprotected, the dancers holding their breaths. The clocks weren't safe. What choice did he have? It was either let Cooley do the winding or let all those clocks die. One by one, all around him. It wouldn't matter if his hearing never came back; there'd be nothing to hear anyway. Carefully, James poked out a bulky finger and started the pendulum on his mother's clock. It hesitated, then swung into its rhythm. It was still alive. He had to find a replacement dome.

James looked at Cooley. "Why aren't you in school?"

Cooley said something, then Ione wrote on the notebook. "Perent/teacher confrences," James read. He wondered about that, wondered if Cooley was skipping school and using him as an excuse.

Then he thought about the tourists. Alarmed, he grabbed for the notebook, but Ione immediately began scribbling again. "It's OK," she wrote. "We closed the Home just until you get back on your feet again. You can reopen on Monday."

No tourists. Mixed blessing; no other people traipsing through the house, but no revenue either. James sighed and threw back the covers. "Come on then, Cooley," he said. "I'll have to show you what to do." Ione grabbed at his arm, trying to pull him back into the bed, but he shook her off. "Ione," he said, the name foreign on his tongue. He wondered how it sounded. "It's not just the stopped clocks that have to be wound. There are others. Some get wound every day. I'll have to show Cooley which clocks they are and where I keep the keys. It's too complicated, I can't do it from here." James' tongue felt clumsy and he wondered if he was forgetting how to talk. Ione frowned, but then she crossed the room to the closet. She looked through the clothes, finally pulling out a robe. She must have understood. While James stuck his arms into the sleeves, Cooley looked under the bed and found James' slippers. They were useless though; his bandaged feet were too fat to fit. James kicked the slippers back under the bed, a move he instantly regretted as pain shot up through his toes to his ankle. He let loose a string of curses that made Ione turn away and Cooley smile. "Sorry," he said when the pain slid away. Then they went downstairs, James leading the way, Cooley taking up the end, Ione in the middle, carrying the tray.

Cooley and James left Ione in the kitchen and moved on toward the office. James couldn't help but notice that everything was cleaned and put back in its place. The bucket and rags were gone, the floor as clean as could be. There was no sign of last night's nightmare. Even the knife was gone. James shuddered, then glanced automatically at his security cameras. Except for Ione in the kitchen, all the rooms were empty.

Fetching the clipboard, James flipped it to the appropriate day. "Here," he said to Cooley, handing her the schedule. "This is a list of everyone that needs to be wound. I have them all organized into groups. Clocks that need to be wound every day, clocks that are 5-day, 8-day, 31-day, and so on."

Cooley seemed to study the list. The tilt of her head reminded James of Diana, the way she used to pore over books, the way she used to pore over him, and he quickly looked away. "I keep all the keys and notes on the individual clocks in here." James pointed to the old card catalogue. Quickly, he explained how it was organized, according to the type of clock and the amount of time required between windings. When he was done, Cooley shook her head. "What?" he asked. "It's really very simple, anyone could understand it. Don't you get it?"

She glared, then found a pen. James flinched when she wrote at the bottom of the schedule. He never wrote on the schedules, that way, they could be used over and over, until a new clock had to be added to the list. Then he retyped each of them.

"U should buy a computer," James read. "Way easier."

He sighed. "I don't need a computer. It's easy. I never have a problem." Checking the schedule, James turned to the card catalogue to start collecting the day's keys. But he couldn't wrap his fingers around the tiny handles of the drawers.

Cooley touched his shoulder, then opened a drawer herself. One by one, checking the list, going back to the card catalog, writing questions on the schedule, she collected the keys. There were twenty-seven clocks to be wound that day. James showed her how to sort the keys by room, using individually marked keyrings. He had her take the index card for each clock out of the drawer, tucking it into her back pocket for reference. James didn't need them, but she might. She was the one who needed to learn.

They started in the living room. A mantel clock waited for them, as well as an 800-day and a cuckoo. It was odd for James, odd and uncomfortable and disconcerting, seeing someone else wind his clocks. Seeing Cooley. "Be careful!" he called out more than once. "You wind, you don't crank!" She snarled back at him, her lips curled, saying God knows what, he couldn't hear, but she eased up, her fingers relaxing, her wrist going soft. The clocks needed a gentle touch, not a bully.

James let her stand in front of the cuckoo clock a good long while. He could see her trying to figure out which key belonged and where it would fit. Her shoulders braced, she was so determined not to ask for help. When her eyebrows descended in a dark cloud, forming a black V, and her fingers began frantically flinging the keys around the ring, James spoke up. Softly. "There's no key for a cuckoo clock, Cooley," he said. "See the weights? It's driven by weights and pulleys. You pull on the three chains. One chain controls the hands, one controls the pendulum and one controls the cuckoo bird." She stared, then put the keys down on a table. There was a resigned set to her shoulders as she began carefully tugging on the chains. "Easy," James said. "It's like you're pulling on the clock's heartstrings." He could tell she was frustrated; he knew she thought she'd never get it. He'd never admit it to anyone, but he stripped enough gears when he was learning about clocks. There might even be a few clocks in the backyard cemetery that were the results of his first unknowledgeable and clumsy attempts. But no one would ever know. No one except Diana, he corrected. He wondered if she ever told anyone. He wondered where she was. She would certainly be a help right now. Though she was an old lady. Old, like him. That was hard to imagine.

Cooley's fingers on the chains reminded James of Diana's; long, slender, tiny-knuckled. A purple-stoned ring glimmered from Cooley's left hand and he remembered Diana's ring. He remembered the coolness of her skin as he slid it onto that finger, that steady finger that never shook or pointed or jabbed. It was just a promise ring, a tiny silver band with threads of turquoise running through it in waves, but it was all James could afford at the time, with the Home so new. He knew that Diana understood what it meant, what he wanted it to be. She took the ring with her when she left. James wondered if she wore it now, the silver embedded in the wrinkles of a much older, heavy-knuckled hand.

Diana used to wind the clocks, back when the Home was young. There weren't nearly as many clocks as now. And back then, it wasn't just James' bedroom that was sealed off, but theirs, the one they shared. He didn't want the tourists to see the bed Diana always forgot to make, the sheets still twisted like their bodies the night before.

James wasn't as worried about the clocks then, as long as they ran, as long as their ticking filled his ears. He needed to be around that sound. He could trust Diana to wind them, to look at him over her shoulder as she did so and laugh. Her sound as sweet as any Westminster chime.

Then she broke a clock, overwound it so the spring sagged and drooped out of the bottom of the base. And instead of burying the clock, James discovered the excitement of searching for parts, digging through backrooms of clock shops or into piles of discarded, disemboweled clocks at the flea markets. He fixed that clock by himself and then moved on to fix others, putting them back together, filling the Home with the noise that kept his blood flowing, his heart beating. And Diana came along for the ride, she tried to keep up. But she couldn't.

Nobody could. Not even a young girl. James looked at Cooley now, standing in front of the cuckoo clock, smiling as the bird popped out and chirped its gratitude.

"This is only temporary," he said, as much to himself as to her. "Only until I get these damned bandages off."

Eventually, they worked their way to the back east bedroom. The birdcage clock was on the list and James stood under it, saving it for last, while Cooley moved around to the others. He craned his neck to see the clock's face, flat against the bottom of the cage, and he was relieved to see it was still on time. It was almost the top of the hour and in a few minutes, the golden bird in the cage would start to sing. It wasn't one of the ones that stopped; James didn't have the heart to ask Cooley which ones she saw, which ones fell silent when he wished them dead. He would find them on his own and he would fix them, if he had to remove his bandages himself. It was his fault they stopped. He would show them that the clock-keeper could still be trusted.

Cooley joined James and together, they craned their necks. Birdcage clocks were unusual, crafted in Switzerland near the end of the eighteenth century. James always figured they were popular until people began to complain of perpetual pains in their necks. The only way to truly see the time was to stand directly under the cage and look up. The clock face couldn't be seen from across the room; you only saw the bird cage. The discovery of the clock was often a great surprise.

This clock was delicate and gold, the bars made from thin braids. They were far enough apart that the bird could easily have flown away, if it chose to, and it looked like it was in the act, its wings spread as it stretched from its perch. The birdsong was actually a music box, so the bird's voice was a twinkly tinny unrecognizable tune. But it was cheerful and the bird always called to James at the top and halfway through the hour. It was like having spring caught in a cage, always ready to perform. James' clock was unusual in that it also chirped the hour. Most birdcage clocks just sang; you didn't know the time unless you stood under it and looked up.

And now James couldn't hear it at all.

Cooley flipped the schedule over and wrote a note. "How do I wind it?"

James pointed to the little stepstool. "This clock's movement is in its base," he said. "When you stand on the stepstool, look on the side, behind the bird. There should be three holes. One is for the time, one for the birdsong and one for the chime."

Cooley nodded, then went to get the stepstool.

James found this clock at a flea market in St. Charles, Illinois. It was a huge flea market, one he heard about for years before he finally decided to pack up the car and drive down one weekend. It was worth it; acres of tables and booths to dig through. He brought home at least thirty clocks that weekend. But this one sat in the front in the passenger seat, safely buckled in, on the way home.

James saw it from a distance. It sat on a table and it looked like an ornate statue of a bird in a cage. He could tell it was light by the thinness of the bars, easily hung from a ceiling, and he wondered if it could be a birdcage clock, and if it was, why the owner didn't have it hanging somehow, to show off the face. Wandering by the table a few times, James glanced at the clock, trying not to appear too interested. It was on the third pass that he caught sight of the three holes at the base and he knew he'd not only found a clock, but a rare one. Stopping at the table, he picked up a few items, and then picked up the clock itself.

James admired the bird, poised, ready to take off. Then he hefted the clock above his head, to get a look at the face. Some glass shards rained down and James dodged.

The glass was smashed. What was left dangled like sharp pointed tears and the hands were missing. The face, unprotected by the glass, was scratched and gouged. But James knew he could replace it.

The man behind the table watched. "Does it work?" James called. The man shrugged. This was a good sign; he didn't know what he had. James set the clock back down and opened a door in the side of the base. Inside, the clock movement was a mess. It would take months to restore it, months to determine what parts were needed and to find them. If James could even fix it at all. He could make the clock look good. But he didn't know if he could start its heart again.

"How much?" James asked.

The man shrugged again. "Two-hundred," he said.

James closed the clock door, poked at it a few times. He must have looked too interested...the price was higher than he expected from a shrugger. So James shook his head, turned as if to walk away. He even took a few steps, stopped, then walked back. "Fifty," he said.

The man laughed. He came over, patted the clock, straightened it out on the table as if he was making it look perfect for the next buyer. "One-fifty."

"It's a mess," James said. "The hands are missing, the glass is broken, and the insides are all in a jumble. I bet you don't even have the key."

The man shrugged.

James sighed, turned to leave and really left this time. He walked down a couple booths, got out of the shrugger's line of vision and waited ten minutes. Then he strolled back. The shrugger was sitting again, reading a book. The clock, James noticed, was shinier, as if the shrugger polished it during James' absence. The sunlight caught the bird and it spread its wings. James needed to get it out of there, take it home, start working on it. "One hundred," he said.

The shrugger looked up from his book. His eyebrows went up, as if he was surprised to see James, but James knew the shrugger was alert and aware from the moment James stepped back to the table. He'd been waiting. And then, mercifully, he shrugged and held out his hand.

The clock was James'.

It took almost a year to fix it. That bird sat, voiceless, on the basement worktable until James thought it would build a nest and roost there. He always tilted the clock when he was done with work, so the face could see out too. That clockface wasn't meant to be buried; it was supposed to shine down on whoever wandered by and looked up. Eventually, the clock was done and the bird sang twice an hour from the back east bedroom. James made sure to stop, at least once a day, and raise his face to the clock, let it tell him the time.

Now Cooley climbed up and James watched her insert the key and start twisting. The clock swung slightly from its hook. "Be careful," James said. "Hold it with your free hand. Don't pull down on it, you don't want the extra weight to pull it from the ceiling."

Cooley made a face, but she steadied the clock. She wrapped an arm around it, as if she was putting her arm around the shoulders of a friend. And that clock nestled right in while she wound.

James was still watching this, seeing the tender bend of her arm, the concentration in her face, when Ione appeared in the room and tugged at his shoulder. She tilted her head several times toward the doorway. James didn't want to leave, there were still over a dozen clocks left to go. But Ione grabbed the schedule and then she wrote on it too. James wanted to scream.

"Let Amy Sue do sum of this on her own," she said. "You need two rest. She'll find you if she needs help."

"I'll just go with," James said. "I'll sit down in every room and watch."

Ione shook her head and took his arm again.

He yanked it away. "Damn it, Ione!" he yelled. "It's my house and these are my clocks! If I'm tired, I'll take a break. But it's me that says so."

Ione's face clouded. She turned and left the room. James felt the reverberation from her feet as she stamped down the stairs and he followed her movements until she was out the door. The slam shook the floorboards. For a moment, James thought about calling out to her, telling her to come back, that he was sorry. But only for a moment.

When James turned back, Cooley shook her head. She wrote on the schedule. "Maybe we both need a break," she said, and then headed off toward the kitchen.

James groaned. At this rate, the clocks would never get wound. He swore at his hands, at the bandages, at Dr. Owen. And he swore at himself for getting into this mess. He never should have tried to fix that damn clock tower. It was just too big.

James went to the kitchen. Cooley stood at the sink, looking out of the window. The clipboard, the keyrings, the stack of index cards were in neat piles on the table. After James sat down, Cooley went to the coffeepot, searching in the cupboards above for a mug. Ione already washed the breakfast dishes. James stared at his bandaged hands, thought about his damaged ears.

The remaining clocks needed to get wound. James hated to admit it, but he needed someone. More importantly, the clocks needed someone. He thought of Ione slamming through the front door. For now, all he had was Cooley. All the clocks had was Cooley; James was useless.

"Cooley," he said.

She turned, her hands cupped around James' mug. He thought her hands must be cold and she was drawing warmth from the coffee.

"The newspaper should still be on the front stoop, unless someone brought it in. Go get it and help yourself to the comics.

Then get your own mug of coffee. And the day-old doughnuts from the cabinet."

She looked at him and beamed, the light of her smile bringing a new, old light to this room. But it wasn't welcome. James knew that lights could go out as quickly as they go on. He flinched away when she touched his shoulder, on the way to get the newspaper.

Then he concentrated on picking up the coffee in his thick fingers, determined not to spill a drop.

CHAPTER FOURTEEN:

FROM THE MOUTH
The Birdcage Clock's Story

Meg felt heroic as she sat down to save her healthy marriage before it needed saving. The book promised she could do it, declared in bold gold letters on its cover, "Rescue Your Marriage!" Given the right directions, Meg knew she could do anything. Decorating books helped her to create a relaxed, yet classic look in her already stunning house. Exercise books kept her always athletic body in shape. And "How To Raise Baby A to Z" hadn't failed her yet. When Alyssa was only four days old, Chapter Three told Meg that the baby should have a nickname, a loving little spark that would always let her know she was special. Meg remembered looking at her new daughter, sleeping in the bassinet. She looked so much like Paul, Meg's husband, and at first, Meg nicknamed her Paulie. But that sounded too much like a parrot, so she switched to alliteration and wordplay and called her Paulerina and Paulie-wolly-doodle and Paulie-Peeps. Eventually, she shortened it all to Peepers.

Peepers was five years old now and insisted on using her nickname all the time, even at school, proof of how special she felt. Books just weren't wrong.

Meg was deep into the first chapter of marriage-salvage when Peepers ran by with a doll stroller. "Peepers, remember?" Meg called to her daughter's back. "No running in the house!" The A to Z book said that a gentle reminder of the rules worked every time. But Peepers kept running. She sang a tune again and again and Meg reasoned that Peepers probably didn't hear the warning over her own lyrical voice. Meg listened closely; the song was unfamiliar. The A To Z book said that a child's song often gave clues to her innermost feelings, her thoughts and her troubles. This song had three syllables and Peepers put the emphasis on the second, roaring it while barely mumbling the other two. "Hmm-TOR-mms," Meg heard. "Hmm-TOR-mms."

She tried to block it out and concentrate on her marriage, but every time Peepers dashed by, all the words in Meg's book blended into that three-syllable sound. Finally, she grabbed the back of Peepers' shirt. "Peeps," Meg said. "Peeps, we don't run in the house. And what are you singing?"

Peepers leaned into her shirt, pulling it taut, her toes straining and her heels lifted with the desire to be in motion. But then she sank back against her mother's knees and accepted a hug. "A song I made up," she said. She patted her flat chest. "Me, by myself. About my new doll."

Meg looked inside the plastic stroller and saw the doll that Paul brought home last night. It was an ugly thing, with green and purple hair, bruised eyeshadow and ketchup lipstick, dressed in frayed bellbottoms and a tie-dyed shirt that proclaimed, "Attitude—My Way or the Highway." Paul said it was supposed to look like a teenager. A Jive-Diva Girl, it was called. When Meg asked why Peepers would possibly want a Jive-Diva Girl, Paul shrugged. "Maybe as an inspiration? Besides, it was on clearance."

Meg shuddered. In her book, "Wise Financing: Making Sense With Cents," it said to never buy anything on clearance. Through some convoluted formula that Meg couldn't quite follow, it showed that clearance items only made the stores richer and the customers poorer.

In the stroller, the Jive-Diva Girl was wrapped in a baby blanket. The blue-lidded eyes looked out of place, peering over the pink bunnies and lavender duckies. "Can you keep it down a bit, Peeps?" Meg asked. "Mommy's trying to read."

Peepers squinted at the book. "Res-kew-Your-Mar-marrrr-marrrry-age," she sounded out. "What's a Mary-age?"

"It's marriage. And it's what a mommy and a daddy have. They're married."

"Oh." Peepers straightened her tugged-sideways shirt. "My song is about my doll's name." She moved away, walking, Meg noted, and whispering her song. Which was worse. Now it sounded like "Psssss-TOR-hissssss."

Meg sighed and tossed the book to the couch cushion. "All right, I give up. What did you name your doll and what's the song?"

Quickly, Peepers turned back and sank down on one knee. Throwing her arms wide, she bellowed, "Clit-TOR-is! Clit-TOR-is! You're the best one FOR us!"

Meg instantly snapped her legs together. Then she tried to relax and return to her original position, but she couldn't remember what that was and suddenly, every position she took seemed suggestive. In the A To Z book, they warned that you should never let your children know when you're shocked or panicked, especially over sexual matters. It could cause the child to have such extensive trauma, she'd never lead a fully developed sexual life.

Meg took a deep breath, then took Peepers by the shoulders. "Do you mean clitoris?" Meg stated the word carefully, using the real pronunciation, with the emphasis on the first syllable. She learned it long ago, in college, when she read the book, "Meet Your Body, Treat Your Body."

Peepers nodded. "Yep, clit-TOR-is. I love that word. Ms. BigBrain taught us." The teacher's name was actually Ms. Barbain, but Paul changed it after Peepers' first month in her kindergarten classroom, a month filled with science experiments and dramatic plays and strange 3-D plastic puzzles. Ms. Barbain insisted on a steady stream of odd supplies, empty 2-liter bottles and button-filled baby food jars, baggies of sand from backyard sandboxes, even plain white bars of soap that Meg learned later the kids carved into animals, brandishing real knives! Meg was appalled, but Paul laughed and changed Ms. Barbain's name and now Meg couldn't get Peeps to say it correctly. The A to Z book said if parents allow their children to ridicule adults, the children would learn to disobey and disrespect.

"You mean Ms. Barbain, Peeps, remember? And why was Ms. Barbain using that word?"

Peepers pulled the Jive-Diva Girl from the stroller and tossed her into the air. The blanket went flying, but Peepers caught the doll by her purple-green dreadlocks. "For learning about our bodies. What makes girls girls and boys boys."

Meg remembered seeing the announcement last week in the kindergarten's newsletter for the "Body Language Unit," but this wasn't what she expected. She thought it was odd that kindergarteners would be taught what it means when people cross their arms or legs or when they lean forward or straddle a chair. Her own book, "How To Make Your Body Say What You Feel," was far too complicated for children. Meg was amazed at how much a cocked eyebrow could say.

But this was something altogether different. This was real life. Meg still quietly asked Peepers if she wiped her hoo-hoo after using the bathroom; she didn't think Peeps was ready for the real thing. Peeps had never even seen her father naked. The A to Z book said children shouldn't be taught what they aren't ready for. Meg would have to call the principal again.

She shut her eyes and pinched the skin above her nose, a method she learned in a stress-relief book. "Peepers," she said, "it's pronounced clitoris, not clit-TOR-is. And it's not a good name for a doll. It's not a name at all, not like Meg or Paul or Alyssa. It's a thing. A body part."

"I know. But it sounds neat." Peepers tucked the doll back into the stroller. "And that's how Ms. BigBrain says it. We saw pictures." She nodded firmly, as if the pictures somehow validated the way her teacher pronounced the word. Then she started to walk away. Over her shoulder, she said, "I heard Ms. BigBrain tell Mr. Parker if we show our someday husbands where our clit-TOR-is is, we'll be happy." Peepers spun around a corner toward her bedroom. "I'm already happy," she yelled, "cuz I have a new doll! Her name is Clit-TOR-is!" She slammed the door.

Meg wondered if the slam meant Peepers was angry. She sat for a moment, then rubbed her temples and pinched her nose again. She made a mental note to talk to Ms. Barbain about inappropriate comments near the presence of children. She was sure there was a chapter on that in the A To Z book and she planned to refer to it. Ms. Barbain had a lot to learn about dealing with children. Then Meg decided to leave Peepers alone for now. The A to Z book also stressed that children sometimes needed their own space…parents too. Meg returned to saving her healthy marriage.

Later, Meg wandered into the kitchen. It was dark enough to start turning lights on, so Paul was due home soon and supper needed to be made. She wondered what time it was and how long she had. She looked toward the birdcage clock, suspended from her kitchen ceiling, and automatically rolled her shoulders.

She bought the clock on their honeymoon when they stopped at an antique mall a mile away from Niagara Falls. Meg saw the golden birdcage, a bird inside spreading its wings and preparing to fly. Fly from what, she wondered. Who would want to leave a golden cage? She touched the bars, felt the fine twine of thin gold braided together. Reaching carefully through, she stroked a wing. She'd never had a pet. She picked the birdcage up and brought it to the cashier.

It wasn't until they got back to the hotel that she realized it was a clock. She thought it might be a music box and when she lifted it above her head to find the winder, she saw the clock face flat against the bottom of the cage's base. There was a key taped to the side and when she wound the clock, the bird sang on the top and half of every hour. It kept pretty accurate time, so they hung it in their apartment for three years, then from the kitchen ceiling when they bought the house. Her book, "Kitchen Savvy: Create More Than Meals In Your Kitchen," said that it was particularly important to have something striking here, one of the easiest rooms to go cliché.

The clock was definitely striking, everyone commented on it. But it was also really annoying. The only way to tell the time was to stand directly beneath it and look up. Every month when she wound it, every day when she stood under it, Meg swore at the inconvenience.

But it was too pretty to throw away and too accurate to ignore. Meg's Thought of the Day calendar once read, "If it ain't broke, don't fix it." So the clock stayed. And Meg never put another clock in the kitchen because it seemed silly and redundant to have two clocks in the same room. So telling the time meant a crick in the neck and a whispered curse each and every time.

Meg rubbed her neck in anticipation and walked toward the clock. Peepers ran past her and looked into the fridge. "When's supper?" she yelled as she disappeared behind the open door.

"Hang on, I gotta look at this stupid clock first." Meg put her hands on her hips and craned her neck. "Probably about a half-hour." Her neck twinged, a shivery pain that ran down between her shoulder blades. "Damn, I hate this clock." She instantly regretted swearing. It was one of those topics in the A to Z book headed with a big scarlet NEVER. It only took one slip for a bright child like Peepers to pick up an inappropriate word. Like clit-TOR-is.

Peepers looked at her, then up at the clock. "Pretty bird," she cooed. "Pretty Seymour, sing so pretty." She smiled at her mother. "Just look at your watch, Mommy." She waved a thin wrist, sporting a bright yellow Winnie-the-Pooh watch.

"Seymour?" Meg looked down at her own silver Liz Claiborne, bought at full price, then back up at the clock.

"I call him that. He's my pet." Peepers went back to the fridge.

Meg shook her head. "Don't have a snack now, Peeps," she said. "You'll spoil your supper."

"Aw, Mommy. Just something little." Peepers held up a shiny apple, her pink fingers curled like ribbons against the red skin.

Meg pulled out her new cookbook. "Don't blame me if you can't eat a bite of your yummy supper later," she said. The A to Z book said you should never make an issue out of food.

The new cookbook was called, "Tempt and Tease Your Tastebuds!" She bought it the other day, with the Marriage book and one other at a sidewalk sale outside Schwartz's Books. Three for a dollar. A bargain. Meg nearly passed them up, thinking of the Wise Financing book, but then she reasoned that the books weren't really in a clearance sale. They were in a sidewalk sale. The signs were yellow and black rather than bright red with slash marks. And the deal only worked if you bought three.

Meg opened a page at random and looked at the recipe. The first direction was, "Blanch your chicken." Meg quickly turned the page.

Peepers leaned on the counter, tilting her head sideways to read the book's title. "Tem-pit?" she asked. "Tastebuds?"

"These things in our mouths that let us taste," Meg said. "And tempt. Make them want to eat." The next recipe called for a double-boiler. Meg turned the page.

"Daddy's tastebuds like sketti and meatballs," Peepers said. She bit into the apple, the crunch sounding like crisp snow under a boot.

Meg shivered and smiled. "Spaghetti," she said. "It's pronounced spaghetti." The next page read, "Set your pastry blender on—"

"And my tastebuds like sketti and meatballs too," Peepers said. "Best of anything." The bird clock went off, breaking into a tinny music box tune that Meg was never able to place. Peepers leaped across the floor, turned a graceful pirouette on bright purple sparkly sneakers, and left the room. Meg heard her singing, "Seymour's a bird, he's my pet, he's my pet!"

Meg started to look up to check the time, but then looked at her watch instead. Her neck relaxed. Her stomach growled and she thought of the long half-hour before supper. After stacking her new book along with the dozen others on the dusty baker's rack, she turned to the fridge.

As she prepared spaghetti and meatballs, she ate an apple.

Meg sat on the couch that night, trying to read her third new book while her husband watched basketball on television and Peepers colored at their feet. Meg looked over Peepers' shoulder and discovered that Paul also brought home a Jive-Diva Girl Activity book and Peepers was busily filling in various mopheads with an atrocious shade of neon green. Clit-TOR-is sat on the corner of the coffee table.

It was hard to concentrate on the book with the noise of the cheers and her husband's accompanying grunts of approval and the skritchscratch of crayons. But she tried. This book was the most important one of the bargain three, called, "Are You Hurting; How To Know For Sure." Meg struggled through the third page of the first chapter, "How To Know Who You Really Are," when Peepers suddenly sprawled over her knees. Meg jiggled her legs up and down, bouncing Peepers, but unfortunately also bouncing the book in the most seasick way, when Peepers suddenly knocked the book out of Meg's hands and onto the floor. She shrieked, "Mommy! Where's it hurt?" She grabbed Meg's face in both hands and repeated at top volume, "Where's it hurt? Where's it hurt?" Meg recognized this as her own refrain from times Peepers ran in crying from playing outside or down in the basement or in her own room. Now Peepers lunged onto Paul's lap, who sat there gaping, and she beat on his chest. "Help her, Daddy! Help her!"

"What?" Paul and Meg both said together.

Meg scooped Peepers up and rocked her. "Calm down," she said. "There's nothing wrong with me, what are you talking about?"

Peepers quickly kicked free and rolled to the floor. She grabbed the book, holding it out of Meg's reach. "Are You Hurting!" she yelled.

Paul began to laugh and he took the book from Peepers. "Sweetheart," he said. "It's just a book. That's all. There's nothing wrong with Mommy."

Peepers stood ramrod straight and tears rolled down her flushed cheeks. "Mommy? Nothing's wrong?"

"No!" Meg reached for Peepers and hugged her tightly. "I'm fine, Peeps. It's just a book I'm reading."

"But then..." Peepers pulled away and again took Meg's face in her hands. "If you're fine, how come you're reading a book about hurting?"

Meg opened her mouth, then closed it. She tried again, but no words came out. Finally, she said, "How about some hot chocolate and popcorn?"

Peepers cheered and leaped off Meg's lap. "Lemme help! I get to put the bag in the microwave!" she said and ran for the kitchen. "Hi, Seymour!" Meg heard her yell at the birdcage clock.

Meg got up slowly, then trembled a smile at Paul. "It's just a title," she said. Before she followed Peepers, she took the book and tossed it behind the couch.

In bed that night, during the Late Show, Meg told Paul the Jive-Diva Girl's name and the story behind it. He laughed. Meg waited a moment, uncertain, then laughed too.

"But can you imagine teaching little kids this stuff?" Meg asked. "And then not using the right pronunciation!"

Paul turned off their television and settled down onto his pillow. "What do you mean?"

"It's clitoris, not clit-TOR-is," Meg said.

"I think it's both, actually."

Meg sighed. "Paul, I'm the woman. I know how it's pronounced. It's not like I tell you how to pronounce penis. Or testicle."

He smiled and closed his eyes.

"Okay, hang on, I'll prove it to you." Meg got out of bed and crossed to the computer desk they shared. She got out her dictionary and paged through the C's. Then she found it.

Or them. Two pronunciations.

She quietly closed the book and got back into bed.

Paul snuggled close. "So?"

"She's right," Meg said.

Paul rubbed his hand lightly over her breasts.

"I can't believe it. Peepers was *right*." Meg started to roll away, but Paul caught her and held tight.

"You know, we've been married for umpteen years now." Paul rose up on his hands and knees. "And you've never shown me where your clit-TOR-is is." He smiled and worked down her pajama bottoms.

Meg laughed. "Well, that's silly, you know where it is."

"Hmmm?" His hands touched her here, then there. His face hovered over her thighs. "Show me, Meg. Where is it exactly?"

Meg grimaced, but took his hand and guided it. "Well, it's right... right...there. OH!"

She gasped and fell headlong into happiness.

CHAPTER FIFTEEN:

JAMES

And so you leave the root cellar behind, yet the root cellar never leaves you. Your collars and leashes stay in that damp dirt, the cage ajar, the belt coiled on its hook on the wall. You walk away one day and you don't look back, yet you still feel the sting of leather on your neck, you still see the dark of closed doors even as you lift your face to the sun.

As you look around, you embrace clocks, but you imagine so much more as you listen to the steady ticking, revel in their song. The seduction of time holds you tightly, keeps you seeking in a hidden sort of way, yet it takes years, years of wondering, years of glimpses and glances and words never said, before you actually touch the softness of a woman. The softness and the curves and the smooth as silk skin and it is like nothing you ever imagined. The rhythm you make together, your hearts alternately racing and slowing down, your skin abrading and applauding, is uneven, yet the most beautiful thing you've ever heard. You wonder at its imbalance and at its perfection.

But every time she reaches out to you, you have to shut your eyes. You can't watch her fingers coming, even though they are poised and tentative, not curled. You can't believe that this doesn't hurt, you can't believe that this feels so good, you can't believe the softness she returns. This softness for you. Just for you.

Imagine.

Yet you feel for its edges. You imagine all along that it will end. Even as you rejoice in the softness and the imbalance and the perfection, all with your eyes closed.

Imagine never believing in love. Imagine never having faith in softness and passion and curves and the silky skin of a woman, even as your body craves it all and cries out for more.

Fear bred from the rage forged in your parallel river keeps you from breathing deeply in your lover's embrace. Instead, your breath catches and gasps and you bite the inside of your own mouth. Because you know, deep inside yourself, hidden beneath your skin, that secret river solidifies and forms an animal. And not just the sad little puppy left leashed in a root cellar.

You were born from an animal. You know that now, and you knew it then, though you could never have said it. And that animal's cruel blood flowed through you even before you breached her body and saw the light of day, connected you to your mother in a way that not even death can sever. You imagine, you know, that her blood coils through you still, just under your surface.

You are your mother's child.

Imagine.

James knew about hidden hardness. He'd seen sweetness turn to wretched steel. He knew that beauty, resting in a pool of sunshine, could raise itself up, tall, and taller, and then bear itself down into an ugliness that stole breath away. His breath, the breath of a child that didn't come any easier with age.

James imagined that it would be impossible to keep the animal hidden forever. As he tended his clocks, he always listened to the ticking of his own heart. Wondering when he was going to explode. Wondering when his mother would awaken, encased as she was within his own skin.

He imagined that no softness could stop her.

Cooley got all the clocks wound by late morning, and when she was done, James was exhausted. It surprised him, but he didn't say so. He didn't want Cooley to know he was tired. Sitting down in the chair in his office, James looked quickly at all the security monitors. Things were fine. There were no tourists, of course, and all the clocks were running. Thinking of his mother's clock, James reminded himself again that as soon as Cooley cleared out of there, he would head down to the workshop to find a replacement dome.

"We're done, Cooley," he said, knowing she stood behind him. "You can head on home now." He thought that would be enough to send her off and he watched the screen, keeping his eye on the front door so he could see her go. When she touched his shoulder, James jumped.

She handed him the notebook. "Do U want me 2 come back 2morrow?" she wrote.

There was no way around it. James didn't know if Ione would be back and Cooley really had the right touch for the clocks. Ione's fingers were lumpy, they would be graceless on a key or curled around a chain. "Yes, come back tomorrow."

She scribbled some more. "OK. I like being w/the clocks. That's Y I like Ione's shop 2. But URS are better." There was something else written too, but scratched out, so James couldn't read it. He thought he saw the word clock though and he pointed to it. She just shook her head. James thought maybe she'd written a thank-you note for fixing her Baby Ben.

She left. When she appeared on the screen, just before the front door, she turned and waved.

James sat for a moment and wondered what he was going to do. There were too many people coming and going in the Home. And he didn't know how to get rid of them. He didn't know how to get rid of his need for them. The only way was to get better, and what was the way to get better, other than this interminable waiting?

Leaving the office, James headed toward the basement door. But then he stopped and looked down. He couldn't work in his pajamas. He could hardly believe he was still in them. James glanced over at the closest clock. A quarter past eleven. Plenty of time left in the day to justify putting on fresh clothes.

Getting dressed was more complicated than James expected. With his hands bandaged, zippers and buttons were next to impossible. He finally managed to get his jeans closed, but the tiny buttons on his shirt left him sweating. Giving up, he found a pullover sweater and wore that instead. Shoes were out of the question...they pressed too hard on his bandaged feet. So he settled for socks, black ones, that at least looked a little like shoes. There were no tourists coming anyway, James reminded himself. It was okay to look sloppy, just for a few days.

James glanced at his mother's anniversary clock. The dancers still moved, but it looked like they were spinning more slowly. And there was a catch, James thought, in the movement of their feet. Too much dust, too much air, and the dome was no longer around to protect them. He hurried down the steps to the workshop.

In the storeroom, James looked through all the glass domes for anniversary clocks, and other types of clocks as well. But as he picked them up, hefted their weight, he knew they were all wrong. His mother's clock was much larger than the typical anniversary clock, and while these domes might fit over the little dancers, their feet would bang against the sides, bringing the whole mechanism to a halt.

James worried about this clock, worried about the possibility that he wouldn't be able to find a replacement dome, worried that the clock would die because of his own clumsy hand. And he worried that his mother would kill him. A thought that was so common, it continued to plague him long after her hands, her voice, her body became even more silent and still.

She's already dead, he reminded himself. She can't hurt me anymore. But still, there was a grip around his throat, like the collar being yanked up a notch. He would have to special-order the dome. In the meantime, he would clean the dancers and all the clock parts every day, making sure that they stayed alive.

As James climbed the steps, he felt fatigue run through his hips to his knees and ankles. He really needed some sleep, but he never slept in the middle of the day. His mother took naps all the time, putting James down in the root cellar first so he couldn't, wouldn't disturb her. James remembered standing at the foot of the cellar steps, stretching as far as the tether would let him go, and looking up at the slot of sunlight coming in between the doors. He wanted so much to be near her, to be in the house, watching her sleep while he quietly got things done for her, things that would make her smile, and he always promised himself that when he was a grown-up, he wouldn't waste a minute sleeping. Though she was so beautiful in sleep.

And now, James' feet dragged on the stairs.

In the kitchen, he punched in the number to his favorite clock shop in Des Moines. He knew he'd be able to get the dome through them, in probably a matter of days. But it wasn't until he kept standing there, waiting to hear the soft burr of a ringing phone miles away that he realized he'd never know when the clerk answered on the other end.

James slammed the phone down and a jolt of pain traveled from his fingers to his elbow. Swearing at the bandages on his hands, at the wounds that brought them there, at his ears and the town's clock tower, he turned and found myself a few feet away from Gene's wife, Molly. She stood in the kitchen doorway, holding a tray. When she smiled, James didn't know what to do, so he let his hands dangle and he stared.

Molly set the tray down on the table and looked around. Then she motioned, moving one hand like she was writing and her other hand was the pad of paper. James nodded and retrieved the notebook from the office.

"Here's your lunch," she wrote.

James wondered why she felt the need to write the obvious, why Gene wasn't here, why he had to send his wife, another woman James barely knew, except for her pie crusts. "Thanks," he said.

She nodded and busied herself with the tray. She pulled off napkins and unrolled silverware and even held up a tiny set of salt and pepper shakers.

"I have my own things," James said.

She took up the notebook. "Now you won't have to wash them. Just leave them on the tray." She shook her head. "Your poor hands," she wrote. "Your poor ears."

James didn't know what to say, so he sat down. Molly began to look through the cupboards and he wanted to moan at yet another violation of what was his. When she glanced over her shoulder, James realized the moan must have materialized from his mind and his heart out his throat. So he shrugged and looked away. When she came across a glass, she held it up. "Milk," James said. Then he added, "Please."

Molly crossed to the refrigerator and got out the carton. But when she opened it, she wrinkled her nose. It must have gone bad again. "Then just water," James said. "And I'll have some more coffee later."

She brought the water and sat down. James didn't want to be watched while he ate, so he waited. She grabbed the notebook again. "It's today's special," she wrote. "Good, spicy chunky tomato soup. Grilled cheese sandwich, three different cheeses, and tomato and bacon too." She probably wrote the same thing on the big chalkboard at the front door of the diner.

"I can see," James said and she blinked. Then she nodded, patted his hand, and left. James called out a thank you, but it was probably too late. He wasn't sure if she heard.

It wasn't easy, but he ate. And Molly was right, the food was good. But James' stomach turned at the thought of rounding another corner and seeing Ione. Or going to a different room and finding Cooley. Seeing Molly heading up the stairs, or Gene and Neal wandering around the workshop. The doctor poking at James' hands, his feet, his ears, just stopping everything up with bandages and more bandages.

James dropped his spoon. He couldn't eat, couldn't breathe, the choke around his neck grew tighter. Shoving the tray away, he placed his face flat on the table and slapped his bandaged hands around his damaged ears. He willed them to hear, willed them to listen, but he couldn't hear his own pummeling as he smacked himself upside the head. In that old familiar way, the way that used to bring stars and colors bright as the sun shining through the slats in the root cellar door. Now, the soft bandages barely cuffed his ears and they refused to open. James gave up, then gave in to sleep, wrapping his hands like root cellar doors around his head to block out the light.

The next day, James sat stiffly in the recliner. Somewhere in the house, he knew Cooley was winding clocks. In the kitchen, Ione was doing dishes. She showed up that morning on Cooley's heels, and when James couldn't stop a smile of relief from creasing his face, Ione nodded, accepting his silent apology. Molly was already by with breakfast. The doctor was due to show up at any minute and so Ione insisted that James stay in one place. "I don't want Dr. Owen too have too serch four you," she wrote. "It's not like we can holler four you. Amy Sue can handel it."

And so James sat there, hoping Cooley would need him. Hoping she would find him. And hoping his ears would suddenly pop like a big bubblegum balloon and he'd be able to hear himself yell at them all to get the hell out of his house.

Women were everywhere. And with them there, the women in hiding, the women James tucked away, suddenly came back. In his head, he could hear his mother. He found himself ducking and darting around every corner, in case she was there, her hand raised high, ready to come after him for whatever he did or didn't do. He slept last night with the light on, suddenly afraid of the dark again.

But James could hear her voice, whether it was light or dark. Now that he couldn't hear the clocks, her voice came at him from all the different recesses of his brain.

"Get the hell out of here, James!"

"Don't let me see your ugly face, James!"

"Bend over! Bend over!"

"Play dead. Play dead for real, James. You're dead."

And so many times, down there in the root cellar, James thought he was. Dead. And then he thought if he could just be better. If he could just be good. If he was quiet, she'd never notice him. But he wanted her to notice him. He wanted her to open her eyes wide and see him and nobody else. James never stopped hoping for that. Not even as the door to the kennel clanged shut or she yanked on the leash, burying the choke collar deeper into his skin.

Now James opened his own eyes wide, looked around the room, letting his gaze touch each and every one of his clocks. James knew if he could connect with them, he'd be okay again. If he could just hear that rhythm again. That rhythm. That rhythm you hear when you press your ear against warm skin and arms circle around you and hold you as if you are the most precious thing on earth.

And Diana was back again too, tiptoeing behind his mother, now that the clocks were silent. And she was right there in the living room when he looked at a tiny ceramic clock on an end table. It was a simple clock, an old winder whose paint was chipped. It was a little flower basket and the face of the clock was surrounded by faded green vines and still-deep purple flowers. James gave that clock to Diana years ago. She didn't take it when she left.

James remembered waking up that morning. He and Diana had been away for the weekend, driving down to Illinois to the Clock Tower Resort in Rockford. The resort was owned by a rich old man who collected clocks and offered them up in the middle of the complex as a tiny, free museum called the Time Museum. James fell in love with the place and he and Diana spent hours there, going from clock to clock. Diana was very quiet on the drive back, but James couldn't stop talking, about one clock in particular, the Gebhard World Clock, a tremendous thing that took over thirty years to build in the late 1800's. James couldn't say enough, and later, he realized Diana couldn't say anything at all.

When James got up on the morning she left, their bed was empty. It was cold, as cold as the root cellar, there wasn't a bit of heat left from her body. James looked around the house, but it was like she never lived there. He checked her closet and everything was gone. He kept at it, trying to find something of hers, a toothbrush in the bathroom, a mug in the kitchen sink, one of her old artsy novels cracked open and turned upside down over the arm of a chair. Her chair, as James thought of it, a recliner just like his. A recliner that now appeared nearly new next to the one he sat in. He thought of her there, almost every night, her legs slung over the side rather than stretched to the footrest, her head tilted back, her voice soft as she talked to James and then guided him to bed.

All she left behind was this little clock. James leaned forward now and took it into his lap. He remembered her finding it at a side-of-the-road flea market. She picked it up and held it out as if she'd just found a secret treasure. In terms of value, it wasn't a great clock, James told her, but she clasped it to her chest and said she loved it and he loved her and so he bought it. He thought she liked the flowers and later, he bought her a big purple bouquet. She placed them in a vase, but then she sat on his lap and showed him the little clock.

"Look at its face, James," she said. "It's the face that's so extraordinary. Distinctive. Like yours. Just look at it."

And James did. Hidden among all that foliage was the prettiest set of gold filigree numbers he'd ever seen on a clock. They twirled on the face and blinked and lit up and sparkled. The hands too curved and caressed, gliding over each number as if it was a child's cheek. The way a child's cheek should be touched. The way Diana touched James.

Now he held his own bandaged hand to his face.

But Diana left the clock behind. James sighed and lifted it to his ear, hoping a whisper would get through.

Someone tapped James' shoulder and he looked up. It was Dr. Owen, who waved and smiled. James replaced the clock on the table. "I still can't hear a damn thing, Doc," James said.

The doctor nodded and picked up the notebook. "That's to be expected," he wrote. "Your ears have suffered through trauma. It may take a while for them to return to normal. You need to be patient." He set the notebook aside and pulled up the small stepstool. Sitting on it, he rummaged through his bag and pulled out his otoscope. He brandished it, then got to work.

James heard the scraping again, or at least he thought he did. It was no clearer than yesterday. His ear itched though and for a moment, he heard his father's voice, from a long time ago, as he bent over a scratch in James' arm, a scratch put there by his mother's claws. James' father had them too, usually on his face. He painted James with some sort of cold yellow ooze, cold that still managed to burn. "When it itches, Jimmy," he said, "that means it's healing. You can't scratch it though. You'll wreck the new cells. Just let it heal." So maybe James' ears were healing.

The doctor looked into the other ear. James touched his free ear and felt the coolness of his own skin. It was like his ear was dead. A dead part of his own body. So he asked the question that he didn't want to ask.

"Doc, is it possible my hearing won't ever come back?"

The otoscope stopped moving. James no longer felt Dr. Owen's breath on his neck. And James knew the answer. Carefully, he shimmied his hand up between his face and the otoscope and eased the doctor away. "Okay," James said. "Okay."

Dr. Owen reached for the notebook. He seemed to spend a lot of time writing, looking up every now and then at James, and at the clocks, then at the floor. Finally, he handed the notebook over. James settled back for one of his medical lectures. The man had one for every malady, he even had them when patients were healthy, so broken ears wouldn't be any different.

"James," he wrote. "It's very possible for you to regain your hearing completely. A week from now, you might not even remember that this happened. Or it might take longer. Your ears are still so red and swollen, I can't get a good look at the eardrums, but I still believe that both burst. They may heal quickly or slowly. Then there's all the tiny little hairs and bones and nerves in the ear that have to recover as well. Think of your ears as being in shock. I can't say with absolute certainty that your hearing will come back. But I think it will. You had good hearing before, correct? I don't remember any hearing aid."

Here, James looked up and nodded. "My hearing was very sharp," he said. "I could come into this room and tell in a second which clock was out of rhythm."

Dr. Owens smiled, then pointed back at the notebook.

"There's always the possibility this will be permanent. But I don't think it's likely. I called the specialist in Des Moines I told you about a couple days ago. He's a friend of mine. He agrees with the regimen of rest, antibiotics and anti-inflammatories. He suggested, however, sending you to Chicago instead of to him. He said there's a great hearing and ear injury clinic there. So we'll think about that."

James closed the notebook and nodded. Dr. Owen patted his shoulder and left. James kept sitting there, thinking about a possible trip to Chicago. He'd never been there, not to stay, but only passed through on his way to other things. St. Charles, to the Kane County flea market. And Rockford, to the Time Museum, the last place where he and Diana were really together. James wondered how far away Rockford was from Chicago. He wondered if the Gebhard World Clock was still there, if it still ran. For a moment, he let himself picture the clock, standing broad-shouldered in the middle of the room, and he saw Diana standing there, leaning over the old red crushed velvet barrier, and she didn't look a day older than when she left. James let himself think she would smile when she saw him and he let himself think that he would smile back.

When Cooley entered the room, James didn't even glance at her, just handed her the notebook and waited for her to give it back.

"I'm done," she wrote. "Everyone is fine."

James noted the "everyone" instead of "everything." It made him hesitate for a moment, attempt to hold his tongue, but then he knew he couldn't. The clocks were too important. He said, "Are you sure?"

She nodded.

James slapped the notebook. "Then you're wrong. You never once came in this room, Cooley, not once. There are clocks that need winding in here." He nodded at Diana's clock. "That little one there, for instance." It was one that had to be wound every day.

Cooley stared, then turned and ran from the room. James nearly got up to go after her, but then he stopped. He didn't expect her to leave, he thought she'd get angry or maybe break down and cry in that way girls do, the way he remembered Diana doing whenever they argued. The clocks glared at him, they needed winding and he might have chased off the one that could do it, and he nearly started to go after her again, but then he met his clocks' stares head on and told them he would manage. Women ran, they left. There was nothing he could do about it.

James puzzled over how he was going to do the winding. He realized Dr. Owen forgot to check his hands and feet.

But then, Cooley came back, carrying the clipboard. She looked at it and frowned, her pencil stuttering in tiny movements that James figured must be checks. Then her shoulders sagged and she reached for the notebook.

James held onto it. "You don't have to tell me," he said. "You forgot the room."

She nodded, then moved toward Diana's clock.

But it wasn't enough. There was too much at stake. "If you forgot an entire room, then who knows who else you forgot?" James looked at the clocks and wondered how she couldn't have known. How could she not hear the hesitation in a tick, a pause in a chime? The gap in the sounds were even more obvious than the complete silence when a clock wound down entirely. That moment when there should be a tick, but there isn't, followed by a quick catch-up tock. It was like listening to someone gasping for breath.

Cooley stood for a second in front of Diana's clock and James watched for her to reach out and pick it up. To wind the winder too quickly, and have the little built-in key fall off in her hands. For the clock to slip free completely and then shatter on the floor. James felt the muscles in the back of his neck tighten and his own fingers twitched, needing to set that clock himself. Needing to make sure it was all right.

But then Cooley swung toward him and snatched the notebook off his lap. Her face was bright red. She scribbled furiously, her pointy elbow shooting into the air like a sword, and then she pitched the notebook at James and ran from the room. Across the entire page, she'd written, "I was only trying to HELP! Give me a fucking BREAK!"

James' hands shook and he threw the notebook across the room while he struggled to his feet. "Cooley!" he yelled. "Get the hell back in here!"

He wasn't even to the doorway when Ione appeared, grabbing James by the arm. He struggled, but he was no match for this large woman as she hauled James back to the recliner. To James' horror, he realized she was wearing her fuzzy slippers and she had the lavender feather duster under her arm. "Dammit!" James bellowed. "This is not your namby pamby gift shop, Ione! Don't dust my clocks with that feather-flayer! It'll gum up the works worse than the dust!"

They were both panting when she strong-armed James into the chair. Her face went white and James saw her mouth moving, saying something, and it looked like it was a snarl. James closed his eyes and brought both hands up to his face, pressing his bandaged fingers into his eyes. "Get out!" he said. "Get the hell out!"

A moment later, his arms were yanked away from his face. Ione slapped the notebook into his lap. She'd turned the page and she'd written in some pretty big letters too. "Look what you've done!" she wrote, with about a thousand exclamation points. Spelled correctly. James figured she was the type to draw smiley faces in her o's as well. He looked where she pointed.

Diana's clock was on the floor. It was in pieces.

James tried to surge out of the chair, but Ione pushed him back in. "What did you do?" James asked, feeling the break in his own voice. He ransacked his recent memory, sure that Cooley hadn't touched the clock before she left. But maybe she did, she was standing in front of it and he couldn't see what she was doing, maybe she threw it before she grabbed the notebook and he just hadn't noticed. "Or was it Cooley? Get Cooley back here!"

But Ione jabbed her finger again, at James, and then at the notebook. James looked, but there was nothing else written. "What?" he said and shrugged. "I read your note! I didn't do anything but tell Cooley the truth!"

Ione grabbed the notebook. She pointed at James, then threw the notebook so that it landed next to the clock pieces. Then she speared the air in front of his face again and he breathed in the truth.

It was James. James broke the clock when he threw the notebook across the room. And it was his third mistake, the third time he let the clocks down, let them be hurt. The teenage boy who knocked over the waltzer. The little girl who grabbed Felix's tail. Within his sight, when he was supposed to be there to protect them. And now it was worse, it was James himself. He couldn't hear the clocks, he couldn't wind them, and now he shattered them.

"Oh, no," James said. He pushed out of the chair and Ione didn't stop him this time. When he sank to his knees next to the pieces, she joined him and began to sweep them up into her large palms.

James could see there was no fixing it. The aged ceramic crumbled to dust. But the clock mechanism was still there and when Ione turned toward him, cradling the mess in her hands, James plucked it out. There was a chunk with the number six on it, or the number nine, James couldn't tell, and there were the hands. He chose those as well. "I'm going to keep these, Ione," he said.

She nodded and stood up, transferring the pieces into one hand. She offered her free hand to James. He hesitated, then accepted her help as he lurched to his feet. Ione picked her feather duster back up and the notebook too, and they left the room.

In the kitchen, James watched as she deposited the last of Diana into the trash can. He thought about stopping her, about telling her to get out the blue velvet, the golden leather, but he didn't. It was too much to explain. He whispered to the remains in his hands, told them that he would do right by them, that there would be a burial in the back yard with Diana's clock properly put to rest in a soft pouch that would cradle her parts, in the royal blue she deserved. It would just have to wait until Ione went home.

Then she sat down at the table with the notebook and began to write.

"That clock was Diana's," James said slowly, trying to taste her name in the air. He wondered how it sounded, if it was as soft and smooth as his voice used to make it.

Ione glanced up. James couldn't remember if she and Neal ever met Diana. Everyone was so busy then, with the town's resurrection, changing it over to thriving clock-themed businesses. "She was a girl," James said. "A girl who lived here. With me."

Ione's eyebrows went up and she nodded. Then she handed James the notebook.

"You have too let people help you now," he read. "While you heel. You have too. Amy Sue did a pretty good job, four her second day. And her first day without you folowing her. Breathing down her neck."

James nodded. He thought of how Cooley called the dwarf tall clock by its proper name, how she said "everyone" was okay.

But even so, if he hadn't said anything, those clocks would have died that night. Would still die, since Cooley ran out before she wound them. They'd stay dead unless James figured out some way to use his fingers again. Or they'd stay dead until the bandages came off. By then, their gears and cogs would be stiff and brittle.

"I'm going downstairs for a bit," James said. "Can you call me for lunch?" He started to leave, then stopped. "Please?"

Ione smiled. She set her feather duster on the notebook and nodded.

James looked at the feather duster. Then he looked at Ione's fingers. They were thick, but they weren't as thick as his bandages. There was no way around it. James reminded himself that the clocks had to come first. "Ione," he said, "would you look at the checklist and wind the clocks in the living room that need it? That Cooley didn't—" He stopped when a frown crossed Ione's face. Rearranging his thoughts, he tried again. "That Cooley forgot. It was just a mistake."

Ione nodded again.

James waited until he was halfway down the stairs before he called again. "And if you see Cooley," he said, "would you ask her to come again tomorrow? Please?" He'd said that word twice now and it still felt like a foreign language. But one he had to learn, while he lived in this strange country for a couple of days. A couple of days only, he reminded himself. He'd made three mistakes. He wouldn't let himself make anymore. He'd force himself to heal.

Then James descended to the workroom, to hover over the heart of Diana's clock and wait to bury the rest.

CHAPTER SIXTEEN:

STEPS TO STAGES OF THEATRE IN THE ROUND
The Ceramic Clock's Story

I t's the ugliest clock in the world that reminds me and I say to my bartender, "It seems to me that everything is centered around twelve." The clock's twelve numbers sneer at me in a golden shimmer. "At the store, we buy a dozen eggs. At the bakery, a dozen doughnuts. A dozen long-stemmed blood-red roses at the florist's." I almost drain my drink, almost, because it's just about one o'clock in the morning and at one, he's going to pull the plug and we'll all have to leave. But he can't kick me out as long as there's a drop left in my glass. I'm a paying customer, after all. "And clocks too," I say, nodding at the ugly clock. "Twelve numbers on the face. Why not ten? Why not fifteen?"

"Could be because there's twenty-four hours in a day, Zach," the bartender says. He glances at the clock and I can see the hour hand sneaking toward the number one.

"Then there should be twenty-four numbers," I say. "Thirteen o'clock, fourteen o'clock, all the way up to twenty-four o'clock. But no, we do a repeat. We stop at twelve and start over, even though it's not a new day."

"Time!" he yells and I tell myself it's in reaction to my argument, but he picks up the clock and waves it over his head. "Time to go home! Work day tomorrow!"

I hate Sundays when the bar closes at one instead of two. The bartender says he does it for our own good, so we can get up in the morning to go to work after a long weekend. Or look for work, in my case. I say he does it because Sunday nights are the nights he puts it to the wife. I've seen her picture…it would take me an extra hour to get it up for that.

"Where'd you get that thing anyway?" I point at the clock as the bartender puts it down.

"Time, Zach," he says.

"I know. Where'd you get it?"

He nods as someone obediently sets his empty glass on the bar. "Present from my mother when I opened this place." He looks at the clock, touches it briefly with the tip of a dishtowel. "She thought owning a bar meant I'd have hanging flower baskets all over the place. A quaint little pub, she called it, a bistro. So she figured a clock that looked like a flower basket would fit the decor." He draws out the last word, giving it two long syllables, making it sound like day-core, and I wonder where a day's heart would lie.

"It's damn ugly," I say.

He looks toward the door. "Yeah, well. What can I do? It's from my mother."

I can still remember when this place opened three years ago. I stopped in on opening night and I've been coming ever since. And now it occurs to me that I don't know my bartender's name. I talk with him every night, I've seen pictures of his wife. I even know who gave him his clock. He knows my name and seems to use it every chance he gets, but I never call him anything. Nobody seems to call him anything. Nobody has to. He's always right there when you're ready for another, slipping a fresh glass on a napkin that's so crisp, it can clean under your fingernails.

"Hey," I say. "What's your name anyway?"

He looks at me hard. "Zach, you've had enough. Let's go."

"No, what is it? I really don't know."

He points toward the window. "Zach, what's the name of this place?"

I picture the blinking blue neon outside. Benny's Barstools. You can't sit on anything in this place but a barstool. Even the tables and booths are set high so that you sit on a barstool to reach them. "I thought," I say slowly, "that you were using alliteration." At his blank look, I quickly add, "I thought you just needed a B-name to go with Barstools. Your name is really Benny?"

"Out, Zach." He reaches for my glass and I snatch it back. "Zach, either drink it up now or it's going down the drain."

I slam it back. "Can't even get what you pay for anymore," I grumble. Sliding off the barstool, I head for the door.

"See you tomorrow, Zach," he calls.

"Yeah, if you're lucky."

He laughs.

Outside, I walk down the sidewalk, then sit on a bench under a streetlight. I wish it was moonlight, but the sky is clouded over. It's one o'clock in the morning and I'm not sure where to go. I think about howling.

1:00. I admit I am powerless over alcohol, that my life has become unmanageable.

Watching the intermittent car go by, I debate whether or not I should go home. I see Benny lock up and walk away, whistling, and I wonder how long it's been since I whistled. Puckering my lips to try, nothing comes out but a dry sputtering sound. Like a motor that won't quite catch.

I could go home, but there's no one there. Kat and the kids left a long time ago. My sheets are so rumpled, even I can't stand them anymore, so I sleep on the floor, pulling our smelly old quilt over my head. Kat is attached to that quilt. One of her sorority sisters made it for us when we got married. I always wanted one of those dual-control electric blankets. I wonder if the dials have twelve settings, miniscule filaments of heat firing up with each notch. Kat wants to have the quilt in her new apartment, but I tell her she has to come and get it for herself. So far, she hasn't shown up. Not in almost a year. Twelve months, I think, and my lips twist and I feel them crack.

Sighing, I stand and head for home. A hard floor is better than a cold bench under a streetlight, I think.

I stop by Benny's Barstools' window and peek in. All the lights are off, but I can still see the face of that damn clock. It glows in the dark. In the luminescent sickly-sea-green, I see the fancy hands rubbing up against the fancier numbers. One-twenty. I blink, making the green blur and the hands disappear, and then I leave.

At home, I notice how everything has changed. It's always the middle of the night or the earliest morning when things become clear. There's a layer of dust everywhere. I can see where my fingers touched, where my knees brushed against tables. There's still dishes in the sink, even though I gave up using dishes months ago. I share this place with spiders now, multi-sized specks of silver and black and brown, hovering over my head in their webs. Kat hates spiders, she always screams for me to kill even the tiniest ones. I never told her, but mostly, I caught them and set them free through a loose screen in our bathroom window.

I feel my eyes fill up and I know it's time for my regular one-thirty in the morning not-very-manly cry. I've stopped fighting it, it hits every morning like this, like clockwork, ever since Kat and the kids walked out. At least it's early in the morning when there's no one around but the spiders to witness it. I sit down in my recliner, but I stay leaning forward, not grabbing the handle that would tilt me back and put my head to rest. Dangling my hands between my knees, I lift my chin and give way. The tears know where to go; I think there are tracks on my face. New tracks, worn over old. I wish Kat was here to kiss them smooth.

I wonder when it all got away. I wonder when I lost control. And I decide it's time. It's time to get it back. Get it all back.

2:00. I come to believe that a Power greater than myself can restore me to sanity.

I am sick of my morning cry, I am sick of the spiders above my head and the dust motes clouding the air. I might even be sick of the fuzziness in my head, but my head is too fuzzy to figure that out. "Jesus Christ!" I mutter, staggering to the kitchen and opening the fridge. I vow to get rid of every bit of liquor there.

Kathie Giorgio

But it's already empty. From last night's tirade? Last week's? Maybe. I can't remember. It could be that I've just depended on Benny's Barstools for so long.

I search through my cupboards, reaching into the gaps where toaster pastries used to be and colorful sugar cereal and lollipops and gummi-fruits that look like the real thing, but taste like candy. I realize I miss the rainbow of the stocked family shelf, the sweetness of soaring sugar counts.

Finally, I find something I can throw away, something so symbolic, it makes my knees weak. A half-empty glinting jar of maraschino cherries, rolling red and shiny in their juice, and a box of plain brown toothpicks. Before she went away, Kat decorated drinks for me with these, trying to convince me that the cherries made the drink special, a stay-at-home special, as special as a bourbon at Benny's. She filled my glass with diet Pepsi, Dr. Pepper, Mountain Dew, then floated the cherries, speared through with the toothpick. In the white sodas, the 7-Up and the Sprite, I could see the tiny trickle of cherry blood. The dark sodas hid it, but I knew it was there. Just like I knew the tastiest soda would never give me a buzz. "Just like Benny's, Zach, see?" she said, handing me a glass she attempted to frost, but only succeeded in making cold and slippery. "There's no need to go out."

I always smiled at her, drank my slippery soda, fucked her until she was stupid with satisfaction and sleepiness, and then I went to Benny's anyway. A warm wife smelling of my semen at home, and a bar that offered real drinks and real frosted glasses and toothpicks with fancy red shredded cellophane at the end. Not just cherries, but pineapple and mandarin oranges. Sometimes salty olives, depending on what I ordered. I thought I had it all.

I think about praying as I fall on my knees in front of the wastebasket. The Sacred Twelve Steps say to look to God, and so I think of television shows where earnest actors look to the skies and pray in soft shaky voices. I clear my throat as the cherry jar makes a solid liquid thunk at the bottom of the basket and the box of toothpicks open and spill, a hopeful whispering clatter. Then I look at my ceiling, the only sky I have, and say softly, "God? I need you. I gotta start thinking straight again." I wonder if I look dramatic and sincere and I imagine swelling music.

3:00. *I make a decision to turn my will and my life over to the care of God as I understand Him.*

I rest my head on the rim of the garbage can. "It's up to you, Lord," I say. "I am your responsibility." That doesn't sound right and so I ransack my brain for the appropriate thing to say, and then I remember. "Thy will be done, okay?"

I think about who God is, how He's changed over the years. When I was a boy, he was this ferocious white-haired giant, pointing a sharp finger directly at me like he was going to puncture my little balloon face the moment a cuss-word came out of my mouth or I decided to lie or I achieved a little-boy erection thinking about what I saw my dad doing to my mom one night. Then for a while, God became a rock-star Moses, scraggly and scruffy and wearing purple robes, his hands forked in peace signs as he rocked and rolled to *Godspell* and *Jesus Christ Superstar*. When I stepped into adulthood, he faded for a while, coming back in blinding bright moments like the births of my two kids and the death of my mother, and mostly now, he is a haze. A powerful haze, a still-purple haze, but a form I can't quite get a grip on.

I feel my brain lurch sideways and I wonder if I passed out, if my memories of Ferocious God and Superstar God are just a part of alcohol-induced hallucination. "Look, God," I say, getting on all fours and crawling toward my couch. "I'll say it again. Thy will be done, not mine, okay? Not mine."

The couch seems twelve miles high, but I am amazingly light after disposing of my cherries and toothpicks. I crawl up and stretch out, resting my head on a pillow that smells of Sunday afternoon popcorn, stale soda and spoiled milk. I decide to stay here; it's more comfortable than my bedroom floor and so I thank God for leading me to this soft discovery. Everything is going to be fine, I think.

4:00. *I make a searching and fearless moral inventory of myself.*

When I wake up, I think it must be morning, but it's only an hour later. I stare at the ceiling and think about how I'd like nothing more than to crawl into my bedroom and curl myself around the warm body of my wife. Reaching over my head for the telephone, I yank it onto my chest and dial her number. Her new number. The number that doesn't have my name linked with hers in the phone book. I'm listed under her and I think of the wrongness of that, of how she should be under me. Under me, sweet and open and ready to take. But Z comes after K, I remind myself, and we are all sworn to following the alphabet. I wonder for a moment why we didn't stop after the twelfth letter. How many are there anyway? I pause for a moment. Twenty-six. Not even divisible by twelve. Kat answers on the fourth ring.

"Sweetheart," I say. "It's me. I really need you. I can't even go in our bedroom anymore, because I know I won't find you there."

"Jesus, Zach," she says and I know she's rubbing her forehead. "You've got to stop making these early-morning phone calls. I'm a working woman now, remember? I have to get up in two hours."

"You shouldn't have to work," I say. She took the first job she could get, a secretary at my kids' school. She told me proudly that they hired her on the spot and now she could earn money and be home when the kids were home.

"I do have to work, Zach," she says and it sounds like her mouth is right next to the phone and I picture her tiny white teeth taking nicks out of the receiver. "Because of you, remember?"

I shake my head. "That's all over, Kat. I've given it up. I'm going to go to meetings again. I even threw away my last jar of maraschino cherries and my last box of toothpicks. Remember those? Remember how you got them for me?"

I expect her voice to soften, but it doesn't. "Were you at Benny's Barstools tonight?"

"Well, yeah. I decided to quit when I got home—"

"Call me when you've been away from there for two weeks, Zach. Two weeks." Fourteen days. The phone goes dead.

I let the whole thing slide to the floor. I think about my wife. I haven't seen her in so long. I try to put a date on it and I can't. I think about my kids, I haven't seen them in even longer. She won't let me, put a court order on me the last time I drove them home when I'd had a few. A few too many, she said, but it was really only a few.

Standing up, I kick the telephone out of my way, relishing the shattered bleat as it hits the wall. I walk briskly to the bathroom and look at myself full-out in the mirror. "You're pathetic," I say. I shake my finger and scowl, thinking of Ferocious God, thinking of puncturing my own face. "You're going to make it better." Instantly, a calm smooths itself over my shoulders and I stand taller. I frown at myself, try to look firm, like I did the day I caught my boy stealing bubblegum. I did the typical march-him-back-and-make-him-apologize parent thing. But a part of me glowed with pride. He pulled it off, after all, in today's world of high-tech security cameras, coded labels and alarm systems, and security guards on every corner. "So what's the best way to make it better?" I ask. "Organize! Figure out what you have to do!" I smile. I know the answers. I can do this. "Let's go make a list," I say to my reflection. "Once we know everything that's wrong, we'll be able to make it right."

I imagine myself in a three-piece navy blue suit, a blue tie with silver diamonds knotted at my throat. Holding a brand new pure leather briefcase in my hand (the old one is too representative of my prior life, so Kat gets me a new one, a blood-red one), I stride to the kitchen table. I nod at Kat, who stops cooking my breakfast long enough to pour me a cup of fresh hot coffee. "Thank you, darling," I say out loud to this glorious image. Then I pull out a notebook. Dreaming of coffee and bacon and eggs and a silk-robed soft-skinned wife straddling my lap, I start on my list.

5:00. I admit to God, to myself and to another human being the exact nature of my wrongs.

After staring steadily at the wall for a few moments, I decide to start with a Game Plan. Every goal can be achieved through a Game Plan.

    1) Figure out where things went wrong.
    2) Fix them.
    3) Find a meeting and stick with it.

4) Get another job.

5) Get Kat and the kids back.

I sit back and flip the page. Now comes the hard part. Shaking my hands, then cracking my knuckles vigorously, I clear my throat before hunching over the notebook. I write until sweat pours from my temples, so I know I must be getting to the crux of the situation.

1) I drink too much.

2) I ignore Kat and the kids.

3) I lost my job.

4) I spend a lot of our money on drinking.

5) I never do anything around the house.

6) I lie to Kat about where I've been.

7) I've lost all my friends except for a bartender named Benny.

8) I lost my license.

9) I put the kids in danger when I drink and drive with them in the car.

10) I slept with another woman, but just once, and I don't remember her name.

11) I don't put Kat and the kids first.

12)

For a while, I leave number twelve blank. I'm not sure what to put there, but I know it's important. It's the sum-up point. I think about Kat, sleeping across town in the twin bed she bought from Goodwill. In a short while, she'll get up, take a hot shower and have some coffee by herself in that tiny kitchen. I remember her getting up early some mornings, just to scrub my back, to wrap her arms around my waist. "Let me clean you inside and out," I would say. "You're a dirty girl." She threw back her head and laughed and I kissed her neck, not minding the taste of the soap.

She always smelled so damn good.

I look at the number twelve on my list and then I fill in the blank. "I broke Kat's heart."

Going back into the bathroom, I recite each of the twelve items out loud to my reflection. I do it again. And again. By the sixth time, my face in the mirror tells me there's a new understanding, a new depth. "And remorse," I say. "I am so sorry." I find myself crying again. It's a different cry than at one-thirty in the morning, a new cry with a deeper tone and timbre. I look at my face in the mirror, study the tears, and think that they look larger, clearer than ever before. It's working, I think, and this makes me cry harder.

6:00. I am entirely ready to have God remove all these defects of character.

"This is it," I say out loud. Crumpling my list, I toss it into the toilet and flush. "They're gone. It's over. It all begins again today." I remember the maudlin, "This is the first day of the rest of your life" motto that appeared on every bumper sticker and cross-stitch pattern and top-forty song in the seventies and suddenly, it all makes sense.

I go to the kitchen and check off Step One on my Game Plan. I make a half-mark on Step Two, because I figure admitting all this stuff is halfway resolving them. Fatigue comes over me, as heavy and smelly as Kat's sorority sister's old quilt, and I tuck my notebook into my pocket. Returning to the couch, I try to catch some z's.

7:00. I humbly ask Him to remove my shortcomings.

At seven, my eyes automatically open and I stare at the ceiling again. No matter how drunk, no matter how sober, no matter how employed or unemployed, I always wake up at seven. I curse the clock in my head. Then the every-morning thought erupts in my brain and drips down to my tongue. I lick my lips.

I want a drink.

A Bloody Mary, rich red tomato juice, sharp clear vodka that goes straight to my sinuses, a stalk of celery as green as spring. They make them at the little restaurant down the street. Vegetables (and vodka) for breakfast.

I moan and roll over, covering my head with my pillow. I picture Ferocious God, but with the wild hair and robes of the rock star. "Please, God," I say. "Take it away. Please make this easy."

I get up and decide to do battle with the craving by pitting it against steamy hot water and Kat's liquid soap. I even use her little loofah. She left it behind, she was in such a hurry to leave. Holding it to my nose, I inhale her and get an instant erection. Jerking off also helps to relieve the craving. I decide, as I towel off, to head the other direction this morning, follow a new road, find a new diner, and order bacon and eggs and hot coffee. I'll have to imagine the waitress in a silk robe.

8:00. *I make a list of all the people I've harmed and become willing to make amends to them all.*

At a diner called Ruby Belle's, the bacon and eggs taste pretty good, the coffee much better. I look quickly at the menu before ordering, half-hoping Bloody Mary will be there, but she isn't. I take that as a sign from God that I'm on the right path.

The waitress, her name is Stacy, according to her crooked nametag, refills my coffee and smiles at me. I admire her and wonder what she would look like in one of Kat's nightgowns. I wonder if the skin behind her knees and inside her elbows is as soft as it looks. Her legs swing open and closed under the short uniform, her breasts beg to be squeezed, tomato-plump in the generous scoop neck.

I open my notebook and stare at it over the lip of my mug. Something looks wrong and I get out my pen, drawing circles around the Game Plan. I circle and circle, trying to zero in on what's wrong, and then I realize it. The kids. The fifth item says, "Kat and the kids." I always think of the kids together, as a single unit. Yet surely I've hurt them both individually.

I think of the last time I had them for a visit, the last time I drove them home to their mother's. I went through a red light and then skidded up onto a sidewalk. No one was hurt, but I remember looking into the rearview mirror and seeing Will's face, gone white like they say it goes in books. His eyes were wide and he looked right at my reflection and his glare refracted directly into my eyes. I tried to laugh, but he only blinked, then looked out the window. After I pulled the car off the sidewalk and we headed toward Kat's apartment, Will said in this impossibly low voice, "Dad, I'm tired of this. I don't want to see you again."

I wondered when his voice changed and then I laughed again, looked at him in the mirror, grinned as broadly as I could to show

I could take the joke. "Aw, c'mon, Will. It was just a little slide. The road's slippery tonight."

He looked back out and I knew he was seeing the dry pavement. At thirteen, he couldn't drive yet, but he knew wet from dry.

"It must be the tires," I said.

"It must be you're drunk," he said. The white was gone from his face, replaced with two giant red stains on his cheeks. He's had those red stains his whole life. When he was born, they were there, like cherry tomatoes on his baby face and I asked the doctor if they were birthmarks. The doctor said, "No, you've got yourself a high-spirited son."

When I pulled in the apartment's parking lot, Will was out before I even stopped the car. He ran up the walk and slammed the door behind him. My daughter, Marie, just shook her head and said, "Bye, Dad." From the way she walked slowly to the door and shut it without looking over her shoulder, I thought better of going in to say hello to their mother.

To my wife.

Later, Kat called me and told me I wouldn't be seeing them again. When I argued, she said she would get a court order and she did. The kids testified that I drove them home drunk several times. When the judge found out I was driving with a suspended license, my fate was sealed. My fatherhood was taken away.

We met in the judge's chambers and it felt like we were in counseling. I told myself we would all walk out cured. Will spoke to the judge straight-out, his new voice deep and steady. I looked at him and wanted to tell the judge about the time Will stole bubblegum and I marched him back to the store. I'm not sure what Marie said, exactly. She spoke so softly, I couldn't hear and the judge had to lean forward, almost folding himself across his desk. Kat sat ruler-straight the whole time, never once looking directly at me. When the judge told me I could no longer see my children, Kat nodded, thanked the judge, and walked out the door, the kids following. I sat and stared at the judge until he told me there would be no cure today.

I used to carry Marie on my shoulders, her fat legs fitting perfectly in the grooves by my neck. She pumped her fists in the air and shrieked that she could see the whole world from up there. And she could see everything that was important; the Santa at the end of the Christmas parade, the home run at the ball game, the nearest porta-potty at the state fair. Once, I stumbled and we both went down and Marie smacked her head on the sidewalk. We had to go to the hospital and the doctor snarled at me as I sat in the waiting room, buying cup after cup of bad vending-machine coffee.

Kat wouldn't let me carry Marie after that, even though Marie begged and begged. She knew it was an accident. So we would sneak away together and I'd carry her then.

Now sixteen, she's almost as tall as me. At the last Christmas parade, I joked and offered to carry her on my shoulders and she told me she could see everything just fine now, thank you.

Stacy the waitress comes back to my table and offers me another refill. I nod, hold out my mug. She bends, just a little, though it's unnecessary, and gives me an eyeful. I take advantage of it and smile at her breasts.

"You know," she says, "I get off at about five."

I sip my coffee, lick my lips. "You know where Benny's Barstools is?"

"Sure."

"Why don't you come by after work? I'm always there."

She dips her head, then walks away, hips swaying to a warm beat I can't help but recognize. I let my gaze linger. And linger. Then I remember I don't go to Benny's anymore.

"Shit," I whisper. Pulling the Game Plan toward me, I put an addendum under number five:

5) Get Kat and the kids back.

Get Kat and Will and Marie back. And if I can't get Kat back, get Will and Marie back. Definitely get Will and Marie back.

Then I underline, "Get Kat back." I need her skin.

9:00. I make direct amends to people wherever possible, except when to do so would injure them or others.

At nine o'clock, I stand across the street from my kids' school. I know that the main office is just behind the front doors and I'm sure that the shadow passing across the blinded windows must be Kat. My mind gives the shadow Kat's face, her high cheekbones and dimpled chin, and then I recognize her gently sloping shoulders, her arched neck.

The sign at the door says visitors must check in at the secretary's desk and so I do.

When she sees me, I tell myself that the look on Kat's face must be joy. Her eyes widen and she gets those tomatoes on her cheeks, just like Will. I smile at her and open my arms. "Hello, sweetheart," I say.

"What are you doing here?" she hisses.

I start to move toward her desk, but she comes around it, grabs me by the arm and pulls me into the hall. "I thought I'd come by and offer you a cup of coffee. Or a late breakfast. Or an early lunch," I say. Looking around, I spot the teacher's lounge. "I've always wanted to see the inside of one of those," I say. "Want to go in there? Is there a coffee machine?"

"Zach, you can't stay here. I have work to do," she says. She yanks on my arm, leading me toward the front doors.

"I wanted to see you," I begin, reaching into my pocket for the notebook.

"Well, I don't want to see you! Not until you've been sober for two weeks, Zach! Two weeks!" Fourteen days.

I spreadeagle my arms when we get to the doorway and she gasps as she pushes against me. She knows she's no match for my bulk, but she tries anyway and I'm surprised by the force of her little body against mine. Finally, she stops and pants, looking down at the floor. "Zach, please," she says.

I look past her down the hall and I wonder where my kids are. "Do you think it would be okay if I take Marie and Will out at lunch hour?" I ask.

She puts her hands to her face. "They don't want to see you, Zach," she whispers.

She's crying and I'm instantly sorry. I put my arm around her shoulders. "Oh, sweetie," I say. "I just wanted to come and apologize. For everything. And I want to tell the kids too." I think of the Game Plan. "Marie and Will," I amend.

She turns her back to me, sliding out from under my arm. "You're always sorry," she says. "Now, Zach, please just go, before someone sees you."

Too late. A man steps out of the office. "Is there a problem, Kat?" he asks. He's bigger than me.

She looks quickly between us. "No, Bob, it's fine. This man was just leaving."

I step forward, sling my arm back around her shoulders, then offer my hand to Bob. "I'm Zach," I say. "Her husband."

Kat looks at me, the tomatoes bursting, before running into the office. Bob just looks at my hand, then shakes his head. "You'd better go, Zach," he says.

"I guess so." I take one more quick look around, hoping the bell will ring and I'll see my kids, but the hall remains silent. I smile at Bob, then turn and leave.

10:00. I continue to take personal inventory and when I am wrong, promptly admit it.

"God, you're stupid," I mutter as I walk down the street to a phone booth. "You should have brought flowers." Kat's favorites, a dozen blood-red roses, a cliché, but something she loves. I picture myself peeking around a huge bouquet and seeing those tomatoes bloom on Kat's cheeks again, but this time with the pink of pleasure. I hear her squeal.

In the booth, there's a torn copy of the phone directory. I find the school's number and scrounge enough change out of my pocket for the call. I don't have much left after the tip I left for Stacy. I felt I had to leave a big one; I'd be standing her up later.

Kat answers the phone. "North High School," she says. Her voice sounds shaky and moist.

"Kat," I say, then pause. She doesn't hang up. "I'm sorry, Kat," I say quickly. "I shouldn't have done that. It was a mistake. I'm a dumb fuck, okay? I'm sorry." Still silence, but I can hear her breathing. I make my breath match hers, then I slow it down, a trick I learned in our childbirth classes so many years ago. I hear her growing calmer, so I take a chance. "Kat?" I ask, making my voice as soft and sincere as possible. "Can I come to see—"

She slams the phone down so hard, my ears ring.

Sighing, I hang up my own phone, then caress the receiver as if it was her cheek. I think about the Game Plan.

2) Fix it.

The best way to fix things, I know, is to go back to meetings, to following the Sacred Twelve Steps. But Christ, I hate going. "Hello, my name is Zach and I'm a fucking alcoholic." I always picture those steps as a staircase. A staircase of words. The words blink and mutter and repeat and after I've said them enough, they just don't mean anything anymore. It's like going to church. For years, you mumble the Apostle's Creed with the congregation, but you just don't know what it all means.

Kat thinks the meetings work and she loves her Al-Anon meetings. I wonder if they have Twelve Steps. I wonder how they do introductions. "Hello, my name is Kat and my husband is a fucking alcoholic." And I wonder who she talks to there. There used to be a guy named Bob and when I got home at night from Benny's, she'd always be on the phone with him. Even if I fucked her silly before I left.

Bob. I stop for a moment and look back at the school. Then I shake my head.

I have to find a meeting. I'll call and tell her about it tonight. Then she'll know I'm serious.

11:00. I seek through prayer and meditation to improve conscious contact with God as I understand Him, praying only for the knowledge of His will for me and the power to carry that will out.

It takes a lot of walking and about a dozen churches, but I finally find one that has a meeting at noon. That only gives me an hour to kill. I'm not hungry yet, after that huge breakfast, plus I know the meeting will have coffee and doughnuts, so it doesn't make sense to spend money on what will be free later. I stand around for a while, looking at the closed door. The meeting is in the church basement and it has its own separate entrance, as if they're trying to weed out the drunks from the saints. Finally, I walk away a little bit and face the street. I hate to look like an alcoholic.

Five or ten minutes pass, so I decide to go up to the church proper. At least, I think, I'll be out of the view of the passersby, who look at me and sneer. Inside the church, I walk up the long aisle. My footsteps echo and I brush my hand over each pew, feeling the softness of the wood. The stained glass windows pour down a colored light and I watch my feet as they splash through puddles of red and green and yellow. When I run out of pews, I look up at the altar.

A big-ass crucifix hangs there, about twenty feet of Christ dangling and dying. At that size, I can see all of him in graphic detail, from the nails entering his wrists and ankles to the wound in his side. He looks down at me and I think how tired his eyes look. "You look like you need a belt," I say. I try to laugh, but those eyes take the sound right out of me.

I look around; there's no one else there. "Okay," I say to the giant Christ. "I'm back for another try. I've gotta get Kat and the kids—Marie and Will—back. And this seems to be the only way to do it." I remember the morning with Stacy, the hot coffee and her full breasts, and Christ's eyes seem to narrow. "I know, I shouldn't have said I'd meet her. It was just reflex, okay? I'm really serious this time. Really."

I sit in the front pew, then awkwardly lower myself onto the padded kneelers. I feel my kneebones sink in and it's not half bad. In my head, I go over the Twelve Steps I've learned time and time again, heard chanted at meetings, read posted over my bathroom sink, on the refrigerator door, and the lowered flap of my car's sun visor (Kat's doing). Somewhere in there, I know I'm supposed to make a bargain with God. I'm supposed to decide to stick it out.

"Look, God," I say, looking back up at the crucifix. "I'll try and get here more often, okay? Maybe I can stop in for a service when I come for meetings. So I'll be in touch. And maybe you can show me how to do this stuff? Can you like, lead the way? Because I'm at a loss here."

I swallow and look at my hands. Carefully, I fold them, letting each finger curl and nestle with the others. "It's supposed to be easy," I say. "Just stop. No more drinks. Like turning off a faucet." I shake my head. "But it's like I have a leak somewhere."

I stay like that for a while. It feels pretty good, in the cool and the quiet. After a time though, even the soft kneepads hurt my joints, so I sit back in the pew. The wood curves, just like it was meant to cradle me.

When the church bells begin to ring, I know it's noon and I get up to head downstairs. I nod at Jesus, do a little bow, then promise to come back.

And I mean it this time.

12:00. Having had a spiritual awakening as the result of these steps, I try to carry this message to alcoholics and to practice the principles in all my affairs.

It doesn't take long to get to my turn. I carefully set my black coffee and chocolate doughnut on the empty seat beside me. Standing, I fold my hands, dangle them meekly at my crotch. "My name is Zach," I say slowly. "And I am…still…an alcoholic." They applaud and for a moment, I enjoy it. I think I feel the breeze from all those beating hands and between those hands and the eyes upstairs, I think I can do it. I can turn off the faucet. I sigh and lift my face.

1:00 Denial

At the end of the meeting, I stand off to the side and help myself to the cheese and sausage tray that someone brought. She's been sober for a year and she thought we'd celebrate by eating something other than doughnuts. The sausage is good and the cheese is that pepperjack stuff I love, so I keep visiting the snack table and taking a few pieces.

While I'm eating, I watch everyone else. And I notice things like unkempt hair, baggy clothes, dark shadows under their eyes. Their hands shake as they hold their coffee cups. They all speak too loud and too fast, and I swear, each of them licks their lips until they're chapped and raw.

I realize, watching them, that I'm not like them at all. Looking down, I admire my khakis and my button-down shirt. No tie today, no work to go to, but I look nice anyway. I've always paid attention to my appearance. I tone my voice carefully and always make sure to speak clearly and slowly. I know that only I can see the slight tremor as I hold my coffee cup. Nobody can be absolutely steady.

Looking at the others, I think of the phrase, "sloppy drunk." And I'm not. Not like them.

After swiping one more handful of sausage and cheese, I crumple up my coffee cup and throw it away. Then I head out, blinking in the light of the afternoon.

2:00. Anger

At home, I wander around, look at the paper, wander some more, attempt to straighten up. I think about how if everything was still okay, I'd be at work, a couple hours away from coming home, but Kat would be here, probably having a mid-afternoon cup of coffee and something sweet. I usually called her about now and she'd tell me what we got in the mail, what we were having for supper. And I'd look forward to coming home.

I look around at the stack of newspapers I just pushed together by the front door, the dishes I scrubbed, draining and drying in the sink, the bed I just made for the first time in I don't know how long. And I think, I shouldn't be doing any of this.

All this. All this emptiness, just because I like to go to the bar at night. I'm here by myself, in a place too big for one, and she's living with the kids in a place too small for three. I think of Bob and up the count to maybe four. She's working and I'm not.

All because of Benny's Barstools?

I'm not a mean drunk, I've never raised a hand to her. Most nights, I left her sated and sleepy in our bed. Most days, I got up in time to say hello to the kids, to head off to work, despite a pounding headache or a queasy stomach. Most days. I had supper with them all the time, I never stayed late at the office on account of work or some woman. Just once because of some woman, and that wasn't at work, that was later. At Benny's.

Mostly, I came home after. And when I crawled into bed, Kat would roll over and curl into me and I would smell her hair and touch her and sometimes we made love all over again. I never let her down, not once, no matter how much I had. She always made it. No whiskey dick here. All drunks have whiskey dick.

My hands begin to shake and I sit down on the couch, folding my fingers against each other, trying to get them steady. I think of the drunks at AA, but I know my shakes are different. Mine are from wanting to strangle someone. I want to strangle Kat.

Snatching the phone from its cradle, I dial her number. She's not home from her job yet, of course, and neither are the kids, so I yell into the phone, into the ear of the answering machine, "I went to a fucking meeting, Kat! I did what you told me to! Now get your ass straight home! I don't deserve this, I don't fucking deserve this!" The phone becomes slippery and I realize my hands are sweaty as well as shaky. "You tell that Bob to stay there and fuck himself, you come home. You're my wife, those're my kids, you come home now!"

I try to slam the phone down, to get that satisfying bang and clang of a phone smacked silly, but the damp receiver shoots out of my hand like a missile and bounces across the floor. I reel it in, hand over hand, and then slam it down, but the satisfaction is gone. The shakes and the sweats are worse and I hold onto my knees and throw my body into a fast rock. When I close my eyes, I see blood-red and I feel a growl deep in my throat.

This shouldn't be happening, I think. I just have to get control of the situation and pull it all back together. I squeeze my eyelids so tightly, the red turns to black and I fall into it like a bottomless night.

3:00. Bargaining

After a bit, the darkness begins to have edges to it and I climb back out. I sit on the edge of the couch and hold my head in my hands. Get control, I think. Take deep breaths. And I do.

Pulling out the notebook, I glance quickly at my Game Plan, then move to a new page. The key to everything is organization, I think, and so I write the days of the week down in a long column. Maybe, maybe, I think, if I just go to the bar one night a week, and so I try to pick one. My hand hovers over each of the days and my pen is like a divining rod.

But there is no day, no favorite day, no day that starts with D for drinking. Maybe every other day. I start with Monday and carefully draw what looks like a wine glass with toothpicked fruit in it. It doesn't look quite right, and I doodle some more, and the fruit looks more real and I draw a little squiggly line for the liquor and then I color it in. I move on to Wednesday and the glass grows bigger and by Friday, it's full to the brim. Then, all of a sudden, I have glasses drawn after every day of the week.

"Shit!" I throw the notebook across the room. "All right!" I yell at the ceiling. "I'll go every night, I have to, it's my right, but I'll only have one drink and I'll come home right after!"

The phone rings and I grab it, thinking again about just slamming it down, a second chance at getting the slam right. Instead, I holler, "Hello!" as loud as I can.

"How dare you call here and shout like that!" Kat shrieks at me. "Your kids heard that message, do you know that? Do you think that makes them want to come home? Do you think it makes me want to come home?"

"I went to a meeting!" I bellow. "I went there just for you! I had to listen to a woman prattle on about how she hasn't had a drink in a year and her whole life is a dozen blood-red roses and she fed us cheese and sausage!"

"One meeting doesn't make you sober!"

"Yeah, well, drinking doesn't make me a drunk!"

We're silent for a moment, both of us breathing heavily over the phone. I think I hear Marie's sobs in the background and there's the slam of a door.

I clench my fist around the phone, force my voice to go soft and mellow. "Look, Kat," I say. "Come home. We'll work it all out, I promise. I'll get resumes together this weekend, hit the employment offices on Monday. I mean it. I'll have just one drink a night at Benny's, maybe even every other night—"

Kat slams her phone in my ear, just the way I wanted to slam her. I hesitate, say, "Kat?" before banging my own phone, then going one better and pulling it out of the wall and throwing it after my notebook. "Fuck!" I yell. "It's just not fucking worth it!"

Lying face down on the couch, I cover my head with the pillow and try to bring blackness around me. I push my nose into the cushion, yank the pillow around my ears, try to soften the blackness into a smooth gray, to smother the air from my lungs.

If I let myself up, I will pull every hair from my head. I will throw things and punch walls and kick furniture. I will say every curse word I know, at least a dozen times over, and my voice will shatter windows.

But the smooth gray tucks me in.

4:00. Depression

"It doesn't matter," I say to the gray, my lips moving against the couch cushion. "I can go to meetings, she doesn't care. I can just have one drink a night, one drink! And come straight home to make her happy, but she won't care. I could give up drinking altogether, but it wouldn't make a damn bit of difference."

I think about our wedding day, eighteen years ago. We toasted each other at the wedding table, our elbows linked, Kat's Bride glass filled with diet soda, my Groom glass with straight whiskey. Neither of us like champagne. She watched me drink it and later she tugged on my arm and asked me if it wasn't time to go. "Just one more," I said. I was enjoying myself, it was my wedding, for Christ's sake. There was music, all my friends were there, they were happy for me. So I had one more and she asked again, and I had one more and my friends started joking about how I was pussywhipped already, not even married six hours. So I had another and she began to cry.

I took her home then and told her I was sorry and filled her in such a way that she'd never forget that night in a million nights. And she smiled at me then, through her tears, there under me, and she asked for more, and I gave her more. I gave her more until she fell asleep beneath me, me still inside her until I shriveled and slid out. Then I poured myself a drink, looked out the window of our new apartment, and wondered what in the hell I'd done.

Now, the pillow slips off my head as I prop my chin on my fists. "I should've known then," I say. "I should've known then and I should've walked out that night."

I let myself cry, just one more time. I think of my kids and I cry. Marie and Will. I remember Will learning to walk, careening into a wall and bloodying his nose. I held my handkerchief to it until it stopped bleeding and he stopped sobbing. I gave him a sip of my rum and coke to calm him down. I remember watching Marie leave on her first date, her walking down the sidewalk with her arm around that scrawny boy's waist and I stood at the open door and glared them away before I set off for Benny's.

And I think of Kat.

And I cry and I think the whole time, this is the last time. I'm done. It's over. There's no need to run up those steps again. There's no one waiting at the top.

5:00. Acceptance

Swinging open the door, the sound and the smell hits me and I take the deepest breath of my day. My stool is there, waiting, and Benny smiles at me. "Hey, Zach," he says. Before I'm even settled, he has my drink squarely in front of me.

"Rough day, Benny," I say, using his name and thinking how comfortable it sounds. The barstool is molded to my ass and the drink fits neatly in the crook between my thumb and forefinger.

"Again?" Benny shakes his head. "Seems like you always have a rough day."

"Same old, same old," I say and swivel in my seat to check out the early crowd. Some are new, but others I recognize and they lift their drinks or smile in my direction. I repeat their gestures. I feel the tension drain from my shoulders and neck and the liquor warms my throat and stomach. When I hear the thunk and rustle behind me, I know Benny has set down a basket of my favorite party mix. He always gives me my own basket, though I share it when someone sits next to me.

The door opens and for a moment, I think it is Kat walking in. But then I see the younger body, the feet neatly encased in white sneakers, the low-riding jeans and belly top. The hair though, the hair could be Kat's. It swings just the way hers does, barely touching her shoulders.

Stacy sits next to me and I offer her my basket. "Benny, this is Stacy," I say. "Set her up with what she wants."

Stacy brings her hands up beneath her chin as she orders and I hear chimes. On her forearm is a load of silver bracelets and they shiver together and sing and shine. I count them. Twelve.

"Of course," I say out loud.

Stacy looks at me, raises her eyebrows.

"Your bracelets," I say. "You're wearing twelve."

She shakes her arm, sending the silver sound into the air. "My favorites," she says.

I nod toward the ugliest clock in the world. "See, it seems to me everything is centered around the number twelve," I say. "Like that clock there. Or a dozen eggs. A baker's dozen. Twelve blood-red roses."

Benny rolls his eyes, but I smile at him as he turns away. Everything slips gently back into place, like pieces of a puzzle or disks and vertebra snapped softly in line. Raising my drink, my lips meet the glass's edge exactly. I put my arm around Stacy's waist and it's like I find a groove and my arm rests against her skin like it's rested there a very long time.

I laugh out loud and raise my glass in the universal signal for another.

CHAPTER SEVENTEEN:

JAMES

nd so it ends, as you expected, this only soft relationship you've known. The only relationship that made you shudder with more than fear, but with love and ecstasy and passion. You never imagined it could really happen. Not to you, anyway.

Because of course you are scared. When it comes right down to it, you are scared of everything. Of everyone. Even of yourself.

Imagine waking up every morning and wondering if this will be the day. If this day will bring the moment that your mind goes around the bend, follows your mother's lead. Imagine wondering every morning if by the time you return to your bed that night, you will be brandishing the other end of the belt. If you will shut the root cellar doors on brimming eyes and know that this time, it's you that left someone down there in the dark. If as you draw the bolt, the sound of that life being locked away will fill you with a jolt of pleasure so deep, you have to sink to your knees in the sunlight.

Because that happens sometimes, in little spits and spurts. One day on your way home from school, a hard day because you'd returned from a week-long stay in the root cellar and found yourself hopelessly behind, again, you stopped to play with a stray cat. At first, the cat rubbed around your legs and you ran your fingers down its knobbed and matted back. The choked purr that came from its throat made you smile. But then you brushed its fur backwards, and backwards again, admiring the plethora of colors erupting from underneath. You didn't know that cats don't like this, and when you did it again, the cat grew angry and sparked its claws at you. Three deep lines of red appeared on your hand, the same hand that was just petting the cat, even though it was the wrong way. Just petting it. And so you took that same hand and molded your fingers in your mother's way and pounded that cat full in the face and when it ran from you, you roared with a sound that came from the dark part of you that was just sick of being hurt. That was just sick of being puny.

And there was the boy in ninth grade who made a comment about the length of your dick when you were in the shower after gym, and you didn't even stop to turn off the water, to rinse the soap from your hair. You pounced on that boy, your skin and his slippery wet, and you rammed him against the wall, brought your knee up against his own diminutive dick. When he folded in half, you unfolded him and repeatedly snapped his head against the streaming white tiles beneath the shower head. The teacher pulled you off, dragged you from the shower and threw you against your locker. The clang of your body against metal crumpled you into an immediate cower, and then the teacher just stood there, watching you, arresting you, as you climbed wet into your clothes. He led you on the long trek to the principal's office, where you were suspended for three days. Your mother never knew. You just slunk into the woods each morning, climbed a tree, and watched the colors of the sky change. It was the most peaceful three days you've ever known. Except you were so alone and you wondered what you were missing.

And then Diana. The one time you raised your hand to Diana, and the look on her face let you know that the animal was there. Your mother stood erect in your skin and she looked out of your eyes and said words you knew so well, but you would never have said yourself. And then your hand connected to Diana's face and you felt the piercing pleasure of attack, the pleasure you only imagined, but were always afraid you'd experience. The unimaginable pleasure of hitting someone you love.

And it happened with your mother too. On the last day you saw her, the day you finally walked away. Your anger met hers and you won. The thrill you felt was palpable as you stood over her, her hand cupped over her nose and mouth, against the sting you put there, and the fear in her eyes made you want to roar again, to watch her run off into the woods like a stray cat.

Imagine being on the other side of the pain for a change. Imagine the unimaginable pleasure of being all-powerful. And imagine never wanting to feel that powerful again.

James didn't have to imagine. He apologized to Diana that night, apologized over and over even after the red mark disappeared from her face, and he never ever forgave himself. Instead, he choked himself down, choked down his mother, and fell into a reserve that remained until Diana left. And it remained still, that distance. The distance between him and anyone who truly breathed in and out and whose tick came from vessels and arteries and aortas, all working together, not unlike a clock mechanism, but not a clock mechanism at all.

A distance that James imagined was absolutely necessary.

James was on the porch the next day when Cooley came back. The house had been quiet for a couple hours, quiet in the sense that nothing moved, besides James and the clocks. Molly delivered breakfast and lunch. Ione stayed until one, then left. The doctor showed up mid-morning and finally removed the bandages on James' hands and feet. James thought the fresh air would feel good on them, but it felt cold, almost like he was being burned with ice. Both his hands and feet looked terrible, with long running gashes that were still inflamed and swollen. Dr. Owen said they were actually a lot better than they looked.

When Cooley walked up the steps, she didn't look at James. She held a box and she kept her eyes firmly fixed on it. When she got to the top step, she sat down and turned away. She placed the box gently by James' feet. He noticed the way she slid her hands out from beneath, one at a time, supporting the box so that it didn't drop. James and Cooley stayed there like that for quite some time. Cooley's shoulders were raised and she sat straight instead of slouched, though from time to time, she rocked left to right, as if an internal breeze set her into motion. James didn't feel any air at all and in fact, it felt like Cooley sucked all the oxygen out of the afternoon. He couldn't tell if she was talking. She could have been saying anything, from apologizing to cussing James out.

"Did you say something?" he finally asked.

She shook her head. Then she reached up and patted her ears.

"Notebook's in the house," he said. "On the kitchen table."

She shrugged and went inside. James immediately bent forward to look at the box, but the flaps were folded. He looked over his shoulder, then touched one of the flaps, intending to sneak a peek. But when he couldn't hear the scraping sound of cardboard against cardboard, he realized he also wouldn't hear when Cooley came back. And he didn't want to get caught. Not by her. James knew better than to be caught doing something by a woman that would be interpreted as wrong.

She came back and sat on the step again, this time facing James. She set the notebook beside her on the porch and then displayed the clipboard. James nodded. "Yes, Cooley," he said. "There are clocks to be wound." He held out his hands. "The doc took my bandages off, see?"

Her mouth opened and James knew she must have cried out. She got up on her knees and took his hands in hers. Her skin was warm and smooth, her palms felt like cushions. As she bent over the cuts and slices and abrasions, for a moment, James thought they might stop burning.

But nothing would make them stop burning. Nothing but time and healing. James pulled away. "Anyway. Even with my bandages off, I'm still having trouble doing the winding. The skin is stiff, see, and it hurts to move my fingers too much. Doc said I should do some things, to work the skin back to flexibility, so I wound the weight-driven clocks due for it. But the ones that need key-winding, I left. All that turning hurts and Doc said I could split the skin open."

That morning, James thought his heart would burst when he reached out to wind a clock, the first one in almost a week. He walked the doctor out the door and then peeked in on Ione in the kitchen. She was busy, so James slipped by and went to the office to get the clipboard. Then he set off for an upstairs back bedroom, where he could wind in peace, without anyone watching.

The clock he chose was a cuckoo clock of sorts. It ran like a cuckoo, but in the door where a bird normally popped out was a circle of children. They twirled when the clock chimed and then played a tinny version of Ring Around The Rosie. James' favorite part, though, was the pendulum. It was a girl on a swing, who sat facing out into the room. Instead of swinging left and right, like most pendulums, this one went forward and back, setting the girl on a forever ride in the sky. It took a special place to hang her, a place where there was room for her forward and back movement. The west bedroom had a niche in one wall. It used to hold an ornate sconce, an elaborate light that just didn't fit with James or the Home. So he removed it and hung this clock at the top of the arch. The little girl in the swing flew backwards into the niche, then out into the room. James kept a tumbling philodendron there as well so it looked like the little girl played over a lush green park. The curved wall was painted blue, giving her a sky.

James watched her, swinging, and he wished he could hear her. He always thought of giggling when he looked at this clock, giggling that was high-pitched, feminine, sweet. The little girl had a smile on her face and James knew she never, not for a moment, missed being a part of the dancing circle of children above, at the top of the clock.

The weights were just above the floorboard, indicating the clock was ready to be wound. James started to reach for the chains, but then stopped, leaned against the wall, and put his ear against the side of the clock. He thought that maybe with the bandages coming off his hands and feet, maybe his ears would magically clear as well. Maybe they stayed deaf this long out of sympathy.

But there was nothing, no sound. James thought he detected the wood scraping against his skin, but he couldn't be sure. The rhythm was there, that vibration, and for a moment, he closed his eyes and leaned into it, tapping his fingers on the wall to keep the beat.

While James couldn't hear the ticking, nor the chiming nor singing nor time-telling, he could still feel the clocks' hearts beating. He pictured himself going around the Home, laying his head aside every clock in the place. His fingers curled into a stiff and painful clench.

It would do, for now. But it wouldn't be enough for long.

Now Cooley nodded and sat back down on the porch. She looked at the clipboard, then wrote in the notebook. "Could U mark which 1s U wound?" it said in her strange alien code.

"Why do you write like that?" James asked. She cocked her head. "I mean, with U's and 1's and things like that, instead of just writing the words?"

She blinked for a moment, then smiled. "I guess I just do it w/o thinking," she wrote. "I'm on the computer a lot. That's how U talk on the internet."

The internet. James shook his head; he'd never been. "Well, I think you can figure out which clocks to wind on your own. If it has weights, I did it. If it has a key, you should do it." He thought of the words he rehearsed all morning, the words he promised Ione he was going to say to Cooley when she came. Now, he wondered if it would be enough just to tell her that he thought she could do it. The other words were stuck somewhere between his stomach and his throat. He kept seeing Diana's clock in pieces on the floor. Maybe he did break it; James knew he did. But he wouldn't have if Cooley hadn't messed up. If she hadn't thrown the notebook at him. If she'd just wound the clocks right in the first place.

But Ione said that kids need encouragement. Incoragement, she spelled it, but James knew what she meant. She said that Cooley needed it especially.

Cooley looked at James, then at the clipboard. She nearly smiled, but he saw her face freeze as she stopped herself. James forced his rehearsed words past the lump in his throat to his mouth. "You've been doing a good job, Cooley."

She turned the smile loose then and as always, her smile brought a change to that darkly made-up face. It was like for a moment, the makeup disappeared and James could see Cooley herself. It struck him this time that her eyes were blue. He wondered if her hair was black under the purple/red dye, or if under the ragged mop was really a blonde who would do those blue eyes justice.

Then she stopped smiling and dark Cooley returned. She shoved the box closer to James, leaned on it with the notebook to write. Then she set the notebook in his lap and started to open the box.

"I brt U something," James read. "It was my gramma's. It stopped working and my Mom pitched it. ☹ I hid it under my bed. Can U fix it?"

James set the notebook aside and looked at Cooley. She cradled a clock in her arms. As soon as he saw that distinctive shape, he knew what it was and his heart misfired. "Cooley," he said and held out his hands. "Let me see."

She hesitated for a second and her lips formed a word James recognized. Careful. James shook his head. "Who would be more careful with it than me, Cooley?" Her eyes widened and she said something else as she handed the clock over. James glanced at the notebook. "Use that," he said. "I can't hear you, remember?"

She wrote quickly. "Then how cum U knew I said careful????"

James wondered at a girl Cooley's age using that misspelling, then shrugged it off. "I saw the word on your lips, I guess." James looked down at the clock, ran his hands over its body.

It was an acorn clock, an American clock made exclusively by the Forestville Manufacturing Company from 1847 to 1850. This one was startlingly beautiful, its acorn-shaped case glowing in a soft rosewood. The two wooden rods that flanked the case on either side were still firmly attached, though one lacked its acorn finial. Looking at the painted tablet embedded in the front of the clock, James nodded. All acorn clocks displayed a scene from Bristol, Connecticut. This one showed what looked like a soft blue pond, complete with a little sailboat. A pale green weeping willow in full leaf hung over the water, and in the distance, a white clapboard house slept in the trees. The tablet was in perfect condition, no nicks or scratches marred the scene. The clock's face was off-white, with solemn black roman numerals and wrought iron hands. It looked sad to James and he lifted it to his ear, trying to find a tick. Then he remembered and sighed. Placing his hands on the front and back of the face, James waited for any reverberation. There was none. This clock's heart was definitely stopped.

He glanced at Cooley. She scribbled away again in the notebook. Opening the door that hid the pendulum, James checked inside. The pendulum was there and it swung easily. When set in motion, James could feel the clock's tick, but it was off beat and irregular, lasting only for a minute and half. He gently turned the clock over. As expected, there was another small door at the back of the face. James opened it and looked inside at the clock's mechanism. He carefully poked some of the gears and cogs. Everything seemed to be there. It was just very, very old and very, very dirty. Apparently, life under Cooley's bed was suffocating it.

Still, it was better than being tossed out in the garbage. James shuddered, then carefully set the clock on a table. Pushing the hands just a bit, he felt their stiffness and then winced at his own. This clock needed to be completely taken apart, cleaned and oiled, then put back together. Not an inexpensive job. Not something a high school kid could afford.

"Cooley," James said. "Didn't your grandmother ever have this clock cleaned? Didn't your parents?"

She looked up at him and her lips twisted to the side. She didn't need to write her answer in the notebook; James knew. And he should have known before asking. Parents that let their daughter look like Cooley would hardly spend the time or money to clean an old clock.

She handed James the notebook, then put one hand at the base of the clock as if to steady it. James read her message.

"When it was at my gramma's, I looked at it 4-ever. Then she died and it came to my house. Only good thing about her dying. I love the picture. I pretend I'm on that boat. Or sometimes I'm under the tree. And I always go home 2 that house. :-P Stoopid, I know."

James shook his head. "It's not stupid, Cooley. And it's a great clock. Do you know there's really only a few of these around? It's called an acorn clock."

She frowned, then pointed at the tablet.

"No, there's no acorns in the picture. But look at the shape, especially around the clock face. It looks like an acorn."

She sat back, squinted, tilted her head and the line between her eyebrows grew deeper. Then she tilted her head the other way and James saw her eyes move around the periphery of the clock's face. He wondered how many times she actually looked away from the tablet, let herself see the clock above, the time, the handsome numbers and hands. Then she smiled and nodded and traced her finger around the acorn shape.

"Right! That's where it is! These clocks were all made at one factory, owned by the man who created this style. All the clocks show pictures of where he lived."

She said something, but James couldn't catch it. He handed her the notebook. "A real place?" she wrote.

"Yes, Bristol, Connecticut."

She nodded, then wrote again. "I want 2 go there NOW!!! ☺"

"Well, anyway, I think I can fix it. Everything seems to be here, but it's old and dirty and dried out. I have to give it an overhaul."

For a second, her fingers tightened on the clock and it inched a little bit closer to her.

"It's okay. That just means I take the parts out, clean everything, then put it back together again. It should run."

She nodded, ran her finger down one of the wooden rods, then pushed the clock to James. On the notebook, she drew a dollar sign and a question mark.

James attempted to drum his fingers on his knee. It hurt, but he kept it up while he thought. Normally, these overhauls cost about two and a quarter. But James knew Cooley didn't have that kind of money and he was sure her parents would die laughing before they paid that much to fix a clock they thought was in the garbage. Normally, if someone didn't want to pay for a repair, James offered to buy the clock at a dirt-cheap price. But he didn't think Cooley would sell. And in this case, the clock was loved. It didn't deserve to be taken from its home. Even if its home was under a bed.

James considered doing the repair for free. He'd never worked on an acorn clock before and his stiff fingers itched as he thought about diving into those parts. Maybe working on this clock would be the healing his fingers needed. They would loosen up, smooth out, as they attempted to bring life to this clock once again.

But then James glanced at Cooley, sitting quietly by his knees. Diana's shards pierced him. Why should Cooley get anything for free? She was getting away with breaking Diana's clock. With making James break Diana's clock, which meant she broke it too. Why should she get a fixed and valuable clock out of all this?

James looked at the clipboard, at the list of clocks waiting inside. He knew they wondered if they were going to be allowed to stutter, to gasp and then to die. Diana's clock was broken, Cooley's wasn't breathing, and there were lots of other clocks whose lives were hanging on someone's fingers, someone who had the ability to wind them.

"Cooley," James said slowly. "It costs a lot of money to fix a clock like this. Over two-hundred dollars." She turned red and made a grab for the clock, but he put his hand over hers, keeping the clock firmly on the table. "You've been working a lot around here, and I'm going to need more help for a while, I guess. Doc says I probably have to go to Chicago, to get my ears looked at. Someone has to keep the clocks running while I'm gone. And I'd like to reopen again too, at least on the weekends when you're not in school." James cringed at that, at people walking through the Home without his overseeing. But the longer the Home stayed closed, the longer James was without revenue, and since the Home was what tourists came to see, the rest of the town suffered too. "Maybe you could just work off the repair?"

Cooley's shoulders relaxed and she sat back down on the step. And she nodded. Then she picked up the clipboard and made a motion toward the house.

"Yes, you'd better get started." James stood and picked up the clock. "I'll take this down to my workshop." She rose too, grabbing the notebook.

Cooley turned toward the living room as James headed for the basement stairs. "Oh," he said, remembering yesterday. He turned back. "Cooley?"

She looked over her shoulder.

"No more outbursts like yesterday's, understand? You work here now. You need to behave yourself."

Cooley opened the notebook and James braced himself as she wrote in huge, swirling movements. But then she turned the notebook to him. "U 2!" blared across the page. She thrust it at James twice, scowled, then turned and stamped away. James couldn't hear the sound of her feet smacking the floor, but the vibrations ran up his legs.

James went downstairs. Setting the acorn clock on the worktable, he prepared to take it apart. Pulling a big fluffy towel out from a drawer, James nested the clock face down on it. The tablet and the glass over the clock face needed protecting, plus James always thought a clock should be as comfortable as possible while he worked on its insides. Finding a small screwdriver, James opened the little door again and set to undoing the screws that held the clock's heart in place.

His fingers complained, they didn't want to move, to make the little fine twisting motions that the clock needed. James swore, and felt himself swear, his body tensing under the words, sweat slipping from his temples. In the time it normally took to remove an entire mechanism, James got one screw out.

Then suddenly, Cooley was by his side. She touched James' trembling hands, then held out the notebook. "Can I watch?" she wrote. "I want 2 know how."

James started to shake his head, but then looked at her hands again. The fingers were supple and smooth, and despite the black nail polish, delicate. They were slimmer than James' and didn't seem to show much strength. But he thought again of the warmth, of the softness and the cushion of those palms. She would be gentle with the clocks, with all of them, but especially with her own.

"Go finish the winding, Cooley," James said. "Those clocks that are still living and breathing have to come first. Make sure you get them all. Then come back here. I'm not going very fast anyway, you won't miss much."

She frowned, looked like she was going to argue, but then seemed to think better of it. She patted her clock again and James felt it relax under his hands. The screw he was working on suddenly loosened. Then Cooley headed back up the stairs.

James waited until he thought she was halfway up. "Double and triple check that list, Cooley," he yelled. "No more mistakes." Then he smiled and leaned back over the clock. He could imagine her expression. Her red face alone would keep the clocks warm.

The work on Cooley's clock went well. Cooley did some of the work herself, but mostly, she just watched. As James carefully removed all the individual pieces from the mechanism, he explained what they were, then handed them over for her to look at, to study. From there, she slipped them into a shallow pan, filled with a cleansing fluid.

"Looks like mechanic's soup," she wrote in the notebook and James told her to concentrate and keep working.

Once, she slipped off her high stool and came around to James' other side. She looked at the leftover pieces from Diana's clock. When she picked them up, James flinched, and she quickly put them back down. Then she pointed at them and frowned.

James focused in hard on a stuck gear. "They're from a clock that broke upstairs."

She touched the number six, or nine, tracing its circle. She adjusted it, making it firmly a six. Then she reached across for the notebook, putting her arm between James and the mechanism. He smacked her wrist. "The 6 looks familiar," she wrote.

James glanced at her. He didn't think it was possible that she could start recognizing all the clocks already. "It shouldn't," he said. "It's from one of the clocks you forgot to wind."

She stepped away. Then she turned her back, looking out the windows into the back yard.

James examined a gear wheel, making sure that each of the teeth was straight. If not, it wouldn't grab on to its sister cog and pull her through. "When you threw the notebook at me, I threw it across the room," he said. "It hit the clock and broke it." James quickly bit his tongue. Ione's word Incoragement forced him to cut off his own words. He was about to tell Cooley it was her fault. But he felt again the weight of the notebook, just before it sailed from his hand. Moments after it sailed from hers. James decided to stay quiet. He knew Ione expected him to tell Cooley it wasn't her fault. But it was. And James' too. They shared in the death.

She looked at James and nodded, then turned away again. He saw in the lowering of her eyebrows and in the stooped set of her shoulders that it wasn't a reassured nod. His shoulders were stooped too, with the weight of the words he didn't say. He knew then that they thought alike. Minds worked that way sometimes. They both wanted to blame each other. And themselves.

"Cooley," James said slowly. "Are you going to help me with this clock or what?"

She shrugged and returned to her stool. She wrote in the notebook for a second, then set it next to his elbow. "Wz it important?"

James thought of Diana, the way she held the clock cupped in both her palms. The way she wound it, with a touch just right, never pushing it past its limit. "All clocks are important," he said.

Cooley nodded. "So what R U going 2 do 2 it?"

James really didn't know. The pieces Ione threw in the trash were already saved and wrapped in their royal blue velvet and buried under the deep purple lilacs in the moon-glazed back yard. But James kept those remaining pieces, the hands, the number six, the mechanism, on his table. He knew they should be with the rest, the clock was dead. Keeping these parts out was like mounting the head of a deer after devouring the rest of the body. Those glass-eyed deer staring out from walls and over doors always unnerved James. It was like the head longed to be with the rest of its body. With its soul. As the clock's soul surely was in the movement.

James glanced at Cooley. He wasn't sure what to say, how to justify not throwing these pieces away with the rest of the clock which she probably figured was in the trash bin upstairs. So James just made some sort of noise. A grunt, he thought.

Cooley wrote again. "Can U put that in another clock?"

James paused, then blinked. For a second, he imagined he felt a beat from Diana's clock's heart, lying cold there on the table. He hadn't even put it on a towel. Then he just shrugged. "One clock at a time, Cooley," he said. But the thought was there now and when he quickly placed a soft towel under the movement and the number six and the golden hands, they all gleamed together. He covered them as if they were napping.

The Home was full of clocks with other clocks' parts stuck in them. But he never transplanted an entire movement before. He never moved one soul to another body.

Cooley's question kept pulling him back to the notebook.

That night, after the house was finally still, James couldn't get to sleep. He told himself to turn off the lights, but he couldn't. Whenever he was in the dark and his sight joined his closed-down hearing, his mother appeared. He knew it was impossible, he knew it couldn't be her. But she was there and he was back in the cold and damp of the root cellar. He hadn't worn a collar since he was seventeen, but whenever that newly silent, familiar darkness covered his face, he felt the leather and the studs again. Or sometimes the cold metal links of the choker. Tightening. Constricting. His throat closed up in the dark, as solidly as the silence blocking his ears.

James couldn't sleep with the lights on and he couldn't sleep because he was thinking about Chicago and what he would find out there, and Cooley winding the clocks without him close by, and what Cooley said about putting Diana's clock's mechanism into another body. And James couldn't sleep because he kept thinking about how close Rockford was to Chicago and how he could maybe take a side trip to the Time Museum and see all those wondrous clocks again, especially the Gebhard World Clock. Maybe, in Chicago, they could fix his ears and then, in Rockford, he could hear those clocks go off. And if his ears weren't fixed, he could watch and if no one was looking, maybe lay his face against a few of them. The caretakers wouldn't mind. They understood clocks there.

And James thought about how the Time Museum was the last place he saw Diana. He couldn't count that real last time, that night when she climbed into bed and turned her back. James realized now, from the way she turned away, the way she curled her arms around her pillow and her hair fell over her cheek and the way her shoulders moved as she sighed, she was already gone that night. Even though he kept talking. Talking, he thought, to her, but talking to nobody but himself.

James got out of bed, wrapped his robe around his shoulders and headed for the basement. He made sure to turn on the light before descending the stairs, flooding even the darkest corners with brightness. Then he sat at the workbench, held the number six in the palm of his hand, the hand that remembered striking a cat, a boy, his mother, and Diana. Four times total. But four times too many. James looked at Diana's heart.

He thought of all the clocks in the Home. Whose insides could he take out, to tuck this one back to life in a different body? But that would be like killing one for another. What would he do with the heart he removed? And what about the clocks that didn't work, that were only shells with their insides buried out in the graveyard? James always hoped he would find the right parts to fix them. But wouldn't a clock rather tick with someone else's heart than just sit there, waiting to be raised from the silent dead?

James looked at Diana's heart, lying there. It seemed sad. But the thought of it ticking away in someone else's body, in a body that wasn't created for it, fully intended for it, seemed wrong. It wasn't fitting. Not for her. She deserved only the best.

James dug around until he found a small box and he lined it with some lamb's wool. Then he put the little number six and the hands and the mechanism inside. Carefully folding the box shut, he made sure there was a small gap to allow some light in. Then he placed Diana on the shelf.

Cooley's clock parts were still soaking in their fluid. They were each going to need individual scrubbing with a new toothbrush, so since sleep seemed far away, James settled down for some work. He decided the acorn clock needed a blue toothbrush, blue for serenity and peace and a long life, as long as the ocean, which is what he wanted to give to this clock, trapped for too long under a teenager's bed. But as he dug through his collection of cellophane-covered toothbrushes, he found his old drawing pad. James remembered placing it there as a lift for the toothbrushes, bringing them closer to the top of the drawer so he wouldn't have to dig so deep. James pulled the pad out, then selected a blue toothbrush and set it next to the pan holding the clock parts.

Only one page of the drawing pad was used and that was to sketch the clock James wanted to create, so long ago. The statue clock, the mother looking at her watch while teaching her little boy how to tell time. James looked at it now, saw the way the mother bent smoothly at the waist, saw her soft skin as she smiled at the boy, and saw the firm concentration on the boy's face as he leaned over his own watch. In the way they touched, in the way she smiled, in the way they both held their watches on slim delicate wrists, there was a connection. It was one James wanted to feel, one he wanted to show the world, but at the time he sketched it, he didn't know enough about clocks to make this statue work.

Now, maybe he did. Maybe James could create a clock. Something just for Diana's heart, so that when it ticked, it knew it was in a special place, where it should be, in a home for nobody else. The clock mechanism was still working, it was all in one piece, so he really only needed to create a new body. A new body for Diana's heart.

For Diana.

But then James flipped to a new page. It wouldn't be the statue clock. The mother/son body didn't fit. Diana's clock wasn't about that. Diana wasn't a mother. At least, not when she was with James, though they talked about it.

James sat and thought. Diana's flower basket clock was ceramic and he had no idea how to make that. But he knew wood and maybe something could come of that. James never carved anything before, but if he could draw the picture, maybe he could find someone else to cut the wood. Neal, maybe, or Gene.

James tried drawing a few things, silly things, like a Valentine heart, a flower, held hands. Then he quickly gave up. His fingers were just too tired and stiff and he needed time to think and consider, to find a perfect form to hold Diana's heart. It helped though to have this idea, to think that the clock's life wasn't completely gone. He could do a transplant.

James went upstairs and turned off the basement light, waiting until his eyes adjusted and he could see the soft glow of the nightlight by the bench. None of his clocks were ever in complete darkness. Then he went upstairs, bringing the drawing pad along. He left it on the bedside table, near his mother's anniversary clock. Touching the pad, James felt the promise of its many blank pages, and then he decided to turn off the light. There was another nightlight in the bathroom and the rosy glow fell into the room, softening the shadows. James decided he would sleep.

And he did fall asleep, but it didn't take long for his mother to find him. He was nine years old again, crouched in a cardboard box in the cellar, when she threw open the doors and came down. "Time to get up, James, naptime is over," she said and James jumped out of the box and trotted over to her, lifting his chin so she could take off the tether and collar.

Then she discovered the mess in the corner. James hoped it was dark enough, that corner, the only one he could really reach on the tether. He thought the dark would hide his secret, but he'd forgotten her sense of smell and her cat's eyes found the source easily.

"James! What did you do?"

James hung his head. "I'm sorry, Mom. I tried to wait, I did, but I really had to go and I called for you, but you didn't hear—"

"You called for me? You know you're supposed to be silent down here! You're supposed to be napping!" Her hand came down, smacking James against his ear and he fell back onto his haunches.

"I know, but I had to go—"

"Come on. Bad boy." She yanked the chain and the choke collar clenched around James' neck. He tried to keep up, but she dragged him over to the corner. Then she caught on to his hair on the back of his head and thrust his face into the pile. "Bad boy!" she yelled. "Bad boy!" She pushed James a few more times, his nose sinking in until it scraped the coldness of the dirt beneath. Opening his mouth to cry, he tasted his own foul mistake. He gagged and choked. When she pulled James over to the belt, it was almost a relief because he knew what to do. Lowering his pants, he watched through his tears as she doubled the belt in her fist.

Eventually, James just didn't feel it anymore. That was always the good part, when his entire body went numb.

When she was through, James started to pull up his pants, but before he had a chance, she grabbed the tether and began dragging him toward the stairs. He tripped behind her, finally losing his pants completely, and emerged half-naked into the bright sunlight. "Mom!" he said, trying not to yell; she hated yelling. "Mom, my pants!"

She swung the tether in a wide arc and James went flying. She stopped when she ran him into a tree. "This is where you do your business, here!" she cried. She came at James, put her hands on his bare skin, pushed him into a squat on the grass. "Here! Do it here!"

"But Mom—"

"Do it now!"

James didn't know what to do. He didn't know where to run. He was bound to her and there was nowhere else to go. There was only her and she seemed to be growing bigger by the second.

So James did the only thing he could do. He peed as hard as he could. He peed out of fear and fury and an overwhelming sense that if he didn't, he'd be killed. She'd pull up on that tether and dangle him by the choke collar and all the air would rush out of his lungs.

Gasping, James woke up, sitting in his bed, his pajamas and sheets drenched, and he knew it was more than sweat. He knew, because this wasn't the first time. It hadn't been the first time in a long time. Waiting a moment, panting, James' eyes desperately tried to adjust to the darkness, drinking in the sparse light from the bathroom. Then he reached over and switched on the bedside lamp.

After cleaning up, after a shower and fresh sheets and pajamas, James settled back down again. But he left the light on. And until he fell asleep again, until his eyes dropped of their own accord and he wasn't even aware of it, James watched the walls, watched all the pendulums moving, back and forth, so slow and steady, and he breathed quietly along with them.

CHAPTER EIGHTEEN:

KISS SO BLACK
The Acorn Clock's Story

The picture in my grandmother's clock always calls and so I slip in and tell myself the tale that is mine, an epic that just grows inside me until I have to say the words out loud to move my own story, my own life, forward. It's my voice that makes it real, just for a little while. "Your face slices into the open air," I say, "the water crashing like a mirror with splinters of bright glass flying everywhere, sounding and flashing like crystal, and the air is cold enough to make you gasp. You tread water and wipe your eyes and then you see the warm little white house and you decide it's time to go home—"

My mother's voice dashes into me like the prism-blue water in the picture, that beautiful picture painted on the rounded belly of my grandmother's figure-8 clock. "Oh, fucking Jesus, I thought I took care of this. Amy Sue, are you at it again?"

I blink. Pulling my gaze away from the blue and the green and the warm white house with the yellow door is like lifting my body, cooled and wet, my limbs heavy with the hug of the resisting water, onto the pebble beach. I don't want to leave, but I look at my mother. She stands in the doorway of the living room, her hip cocked, a cigarette lit and dangling from her lower lip. I tug my sleeves down to my wrists, check the tiny buttons, just in case.

My mother sucks smoke, then crosses over and grabs the clock off the mantel. I wince as she jams it under her arm, the way she used to carry my cat when he tossed another hairball. She always threw him outside until he never came back and I reach out to rescue the clock as she walks by. It only takes a second for her cigarette to touch the back of my hand. I jerk away.

Trailing her into the kitchen, I press my lips against the burned skin, cooling it. "I was just putting the clock back on the mantel," I say, muffled. She ignores me so I put my hand behind my back and speak more clearly. "What was it doing in the kitchen anyway?"

She sets the clock on the counter by the back door. "I'm sick of you mooning over it, talking to yourself like a fucking looney. It's going out in the trash tonight."

"What?" I take a step toward the clock and she instantly gets between me and the counter. No matter which way I move, she's there, blowing smoke in my face, making my eyes water. The ash from her cigarette drops and we both look down, but I'm wearing shoes this time. She jolts forward, aiming for my cheek, but I duck away. "The clock's outta here," she says. "And your looney tunes are over." She laughs.

I don't find it funny. I don't find anything she says funny. "Mom, you can't get rid of that clock! It was Grandma's! It might even be worth something."

"This old piece of junk?" She turns and nudges it closer to the edge and I cringe, waiting for a crash of shattered glass and chimes. "Nah, nothing your grandma had was worth much. Not a damn thing." The clock teeters, but my mother stops and steps away. Then she brushes her hands together, like she's cleaning them or she's done a good job at something. "What are you doing down here anyway? Get your little blonde ass upstairs and do your homework." She starts digging through the fridge.

I look at the clock and long to just shove my mother out of the way, grab it and run, but I know that won't work. She'd catch me and break it and break me too. But there's no way that clock's going out in the garbage. I try to toss it a promise and then I run upstairs to my room.

I have no homework and even if I did, I wouldn't do it. Not now. I turn on my computer and glare at the monitor, willing it to boot up faster. Eventually, it goes through its color contortions and dings and rings and then I'm on the net and looking for his email and it's there and before I even finish reading it, his Instant Message box flies open to me on the screen and his welcome shouts all the way across the country.

"{{{{{AMY SUE!!!!!}}}}}"

Those little brackets mean the world and I accept my online hug as if it was his own arms around me, wrapping me so tight, I can't breathe, and I pound in my return message, adding kisses which I picture as a wet twisting of tongues and lips:

"******{{{{{{MARCUS!!!!}}}}}*****"

"Howzzit goin, girlfriend?" he asks.

"Terrible," I answer, then fill him in on my mother's latest. "That clock wz my grandmother's," I type. "And I luv it. Gramma and I told stories about its picture. But she died and it's MINE."

"It'll B OK, baby," he says. "Really. I'll get u another 1. I'll look on eBay."

I smile. Marcus is so sweet. I've known him for about six months now and he's the closest thing to a boyfriend I've ever had. He says he loves me and I know I love him. He's from Vermont, out in the middle of nowhere, he says. I tell him he's never been to What Cheer, Iowa.

"BRB," Marcus says, "thirsty."

"K," I type, then read his email. He writes like poetry and there's three paragraphs of nothing but I love you's, in all caps, in bold, in italics, in six different kinds of fonts. Rolled and scrolled together like a thought that never leaves his mind. And he says by next week, he should be able to buy himself a bus ticket. I close my eyes and pray it's one way so he never leaves me once he's really here and his brackets turn to real live hugs in his real live arms. I set my computer to printing. I want to read his email again tonight before I fall asleep.

Under the sheets, in the dark, I'll wonder if he'll do the things he says he's going to do.

"BAK!" he announces and I type in a smiley face. Then he says, "Could u use sum luvin? Make u feel better? Cuz I'm burnin 4 u, girl."

"Wait," I answer, then go stand by my doorway. I can smell supper and there's clattering going on in the kitchen, so I figure I'm safe. I shut my door as quietly as possible and push the little button that locks it. I hope the click doesn't echo over the pots and pans, bringing my mother banging at my door, demanding what I'm doing in my very own room. It's my room, I always want to tell her. I'll do as I please here. But I know I can't, it's her roof I'm under and no place is truly mine.

Then I sit back down at the computer. "K," I type. I unbutton my jeans and slip my hand inside.

A few weeks ago, Marcus suggested cybersex. I laughed at first, told him I was a virgin, online and live, inside and out, and he told me how perfect that made me, how that made me his and nobody else's. He told me to sit back and touch myself, like he somehow knew I did in my room at night, and he would type things that he wanted to do to me and I should read them and see if they made me feel real good. And they did. Now I watch the words continually scroll across my monitor and I think about his tongue and his fingers and his dick and my own hand moves faster and then for a moment, I have to shut my eyes, shut out his words, and just fall into the throb and the heat of it. Then I lean forward and type, interrupting his stream, and I say, "Marcus, O, Marcus, get here soon!"

"Cumming," he answers.

Under my blanket that night, I read Marcus' email and count the I love you's. I keep coming up with 648. I count until almost two o'clock, knowing my parents are usually unconscious by then. I heard my father take out the trash at about ten and I cried, thinking of that clock all crunched together with my mom's cigarette butts and their bottles and cans and what was left of our supper.

Slipping out of bed, I carefully open the door to my room. The hallway is dark and there's no light in the crack under my parents' door. I sneak by and down, then let myself out the back. Running to the end of our alley, I start digging through our trash. The clock is at the bottom of the nastiest heap and I scoop it out, give it a quick hug, then carefully retie and replace the garbage bag.

Back up in my room, I turn on my bedside light. The clock isn't too bad, I just grab some tissues and wipe it off. Then I pull a box out from under my bed. It's full of all the things I've kept from school, rescued from my mother, artwork and journals and papers with good grades. I dump all of it into my backpack and then carefully place the clock inside the box.

Trailing my fingers over the picture of the lake and the long stringy hair of the willow tree, I half-shut my eyes. "You sit under the tree, reading poetry," I say. "It's spring and it smells warm and there's just a little bit of a breeze blowing through your hair." I touch the little red boat on the lake. "Then Marcus comes in his boat. He sails to you and you smile and put down your book. He steps through the cat tails and the sun is in his brown hair and you know he's smiling just for you. He comes over and takes your book away. He kisses you, leaning you back until you're flat on the grass. Then he tells you it's time to come home, to that little white house in the woods, it's time to come home to him."

I pat the face of the clock before shutting the lid and carefully sliding the box under my bed. It's safe now and I know I can sleep.

The next day after school, I sit on the floor of my room and sift through all the emails I've received from Marcus. My computer hums quietly, the screen sending shivers of rainbow light over my printed pages. Marcus isn't on, but I know he has a basketball game today and so he'll be late.

My clock barely peeks out from under my bed, just enough so that I can see the little picture. If my mother comes up, I can shove the box under before she sees it. She's downstairs, like usual, and I was able to sneak by without her noticing. Her music blasts from the stereo, some loud hard rock junk that I just can't stand. She still uses record albums, her groups are so old. I know without looking that she's lying on the couch, one hand thrown over her eyes, the other dangling her cigarette over all the scorch marks in the carpet, and she's "singing" along with the noise. Sometimes she nabs me and makes me sit and listen, as if I'll learn something from those lyrics. Sometimes she kneels in front of me and spits the words right in my face, as if she's trying to pound inside my head whatever it is she wants me to learn.

And sometimes, she does just that.

I always cross my fingers and wish on the way home. I wish she's gone. I wish she was killed in a car crash, burning every inch of skin on her body with spots of scorch like the spots of a leopard, and I wish she didn't die immediately. And I wish for my dad to be there too, all folded up in the glove compartment.

I shudder and look at the clock. I hate when I think things like that.

Concentrating on the picture, I say, "You're sitting on the porch of the house." For a moment, I wonder if my mother would be different on a porch like this one. It's wooden and white and I imagine wicker rockers and tall glasses of lemonade or iced tea. But that would need a mom in an apron, or at least with a smile, and that's not my mom. It would mean a mom who loves me and she's not that either.

She says when she found out she was pregnant with me, the doctor said she had to quit smoking and drinking. Low birth weight, he said, birth defects. My dad never makes my mom do anything, but somehow he made her quit for those nine months and she says it was the worst hell of her life. And that when I was born, I made the hell stay. No sleep, she said, have to change the baby, feed the baby, shake rattles in its face. Dress it right, send it to school, go to parent-teacher conferences. Always something for the baby.

My mom still smokes and drinks now, she always has, so I don't keep her from that anymore. But she says I keep her from herself. Even though I don't want her. I don't want her at all.

I shake my head and refocus on the picture. The white wooden porch with no mom at all, just me. "It's fall and the leaves are beginning to come down. You look at them and think of the colors, naming them out loud. Burnt orange and cinnamon, honey gold and deep, deep russet. And you think about how the world outside this house is like a poem or a picture you'd like to paint. The lake is still blue, but a cloudier blue with the coming of fall, as if it's preparing for the frozen white surface of winter. The willow leaves are yellow, a yellow like sunshine, reminding you of afternoons under the curtain of soft branches in the highest heat of the summer." I glance up at the computer, in case I missed Marcus' arrival, but he's still not there. "And inside, sitting at a rolltop desk that he built himself, is Marcus, working on a poem just for you. For a book he's writing, a book about you, another book for the bestseller list." I stop and smile.

I only recently included Marcus in my clock world, the world my grandmother introduced me to. First, it was my grandmother and me, then it was just me, but it was still perfect, the silence and the lake, the spring and summer winds through the willow branches, the little boat where I lay back and studied the sky full of stars on long fall nights. But after Marcus and I became lovers, I decided I didn't want to be alone there. It was even more perfect with him. He would spend his days writing and I would spend mine painting. And the nights were just for each other.

"You wish you could paint everything you see this afternoon," I say and my fingers twitch. I think about taking an art class. I can take one elective next year when I start high school.

Sorting through Marcus' emails, I find one of his first, where he described himself to me. "I'm just under 6 ft," he wrote, "so I'm not very tall. Not as tall as girls usually like anyway, but I'm tall enough 2 play a decent game of b-ball. I play pretty much every day and my team's not 2 bad, especially 4 freshmen. I've got brown hair and I wear it long, usually pulled back in a ponytail. Brown eyes 2. I'm in pretty good shape, since I'm an athlete. I luv poetry. Maybe I'll write u a poem someday. A luv poem. I know I already feel something 4 u."

I met Marcus in a chatroom for fans of boy bands. I loved being in that chatroom because I was like everyone else and it felt like no matter what I did, I had friends who were like me. And then Marcus showed up and he was the only boy there and at first, none of us knew what to do. But he seemed to really like music and he knew a lot about it too. He started emailing me and then IMing and then he just became a part of my life.

My computer creaks like a door and when I look up, there's Marcus. Quickly, I put his emails into my clock box and gently put it back under my bed. Then I run to the computer just as his IM floods my screen.

"{{{{Amy Sue!!!!!}}}}}"

I notice his use of lower case instead of all caps and I respond in kind.

"******{{{{{Marcus!!!! }}}}}*****"

Sometimes, he's a little low-key, a little serious, and I'm afraid I'm not smart enough for a poet. I wonder why he never includes kisses in his greetings, but then I push it out of my mind. He kisses me often enough when we're making love.

"Guess what, baby?" he writes. "I bought my bus tickets! C u this weekend!"

I stop and I stare and then I read those words again. I've been waiting for them, waiting forever, but now that they're here, I can hardly believe what I see in Marcus' italicized gothic font. I tap the screen to make sure it's real, the way I pinch myself sometimes to stay awake in school. "Wow, that's GR8!" I type. "Now I just have 2 figure out how 2 c u."

He's quiet for a moment, then he says, "Well, u better! I'm coming all this way! I get there Fri nite at 10. Can't u sneak out? Tell a friend 2 cover 4 u."

I shake my head. "There's nobody," I type. "I kind of stick 2 myself. There's stuff I don't want people 2 c." I think of my arms and tug my sleeves down to my wrists. I glance at the back of my hand.

He's quiet again and when he stays quiet too long, I get scared. I can't lose him. "I'll find a way, Marcus," I type. "I LUV U!"

"I luv u 2," he says right away. "I can't wait 2 c u. 2 hold u. Will u show me the stuff u don't want others 2 c?"

I think about that. I think about how we make love and how, when we see each other for real, there won't be a computer screen between us. If we really truly make love, the way he says we will, then I'll have to be naked. Completely. And it might not be dark.

"Amy Sue?"

"Yes," I type. "Yes, I'll show u. But Marcus?" I stop. I don't know how to ask and Marcus' question mark appears like a black snake on my screen. "Marcus, I might need it 2 B dark that 1st time."

He types in a smiley face, then says, "OK w/me, baby. All that matters is that I can have my arms around u. I'll B able 2 feel u, even if it's in the dark."

For some reason, I begin to cry. I'm glad he can't see me.

"Make sure u meet me at 10," he says. "The bus lets me off at the intersection of Main St. and Cheerful Ave. By some restaurant. Do u know where the station is?"

I laugh, which makes the tears start to go away. "LOL! This is What Cheer, remember? The bus just stops at a parking lot downtown, at the Tick-Tock Quick-Stop Restaurant. Really. Where r u going 2 stay? There's no hotels here."

The next face he types uses an O for the mouth, so big and gaping like he's finally realized he's coming from the middle of nowhere to an even bigger middle of nowhere. From zip to zip. To find me. "I'll figure out something. Maybe I'll sneak into yr house and sleep in yr bed w/u."

The thought of him here makes me shake. I picture my mother, on the other side of the locked door, screaming and swearing while Marcus takes me for the first time. I picture myself yelling, "He loves me, Mom! He loves me!" while he covers my face with kisses and then I can't yell anymore because he's kissing me on the mouth, hard, his tongue sliding around mine. I squirm in my seat, then type, "That would B 1derful, if u cd. But I don't think so."

"You know what I'd do if I cd? If I cd get u there, in yr own bed?"

"What?"

"Sit back, baby, and lemme tell u. But this time, if u can, type in when yr cumming, so that I know. So that I know I've got u. And maybe I can cum at the same time."

And I do. We make it together and it's the best feeling I've ever had.

"Mom?" I say at supper that night. It's just take-out, Dad stopped by the restaurant on his way home. "There's a dance at school on Friday night." There is too and I try to remember the theme. "They're calling it Spring Fling."

She grunts, then goes back to shoving potatoes around her plate. I glance over at my dad and he looks at me while he chews on a drumstick so I point my words at him. "Can I go?"

He nods toward my mother. She leans back in her chair. "Spring Fling, huh?" she says. "How cute."

I swallow. "I can't help what they call it."

"I suppose some young stud is taking you."

My father freezes in mid-chew. But I shake my head so he looks away. "Just a bunch of girls I've been hanging with. And we thought…we thought we might stay over at someone's house, if that's okay. Not here, I mean. A sleepover."

She lights a cigarette. I watch the tip flame up, then soften to that orange glow. I know that glow is even hotter than the flame. I know that for a fact. She inhales deeply, then releases a stream of smoke through her nose. I wonder if that burns too. "Yeah, go," she says. "Maybe your dad and I can get it on without you here. Give us a night of ro-mance." She bats her eyes at my father and smiles, her lips stretched so wide, I wonder if her face will split. "How's that, honey-babe?" she says, reaching under the table and doing something that makes him squeal like a pig. He grins back at her and I leave the table in a hurry.

I should've known. When you barely exist, it's easy to sneak away.

I hang at the dance for a while, so if my mom asks later, I can say I was there. Though she probably won't care. Besides, there's nothing else to do until ten o'clock when Marcus' bus arrives.

I watch the kids dance, some doing pretty good, others just jumping and wiggling and shaking their arms. I wonder which I would look like if I got up to dance. A couple boys ask me and I say no. Nicely, though. But I'm taken. Marcus is coming.

At nine-thirty, I go into the girls' restroom to brush my hair and check myself out before the walk to the bus stop. I'm thinking I look pretty good. I pulled on my low-riding flares, light blue, and I've got on a pink long-sleeved t-shirt that says Angel Baby. Marcus always calls me baby, so I think he'll like it. I brush my hair, smoothing the waves over my shoulders and wish for the thousandth time that I had dark straight hair. Serious hair. Not this goofy baby fuzz cheerleader hair. I cross my eyes and stick out my tongue at my reflection.

A girl behind me laughs and I see her in the mirror. She grins at me and pats her own hair, dark black and stick-straight. "Hello, Blondie," she says. She thwacks me on the head with flicked fingers. "Little Miss Fucking Curly Locks."

I step away.

She flicks me again. Her fingernails are sharp and they flash black in the air. "You can change it, you know."

I look at her, but I don't say anything. I don't know what she wants. Her hair is really, really dark. It's like the night in March in the middle of nowhere, Iowa.

She touches the ends, like she knows what I'm thinking. "It's a dye job. And I straighten it. I'm just as blonde as you, really." She vamps, flips her hair between twisted fingers. "You'd never know, wouldja? Little Blonde Bimbo Babe. Better not tell anyone."

I know who she is. Her name is Reggie, though she was Regina in grade school. I remember her from kindergarten and she was blonder than me, almost white, her hair poofed around her head like a halo. She's pretty tough now, hangs with the rougher crowd. I look at her baggy jeans and black leather shirt, ripped out at the elbows.

She shoves her sleeves up with those pointy nails. "Bet you'd never change it though. You're too chickenshit. Little Yellow Chickie Hair. You're Amy Sue Dander, right?"

I turn back to the mirror, not sure if I should be flattered that she knows my name. My hair has frizzed out already, lifting off my shoulders like a fluffy yellow dandelion.

"You wanna blow this action?" Reggie says, looking at my reflection over my shoulder. "It bites the bag. My friends and I are heading out to this place we have in the middle of Old Man Yanker's cornfield."

I flush with pleasure at the invitation, but hesitate a second, wondering if there's enough time before Marcus, wondering why she's asking me. But then I shake my head. "I can't. I have to meet this guy."

She shrugs. "See, I told you. Chickenshit. Later, Bimbo Babe." She flicks me one more time, her fingernail catching one strand and yanking it from my scalp. I flinch, but refuse to let my eyes shine with tears.

After she leaves, I take a deep breath and smooth my hair one more time. I look at my bellybutton and think about a ring and I wonder if Reggie has one. Then I shake the thought away and head out. The noise of the dance smacks at my ears and I see Reggie and a bunch of black-clad kids leave through the back door of the gym. I go out the front.

The further I move from the school, the quieter it gets. Downtown What Cheer is dead at night, no stores stay open, even the restaurant closes at nine. There are no cars. Walking toward the stop, I think about actually seeing Marcus, seeing his real smile, not a computer emoticon, and then feeling his very real arms around me. I'm not sure where we're going to go…but I don't care. We'll be together. It's warm enough tonight, I could just take him to the park. There's a shed, all the kids use it. Or even back to the dance. I wonder if I could find Reggie in the middle of a cornfield.

There's a bench outside the restaurant and so I sit down. I cross my legs this way and that, settle my arms on my lap, then on the back of the bench. I wish I could see what I look like.

I hear a rumble and I see headlights coming down the way. Standing up, I clear my throat, then quickly smooth my hair, tug down my shirt, check my sleeves. The bus pulls up and the door opens. One man gets out and I look behind him for Marcus. But there's nobody. The driver waves, then shuts the door and pulls away.

No Marcus.

The tears well up again and I look at the man, standing there. He hasn't moved. He's wearing an old letter jacket and I see a red W on it. But it looks like he can't snap it shut anymore. He turns for just a second, to check out the names on the street signs. And I see his brown ponytail.

He looks at me and smiles. I step backwards. "Amy Sue?" he says. "Baby? Is that you?"

"Marcus?" He has to be about forty years old.

"Yes, it's me!" He reaches toward me, but I dodge away. "Amy Sue? What's the matter?"

"You can't be Marcus!" I blurt out. I move around, put the bench between us. "Marcus is a freshman, he plays basketball!"

"Oh, Amy Sue." Marcus sits down on the bench. "You misunderstood. I'm a teacher, I teach freshmen, and I coach basketball at my school, Burlington West. I thought you knew."

I stare. I think about all I've told him, all we've done together. I look at his hair, trailing down his back. He removes his hat and I see a bald spot. "I'm sorry," I whisper.

His arm dangles over the bench back, his fingers stretching toward me. "Well, it doesn't have to be bad, does it? We're still friends. I'm still Marcus, you're still Amy Sue. I'm just…not what you pictured. But we've shared a lot of things."

I nod.

"Look, come sit down. We'll just sit here and talk. Unless we can get some coffee." He motions toward the restaurant.

"It's closed."

He blinks. "You're kidding. Is there a Starbucks?"

I laugh. "Welcome to What Cheer, Marcus. Home of the Big Lie. It's not cheerful at all."

He laughs too and I feel a little better, so I sit down and we talk.

And he *is* Marcus. He's just like he was online, only older. And he looks different. But his laugh is there, and his smile, and his voice is as low as a lullaby. If I close my eyes, I can still picture him, the Marcus I knew online, and he had that voice, so soft when he called me baby. He begins to recite a poem, a poem he wrote for me, and it's full of those low sounds, soft s's and f's, and I close my eyes and sink into it, like the lake on my grandmother's clock.

"What is it, baby?" he asks.

I open my eyes and see him.

"So how is your mom?" he asks. "You got out of there okay?"

"She thinks I'm at a school dance." I shrug. "And then I'm supposed to be going to stay at a friend's house for a sleepover."

He reaches forward, touches my hand. "I wish I could get you out of there, Amy Sue," he says. "You don't deserve to be there. You deserve to be someplace warm and safe, where you can do what you want, be what you want. You shouldn't ever be hurt."

I feel the tears again, but I blink them away. Or I try to. But then they come too fast for me to stop. He's saying just what I wanted Marcus to say.

"Amy Sue?" He leans forward, touches my cheek. I watch as he puts his fingertips to his mouth, tastes my tears. Then he presses his forehead to mine. I start to pull away, but his hands steady my shoulders and I stay. "Show me," he whispers. "Amy Sue, show me the stuff you don't want others to see."

I swallow, then reach down and tug back my sleeves. Under the streetlight, my skin shines, spotted and scabbed, and he gasps. Then he takes one of my arms and he holds it, supports it, one hand at my elbow, one at my wrist.

When he begins to kiss my arm, I close my eyes. I know exactly where he is, which scar or scab or scorch his lips touch. When he starts on my other arm, I begin to tremble.

"I want to make it better," he says, putting his face against mine again. He kisses my lips and for a moment, I respond. "I love you, Amy Sue."

I remember then who he is and who I thought he was and though I don't want to, I jerk back. He's old enough to be my father. He sighs and leans away and my body cools without him. "I'm sorry," he says.

We don't say anything for a moment, and then I pull my sleeves back down. "It's okay," I whisper. Then I look at my watch.

Marcus stretches and stands up. "Guess we better start thinking of a place to stay." He doesn't look at me, but I know what he's thinking. And I'm not sure what to do. What it is I want.

"I'll show you where the park is," I say. "There's a shed there, everyone knows about it. It's for the maintenance man, but he keeps a cot in there and he takes naps. We…or you…can probably sleep there. He doesn't work on the weekends."

"It's not locked?"

"It's been busted for years."

We start to move down the sidewalk. He takes my hand and I don't pull away. It feels sort of good. He has a big hand and it's warm. "I might just head home then," I say. "I don't know."

He doesn't answer and I wonder if he heard me. As we walk, I look up at the sky. The stars are bright, like spring makes them new too, like the green grass and flowers. Marcus looks up as well. "It's beautiful, isn't it?" he says. "I like the Iowa sky."

"What's the Vermont sky like?" I ask.

"Closer," he says. "Closer and wider, with just a streak of classic rock." That's just the sort of thing Marcus would say, something that I don't quite understand, but that sounds pretty anyway. He moves steadily beside me and his hip bumps into mine every few steps. Then he slips his arm around me and though I hesitate, I put my arm around him too. We fit and for a moment, I'm happy.

We walk through the park and I point out the duck pond, the playground, the sandpit where I used to play for hours. I take him the long way, trying to give myself some time, trying to figure out what to do. We get to the shed and I open the door. The moonlight falls in, letting in just enough light to see the shape of a cot. "Well, this is it," I say. "It's not a hotel, but it's What Cheer's finest."

Marcus laughs, sets his backpack down on the floor. He turns to me and he waits.

I hesitate. I want to kiss him, but I don't. If I close my eyes and he kisses me, he'll be my Marcus again. But every time I look, it'll be this man. "I…I don't know. I guess I'll see you tomorrow, okay? Just stay around here somewhere and I'll find you."

He reaches for me. I close my eyes, give in this time, drown myself in it, smell the old leather of his jacket, feel the warmth and strength of his arms. I kiss him for just a moment, feel his lips open, then the warm wet lick of his tongue. And I keep my eyes closed and open my mouth.

That's when he grabs my sleeve.

I try to pull away. He kisses harder, his teeth scrape against my lips, my tongue, and I hear him moan, guttural replacing soft. With his foot, he shuts the door and then he lowers me onto the cot.

And that's when I know what's going to happen. I try to scream, but he keeps my mouth covered with his, kissing me harder and deeper, a kiss so black, I feel like I'm falling into that March sky. His hands push my shirt up, my jeans down, and I feel him full against me. Then he rears back, his hand over my mouth, and he says, "It's dark, Amy Sue, like you said you wanted. I want to make it better, baby."

His mouth comes back over mine and he shoves my legs apart. I scream, scream as loud as I can into the cave of his mouth and I hear it echo down his throat, down to his stomach, battering his insides as he enters me. And I don't know what else to do, so I scream and scream and scream. Filling him. Filling him with my noise and my pain as he fills me.

The sun is just starting to come up when I let myself in the house. I try to walk quietly up the stairs, but I'm so tired, I stumble. When I reach my bed, I fall in and begin to cry. I put my hand over my crotch, where I'm so sore and my panties are stiff with blood and I don't know how to make the pain go away.

My door opens and when I look up, my mother stands above me. "Mom," I choke out. "Mom?"

She looks at me, takes me in, lying there crying with my hand in my crotch. Her nose twitches and she frowns and I think she smells my blood. Then she slowly raises both her arms above her head. I watch each finger, both thumbs, one right after the other, curl in and form fists. And then she brings them down in an avalanche.

I try to roll away, but she climbs on me, straddles me, and there is no escape.

There is no escape.

And I open my mouth and scream again, this time into my room, as empty and futile as in the shed, my voice swallowed by Marcus' mouth.

I scream until there is no voice, I have no voice, no body, no me. I'm gone. I'm just gone. I close my eyes and wait for it to be over.

When she leaves, when it's been quiet for a while, I slide onto the floor, next to my bed. Carefully, I pull out the box. I lean back and stare at the belly of the clock, at the softly painted picture. I trace it all with my finger. I have no voice, but my raw lips move anyway, and in my head, I hear myself, a whisper.

"You come out of the house and stretch, lifting your hands as high to the sky as you can. The willow tree's branches weave into each other in the wind and the tips seem to curl and flick, waving at you. You look down at the lake, the blue scalloped with waves, and it all seems to beckon. And you answer. Like you've always wanted to do. You answer. Walking to the lake, you stop for a minute to pat the little red boat. You leave your favorite book of poetry there, resting on the seat, the oars crossed over the bow. And then you walk into the lake, feeling the warm water rise and touch, rise and swallow you down.

"And you drown. You drown and you drown and you drown. And you are so happy."

Carefully, I fold the clock in my arms, bring it to my chest, and hug it as tightly as I dare. I close my eyes and dream of this place, dream where I can be happy, where all is warmth and water and blue and green and gold. And there is no one else but me in my clock and water world.

No one at all.

CHAPTER NINETEEN

JAMES

And so she left with her softness and curves and smooth as silk skin, and things return to your kind of normal. A world focused on clocks, on their hearts and minds and their need to be cared for. And like before, clocks don't raise much of a fuss in your life. As long as you keep them wound and cleaned and balanced, they're happy, and as long as they're happy, you're happy.

Except now it seems like you never were. You try to remember when.

The only voice in the house is yours when you murmur to the clocks, or when you specify directions to the tourists. The tourists' voices ring out from time to time, and then all falls silent again. There's no melodic voice, singing your one-syllable name in a variety of octaves, soprano for excitement, alto for serious conversation, tenor for that certain invitation to bed. And bass for the guttural sighs experienced there. And as for warmth, well, the sheets have never been so cold.

Your normal life no longer seems so normal. Your normal life now seems empty. Even though you never expected to receive such a gift as a partner and a lover, even though you never expected that gift to stay, there is a new hollow in your life. A hollow that echoes with the experiences of intimacy in all its forms. You tell yourself to fill that hollow with clocks. Because, after all, clocks never hurt you. That's why you fell in love with them in the first place.

Fell in love. Imagine.

Climbing unknowingly onto the five steps of grief, you argue your way through self-righteous denial—*she'll be back*—and then get hung up forever on anger, leaving the other three steps unmounted. How could she do this? She knew you, she knew everything about you, everything you dared tell. And there are things that you don't dare tell, but how can you ever give voice to that? It seems to you now that all women bring hurt and desertion with them, even as they bring soft skin and soft voices and love.

So you stay in anger. And who could possibly blame you? How could anyone expect anything else but a constant flow of rage through you, recycled over and over again through the beat of your own heart and all the years of your life.

But only you know the full map of that flow. That river. Thunderstorms of fear fill your river of anger, and that in turn empties into the ocean hidden away in the deepest part of you. That profound sadness. Imagine all the blue and all the shades and all the salt. At times, you feel that you're drowning.

How can any woman change the direction of that river, alter the logic of geography? How can any clock? Only an earthquake can change the current, and only for just a little while. Then back to the same path through worn-out and eroded banks. The force of an earthquake is no match for the depth of an ocean.

Imagine.

James knew what it was like to wake in the night and gasp for air, pulling away from that drowning ocean. And he dreamed that he could turn away from it, step out and shake himself dry in the sunshine, by surrounding himself with all that he loved, all the clocks of the world, and by caring for them. The comfort of that sound first heard in the dark of a root cellar multiplied itself by the hundreds and James couldn't imagine a life without the steady tick, the constant reminder that something else was out there. He wasn't alone, even when nothing else breathed next to him.

And as time went by and Diana became more and more of a vapor, he couldn't dream of a life with another person either. Surrounding himself with that person and caring for her, and she caring for him. The comfort. It was a fairytale, mostly dimly remembered, and then with a stunning clarity at times, when he threw himself out of the ocean in the middle of the night, gasping, and remembered the calming stroke of a palm, the whisper of a breath in his ear. But then there was nothing but the ticking of clocks and he had to reach for them again. Reach for them for years.

Now imagine there is nothing to hear.

Nothing.

Imagine.

Standing by his car, James tried to feel that it was right for him to go. He had his back to the house, to all the clocks, and he wondered if Cooley was truly up to the task, if Ione would be able to handle it if he was gone far into next week. It was Saturday morning and he planned to make the five-hour drive in one fell swoop. The appointment at the clinic was early Monday, which gave James Sunday to get his bearings and look around. With the car at the ready, though, it felt different. Cooley gently placed his suitcase in the trunk; his maps were in the front seat, courtesy of Neal. And suddenly, James wondered if he should leave on Sunday instead. Sunday night. Maybe even the middle of the night so that he would arrive just in time for the appointment. And then turn right around and come back home, before anything had a chance to go wrong, before the clocks stopped, before they learned to live without him.

Trying to shake this off, trying to remind himself that he needed the time to relax before the appointment, and that if he came home right after, he wouldn't be able to see the Time Museum, James walked around the car, checking the tires, wiping the mirrors and brake lights. His worries switched to driving without being able to hear. How would he hear sirens or if the car was making an odd sound? The night before, Ione argued with the others, waving her arms around, insisting that someone needed to accompany James to Chicago. He could tell what she was saying by her flushed cheeks and her busy hands, pointing first to Dr. Owen, then to Gene, to Neal. For a while, she even patted her own chest and James wondered what it would be like to go to the Time Museum with a woman armed with a purple feather duster. "Ione," he said then. "You're not going with me. You're needed here."

They all stopped and stared then, for a blank-faced moment before their mouths burst into rapid flapping. Dr. Owen grabbed the notebook and wrote, "James! You can hear?"

"Of course not," he said. "I just figured out what you were talking about. I have to go to Chicago. I can't hear. You're all thinking that I shouldn't travel by myself."

Dr. Owen started to write something, but then he just nodded. Ione sat down. Cooley's legs stretched like sticks on the floor, her back in a corner, her hands folded neatly in her lap. She watched the adult faces as they spoke and from time to time, she glanced at James. When she did and she caught him watching, she smiled.

"Look," James said. "I'm sure other deaf people drive. It's not like I'm blind."

They all said something, but it was Dr. Owen with the notebook. He wrote while they talked, then handed the notebook over. "I'm sure you can drive, James," he said. "Your other senses have probably become a lot more acute. While you're driving, make sure you check your mirrors constantly. And trust what you feel in the vibration of the car. You'll feel it through your wrists and fingers on the steering wheel, through your legs and hips for the engine and tires." So the good doctor could lecture on car anatomy too.

James nodded, then announced it was time for them to go. He needed sleep if he was to make the drive alone. Trying to feel like he had everything under control, James assigned tasks. Ione was watching the Home during the weekdays and Neal would be in and out to check on her. Molly was a backup for Ione, should Ione be needed somewhere else and then Gene would check on her. Cooley would be in after school to work with the clocks. If James was still gone by the next weekend, Ione and Cooley would work together, with Ione focusing on the visitors and Cooley on the clocks. James hoped their two sets of eyes could do what he'd been doing for years. They needed to be everywhere at once.

Before she left, Cooley stopped by James' side. She had the notebook. "I cud go w/U," she said. "I cud miss school."

James frowned at her and shut the notebook. It was all the answer she needed. He felt the force of her footsteps through the floorboards.

Now he turned back to the house, wondering if he should go through one more time, check the pendulums, check the hands, make sure all was well. He thought about taking a clock or two, placing them beside him on the passenger seat to keep him company, but he worried that the jarring of the road could knock them out of whack. James faced the car again, reached in the open window and touched the steering wheel, warm from the sun, and he told himself this was his chance to be on his own again, to make his own decisions and be his own companion. He'd come to realize that these people cared, but that didn't make him relish their company all that much more. Though at times, it was nice to have them around to talk to.

James hoped that in the silence of the car and in the strange hotel room, his mother would return to her grave. Maybe in new surroundings, she would finally leave him alone.

He opened the car door and looked up. Cooley was in the house somewhere and Dr. Owen, Neal and Ione stood on the porch. They shouted something and smiled, so James waved. Then he started the engine. He could tell it was running by the vibration and he thought maybe Dr. Owen was right. Driving off, he resisted the urge to look back through the rearview mirror. He knew they were all waving. He knew the clocks inside continued on their way. Some, he thought, might have a worried sound in their mechanisms, a pause in the pendulum, a shriller sound to the chime. He told himself they would be all right. In his head, his voice was unsure and hollow.

James always enjoyed driving, enjoyed the silence and the easy motion. But the silence was truly deep this time and he found himself straining to hear anything, the smallest of noises. He turned the radio on, hoped, and heard nothing. James never played the radio in the car, other than when he had to listen for Iowa's many weather bulletins, but now he found himself wishing he could turn the radio down because it was too loud. He wanted something to be too loud again. Something other than the silence and his own thoughts. Other than his mother's voice.

He began talking to himself, reciting the sounds he missed. He could feel his lips move and the slight burn of words in his throat. "The trees are moving and I have to keep straightening the wheel," he said. "It must be windy. There is the whoosh of the wind pressing up against the windows. The engine is humming, my keys are jangling from the ignition." When a truck passed, appearing out of nowhere, James jumped and reminded himself to check the mirrors. "There's a roar," he said and he imagined a lion as the six big wheels tore up the road. He thought he felt the extra vibration through his seat.

His initial thought at lunch was just to go through a drive-through and eat on the road. But when he pulled up to the loudspeaker, he realized he couldn't hear when the people inside were talking, asking what he wanted. "I'm sorry!" James yelled out the window toward the microphone. "I forgot I can't hear. I'll have to come in." When he drove through the checkout, he ducked his head, sure everyone inside was laughing.

He didn't really feel safe until he got to the hotel. Turning on the television, he stretched out on the bed. The faces on the screen, moving and talking and waving their arms in a black silent void, kept him company. He thought about phoning home, to let everyone know he arrived safely and to make sure that everything was okay, but then he realized he wouldn't be able to hear when someone answered.

Restless, James' eyes wandered the walls and he knew he was looking for his clocks. James needed something to watch, something with rhythm. But there was nothing on these walls, nothing but screwed-on scenic paintings and a mirror. James sat up, feeling dizzy, and grabbed onto the bedspread. Planting his feet on the floor, he tried to feel grounded, but things blurred all around. Swinging his head, his eyes darting, James noticed a flash of red and zoomed in on it. It was the radio alarm clock next to the bed and the colon between the hours and minutes flashed the slow beat of seconds passing. Sliding onto the floor, James knelt in front of the bedside table and watched the dots blinking and he put his hand on his chest and felt his heartbeat. Eventually, the room stopped spinning and James' whole world slid down onto those two dots. He controlled his breathing, wiped the cold sweat off his forehead, then climbed back onto the bed. Rolling onto his side, he turned the clock so that he could keep watching it.

It was going to be a long wait until Monday.

Sunday, James ventured out for a little while. Chicago was so big, he shrunk to nothing and didn't go much farther than a couple blocks. Just far enough to find a restaurant. He carried his notebook in case he needed someone to answer a question or give directions.

On the way back to his room after lunch, James spotted an antique store down a side street. Abandoned Here, it was called. James liked the sound of that and so he went inside. A man behind the counter smiled around his cigar and then said something, but James just lifted his hand in a wave. The store was bigger than it looked on the outside and James roamed down the haphazard aisles. There didn't seem to be any left or right, up or down, just aisles spreading this way and that and then intersecting with others. It didn't take too long for James to get lost, but he felt okay. He knew he was in this store and he saw a few clocks and so he knew he was among friends. The aroma of the man's cigar, a rich rum and tobacco smell, followed wherever James went and at times, he took a deep breath and drew it deep into his lungs. James' father used to smoke a cigar and the scent calmed him. He tried smoking one himself when he was seventeen, but he couldn't handle the taste. It was amazing how the taste of something could be so different than the smell. Yet James liked tobacco shops and often stopped in, just to breathe and remember small glimpses of his dad. Sitting in his father's lap, his voice deep around James, reading a story. Playing with James on the nights his mother disappeared, giving him a bath, making bubbles into tall wet hats or fragrant necklaces that dripped down to his chest. Tucking James in at night.

James remembered well the morning his father left, a foggy morning when James was eight years old "I know what happens, son," his father said and he ran his finger around James' throat, touching the latest collar burn. "I'm going to find us a place far away and I'll get it all set up. Then I'll come back for you." He paused for a moment and then answered the question that was held back, incoherent, by a voice choked with little boy tears. "It won't be for much longer. I might have to sell the car to get us somewhere and we'd have to walk to get away and that's just too far for a little guy like you. I'll get as far as I can, then sell the car and walk farther, get us a place, then I'll figure out how to get you."

James wanted to say that he could walk just as far as his father could, that James could run to keep up, and that if he couldn't, he could be carried on his father's shoulders, the way he did sometimes, making James feel tall and strong with his father's body like his own flowing beneath him. But James' voice remained stuck as if he still wore the collar, sealing off his breath. So James just closed his eyes and when he opened them, his father was gone.

James kept waiting for him to come home. All through the progression of collars, from leather to choke, to a cage, a tether, beatings with a brush, then a belt. James was seventeen when his mother told him his dad was dead, struck by a truck as he walked on the side of a highway nine years before, in the early morning when there was a fog. A fog that hid him, kept him from finding a place far away that was safe and quiet, that had no root cellar. James cried and hated crying because he was seventeen and too old for such things, and he told his mother that she lied, that his father was coming back, coming back to get him. She laughed and said he was buried in town, in the little cemetery behind the Catholic church. "Go and see," she said.

"Then why don't I remember a funeral?" James asked.

"I didn't have one," she said. "Just buried him, because I had to. He didn't deserve it, he was running away. What kind of a boy wants a father who leaves him?"

Something in her voice, so deep and derisive, so hateful, made James stand straight that day, straight for the first time in his life, pull all his nearly adult bones in order, throwing off the beaten slump, the rounded shoulders, the lowered head. And he realized he looked down on her. She came to the bottom of his chin. She looked up too, seeming to recognize James' height for the first time, and for a moment, her face changed from its feline sneer to the glistening wide eyes of a rodent. James knew the look, he felt it on his own features often enough, saw it on his face when he combed his hair in the morning before school and found her in his reflection. It was fear. Yet then she slitted her eyes and the cat came back and she silently pointed toward the root cellar.

James hit her. Just once, but he hit her full in the face. It was enough to knock her backwards on the ground and she lay flat on the grass, her nose flowing red over her lips and teeth. And then James left.

It was as easy as that.

So easy that he wondered what force held him, curled in a box in the root cellar, for all those years when all he had to do was take off the collar and run. Run like his father.

His father who was supposed to come back. And save James. It never occurred to James to save himself until the hero was gone. Buried without ceremony in the back of the Catholic church.

And now in this shop, in the middle of Abandoned Here, the cigar smoke wrapped itself around James and he felt his father's hand again covering his own. James welcomed him in, even though he was so, so late.

Turning a corner, James found himself in an aisle that looked familiar and he realized he must have gone in a circle, an odd angled circle. He was about to turn down the opposite way when a movement caught his eye. It was a gold flash, a wave from a bottom shelf and he bent down to look. And he found a skeleton clock.

James didn't like skeleton clocks because of their nakedness, baring everything they had to the world. When he lifted this clock from the shelf, he could see its entire workings; there was no shiny gold or wood skin covering its most private of parts. It was undressed and as such, vulnerable. It was mounted on a black and white marble base and a glass dome fit snugly over it, tucked into grooves in the marble, to protect all the exposed parts from the dust and grime in everyday air. James was always put to mind of strippers when he saw this type of clock, strippers moving on a stage, all the parts undulating and swinging and swaying. James was never in a strip joint, but he could imagine and these clocks left nothing to the imagination.

But this time, when James raised the clock to a higher shelf so it was eye-level, he felt something different. It stood stocky and solid and its plates and metalwork were cut in a gothic cathedral style. Everything was erect in this clock, moving skyward, and James could see every cog and pinion moving, interlocking, pushing the clock's life ahead second by second. The pendulum, round and smooth like a jeweled belly button, swung seriously left to right and James' eyes settled on it and his heart moved with it and in a second, he and the clock were connected.

While this clock was naked, it was splendid and it held everything it had toward James. While he watched, it glowed, and its movements matched James' breath and settled him into safety. Carefully, James lifted the glass dome and then turned the clock, getting as much of its workings into his vision as possible. The feel of the gears beneath his hands made him shiver. James wasn't home, but home was here, present in the bare bones of a clock.

He didn't even check the price. He didn't care.

Cradling it against his chest, James moved slowly through the rest of the store. There were plenty of clocks, all old, all in various states of repair. Some moved happily and clearly, others had hands that were stuck on a permanent hour and minute. Most were very reasonably priced. James saw by the other objects around the shop that clocks were not a specialty for this storeowner...the high-priced items were stained glass figurines and windows and lampshades, all throwing paths of red and green and gold light on the floor. One path glowed marvelously purple and James looked up to see a huge arch of window, standing free from a wall, apparently extricated from a church. James thought he was near the center of the store and there was a bright light shining from somewhere, through this misplaced stained glass, and the thing shone with a life of its own.

While it and the other pieces were beautiful, they weren't clocks. And it was to James' benefit...the proprietor didn't know how much to charge. James knew he could probably talk the prices down even lower, but standing there in the purple light, he decided not to. The items were Abandoned Here and the cigar-smoking man saw fit to care for them. The clocks were already priced much lower than they should have been. James didn't want to take advantage of a good heart.

Working his way back to the counter, James set the skeleton clock down. "Would you by any chance have a good-sized cardboard box?" he asked the man. "I collect clocks and I've seen a good number I'm interested in and I can't carry them all." The man nodded and scrounged beneath the counter, coming up with a solid box. "Thank you," James said. The man answered around his glowing cigar and James shook his head. "I'm sorry, I can't hear. I lost my hearing recently through an accident." James handed over the notebook. "Can you write what you just said?"

The man frowned for a second, then grabbed a pen and began to write. The cigar was clenched tightly in his teeth, the smoke curling like a gray coil to the ceiling. Then he returned the notebook. "You can leave this clock up here if you want," he wrote.

"Oh," James said and looked at the little skeleton. He was torn about leaving it, it felt so good against his chest where the movement swung in time with his own pulse. But it made sense to leave it there, rather than jostling it around the store. "You won't sell it to anyone else who comes in?"

The cigar man shook his head.

"All right, thank you." James patted the little clock, then moved around the store again. The clocks were hard to say no to and it didn't take long before the box was filled. Retracing his steps to the counter, James requested another. The cigar man raised his eyebrows, but said nothing.

James was on his way back with the filled second box when he spotted one more clock. It was tucked away on a corner shelf, near the back, but the light shining through a red pane of stained glass caught it and its wood turned to fire. James set the box down and carefully scooped the small clock up.

It was an exquisite miniature mantel clock. It fit neatly in James' open palms, its humpback rising in a sensual curve. The heft and shine of the wood bragged it was mahogany and the clockface was a dim brass, just begging to be polished. The roman numerals were etched and graceful and the hands were a swirl like filigree. But holding it, James felt something was missing. He held it to his cheek. No rhythm. James felt nothing at all.

Turning it, he opened the little back and saw that the insides were completely cleared out. This clock was basically just a case, a shell, all the heart and soul of it gone. James stood there for a second and thought about this, this glorious body of a clock compared to the bare skeleton of the one who waited on the counter. He touched it again, running a single finger gently over its body, then cupping his palm over the rounded mound of its curve. In an instant, James was transformed back to a warm bed with Diana. His hand over this wood could have been over the softness of her breast and James felt his pulse quicken.

And then it hit him.

This clock was small, a miniature, a clock movement inside had to be a certain size. A size like James had at home, resting on a bed of lamb's wool. Diana's clock. Diana's clock movement tucked away inside this body that reminded James of the warmth and softness of her breast. Her heart making this brass face glow again, the hands move like a smooth caress over the numbers.

James stroked the clock again and had trouble breathing for a moment as everything shifted and settled back into place. Then his body relaxed, each muscle shaking loose and then wrapping itself around his bones. It could all work.

Returning to the counter, James set the box down. "That's it," he said to the cigar man, who laughed. The man reached for the notebook and wrote, "That's IT? You've about picked up every clock in the place."

Together, James and the cigar man took newspaper and tucked it in and around the clocks to protect them on the way back to the hotel and later, to home. James was careful with them all, but especially with the skeleton and the miniature mantel. There was everything to protect in the skeleton and nothing at all in the mantel, but he felt they both needed him and so they got an extra cushion of paper.

When the men were done, James realized he now had two large cardboard boxes to carry back to the hotel, still two or three blocks away. "Can I make a couple trips?" James asked the cigar man. "I'm staying at the Rest Easy and I don't think I can carry these all at once. Not safely, anyway."

The cigar man shrugged, then turned a closed sign on his door. He set the plastic hands of the "Will return" clock sign for a half hour. Then he handed James a box and picked up the other and led James down the street. James trailed the aroma of the cigar all the way to the hotel. When they got there, James tried to pay the cigar man an extra ten for his help. He shook his head, reached in his pocket, pulled out a cigar and tucked it into James' outstretched hand. Watching the cigar man go, James held the cigar under his nose and breathed it in. All these years and James never once thought to buy a cigar or some tobacco and just smell it every now and then, to bring the memory of his father warm and safe into his home. James tucked the cigar tenderly into a pocket of his suitcase.

While he knew it was a waste of time, James set out each clock in his room. They would all have to be packed again when he left, either for Rockford or home, but he didn't care. The ones that worked ticked away on the bedside stands, the television, the table, the floor. James felt the vibrations under his hands and against his cheek. The pendulums moved and he swayed with them and felt at home. The clocks that didn't work still got a breath of fresh air and he polished them as best he could with the towels from the bathroom.

The maid would have a fit.

The skeleton clock and the mantel sat next to each other on the dresser, where James could see them easily from any place in the room. Glancing at the blank television, James stretched out on the bed and watched the sunlight play over these new old clocks. When the bright sun and the swirled wood and the gold and silver pendulums began to blur and blend, he closed his eyes and napped like a child. Like the child he never was. James never was able to sleep in the root cellar.

In the morning, James sat awhile over his free doughnuts and coffee. He kept reading and rereading the directions to the Chicago Center for Ear, Nose and Throat that Cooley found on that internet. She booked James this room and then printed directions from the hotel parking lot to the clinic. It looked easy enough to get there, but James couldn't stop reading the step by step directions. Driving in this big city was nerve-wracking, especially without hearing. He couldn't tell when there was traffic, when there was a break, when a taxi or a bus might be bearing down.

At home, James mostly missed the sounds of the clocks. Here, he missed the sounds of everyday life. It felt like he was in a vacuum.

Finally, with one last cup of coffee, James gave the skeleton and mantel clocks a pat, nodded at the others and set out. The directions said it would take twenty-five point eight minutes to get there, so he gave himself an hour. He figured even computers couldn't predict the traffic.

In the car, James clenched both hands over the wheel and with his thumbs, he held the directions in place where he could see them easily. He wanted to stare up at the skyline, no longer far away, but right there on top of him, buildings that went up higher than he could see out of the windshield. But he was so nervous, his eyes wouldn't leave the road for more than a few seconds at a time. Placing himself into the right hand lane, James decided to stay there until his exit, holding the speed at ten miles under the limit so he would have time to read all the signs. If the other drivers honked, he didn't hear them. If they glared or made rude gestures, he didn't see it. Fear and bad ears kept James on the straight and narrow until he rolled down the exit ramp and turned to the right. Then he slid effortlessly into the parking garage of the Chicago Center for Ear, Nose and Throat. For a moment, after shutting the car off, James allowed himself to shake. Shake as a delayed response for what he just drove through, and shake in preparation for what was ahead.

James knew there was a chance that this special doctor would say he was never going to get his hearing back. Whenever he thought about it, it was like a big black box just descended over him and shut him in. It was like deafness was black, a word and color more fitting for the blind. But without sound, the world seemed black and box-like.

There was also the possibility of surgery. James thought of a knife against his ears, puncturing holes until sound flowed through, like air to a jarred butterfly. Or maybe the doctor would say it would be all right. Just all right. Doc Owen kept saying that, he said it just needed time.

At home, there was plenty of time. It was everywhere, on every wall. James just needed to be able to hear it passing.

Inside the clinic, the hallways were brightly lit and James followed the green path to the ear section. A lot of people were talking by waving their hands around and James wondered if he could learn that, at his age. If he couldn't, and if this deafness didn't lift, he would go through a small fortune in notebooks. But James just couldn't imagine talking to someone by watching their hands, seeing them spell out whole sentences with their fingers. James wanted voices, including his own. He wanted to hear himself speak. Hear somebody answer.

At a reception desk, a woman smiled at him. "Hello," James said and wondered if she looked surprised because he could talk. "I have an appointment with Dr. Carson this morning."

She said something as she looked down at this big sheet of paper, graphed out with hours and half-hours. "Excuse me?" James said. "What? I'm sorry, I can't hear." He handed her the notebook, which she looked at for a moment, then she smiled again and nodded. She wrote quickly.

"Please have a seat. Dr. is here, but a few minutes behind. Help yourself to coffee."

James nodded, then poured a cup from a big urn in the center of the room before he sat down. He didn't really want any more coffee, but free was free. He held his hands around the cup, warming his fingers, cold even though the temperature was fine in the waiting room. As he sat there, James wondered how he would know when they called his name. He blinked, and then before his eyes, he saw himself still sitting there after dark because he never knew they were looking for him and they never knew who he was. Quickly, he got back up and went to the receptionist.

"How will I know when they call me?" James asked. He wasn't sure, but it felt like his voice trembled. "I mean, I can't hear."

She accepted the notebook and wrote quickly. "I'll get you," she said. "I know your name."

James nodded, but worried anyway. She might be away from the desk when they came for him, off doing whatever it was that receptionists do when they're not at their posts. She might be on the phone. James started to leave, to return to his seat, but she reached out quickly and grabbed his hand. Still holding on, she searched under the desk, then handed James a chocolate chip cookie. She pointed at his coffee, making dunking motions. And suddenly, James relaxed. A cup of coffee, a sweet, and someone who knew his name. Someone who fed him and wasn't going to leave until he was taken care of. "Thank you," James said, then went to sit down.

He was just licking the chocolate off his fingers when she came to stand in front of him. Motioning, she led James down the hallway and deposited him into a room. Dr. Carson came in before she even closed the door.

James had to explain the whole accident again, even though he knew Dr. Carson just talked to Doc Owen about it a few days ago. James hated thinking about the accident, hated the thought of those smashed baby birds and the feel of that big clock's chime attacking him, pressing him to the floor. He told the story as quickly as possible and then held still and quiet through the examination. This doctor was much more thorough than Doc Owens, pulling James' ears this way and that, sticking the otoscope in so deep, James felt it in his throat. He wondered if the doctor was going to crawl inside, investigate James' canals and eardrums like a lost man in underground caves. Finally, Dr. Carson sat down and wrote in the notebook.

"Your ears look about as I expected," he said. "You've had a severe trauma and both your eardrums definitely burst. There are also little intricate hair cells in the ear that interpret sound vibrations, allowing us to hear in the first place, and these little hair cells have undoubtedly been damaged. All of this takes time to heal. I agree with Dr. Owen's regimen of anti-inflammatories and antibiotics, though I think maybe even a decongestant can be added, in case there's some fluid build-up. It's possible your ears are too swollen to drain properly and that's causing some of the deafness."

James handed the notebook back to the doctor. "Will I hear again?" James felt the words leave his mouth and he pictured them hanging there in the air, black and round, swollen with their silence. Dr. Carson looked at him, then shrugged.

He shrugged. How could a doctor shrug? They're supposed to know so much, it was supposed to either be a yes or no . A shrug left James no better off than he was before. But then the doctor wrote some more in the notebook. James leaned forward, hoping to see a yes written in capital letters and underlined.

"Let's run a few tests, see what I can find out."

James' words in the air changed to gray, but they were still there. He followed Dr. Carson to a large room filled with what looked like booths. Dr. Carson handed James over to another white-coated man, then he waved at James and pointed to his watch. James nodded and followed the whitecoat to one of the booths. The whitecoat wrote in the notebook.

"We're going to test your hearing. It might seem like you're sitting there for some time as I go through the sounds, until I find a level where you are hearing. You might not hear anything at all. I'll come and get you when we're done."

James sat down at a counter covered in some type of fuzzy rough material. Through a gray window, he could see into an adjoining booth where there were a lot of dials and switches. Whitecoat put a set of headphones on James, a strange set of headphones that actually reached deep inside his ears. They made James itch. Then Whitecoat waved and pointed to the window before shutting James into the small booth. The air was sucked out with him and James gasped, wondering if he was locked in, and it was like he was suddenly thrown down the cold cement stairs of the root cellar. There was no strip of light shining around the door and James started to run to it, but the headphones yanked him back, kept him in place. Like a tether. A tether on his ears instead of his throat. James put his hands to his head and gagged, then threw off the headphones and hit the door. Panting, he wrestled with the doorknob, but it wouldn't open. He was locked in.

He was just short of screaming when the door flew open and whacked him in the head. James fell back on his haunches and looked up into the bright light, only barely seeing Whitecoat standing there. The light hovered around him like a halo and the air was fresh and cool. James swallowed it in big gulps. He knew there were sounds coming out of him, and he knew what they were. The terrified whimpers of a puppy.

Whitecoat helped James up and led him back to the seat. He rubbed James' back and then looked at his forehead. Whitecoat's fingers ran lightly over a sore spot that James knew was going to get worse. Whitecoat shook his head, then reached for the notebook.

"James," he said, "it's just for a few minutes. I know it's close in here. Look through the window this time and in a moment, you'll see me. I promise, I'll come and let you out. The air will feel different in here as I leave. The room is pressurized, like an airplane."

Whitecoat replaced the headphones, patted James' back one more time, then left. James watched the door close, then shut his eyes and pictured Whitecoat walking through the big room to the window. When James opened his eyes, Whitecoat was there. He waved. James focused on him, on the light and the air around him, as he began to twist various dials.

It was a long time and there was nothing. Whitecoat kept looking at James, then looking back down at the panel. James wondered if he should be doing something, shaking his head, holding his hands out, palms up and empty. His forehead throbbed and James reached up and touched it, just once, and Whitecoat seemed to startle, his eyebrows arched up under his hairline. James quickly put his hand back into his lap and shook his head. There was just nothing. The sound of nothing, hollow and black and still.

But then James heard it, a pinprick in the darkness. It was quiet and tinny and shrill, but it was there, like the sound a dime makes when it falls on the floor. James' right hand shot up, all by itself, and clasped the headphones. Whitecoat frowned like it was another false alarm, but then James tapped the right side of his head, tapped it and wanted to whoop. Whitecoat grinned and began flipping dials and switches like a great mad organist.

James raised his right arm, his left, his right again, and then the first time he raised both hands, raised them high in the air and waggled his fingers to the rhythm of the sounds rising out of the dead darkness in both of his ears, Whitecoat did a little dance, twisting in the booth, shaking his fanny. The sounds grew clearer, little bells, ringing and singing and playing a discordant song in James' head.

Then Whitecoat bowed, a conductor at the end of a great performance, and he turned two knobs with a final flick of his wrists. The blackness fell over James again, hitting his ears like a wind tunnel. All the chimes blew away and he was alone again. Whitecoat left his little room and as James watched him leave, he suddenly fell headlong into tears. He tried to contain them, but they flew out like an Iowa thunderstorm. James' eyes squeezed shut, he wailed and he didn't know Whitecoat was there until he wrapped his arms around James.

"I'm sorry!" James sobbed, leaning into his coat. "I'm sorry! It was just so good to hear something again!"

Whitecoat patted James' back, over and over, and eventually helped him to his feet. They walked back to the examining room and Whitecoat stayed with James, his arm around James' shoulders, while Dr. Carson wrote in the notebook. The receptionist was back too, with a cup of water for James, which he gulped. Somehow that soothed him and he was able to calm down to the occasional shudder.

Dr. Carson finished writing and he smiled at James before handing over the notebook. "The news is good, James," he said. "That you were able to hear anything at all is wonderful. Hearing those sounds shows that your hearing mechanism is still intact, although it's not functioning perfectly right now due to the swelling and the healing of the eardrums. What will probably happen is that certain sounds will eventually start breaking through. You'll hear a siren, an alarm clock, bits and pieces of someone's voice. It may sound like a radio while you're trying to tune it. But I think it will all come back."

"You think?" James said and Whitecoat's arm tightened around his shoulders. "You *think*? Probably? You can't be any more definite than that?"

Carson shrugged again and James wanted to hit him. Rage soaked him black and pure as his deafness and he wanted to hit the doctor full in the face.

"How long?" James said. "How long, if it does come back?" His voice felt low in his throat. He was snarling.

Carson grabbed his wall calendar. He pointed to a week, then two, then flipped the calendar ahead a couple months, then fanned through the entire year. It was the same as a shrug.

James forced the anger back. He needed answers and it was too hard to talk through a rage. "Will I need hearing aids? I mean, if it comes back." He cleared his throat, trying to feel steady, trying to feel as if his voice was strong. "Do you need to see me again? Is there anything else I can do?"

This time, Dr. Carson retrieved the notebook and wrote some more. "You didn't need hearing aids before, so you probably won't need them now. You only need to see me again if two months goes by and there hasn't been significant improvement. The only thing to do is to continue with Dr. Owen's regimen…and wait."

"Fine," James said. A timeline. At least there was a timeline. Two months and there should be significant improvement, whatever that was. James moved out from under Whitecoat's arm. Whitecoat crossed his fingers, waved, then left the room.

James grudgingly shook the doctor's hand when it was offered, then followed the receptionist back to the waiting area, where she raised one finger in the air. Wait a minute, it said. She poured another cup of coffee, put a lid on it, then reached under the desk and handed James one more chocolate chip cookie. She made walking motions with her fingers. For the trip home.

Two nice people working for a jackass who couldn't make up his mind if a patient was alive or dead.

"Thank you," James said again and then he turned to leave. While the silence was all around him again, he tried to picture it as a shade of gray, instead of black. Gray, like a mist or a fog. Something that would definitely lift and leave the air bright. Or that would keep him from being seen by a fast-moving truck.

James decided to stay the night in Chicago, then leave in the morning for Rockford. Cooley only gave him the directions to Chicago and the Center for Ears, Nose and Throat, so he had to seek out a gas station to buy a map. The trip didn't look that hard, though it was always difficult to figure the sizes of roads from the blue and red lines on a map. But James knew he was heading out of a big city and that was enough.

James sat on the bed that night, looking at the clocks and wishing he could call home. He wanted them to know that he was probably going to be okay, that word "probably" figuring bigger and bigger in his head as the night went on. He stared at the phone, thought about dialing it, about waiting what would feel like an appropriate amount of time and then shouting into whomever's ear was hopefully on the other line. But he couldn't trust that, he couldn't count on anyone picking up the receiver. James didn't have an answering machine.

Glancing at his watch, always more accurate than any of the clocks, James saw it was only seven o'clock. It was possible Cooley was still there, doing the winding. He walked down the hall to the check-in desk. "Hello," he said to the young boy behind the counter.

He looked at James and nodded.

"I'm wondering if you could do me a favor." James handed the boy the notebook. "I wrote my home number on there. Could you call it and see if anyone answers? I'm deaf, so I can't hear if someone picks up. If they do answer, could you tell them my doctor's appointment went fine and ask them if everything is okay there?"

The boy glanced at the notebook, then shrugged. He said something and turned away.

"I can't hear," James reminded him. "What did you say? Will you call?"

The boy turned back, a scowl on his face this time. He grabbed a pen and wrote heavily on the paper. "I'm BUSY!"

James looked over the counter. There was only a comic book there, but the boy quickly whisked it away. "Listen, buddy," James said. He pulled himself up to his full height, which wasn't much, but at least he was taller than the boy. "This is very important. Now, you're supposed to take care of your guests and that includes those who can't hear. Do you want me to talk to your manager?"

The boy stood there a minute and James could see he was thinking, wondering if he should call James' bluff. James tried not to tremble.

Finally, the boy took the notebook. James leaned as far over the counter as he could, to make sure the boy was really pushing the buttons on the phone. "If someone answers, tell me who it is," James said.

The boy glared, but continued dialing. Eventually, James saw his mouth flapping and he wrote on the notebook. "Kooly."

"Good!" James said. "Tell her my ears are probably going to be okay. Probably. And then tell her I won't be home for a few days yet, I'm going on to Rockford."

The boy nodded, talked, then wrote some more. His scrawl was so bad, James could barely make it out. "She says good. Wants 2 no Y U R going."

He wrote like Cooley and James had no idea what he was saying. "Yur?" James said. "Wants to no yur going? What is that?"

The boy rolled his eyes, then wrote more clearly. "She wants to know why you are going to Rockford."

"Oh!" James said. "Y U R! Why you are! I get it." James nodded. "Tell her I'm going to a famous clock museum. And ask her if everything is okay."

The boy talked some more, then hung up the phone. James was about to protest when he picked up the pen. "She said is OK."

James sighed. That was as much as he would get. "Thank you," James said. He started to walk away, then stopped and handed the boy three dollars. "For your time," James said. "Buy yourself a real book and learn to read."

In the morning, James carefully boxed up the clocks and loaded the car. He put the skeleton clock and miniature mantel in a little box that fit in the front seat. James wanted those next to him as he navigated his way to Rockford. James couldn't hear them, but he knew they were there and they kept him company.

CHAPTER TWENTY:

GO GENTLE
The Gebhard World Clock's Story

"Do not go gentle into that good night...
...Rage, rage against the dying of the light."

His words pressed against my ear in bed that night, but the words were formless, a hum that wasn't intended for me. His hand was on me, his arm cradled between my ribs and my hip, and he stroked my breast as he spoke. But while his touch aroused my skin, brought my nipple to full attention, I knew it wasn't me he felt under his fingers.

He felt a clock. He was winding it, pulling on a chain, twisting a key, tenderly adjusting a fragile filigree arm to the correct time. And in his voice, instead of my name, I heard the chiming of the hour. A tenor chime, sounding out into the night for anyone who heard it, but no one in particular. Certainly not for me.

Do not go gentle into that good night, Dylan Thomas wrote, and I thought about that, thought about raging and shrieking, stamping my feet, smacking James' face, bringing his full attention back to me, to me, the one who lay in his bed. Not the clocks that stood in the hallway or hung on the wall or sat and squatted and crouched on tables and shelves in every room. I thought about raging against the dying of the light, our light, the light that fell on James and me these three years.

But this was James. And even as I raged inside, waged a war of words tipped with bayonets, I knew I would go gentle. There was no other way to be with James. There was no other way for James to be but gentle. My skin knew that. Every cell in my body knew his touch and even his voice was soft.

I would go gentle. But I would go.

"James," I whispered. "James, it's getting late. Time for sleep."

His hum stopped for a moment, his thumb and forefinger gripping my nipple, arrested in the movement of pushing time forward. He relaxed, his hand opening and settling onto the curve of my breast, and he curled into me for the night. "I love you," he said.

Those words always got through. Several times a day, they seemed to work their way up through his distraction and obsession, rolling off his tongue, breaking out between his teeth, and each time, it made my belly go soft. But I had to start thinking about all those other times, those long minutes and hours when he was away from me, even within the walls of our home. Moving from clock to clock, adjusting and winding.

I knew he said those same words to them. But I liked to think that the timbre of his voice changed, just a bit, when he turned his attention to me. I liked to think that.

Eventually that night, I rolled out from under his heavy arm and went to sit on the rocker across the room. I wrapped myself in a blanket and stared at James in the grainy gray half-light created by a sliver of moon against white snow outside. A nightlight glowed from the bathroom and I went to turn it off, not wanting the gold halo to reach James, wanting to see him for who he was. I reminded myself to turn it back on before I left. Without a nightlight, James was terrified of the dark.

So I sat and studied him sleeping unawares, his arm resting quietly on the bed where my body used to be, where only my heat remained and was surely dissipating. He didn't seem to notice that I was gone. His posture didn't change and his face remained relaxed and calm, his lips curved in a sweet half-smile.

I thought about our weekend. We'd just gotten home from a trip to Rockford, Illinois, where we visited the tiny Time Museum, a museum devoted completely to clocks. It sat squat in the middle of a hotel complex, the Clock Tower Resort. James and I checked in on Friday afternoon and stayed until the museum closed at four on Sunday. He spent almost the whole weekend with the clocks. I spent some time there too, it was fascinating, but I also swam in the pool, looked around Rockford, and ate at restaurants while staring at the blank setting across from me as time and time again, James was late or forgot to show up entirely. I lounged in our bed part of Saturday afternoon, stretching out in the luxury of king size, and experimented with different styles of masturbation when he didn't join me. Later, at the hotel gift shop, I bought a silk nightgown with clocks all over it and he delightedly identified each clock before pulling it over my head and identifying me. But Sunday morning, even though I slid the nightgown back on and struck a seductive pose, he waved at me and headed for the museum. I packed our things in the car and then went to join him.

By then, I knew exactly where to find James. Although he spent some time admiring all the clocks, he always gravitated to the center of the museum and then he stood there, frozen, his hands in his pockets as he took in the Gebhard Astronomical and World Clock. Every now and then, he whispered something and after the first couple times, I didn't need to hear him to know what he was saying. He whispered, "Look at it. Just look at it."

But I stood in the archway and looked at James instead, dwarfed in front of this massive clock. It resembled a pipe organ, something that belonged in a cathedral somewhere, bellowing out hymns in a voice that vibrated the floor. The oak case glowed and climbed upwards in three distinct columns, each housing instruments shiny with purpose. The clock was as intimidating as it was beautiful and when I saw it for the first time in Friday afternoon's sifted sunlight, I took a step backwards. James grabbed my arm and explained all the different functions. His voice was low and reverent and again I felt like I was in a cathedral.

There were dials and faces that showed Mean Time, Solar Time, Star Time and Decimal Time. On the right side of the clock was a globe, presenting the exact position of the earth at that particular moment in space, and a band ran along the equator, showing what time it was at any point on the planet. On the left side was another globe, but this one bristled with stars and the white lines of constellations. A perpetual calendar sat square in the clock's belly, a little notch that reminded me of a bellybutton. In a window near the top of the clock, a mustard sun moved in a graceful arc, replaced with a glowing moon at night. There was a barometer and below that, a planetary system showing the sun and six planets, the only ones known at the clock's creation. They all moved in a cautious and painfully correct revolution around the sun.

"And all of it," whispered James in my ear, "all of it built in thirty years, from 1865 to 1895. No computers, no calculators, all by hand and by thought. Just look at it."

It was the animated figures that grabbed my attention, and James' too. Our first night there, we stayed until six so we could see the clock set off. Because it was so old, the clock was only run a few times during the day, so as to keep it in working condition, giving it less chance to break down. We sat on a bench and watched as a museum employee started the figures on their rounds. He let the clock run from six to seven, so we could see it in its natural form. The clock's hands were set at eleven and we were told to pretend that we were on our way to midnight.

On the quarter hour, an infant in diapers crawled out and dinged a bell once. On the half hour, a child ran out and rang the bell twice. Three quarters, and an adult appeared and the bell sang three times. And on the hour, an old man seemed to stagger while he struck the bell four times. With the first three, a guardian angel appeared over the figures, her hand outstretched and protective. But she stayed away from the old man and instead, another angel appeared and turned an hourglass over while a hooded creature, carrying a scythe, rang a deeper bell the correct chimes for the hour. Every hour, that old man died, and every hour, a new baby was born.

At midnight, more of the clock spun to life as Jesus' twelve disciples started a march in a circle. Jesus stood above, smiling, his face solemn and sweet, his hands spread, palms turned up. All the disciples bowed to Jesus, except for Judas, who quickly turned his back. Then, as Judas skulked after the eleven, slipping back into their homes inside the clock, a raven popped out of a different archway, above and to the right. I felt James shiver as the raven opened his beak and crowed three times, a raucous sound in the softly ticking museum. Jesus' room darkened.

We sat, silent and amazed, and then the employee pointed out the matching archway on the left, where a bugler dressed in blue stood, his trumpet resting at his side. On New Year's Eve at midnight, the employee explained, the bugler raised his trumpet to his lips and blew in the start of a new year, a new chance. Another year of telling time in every possible way, through numbers on the face of a clock, through stars, through planets. Another year of old men dying and babies being born, of Jesus smiling at his disciples, even as one turns away, and then that cold sharp rasp of a raven's call.

"Please," James said on that first night. He dropped my arm and moved toward the employee, who looked startled. "Can I just touch it? Can I feel the ticking before you shut it down for the night?"

The man started to say no, but he must have seen something in James' face. The same thing I saw when James first woke every morning, when he opened his eyes and looked out and for a moment, didn't recognize a thing. For that moment, he looked scared and his eyes shimmered and his mouth opened as if to call for someone. In the Time Museum, he seemed to call for that clock and after hesitating, the employee nodded.

I watched James walk past the velvet barriers holding the public at bay. He moved to the center of the clock and I suddenly pictured it folding in, catching James up in an embrace. He held out his hand and touched the clock, just above its bellybutton. Then he lay his face against it and closed his eyes.

It happened so fast, but I saw it. He smiled. The smile that you see on a child's face when he curls up in his mother's lap and nestles between her breasts.

When the employee cleared his throat, James straightened, then came right back to me. He walked with me out of the museum and to our room. "I connected with it, Diana," he said. "That clock has a soul, they all have souls, and I connected. I felt its pulse."

He made love to me that night, in that hotel bed, even before I bought the clock nightgown. And I shuddered beneath him, feeling his strength all around me, feeling that connection, knowing he was there with me in that moment, in that bed, his eyes looked into mine and we were together in the way I'd grown to cherish over three year's time.

But when he curled into me later, talking and stroking my breast in the usual way, the familiar way that used to blanket me but now left me lonely, I knew he was away again. His voice, his thoughts, were with that clock, locked into the immensity of its heart.

I wished that night, as I wished a million times before, that he could tell me more of his past. More than a story about a father who left and then died, a mother who, he said, wasn't "all there," but he would never explain what was missing. I wondered if he could tell anyone. I wondered if he could tell a clock. I wondered why he couldn't tell me.

I loved James.

And the whole weekend was like that. I came upon him there too many times to count, in the clock museum, standing before the Gebhard clock. "James," I said. "Let's go eat."

"Just look," he whispered.

"Let's go shopping, let's go swimming," I said. And once, I looked around quickly, then licked his ear while running one finger down the zipper of his pants. "Come to bed with me, James," I said.

"Just look at it."

And then I said it, just loud enough so he could hear, and just to see if the shock of it would work its way through, if the hard sound of the word would bring him back to me. "Come fuck me, James," I said. "Let's go fuck like dogs."

For a moment, he trembled and I thought I had him. He started to turn toward me, but then he stopped. "A raven at every midnight," he whispered. "Just look."

I grabbed his hand then and squeezed it as hard as I could. "I love you, James," I said. I said it loud. I told the whole museum and every clock heard me.

He looked at me then, looked at me clear like he did during lovemaking. And there was that smile, the smile I saw as he pressed his cheek against the heart of the clock. "I love you too, Diana," he said and those words were mine alone.

But then, he turned back. He turned full away and his back was to me and I could barely hear his voice, I wasn't even sure if it was me he was talking to. "Just look," he said and began again to name off all the functions, listing the dials and faces as lovingly as if he recited a poem.

He didn't notice when I walked out of the room.

On that Sunday morning, car loaded and ready to go, I moved out of the archway and found a nearby bench. I sat and watched him watch the Gebhard clock until the museum closed at four. I didn't leave to eat and neither did he. When I saw one of the employees moving toward the closed sign, I took James' hand and led him away. During the drive home, he kept talking about the Gebhard clock, as if it was still there, still looming in his vision.

Now, as the grainy gray light brightened into a pale rose, I began to pack. I didn't have much, mostly just clothes, and I could fit them all in our suitcase, left out from our final weekend. I closed it and set it by the bedroom door, then stood before James.

Carefully, I tucked the clock nightgown into James' arms, so it lay where I should be in the bed. I took one sleeve and placed it on top of James' hand, like the touch of my own fingers against his skin. As he stirred, I kissed him once on the lips and felt his warm response. "I love you, James," I said and he settled more deeply into sleep, pulling the nightgown closer to his naked body. He had an erection and I thought of the raven, appearing every night at midnight. I draped my nightgown so it covered this most vulnerable part. Covered him and kept him warm.

I turned on the nightlight before I left, gently. I left without raging at the dying of our light. I left in tears. But I left.

CHAPTER TWENTY-ONE

JAMES

So you live in silence then, silence while the rest of the world moves in full voice around you. Figures of perpetual motion swirl through a flat environment where nothing reverberates, nothing resounds, nothing echoes. Even your clocks speak and sing and share their heartbeats with the world, but you can't hear a thing.

Yet how is this different, really? You've always lived in a world of silence. Imagine never being able to tell anyone where you came from, how you came to be. Imagine never telling anyone who you are, because to do so would be to let loose with a string of secrets, horrible secrets, that most people would never choose to believe. Secrets that only happen in nightmares or on the front pages of newspapers. Not to someone who lives across the street.

How to even work such a thing into a conversation? "Where do I come from? Well, a root cellar mostly." Or, "Gosh, that's a lovely collar your poodle has. I used to wear one just like it."

To this day, you still wear high collars and long sleeves, even in hot Iowa summers. There are a few remaining marks on your skin, probably not something anyone would notice, but you need to make sure they never do. So even your body, you hide.

Your whole life is about silence and secrets and deeply hidden places.

And you saw what happened when you risked it all. When you showed your skin to a woman, let her touch it, let her love it, and you learned of the wonderful warmth of sleeping naked with another nude body pressed against yours. Skin to skin, thighs to thighs, arms wrapped and clasped around each other. She saw your body, made love to it. Made love to you.

And you even slipped and showed her the side of yourself that most scares you. When the rage comes, when it hurls out of you in a flare of shouted words and raised fists. She saw that, saw it only once, but she felt what it was like under your anger. Even though the anger wasn't ever for her. And she said it was all right. That night, she curled against you and she wept, but she said it was all right and her skin was warm. You detected no change, no stiffness.

You never said the past out loud though. Nothing beyond a few general answers, brushed-off explanations. How could you tell her about your mother? How could you tell her about tethers and kennels and plastic food dishes and water tins? There was never anyone you could tell. Not the teachers or the other children or the doctors or grocery store clerks, bank tellers, or people who smiled at you on the street. Not even the friendly flea market folks. Not with anyone you've ever had contact with. Not with any of the people you've so wanted to care for. The past is silent. You are silent.

Yet somehow she still knew. She must have known. Through the faded marks on your skin, the raised voice, the single sharp blow, she must have figured it out, witnessed the unimaginable, and left. Face to face with the truth, the unspeakable, she left you all alone in the middle of the night. Left you in dark silence. Not a word between you. Not even goodbye.

Imagine.

James knew silence well. He lived side by side with silence, took it to bed with him at night, carried it on his tongue during the day, like a hard candy that was sour and never ever went away. Throughout his life, he made sure that people only knew him in the present, just in the moment, and nothing more. They didn't know his past, they wouldn't know his future. He was rather like a clock himself...ticking forward, moving ahead in time, but really only there in the everyday world when someone looked at him, nodded in his direction, then moved on.

Silence and loneliness are not easy company.

It was late when James checked into the Clock Tower Resort in Rockford. He told the desk clerk he would be staying a couple days, then he unloaded and set up the clocks and went to bed. He was tempted to sneak down into the belly of the resort and look in the closed doors of the Time Museum, but he knew it would be dark and he wouldn't be able to see a thing. Still, James wanted the Gebhard Clock to know he was there. And in some odd and impossible way, he hoped he would run into Diana.

The only time James was here, Diana was with him. When she disappeared, she left behind a silk nightgown, purchased at this resort's gift shop. It was covered with clocks. James unwrapped her that weekend like she was a present just for him. A special gift. Which she was. When she left, James slept with the nightgown for a couple months. He hoped she would come back. When she didn't, he threw the nightgown away. James tried to throw her away, but he just couldn't. He thought of her almost every day, especially when he wound her clock.

So James fell into the hotel bed and a heavy sleep, secure in the knowledge that a few floors below, clocks moved in subtle precision through the night. The Gebhard Clock, James knew, was silent. It was only allowed to run a few times during the day, the curators said to keep its maintenance to a minimum. James wished he owned the clock. He would give it a room of its own. It would take up the entire space. And James would let it run all the time, the way clocks were meant to, and each day, he would tend to it to make sure it was all right. He didn't understand why the museum people thought shutting the clock down would keep it moving. Its joints would stiffen after so much stillness, like James' knees and elbows when he got up in the morning.

James vowed to talk to them about the clock's maintenance the next day. He pictured them suddenly giving the clock to him, sending it to the Home for purely humane reasons, and then that big old clock would hunker down in its private room and run and run and run. James fell asleep, thinking about its new and multi-faceted voice blended in among all the others.

Perhaps it was the clock's proximity that made James dream of it that night. He saw all of its faces and globes, its dials and instruments. He went from one to the other and told himself the time over and over again. He saw where the earth was on its axis, where the stars were in the night sky, saw the position of six different planets around the sun. James saw a child grow old and then die, hidden within the folds of a hooded figure's cloak. And the twelve disciples bowed to Jesus, all except Judas, who looked directly at James. When the raven opened his mouth to crow, James didn't hear a thing. The raven became angry and crowed louder, shutting his eyes and straining so hard, he fell off his perch. He broke into pieces on the floor and Jesus wept and while the bugler blew taps, James wondered where he would ever find a cuckoo bird big enough to fit in that clock.

James woke in a tangle of strange sheets and a too-thin blanket. Sitting up, he grabbed the miniature mantel clock and held it while he looked around the room at all the others. Their pendulums moved steadily and James slowed his breathing and relaxed. It was four in the morning, but he knew he wouldn't get any more sleep. He had to see the Gebhard Astronomical and World Clock.

Pulling on his robe and slippers, James pocketed the room key. In the hallway, he carefully held the door as it closed, so its echo wouldn't disturb any of the other guests. Then he started making his way toward the museum.

James hadn't been there in over forty years, but he still remembered the twisted path. Taking the elevator to the first floor, James went down the hallway past the swimming pool. It was empty, but the water still shivered as if someone was there. Turning a corner, James went past the darkened restaurant, then down a ramp, then a circular flight of stairs. At the base, he stopped.

There was no Time Museum. Just a big room set up like a banquet hall, filled with white-clothed tables and deep blue chairs.

James must have made a wrong turn. He reasoned that a big place like this one probably had dozens of identical passageways.

Quickly, he retraced his steps back to the elevator. Setting out again, he walked past the pool. There was only one pool in the resort, so up until there, the path had to be right. Then, instead of going by the restaurant, James went the opposite way down the hall.

Another ramp, another circular staircase. And the same banquet hall. James could see the first staircase on the opposite side. But this time, a man stood on the bottom step, looking at James. "Shit," James said, he hoped softly, and watched as the man approached.

He said something and James shook his head. "I'm sorry," James said, "but I can't hear. I had an accident a while ago and it took my hearing. It's probably coming back." He felt like the more he said this, the more likely it was.

The man stood for a moment and James read the name badge pinned crookedly to his left lapel. Philip. Philip laced James' arm through his and led him away. They went up the second spiral staircase and eventually came out at the front desk. Philip rummaged around and produced hotel stationary and a white pen with "The Clock Tower Resort" printed on it in big black letters. All of the O's looked like clock faces. "Were you looking for something?" Philip wrote. "Can I help you?"

"Yes," James said. "I know it's late, but I wanted to check out the hours of the Time Museum. I wanted to be there at opening in the morning."

Philip shook his head and James' heart hesitated. He watched while Philip wrote another note.

"The museum hasn't been here for years. The owner auctioned off a lot of the clocks and the rest were sent for exhibit at the Chicago Museum of Science and Industry." He handed a brochure over with the note.

"Years?" James' hand shook as he took the brochure. He couldn't imagine it. This was the museum's home. This was where the clocks lived. James remembered the employees, bustling around, winding and checking to make sure everything was fine. Where did they go? What parts of the world were the clocks in now?

James fumbled with the brochure, trying to open it. "The Gebhard Clock?" he asked. "The Gebhard Astronomical and World Clock?"

Out of his peripheral vision, James saw Philip's fingers flicker and wave. He was talking again, the idiot. Then one finger flipped a page of the brochure and pointed. There was a picture of the Gebhard Clock. It was surrounded by neon and chrome.

It was in Chicago. James just came from Chicago and he didn't even know it was there. He didn't hear it. It didn't reach out to him.

But how could it? James was deaf.

He thought of all the clocks in the Home, even the ones in his hotel room, still touching him although he couldn't hear. Briefly, James touched his chest, feeling for his heart.

But that Gebhard Clock, it stayed away. All these years, James thought of it, pictured it, dreamed that he had a connection with it. Against his cheek, James could still feel the pulse of its pendulum when he leaned his face against its immense wooden body. The pulse and the warmth, the steady rhythm of the huge heart of that clock, allowed to beat only so long each day.

But it never even let James know that it moved. It didn't even let James know when he was within a few miles of it. Imagine.

James thought again of his clocks at home and suddenly, he wondered if they even knew he was gone. If they knew he left one day, left in the sun of mid-morning so they could see him, so they could see he didn't disappear into a fog. Because of them, James would never let the fog take him.

Choking out a thank you, James shoved the brochure into his robe pocket and went back to his room. He locked the door and stumbled to the bed. It was after five now and still dark. Pulling the blanket up to his chin, James shivered, and he held the miniature mantel against his chest. He watched the skeleton clock, seeing each gear move, each cog slip into place, the pendulum moving at an even back-and-forth.

James remembered that weekend with Diana and with the Gebhard Clock. Diana watched as he begged the employee and then slid with his permission up against the clock's solid wall. James' hand touched the wood and it was warm, as warm as living human skin. When he pressed his cheek against it and felt that pulse, something resonated and he closed his eyes and fell into a darkness that wasn't cold and silent, but full of sounds. The beat of a heart. The rushing of blood. The whisper of skin against skin, the touch separate from James but still there, going over his head, his shoulders, his hips. His legs threatened to buckle, but James stood there and listened and felt that warmth and knew he was where he always wanted to be.

James felt something from that clock. He felt something from every clock, but that particular one, in its immense size, brought the feeling all around him. It loved James and he could hear it with every beat of its heart.

That's what James had thought. But now, he didn't seem to matter.

James clutched the miniature mantel and even though it didn't have a pendulum, it didn't have a heart, he still felt its warmth spread to him. All the clocks in the room seemed to close in on James, a soft protective circle. They were there, it wasn't his imagination, and he felt grateful.

James needed to get home to his clocks. To all of them. He needed their embrace.

But there was more.

When he thought of his clocks now, James saw Cooley's thin back, her bright purple hair shimmering with her body's effort to wind a clock. He saw her long fingers, wrapped around a key or a chain, and he saw those same fingers guided by his as she helped him insert a piece into her acorn clock. He saw Ione, her lavender feather duster in a back pocket, busily polishing clocks in the living room, the den, the dining room and bedrooms. He felt her arms around him again, pressing James to her chest as he shook in fear and frustration. He saw Gene at the diner, cooking his dinner, and Molly delivering it, complete with two slices of pie, one cherry, one apple. Neal looking in the back door. Doc taking his pulse, patting his shoulder.

And everywhere, everywhere in his mind was Diana. James felt her lips again, her arms, and the most secret parts of her body. He saw her smile, her frown, felt her come up behind him and wrap her arms around his shoulders as she whispered outrageous things in his ear. Outrageous things that made his heart beat in a new rhythm.

And as much as James felt her, the texture of her absence was ten times greater. The more he felt her, remembered her, the more he realized she was gone. He let her go.

At the resort that last weekend, James felt her behind him as he stepped up to the Gebhard Clock and he felt his connection with Diana break as he closed his eyes and allowed himself to fall into that dark place. His heart changed pace again and this time, it echoed that clock, shuddered, then beat evenly within its broad shoulders, and Diana, their rhythm severed, spun away.

James wished he asked her to stand next to him that day. He wanted her cheek near his as they both listened to the great clock's heart. He wished he had that clock nightgown to hold, along with this little clock in his arms. He wished her body was still in that nightgown, her breast under his hand. The nightgown would be old, she would be old, but it just wouldn't matter.

James had to get home. He had to put Diana's heart into this little clock and feel its beat again. And he had to see them all, touch them all, even if he couldn't hear them.

All of them. Not just the clocks. James needed the flesh and blood warmth of everyone. They couldn't spin away.

James left the next morning, even though he had no sleep. Philip was off duty so he explained to the daytime folks at the front desk that since the Time Museum was no longer there, he had no reason to stay in Rockford. They didn't make James pay for an extra day. He loaded the car and headed toward home.

He thought he could make it the whole way, but around noon, his eyes kept threatening to close. Finally, he pulled over at a fast food joint, had lunch, then curled up in the back seat of his car. Exhaustion crept over James like a blanket, a full thick blanket, not the too-thin one at the resort, and his bones sunk into the seat and he fell asleep.

When James woke up, it was still light, but it took him a few minutes to get oriented. Eventually, he sat up, let himself out and walked slowly into the restaurant to use the restroom. He bought a cup of coffee and a hot apple pie for the road. It was only four o'clock...it would be six by the time he got home.

Despite the sleep and the coffee, James still struggled. There was nothing more boring than driving through Iowa. But partway through, he began to notice something odd. A whang sound, something electrical, that blipped in and out of his consciousness like a mosquito. James kept questioning if he heard anything or if it was just the messed-up jumble in his head. It kept popping in and out at uneven intervals and finally, James pulled over at a wayside to listen.

Turning his head in every direction, James tried to hone in on the sound. He needed to know if it was there at all. Maybe it was a phantom sound, like the phantom pains people have when they lose a limb. But then James began to capture it. It was low and he kept bending to hear it, and it was to his right, so he tilted and tilted, until he was face level with the car's stereo system. And that's when he saw it: the bright green numbers of a radio station. The car stereo was on.

Quickly, James pressed his left ear against it. There was something, but it was soft and it seemed to stay just out of his reach. Then he twisted himself into a pretzel and put his right ear against the radio. And the sound burst through. Electric guitar, James thought, and a drum. It zinged around inside his head and he tried to clear it, to make the sound louder and constant, but it faded and shot back like a ping-pong ball. James listened for a while, closing his eyes and hearing the sound as the color blue, dancing back and forth across his eyelids.

It was all coming back. There was no probably about it.

Then he took off again. If James' hearing was coming back, he wanted to hear his clocks. He had to hurry now, but he could still be there before the six-o'clock chime.

When James drove in, only a few lit windows welcomed him home. But when he stepped out of the car, Cooley threw open the front door. She ran down the path and before James knew it, she had her arms wrapped around his waist. He hesitated a moment, then hugged her back. She was so thin, he could feel every bone.

It felt odd holding her. James touched the backs of ribs and shoulder blades, sticking out sharp from her skin to his, but he felt something else too. Warmth. She sent out a heat that was foreign to James. She wasn't like Diana or his mother, or even Ione. The heat wasn't the roll of passion or the sear of hatred or even the snugged-up feel of comfort. It was something else. Something new and young and vibrant. There was a throbbing in her too, a steady bump that resounded from her chest to James and there was an echo where her wrists pressed into his back. Her heartbeat.

James held her just a bit longer, to feel that young life which he never felt within his own skin, thrumming through his own veins, and then he stepped back. She smiled at James and looked quickly away.

Ione and Neal came around the back, Ione pulling on her coat, apparently getting ready to leave. Then they caught sight of James and hurried over to the car. All their mouths were moving, but nothing got through. James wished they sounded like electric guitars.

"Wait!" he said and held up his hand. "I still can't hear, although I'm going to. Let's get inside and get the notebook out. Everyone grab a box."

With all those hands, it didn't take long to unload the car. Cooley was the first to find the notebook and she started scribbling in it. Then she handed it to James.

"Y R U home????? U said U'd be gone 4 a couple days!"

James explained about the Time Museum while Ione grabbed the notebook and then Cooley grabbed it from her. Eventually, it returned to James.

"So you're hearing is going too be ok?"

"U shud have checked B4 U left! I cud have looked on the internet!"

"My hearing is going to be fine," James said. "The doctor said just what Doc has been saying here. He said sounds would come back to me gradually." James started opening boxes. "On the way home, I began to hear bits and pieces. Mostly with my right ear."

They pressed toward him, all talking at once, and suddenly, while James was happy to see them, he also wanted to be alone. Even in his silence, this was still too much commotion for him to handle. He just wanted to tinker with the clocks, eat some supper, and go to bed.

"Hey," he said and patted everyone's shoulder. He left his hand on Cooley, drawing her a little bit closer. "If it's all right with you, I just want to unpack and go to bed. I'm really tired. Would it be okay if we all just talked tomorrow?"

Cooley and Neal nodded and Ione wrote in the notebook. "Of course you should rest," she said. "Their's leftover stew in the crockpot." Then Neal and Ione headed for the front door.

"Cooley," James asked, "are all the clocks wound? Do I need to know anything?"

She shook her head and gave the A-okay sign with her fingers. Then she hugged James again and for a moment, he relished it. Her head fit neatly under his chin and he felt her relax against him. James patted her back. Then she smiled and left.

Moving through his house, James began to find new homes for the clocks from Abandoned Here. He made notes on the clipboard so that he could add them to the daily schedule. He wound each one and felt the cases for the steady vibration as they resumed their work.

After a bit, James only had the miniature mantel and the skeleton clock left. He knew the mantel was going down in the workshop for now, it had to be fixed, but what about the skeleton? He set it in several places, including next to his mother's anniversary clock on his bedside table, but nothing seemed to work. The skeleton didn't feel settled. Eventually, James brought both clocks down to the workshop and placed them on his bench.

Cooley's acorn clock rested on its towel, almost completely put back together. James would finish that first, then start on Diana's clock. He pulled out her remains, the movement and the gold six and the hands, and brought them to the mantel. It would work, he could see it. The movement could be mounted inside the mantel. Some soldering and connecting, and both clocks would live again. He thought about that, Diana's movement in a foreign body, the mantel clock accepting a foreign heart and both of them working together. He touched the mantel's case and it sent its warmth through his fingers. The desire to run was there. It would work. And somehow, James would incorporate the number six and the hands. Even if they just nestled inside the clock's case.

But what about the skeleton? James sat down at his workbench and watched it, its artful precision open for all to view. It was like seeing a person made of transparent skin, exposing all the bloodwork and muscles and organs within. The clock was constant motion, the teeth of various wheels fitting into each other, the cogs moving ever forward, pushing the pendulum, the pendulum pushing the hands. This clock was an open diagram on how time passed.

James blinked. Then he looked around.

Other than clocks in various states of repair, this room had no timepiece. James always used his watch down here. Yet in front of him, there was now a working model of what he strived for: a cleanly performing clock. No hesitation, no skips or jumps ahead. Just time moving solidly before his eyes.

What better place for this clock than in the workshop?

Carefully, James constructed a worthy pedestal. Setting an old but sturdy wooden box upside down on the lefthand corner of the workbench, James covered it with some black crushed velvet so that no sign of the knotted wood peeked out. Digging around in another drawer, he found a lace doily, probably picked up at some estate sale or another, and draped it over the velvet. Then the skeleton clock settled down on its perch. It was an odd slice of elegance on an old workbench, but it worked. The skeleton clock would help him to resurrect more and more of its extended family, starting with the acorn clock and the miniature mantel.

Satisfied, James went upstairs to unpack. When he put the suitcase away on the top shelf of his bedroom closet, he truly felt like he was at home.

Before shutting off the light in final preparation for sleep, James reached inside the bedside table for his drawing pad. He needed to say goodbye to the clock he knew he would never build. Flipping to the correct page, James looked at the picture of a young boy learning to tell time at his mother's knee. James held it for a bit and his hands began to shake.

He didn't learn how to tell time at his mother's knee. It's hard to tell time in the underground darkness of a root cellar. It was James' third grade teacher who discovered he didn't know how to tell time when she incorporated time-telling into math word problems. James stared at his math sheet that day, reading the words that told him to give the number of minutes passing between 2:10 and 2:35, 5:30 and 7:10 and he had no idea what the answers could be. He heard people refer to the time, but he didn't know how that connected to the numbers on a face of a clock. Going around the room, calling on students, Mrs. Bernicky finally came to James. "James," she said, "read problem number twelve."

Carefully, James said, "Grace leaves for the store at 10:20. She gets back at 11:10. How long was Grace gone?"

The class waited for the answer. The silence pushed against his chest and he had difficulty breathing. He tried to figure it out. If he did it like a regular math problem, 1110 minus 1020, he got ninety. "Ninety minutes?" James whispered.

The look on her face and the suppressed snickers of his classmates told James how wrong he was. Mrs. Bernicky made him stay after school that day, which terrified James because he knew he'd miss the bus. If he wasn't off that bus and down in the cellar in his cage when his mother woke up from her nap, James would be in huge trouble.

But the stuff Mrs. Bernicky showed James fascinated him. She brought out a big red molded plastic clock with bright blue hands. The numbers were blue caps that lifted off the clock, showing the number of minutes underneath, so under the one was a five, under the two was a ten, and so on. She explained the difference between the hour and minute hands. Although the plastic clock didn't have one, she told James about the sweeping second hand too. "Over the next few days," she said, "I'll show you when to say how many minutes it is before the hour, or when it is a quarter past or half past or quarter to." That sounded wonderful to James and he loved the way the clock hands neatly sliced the day into manageable pieces. If he could just get through his day, five minutes at a time, he would make it.

"We'll do this again tomorrow, James, okay?" she said and James followed her gaze to the big flat-faced clock at the back of the classroom. Its solid ticking accompanied his thoughts throughout the day and now he knew what to call those sounds…seconds. He could count them and follow them into minutes and minutes into hours. James looked at the clock and figured out the time. 3:25.

"Mrs. Bernicky, what time does school get out?" he asked.

"Two-thirty-five," she said. "How many minutes ago was that, James?"

She smiled, but James' heart froze. He knew now that fifty minutes had passed. He would have to walk home from school and it would take forever to get there. He tried to answer, but he couldn't. Instead, his eyes filled up with tears. James hated crying, but it seemed to sometimes come over him as a force he couldn't control.

"What's wrong?" She looked at the clock again. "James, do you take the bus or are you a walker?"

"I take the bus," he whispered.

"Oh, and I've made you miss it!" She quickly got up and threw some things into a big leather bag with a buckle that she brought with her every day. "Come on, I'll take you home. Can you show me the way?"

James nodded and tried to swallow his tears. All he could hope for was that his mother was still napping and he could slip into the root cellar and she'd never know that he was late. He was buttoning up his jacket when Mrs. Bernicky handed him the toy clock. "You take this with you," she said. "You can practice with it tonight."

It felt like the most precious gift in the world, even though James knew he couldn't keep it. All the way home, he balanced that plastic clock on his knees, moving its arms, pulling out the numbers and seeing the time passing underneath. When they got within sight of his house, James slid the toy under his jacket. He knew he had to hide it from his mother.

As Mrs. Bernicky pulled up to the front door, James' heart fell beneath the car's tires. His mother was standing on the front step.

After getting out of the car, James stood behind Mrs. Bernicky. "Hi, Mom," he said because he knew Mrs. Bernicky expected him to say something. His mother didn't say a word.

"I'm sorry James is late, I hope we didn't worry you," Mrs. Bernicky said. "He was having a little trouble in math and I kept him after to work with him on it. I didn't realize he was a bus student."

James peeked around his teacher's coat. His mother wasn't looking at him, she was staring at the ground.

"Did you know James couldn't tell time?"

His mother shook her head without raising it. "I guess I never thought about it," she mumbled.

"Well, I'd like to work with him to help him catch up, if that's okay. Could I keep him after school for the rest of the week? I think that's all it will take." Mrs. Bernicky hesitated, then stepped a little closer. James shadowed her. "He's really very bright, you know."

James saw his mother's mouth twist. Mrs. Bernicky stepped backwards and bumped into James and he knew she saw it too.

"You can have him," his mother said.

Mrs. Bernicky nodded and then turned. "See you tomorrow, James," she said. She bent down so she was face to face with him and she smiled. He smelled mint and something flowery. "Remember to practice."

Then she left and James was out of her shadow, standing in the sun, but he felt like all the warmth was sucked out of the air. He stood there, listening to the car get further and further away. Then he looked at his mother.

She met James' eyes. And she pointed toward the root cellar. So he went. But even in the dark, that little plastic clock kept him company. He could feel its hands and he moved them forward. Like a blind boy, he lifted the caps, then felt the numbers underneath. Five minutes. Ten. Fifteen. Time was always moving forward to where he could escape.

James still had that toy clock, he never could bring himself to throw it out, even when he grew too old for toys. Setting the drawing pad aside, James got out of bed and went to the closet. He kept the clock in there, in a box on the floor, away and out of view. For a while, he even hung it on the wall of his bedroom, but when Diana started staying over, he took it down. It was too embarrassing to have a toy on the wall, plus he didn't want her to ask any questions. She always did anyway and James didn't need something to start a conversation about his past, about his childhood. Diana wanted children. James could never tell her. He could never let her know about his mother, about the parts of his mother that flowed through his own body, his own blood.

Now James unearthed the clock and brought it back to bed. Mrs. Bernicky never asked him to give it back. He felt like he stole that clock, and that bothered him because he liked Mrs. Bernicky so much. But that clock kept him such good company, James couldn't return it.

In bed now, he moved its hands, watched time going by. The little number caps still lifted out easily and he looked at the minutes preserved below. His mother gave him a watch for Christmas that year, a Mickey Mouse watch, which surprised and delighted James. She never gave him anything, but that year, when he woke up in the morning, it was there in a little box on his dresser. No ribbon or paper, but it was there. James looked at it for a while, wondering if it somehow came from his father, and for a few seconds, as James set the hands and pushed in the stem that set the watch forward, he let himself believe it. James knew better than to say anything, so he just carefully strapped the watch onto his wrist and wore it to breakfast. Mickey told time by moving his arms and pointing at the numbers and James laughed at all the uncomfortable positions he got into. His mother never said a word.

With that watch, James discovered another wonderful way that time could help him. When he went out to the root cellar that Christmas day, it was cold and the coldness made it seem even darker. As he curled up in his cage, trying to stay warm under his jacket and a thin baby blanket, James heard the sound of a new ticking, harmonizing with the Big Ben alarm clock at his side. The lighter than air tick came from his watch and it filled up his ear and a part of his heart and suddenly, he wasn't so alone. There was more sound.

James wished he could hear that sound now. He still had that watch too, tucked away in one of the dresser drawers. It still ran. But a grown man doesn't wear a Mickey Mouse watch, even if it did come from his mother, even such a mother as she was.

Now, James set aside the toy clock and looked again at his sketch. He noticed some odd shadings and markings and he rubbed at them and then realized they came from a drawing on the next page.

But James' drawing was the only one in the book.

Slowly, he turned the page. It was a penciled picture, beautiful, with lots of fine detail. A little girl stood before James, wearing ripped-knee jeans and a t-shirt with a star on the front. Her face was downcast and she studied a little watch on her left wrist, held up to her chin. Next to her stood a grandfather clock. The picture was so clear, James could see that the time on the clock matched the watch.

He ran his fingers carefully down the page, not wanting to smudge it, but wanting to figure out who drew it. As if his fingers could detect who held the pencil.

At the bottom left, on the sole of the little girl's untied sneaker, James found it. Three initials. ASD. He went through each of the people who'd been in his house while he was gone, and none of their names matched up. But when James ran through them again, thinking of each person, he heard Ione's voice. She turned to James and said, "You shouldn't have yelled at Amy Sue," and "Amy Sue needs encouragement." Amy Sue Dander.

Cooley.

CHAPTER TWENTY-TWO:

FISTFULS OF MAGIC
The Skeleton Clock's Story

When Marcus lost his job because a melon-breasted girl told the School Board about his collection of photographs of nude junior high school girls on the computer in the classroom where he taught eighth grade English, he didn't think it would be a big issue. He coached a winning basketball team after all, and sports are important, and everyone knew that the English teacher who crooned Sylvia Plath's poetry to rapt prepubescents and who wore a ponytail down to the middle of his back was cool, and so he was invaluable. Those pictures? Who knew how they got there? He did, but who else knew?

So Marcus left the school, confident that he'd get his job back in a few days, when the fuss blew over. But then a few days passed, and a few weeks. A couple months and he was looking for a job. But no one was looking for him. He looked everywhere, from other schools to jobs in factories, in retail stores, in 24-hour convenience marts. Being fired from a public middle school mid-semester seemed to raise red flags with employers.

In desperation one afternoon, Marcus stopped at a little house in town that had a flashing sign by the front door. "Tarot," it read. "Crystal ball. Tea leaves. Stop inside." An old lady turned off her television set and invited Marcus to sit down at a card table covered with black velvet and last night's supper. He chose Tarot, and she flipped cards in a quirky pattern and told him that his life had taken a turn for the worse recently and that he had to forge a new path. Which Marcus already knew. But as he left, she pressed a green candle in his hand, told him to burn it every day, that it would bring him good fortune. And that it cost five dollars. He paid, went home, and lit the candle.

As the days passed and the candle burned further, Marcus began to consider it more and more. The power of fire. Mysticism. Magic. That woman, just by scattering a few cards, was able to make enough money to support herself and her house. There was magic there. And five dollars for this little candle!

The bills were piling up. The phone was cut off and with it, his computer line which led to chatrooms with the young girls he missed so much. Marcus sat and worried and looked at his diminishing candle. Then he went to the Dollar Store. Maybe he needed more bang for his buck, more magic for his money.

So he bought candles. Dozens. Green for money (obvious, and backed by the fortune teller), yellow for fame (if you're famous, you're a star and stars are yellow) pink for good health (in the pink!), and purple for a long life (royalty wore purple, and royal lineage went on forever). Marcus reasoned that if he could just keep them all lit, good things were bound to happen. But keeping them all lit proved a challenge. More and more, he began to stay home, watching his candles, making sure his future was guaranteed.

Then one afternoon, while watching a movie, Marcus made a wonderful discovery. The movie was an old one, a black and white, but everything was black and white on Marcus' t.v. At a moment of high drama in the movie, Marcus coughed to the swelling music and a dab of phlegm flew across the room and hit the television screen. Right on the starlet's deep-Y cleavage. Bullseye, Marcus thought, and pumped his fist in the air.

The lit candles flickered and the problem candles sat in Marcus' lap, wicks clogged with wax waiting to be dug free. Marcus used the knife he buttered his toast with that morning and he planned to use it later to slice the film of his ninety-nine cent t.v. dinner, this week's special at the Save-A-Lot. Plus he had a coupon which brought the price down to forty-nine cents and with the remaining money, the saved money, he splurged on a York Peppermint Patty, something he saved special for dessert.

Whittling at the candles, Marcus stared at the television where an old woman and her daughter stood behind his phlegm smear and in front of a grandfather clock. The camera focused in on the pendulum. It wasn't moving. "It stopped this morning when he died," whispered the woman. "Just like it stopped on the day your grandfather died."

Marcus pondered that idea. A clock that stopped when someone died. His eyes flickered around the room and he counted the spots of color, although he already knew the sum. There were more purple candles than any of the others. A long life. A clock stopping could stop it.

Pulling himself out of his chair, Marcus walked around the house, tallying the clocks. On the television sat the clock from his ex-wife, a gift on their first anniversary, a silver heart with the words, "love you for all time" scrolled around the edges. There was an AM/FM clock radio in the bedroom, green digital numbers glowing throughout the day or night, even when the power went out, because it had battery backup. Marcus chose it especially because he never wanted to be late for a day with his students, especially with his girls, and he never was, until now. In the kitchen, there was the special catalog splurge, a clock featuring Harley Davidson motorcycles, a different hog for each hour, the clock's chime the growl of an engine, bought to celebrate the raise a few weeks before the melon girl tattled. You regret telling the bitch now…you thought she was different. Thought the lowcut t-shirts and spread legs in mini denim skirts and the quick kiss and grope in your car one afternoon after she cried and confessed her crush meant she would understand, would lay on your bed the way those porn girls did, and like it.

All of the clocks ran and told accurate time. But Marcus didn't feel any supernatural mumbo-jumbo going on between him and them. He figured he'd live even if they died. He knew for a fact that he lived when the silver heart's second hand froze for an entire eighteen hours before he inserted new batteries, \$1.99 double-A's on special at Walgreens, down to a buck-fifty with his coupon.

So Marcus sat back down and thought some more about the clocks, about dying or not dying. And he wondered what would happen if there was a connection with a clock, a magic connection, and the clock could stop and stop him as well. But if it kept running...

Forever?

Marcus sat forward and shut off the television so he could think. If a clock ran forever and it had a magic connection with the owner, then the owner would live forever too. He'd seen a lot of old movies and read old classics where clocks stopped when their owners died, but why not the reverse?

Because no one ever thought it through before? Never thought outside the box?

Marcus smiled and pumped his fist in the air.

But what kind of clock? The clocks he already had were worthless for that sort of thing. He loved the silver heart, but if it didn't help his marriage to last, how could it help him to live? And he loved the motorcycle clock too, but in a different way. Each time it growled the hour, Marcus felt a surge of power, as if he straddled a hog right then, flying down the freeway. But motorcycles didn't seem appropriate for sustaining life.

So Marcus studied the candles. Maybe a purple clock, like the purple candles? A grandfather clock like in the movie? And then he decided he'd just know. Just like he knew which girl to chat up on the internet, which girl to keep after school for extra credit. Just like he instinctively knew what color candle to buy for every need. Marcus even bought them without coupons, that was how strongly they reached for him, knocked him over. Granted, the candles hadn't provided for everything yet, but it was difficult to keep them all burning at the same time and if just one sputtered out, then the magic was gone, like a bad bulb in a Christmas tree string. But still, there was that day when Marcus had all the green ones burning at once and he found a twenty-dollar bill on the sidewalk. Another time, he had the yellows lit for twenty-four hours straight and then he witnessed a car crash and the police officers quoted him and his name got in the paper.

Though the red candles in the bedroom, they never got Marcus anywhere. Since his wife left and the melon girl tattled, he always slept alone. Shaking his head, Marcus settled in to the project at hand. There were still seven candles to unclog, but he set them aside and placed the fixed ones back in their places, their wicks lit and dancing. After making sure that all the rest of the candles were burning throughout the house, Marcus stuck the remaining seven in his various coat pockets and left. If the candles weren't in the house, they couldn't be counted among the ones that didn't work.

So where to go to find a clock? Marcus hit the clock shop downtown, an obvious choice, but nothing there felt right and besides, the prices were way out of an unemployed teacher's league. Marcus never knew clocks could be so expensive. A lady in a green dress tried to talk him into a payment plan on a beautiful grandfather clock, almost like the one in the movie, although it was oak instead of black and white, but he had to turn her down. Choosing the hardware store next, he found a few nice shop clocks, shaped like saws and hammers and busty, big-butted women. Marcus studied those for a while, especially one woman in particular, sitting with her arms braced behind her and her breasts thrust out. But those all ran on batteries and Marcus just wasn't sure about that. Until he got a job, his life would be dependent on whatever battery coupons he had that week and what would happen if the clock started to run down when he didn't have enough money to buy them, even with a coupon?

So Marcus kept searching through the Hallmark, the Dollar Store, even the Walgreens and the Save-A-Lot, until four o'clock when he stopped at a Kwik Trip and bought a newspaper and a plain cup of coffee. He still felt great about his lifesaving discovery, a miracle, really, even though he hadn't found the clock yet, so he splurged and bought a chocolate-chocolate chip cookie too.

Sitting outside behind the convenience store, Marcus leaned against the wall and opened the paper to the classifieds, like always, but this time, he looked at the For Sale ads instead of the Help

Wanteds. There were a few clocks and he closed his eyes after reading each description, waiting to see if any leaped out at him, but none did. In a way, he felt grateful…there wasn't a clock in the paper going for less than two hundred dollars. Deciding to skip the job ads, Marcus moved back to the sidewalk and sniffed the air like a dog.

And something pulled him to the left. He felt it. Distinct.

Before he even entered the Goodwill, the magic gripped him. His skin pebbled up and his fingers itched, reaching for the mystical connection. But wandering up and down the aisles, Marcus saw nothing. Just the usual collection of mismatched plates and glasses, kitschy welcome signs with missing L's, black and white t.v.'s just like the one he had at home. Then he was drawn toward the showcase. It was usually full of old costume jewelry and maybe some broken pottery or tarnished silver, but today, there was something else. A clock.

A miracle.

Marcus stared through the glass at it for a while, wondering if the clock was really all together. He could see every part because there was no wooden case hiding the insides from view. The clock was as bare as the girl in the blown-up photo from the internet on his bathroom wall. Marcus liked to light her with bright white candles, white for purity, because when he found her, when he found just the right one, she would look just like that and still be a virgin. Marcus looked at her every night when he took his bath and then he thought of her among all the red candles in his bedroom and sometimes, it was like she was really there.

Marcus decided the naked clock must work because every part was moving, a burlesque of timekeeping as the pendulum swayed back and forth, directing all the wheels and gears behind her. Marcus knew it was the other way, the gears directed the pendulum, but still, the rhythm was so strong, it was easy to believe otherwise. Marcus kept putting his face closer and closer to the showcase, his breath fogging up the glass, and he wondered if this was the magic connection. Did she want him?

Then it struck him. Of course this was the clock. What better for life-sustaining than a clock with everything exposed? If a part was about to break down, he'd know it at the first rub, the first creak, and he'd fix her before she even had a chance to stop. It was just so obvious.

When the tomato-breasted clerk asked if he'd like to see something, Marcus pointed to the clock. As she retrieved her, she bumped her against the counter and Marcus shuddered, but the clock still ran. She was brass and shiny and Marcus thought how pretty she would look with all the candles lit around her. If he kept lighting the candles. Why would he need candles when he had eternal life?

The price was five dollars, the same price as almost a whole week of his suppers on special at the Save-A-Lot, but Marcus paid quickly. He knew he had to show the clock that he understood the magic connection. He was prepared to sacrifice the almighty dollar and possibly a week of dinners in exchange for the clock's gift, the gift of blood that flowed and replenished in a consistent rhythm of time, a heart that shadowed every move of the pendulum.

Then the clerk pulled off the protective glass dome and reached for the pendulum. Marcus gasped. "No!" he said and snatched the clock away. "I'll just carry her like this." The tomato-breasted clerk warned that the clock would probably break on the way home if it wasn't stopped and properly packaged and it couldn't be returned, but Marcus knew she wouldn't, he'd make sure of it. He had his life in his hands.

It was difficult, walking home, balancing the clock on cradled arms and stopping every few minutes to make sure she was running and not just jostling back and forth. A few times, the pendulum smacked one of the four golden legs that stood the clock on its pedestal and when that happened, Marcus swore he felt his heart banging into his lungs. But he made it home, both he and the clock in one piece, though he was breathless and worn out.

Wandering throughout the house, Marcus tried to decide where the clock should stand. It needed to be a central place, a place where he could keep an eye on her even if he wasn't in the room. The kitchen opened to the living room and he could see her there if he moved the chair at the table closer to the archway. He always kept the bathroom door open so he could watch the t.v., which meant the living room was in plain sight from there as well. So the living room was the ideal place and Marcus wished for a moment that he had a pedestal, something large and carved and ornate, something fitting for a life-saver, a life-sustainer. But then he wondered about the bedroom, out of sight down the hall. And what about sleeping? What if the clock stopped then?

It wouldn't be a bad way to die, during sleep. Better than a painful heart attack or a knock-you-off-your-feet stroke or getting hit by a bus. But this wasn't about dying well, it was about living forever. Marcus set the clock on a fresh new paper towel, the pattern pretty and purple, centering it on a table near the recliner.

If he was going to live forever, he would never sleep again.

Marcus thought about that for a while, watching the clock tell his life's time, and his eyelids already felt heavy. He thought about never shutting them, about never sinking again into a gray mist speckled with the green of money, the yellow of flashing cameras and the silver of microphones, the pink to red to purple of sex. Hot dreams of lying with the just sprouting bathroom virgin on a bed surrounded by flames and melting into her body, her skin as warm and smooth as wax. And then he decided sleep was worth the risk. If the worst thing that could happen was an orgasmic death in the arms of his pornographic virgin, then it was okay. What a way to go, really.

Except Marcus didn't want to die.

Before sitting down, he had to unload the seven candles in his pockets, so he arranged them around the clock. Carefully, he freed each of the wicks, then lit them. The flames flickered against the glass dome, the shiny brass, and Marcus sat back and confirmed the clock's beauty. The sight made Marcus feel warm. Already his blood flowed more smoothly and he felt his heart rate slow, his breath even out as the clock took over. Marcus felt so much better.

In the kitchen, he used the butter knife to slice the film on his t.v. dinner. As it cooked, he snuck peeks through the archway to make sure the clock was still running. Marcus ate propped in his recliner, putting the television on, and then he spent the night supposedly watching sit-coms and sports events, but really studying the seductive sway of the pendulum's hips. It was amazing, really. He felt like he was humming with a new life. Ticking.

Eventually, the glow of the candles, the clock's serenade and the lowered volume of the television put Marcus to sleep. He woke with a start, checked the clock, went to sleep again. Woke with a start. He didn't have a single dream, his moments of sleep were too short. When morning came, Marcus still swore he felt his veins opening, his heart beating with a new strength and purpose, but he was very, very tired.

How many nights had he spent waking up to check the candles? Or reading all the out-of-reach jobs in the classifieds? Or refusing to answer the jangle of the phone because of the bill collectors; that is, until the phone was disconnected, bringing with it a sad, but welcome peace? And now there was this clock.

Which might not even work. Maybe she wasn't saving his life at all. Marcus closed his eyes for a second and remembered that moment when the clock took over, when he felt something open in his body, a dam holding in all the evil, the bad luck, the ill health, death lurking somewhere within his own skin, and it all washed away. The magic connection was there, he just knew it.

So it was okay to sleep. The clock would watch over him. She almost seemed to nod and Marcus wanted so much to believe.

But in his mind, a doubt still squirmed. It poked Marcus in the neck and in the back of the eyelids and although he wanted to lie down and sleep the morning away, he decided he needed reassurance.

Getting up, Marcus dragged through the house, checking the candles. A few burned out overnight, especially the ones in the bedroom where he always had a window cracked. He relit them, then made a pit stop in the bathroom, saying good morning to the virgin as he stood next to the toilet. He pretended that he felt her nubile admiration and he gave his penis an extra healthy stroke and tap, just for her. When he got to the kitchen, the bread was moldy, so he made a breakfast of last week's day-old bakery and coffee made from yesterday's grounds. They would be replaced with fresh ones tomorrow.

As he waited for the coffee to brew, Marcus stood in the archway and watched the clock. He tried to think of a way to test her effectiveness. He scanned the kitchen, as if the dirty dishes or empty cabinets or the dozen lit candles would give him an answer. And in a sense, they did. When his eyes landed on yesterday's butter knife, a flame reflected off the blade and he felt a new level of magic shimmer into his skin.

And he realized a butter knife just wouldn't do it.

Collecting two stiff muffins, a cup of coffee and a clean steak knife, Marcus returned to the clock. He ate his breakfast with her, savoring every bite, because having a new life taught him to appreciate all things. The muffins were sweeter, the coffee more fragrant and even the knife shone prettily in the candlelight. The handle was a solid black, the blade a toothy silver. It smiled at Marcus and he smiled back. The clock ticked confidently, pushing Marcus' heart forward into each new second.

So Marcus finished his breakfast and then picked up the knife. He felt afraid for a moment, but just for a moment, and out loud, he apologized to the clock for doubting her. Then he stared at her, stared straight past the pendulum into her innermost workings, into her soul and his own, and he concentrated. He watched everything move forward in that clock, keeping perfect time, keeping him on his steady life path. And Marcus held the knife to one wrist.

He felt it as he sliced, but he kept his eyes on the clock and sure enough, the pain went quickly away. Marcus sawed back and forth until he hit something solid. That was deep enough, and then he switched hands. It was hard to hold the knife, his hand was slick and loose, but he didn't look down and he started sawing again. Until that bone was reached.

And there was still no pain. Marcus lifted his arms high above his head, thrusting both fists in a victory celebration, and the blood flew into his eyes. He saw then the mess he'd made and for a second, his heart skipped and shuddered. He quickly focused again on the clock, but while he tried to concentrate, his eyes blurred.

His blood was flowing smoothly again, and there was nothing left to dam it.

Marcus cursed.

As he slid to the floor, Marcus made sure to knock over the clock so that she fell with him, landing next to his head with a solid thunk and with a few candles too. There were sparks and through them, Marcus saw the clock's workings slow and stop.

Like the movie. At least there was some magic in that.

CHAPTER TWENTY-THREE

JAMES

And so as you grow older, you settle into your solitary life. You find solace in your clocks and in your home and even in the distanced comfort that the little town you live in provides. There are people who smile at you, shake your hand, and claim to make your acquaintance. And though you know the truth, you still gather whatever warmth you can while keeping your life carefully to yourself.

It's the nights that are so cold. Even as the clocks gather around you, fill the emptiness with chatter and song, there is only your own skin to keep you company.

Inside you, the rage slithers down the river of the parallel veins. And you wonder sometimes if it's thick, thick like cholesterol, gumming up your blood. Gumming up your life. But as long as that river is alive, as long as your mother flows within you, you have to be on guard.

Late at night, when you sit in your living room, watch the fire, and listen to the clocks, you fold your hands in your lap and you hold very, very still. You can feel the thrum of that hidden river, follow its pulse from your mind to your chest to your fists and feet. Your mind thinks unthinkable thoughts sometimes. Like the time it burst and your thoughts roared with the profound pleasure of watching someone else's face bloom red and blue and purple. Your chest sears with the strength and desire to harm and it sends the anger to your extremities, turning them into weapons. And sometimes, in the darkest of nights, you have your dream of sending someone else to the root cellar. Sending a child who looks amazingly like you, but isn't you, and you burn with the wonderful ache of power. But when you wake, you are soaked through with shame.

You know how it feels, to be locked away like that. How can you possibly want to do it to someone else? Even in your deepest most hidden place? You wonder if burn victims wish for blisters on their wives, if cancer patients dream of tumors sprouting on their sons' brains.

Imagine.

You are so ashamed.

You consider sometimes as you sit by the fire, your hands folded in your lap, who you would have been if only your own blood flowed through you. If your mother wasn't there at all. You imagine what it would have been like to be in a different family. Would you have learned to play? To sing at the sky and swing through leaf-laden branches, watching the sun fall in dapples over your favorite pair of jeans? The jeans a different mother shook her head over, but still washed and left on the foot of your bed so you could find them in the morning on days when the outdoors called and you could run and hide as a game and only as a game. Would you have dated a few girls in high school, kissed in movie theaters and in dark parked cars and sometimes, even behind the closed door of a special girl's bedroom while her parents were away? Would you have gone to college and learned everything you ever wanted to know, everything you ever questioned and wondered about?

And married. Married a special girl, maybe the same special girl from high school, and you would have had children. A boy, a girl, maybe more. And the only door you would have closed would have been those to their bedrooms, at night, softly, after kissing them with lips so light, they never stirred beneath their blankets. You wouldn't even own a root cellar.

Imagine.

Instead, you live alone in a house full of clocks. Clocks which you love and which love you. You do what you love, search for clocks, save clocks, present them to the public and protect them from the same. Yet every night, as you sit surrounded by those you love, you ache with a loneliness that you can't imagine anyone else feeling. Not as they live their lives of laughter at dinner, kisses at bedtime, and spooned bodies before falling asleep.

James knew that ache, as he knew so many different kinds of pain so very well. Too well. Sometimes, he wondered if there was any other way to be, but in pain. He sat at night and listened to his clocks and to the flow of his hidden and secret anger and he tried to imagine what his life could have been. Who he could have been.

Imagine.

Oh, imagine.

The next afternoon, Cooley helped wind the clocks. James' fingers were completely healed now and he could do it himself, but she just kept hanging at his elbow. So James told her to make use of herself and get to work.

"You know," he said as he watched her wind a mantel clock, "I can really do this myself now. You don't need to come over anymore."

She shrugged and kept winding.

"Why aren't you hanging out with your gang?" For a moment, James saw Cooley again, sauntering down the street, surrounded by those black-clad kids. He remembered their sneers and their loud voices, Cooley's among them. The voice she had, the snarl in it, her words bitten and sharp. When she looked at James now, he could still see that Cooley, but there was a difference too. There was something going on with her eyes, with the way she held her mouth. He wondered if her voice had changed, he wondered if it was softer.

But there was a part of James that didn't want to know. It would be so much easier to keep Cooley where she belonged, with the gang of kids he hated, than to learn how to like somebody, how to behave when he liked somebody. With Ione, with Gene, even with Molly and Neal and Doc, James could fake it, he could reflect off of what they did to him. But Cooley was different. She was still new, still fresh-faced under the too-dark make-up she wore, and anything James did could hurt her and the hurt would show in her eyes. And anything she did could hurt James too. It would be better if she stayed where she belonged, and James as well.

She shrugged again, then crossed the room to get the notebook. James busied himself winding. "I'm mostly here," she wrote. "They think I've gone weird or something."

"Well, there's not all that much for you to do here," James said. "I don't really need an employee, unless I'm away for the weekend or something."

She just turned back to the clocks.

He watched her, watched her young arms turning the keys, pulling on chains, saw her bend easily to get the clocks on the lower tables and shelves. She smiled as she worked and he saw her lips move. She was talking to the clocks. James wished he could hear what she said.

And he realized that he didn't want her to go. It had been a while since he didn't want someone to leave and he didn't know quite what to do. So James walked quickly out of the room.

Ione was in the kitchen, cleaning up the lunch dishes. He didn't need her to do that anymore either, but Ione seemed to have taken up permanent residence. Her form at the kitchen sink was a familiar sight now. It was like she belonged, her body pushing a worn curve in the edge of the countertop as she leaned over the sink. If James walked by outside and saw her face in the window, he wouldn't be startled. Wouldn't be startled to see another face in the house where he'd lived alone for so long.

Ione placed a cup of coffee in front of James and when he picked it up, his hands shook. Coffee slopped over the edge of the cup onto the table. In a flash, Ione wiped it up. Then she placed her hand on his shoulder and looked at him, her eyebrows raised. James knew exactly what she was asking. Are you okay? Are you okay, James?

He asked himself the same question. Then he took a sip of coffee and closed his eyes. It took a moment, but he nodded. He wasn't sure which motion his head would take, a nod or a shake, until he started, but then his chin dipped forward. James felt Ione leave and when he opened his eyes, she was back at the sink. He knew she was humming, her hips swayed with her own song, and he wondered what it sounded like. He wondered if Ione could sing.

Cooley walked in and sat down. She had the notebook clutched in both hands. James could see big handwriting on it again and her mouth was drawn tight and her knuckles were white. She said something to Ione who came and looked over her shoulder at the notebook. She said something too and Cooley nodded, her eyes closing. She slid the notebook over to James.

In big black letters, diagonally across the page, Cooley shouted, "DON'T U WANT ME HERE ANYMORE?" James was about to hand the notebook back when he noticed smaller letters at the bottom of the page, on the last line and crammed into the right hand corner. She said, "plz don't send me away."

James' hands shook again and he set the notebook down quickly. Please don't send me away. Please don't send me there. How many times did he think those words, say them, as his mother pointed to the root cellar? Too many times, because they stopped being words after a while. They became a feeling, a cramp in his lungs, a cramp that got worse after he got into his cage and raised his nose to the dirt ceiling and howled.

He looked at Cooley. She faced James, but her eyes were still closed. He wondered if she wanted to howl. He wondered what root cellar he'd be sending her to if he told her to leave. There was so much he wanted to say, but so little he could actually muster. "Yes," James said softly. "Yes, I still want you here. I can always use the help."

Cooley's eyes flew open and for a moment, James saw a joy that soared right through his body. Part of him wanted to jump up and grab her then, dance her around the kitchen. And another part wanted to run away as fast as he could. This girl needed to be wanted, needed to be welcome and necessary, and James just didn't know where to start. If he could wind her and set her time and stick her in a corner, he could do it and do it well. But looking at her, James knew there was going to be more to it than that.

Ione patted Cooley's shoulder and said something and Cooley looked up and laughed. Bits of her laughter broke through James' ears, a staccato sound, high-pitched and sharp. He closed the notebook so he could shut the need away for a while. "We should get some work done on your clock," he said and headed for the basement. On the way down, James felt Cooley's weight reverberating behind him. She was like his shadow. At the workbench, she sat on the stool next to him, the notebook resting in her lap. She chewed on a pencil as she watched James work and listened to every explanation as he cleaned the parts and settled them into place.

James stopped about an hour and a half later, when all that was left was to wind the clock, attach the pendulum, get it going. Setting the clock upright, he turned to look at Cooley. Her eyes were focused on the painting on the front of the clock and she was smiling, a soft smile that made her seem like a child again, a six-year old sitting expectant in front of a storybook. James looked at the painting too and admired the soft greens and yellows of the willow tree, the pale blue of the lake. Cooley touched his elbow and then pointed at the little cottage tucked in the back of the painting, almost hidden by the trees. She wrote in the notebook, "I want 2 live there." She hesitated a moment, then added, "Just me. And some clocks. It would B perfect."

James thought of his house, the Home, not hidden by trees, but in the middle of a small town block. Yet he knew the feeling. For a long time, this house might as well have been in the woods, far away from everything.

James pulled out the drawing pad. Opening it to Cooley's picture, he set it in front of her on the workshop bench. Her fingers immediately got jumpy, ruffling the edges of the notebook paper, and they sat that way for a while. James was in silence, but he knew the paper must be making a whisking sound that echoed around the basement walls.

He finally figured she wasn't going to volunteer anything. "You do that?" he asked, pointing to the drawing pad.

That was all it took. She bent over the notebook and wrote like mad. While James waited, he opened his drawer of spare clock keys. Finding the right one for the acorn clock, a number six, he began to wind.

Finally, Cooley threw the notebook on the bench. She turned her back. James studied her for a moment, noting that her shoulders were steady; there were no sobs. She just sat straight, her body braced. He picked up the notebook.

"I'm sorry I went thru UR things," he read. "I did it 1 afternoon while U were gone. I just wanted 2 look. And I found that pad. I liked UR picture but it wasn't right. I had 2 fix it. There shouldn't be a mom. The mom made it wrong. Moms don't do stuff like that."

James blinked, then turned back to his own picture. A mother teaching a little boy to tell time. The mother's face was his mother's face, drawn as closely as he could remember. But he knew his mother didn't teach him to tell time. He knew that better than anybody. But he thought other moms did. He thought Cooley's mom did.

"Cooley," he said and her shoulders hunched. "Cooley, what do mothers do?"

James waited. After a bit, Cooley straightened up again. Then she turned. Her eyes were huge. Then, one arm at a time, she drew her sleeves back.

The room lurched sideways.

Scars ran from her wrist up to her elbow, then disappeared under the tight grip of her sleeve. Some scars were white and thin, others gray, and some an angry, angry red. There were dots and streaks and James could almost smell the smoke. He could almost feel her skin burning, peeling away from her flesh. A knot grabbed at his throat, the familiar feel of the collar. "Oh my god," he said softly, and then louder, "Oh my god!" James grabbed her and she came flying and he held her as tightly as he could. He felt her shaking and he knew the insides of her arms were pressed against his back, the scars rubbing into his shirt, and he wondered how she could take the pain.

But James knew. He knew. Sometimes, the pain is the only thing left that you can feel.

Reaching behind Cooley, James started the pendulum on the acorn clock. He moved the minute hand until it just barely touched the twelve. Cooley gave a great shudder and James knew the clock began to chime.

After Cooley left, James thought about what to do. She hadn't said anything else before she left, once she stopped crying. But James knew it was her mother.

He sat at the kitchen table and drank a cup of coffee. His supper, delivered by Molly, sat on the counter. He hadn't touched it yet. Molly knew she didn't have to provide meals anymore, but she said she wanted to, just to welcome him back home. And that night, James was relieved. He was too tired to think about cooking. He was too tired to eat. But having someone deliver it made him obligated and eventually, he got up and warmed the meal in the microwave.

Ione came in just as he was pushing mashed potatoes around on the plate. She'd already left for the night and while James was surprised to see her, he didn't jump. She glanced around the table, then looked at him, her palms raised. James knew she was looking for the notebook. "I think I left it downstairs," he said.

She shrugged, then picked up her pink sweater from the chair across from James. She waved it. She'd forgotten her sweater. James nodded, then set down his fork.

Sitting down, she pointed at the dinner plate. Then she pointed at James, her eyebrows raised.

"I'm okay," he said. "Just not hungry, I guess."

They sat like that for a while. Suddenly, she leaned forward and looked James straight in the eyes. James shrugged and sat back. "I'm worried about Cooley, Ione," he said. "There's…well, there's a lot going on at her home."

Ione nodded.

"You knew?"

She looked around again and so did James. Neither wanted to make the trip down the basement stairs. Finally, she got up and fetched a paper towel. She pulled a pen out of her purse and began to write. Her words bumped over the raised texture of the paper.

"Amy Sue's mom is no secret around town. We all no she's a bad person."

A bad person. James pictured this woman, someone whom he couldn't put a face to, holding Cooley's arm and lowering a cigarette onto her skin. Watching Cooley smolder. Watching her own daughter cry in pain. "Not a bad person," he said slowly. "A monster." James said the words with a certainty that weighed his tongue down in his mouth. He knew about monsters.

Ione wrote again. "Not a monster. She sleeps around a lot. Not just her husband. She drinks. Sleezy. It's not real nice for Amy Sue."

"Ione," James said, then leaned forward and grabbed Ione's hands. She stared at him, her eyes wide. "Ione, she's hurting Cooley. Her arms are all scarred. Cigarette burns." He released Ione's hands and she fell against the back of her chair. "I'm sure there's more too. A woman like that wouldn't stop with cigarettes."

Ione wasn't looking at James anymore; she stared at the air. Her lips moved and from the way they trembled, he knew she was stuttering. She was trying to say that she didn't know.

"No one knew, Ione," James said quickly. "Unless Cooley told you, you just wouldn't know. She hides it."

Ione blinked, then leaned forward to write. "I always wundered why she wore long sleeve shirts all the time," she said.

James nodded. Then he joined her in staring into space. "I have to do something, Ione," he said. "I just don't know what."

Ione scribbled some more. "Call the athoritys?" she asked.

"No. They'd just take Cooley away. She doesn't want that." And James didn't want that, though he chose not to say it aloud. He drummed his fingers and wished he could hear them, but the sharp feel of the table against his fingertips helped. He hit them harder, then harder, until Ione reached out and pressed his hand flat. The sudden stop forced the words at the tips of his fingers, the words that echoed through his head, out of his mouth. The rhythm was strong, two syllables pounded by four fingers and a stabilizing thumb, though he doubted their sensibility. "Live here," James said, then completed the thought. "I think she should live here."

Ione patted his hand, then shook her head.

"Oh, I know. I know it would look odd. A teenage girl living with an old man. But she'd have her own room and she'd be fine. She likes it here, Ione. After living in a place like that, she needs to live somewhere she likes."

Ione shook her head again, then wrote on the paper towel. "Not proper. She culd live with me and Neal."

James pictured Cooley sitting in a bedroom, her feet curled beneath her as she watched Ione dust everything with her lavender duster. Then he saw Cooley stretch her legs out and on her feet were a matching pair of pink fuzzy slippers. On her bedside table was a ceramic clock in the shape of a poodle and he knew it was battery-powered.

James wiped his eyes to clear away the vision. "No, Ione. She needs to be here." He carefully rubbed her words on the paper towel, tracing the letters. "See...I understand her, Ione. I...well, I know what it feels like. Okay? Can we leave it at that?"

Ione's mouth hung open and James saw her glance down at his arms. There were no scars there, but he crossed his arms quickly. Ione tugged at his wrists and for a second, James resisted. But then he wondered why. There was nothing. Not physically anyway, not where she could see. There were still old remnants of collar burns around his throat, but age and sagging skin helped disguise those. And the signs of the beatings were well hidden, tucked away behind layers of clothes. Slowly, he opened his arms and laid them flat on the table, palms up. His skin shone clean. "Not exactly like Cooley, Ione." James tried to think of what else to say, what words would express what he meant without giving too much away. His mother was dead. There was no need to exhume her, to expose her to other people. It was enough that she still lived in his mind, flowed through his body. "Different people have different ways, I guess."

She wrote on the paper towel. "Your mother?"

James nodded.

She sat back and closed her eyes. Her chin trembled. Then she reached out and patted his hand again, quickly, rat-a-tat pats. She returned to writing. "You'll never get her mom to agree," she said.

James grabbed the paper towel and crumpled it, feeling it crush inside his fingers. "Then I'll have to convince her," he said. It made James think about that one moment, that one time that he drew back his fist and hit his own mother. The way she staggered, then fell to the ground. And he thought about how he was able to walk right past her then, walk away, and she never even said a word.

James had to find that strength again. He looked at his curled fingers, gripping the paper towel.

Ione pulled away from the table. For a second, she stood there, hugging herself. Then she stepped behind James and wrapped her arms around his shoulders. James felt the embrace and let himself relax into it. He knew she was saying that she would help, that she and Neal would come with him to Cooley's house, if that's what he wanted.

"I'm going to fetch her myself," James said. "But I will need help getting this house fit for a young girl. You'll have to tell me what she needs."

Ione planted a kiss square on the top of his head and James thought about how he always wanted his mother to do that sort of thing. He watched Ione go, then got up to dump the rest of his meal down the disposal.

Going into the living room, James built a fire, then sank into his recliner. He watched the fire and he watched the pendulums and he thought about things. He thought about Cooley and what it would be like to have her living there. He thought about what it would be like to have anyone living with him. Cooley knew the clocks, she was getting better at it every day, but would she stay out of his way? Would she be underfoot all the time? James looked over at Diana's recliner and pictured Cooley's thin body there, her feet up in a way that Diana's never were, her lap full of homework. She'd probably be full of questions that he couldn't answer.

James wondered what room he should put her in. He wondered if she would stay there and leave the rest of the house to him. Which he knew wouldn't be good, but every time he pictured himself coming around a corner and seeing Cooley, bumping into her as she came out of the bathroom or as she slid down the stairway banister for a snack, James cringed. He was used to living only with his clocks and at times, running into shadows and shapes and scents of the past. What was he going to do with flesh and blood that didn't eventually go home?

James must have thought himself to sleep. But at midnight, he woke up. Or something woke him up. He knew it was midnight.

Because he could hear the dwarf longcase clock. Her alto voice came through his fog, cutting through soft and gentle, just enough to let James know she was there. He turned his right ear toward her and he heard her more clearly, and a few other voices came through as well. But it was the longcase, the grandmother clock, that reached out to James first. He held absolutely still until her song was over and the silence descended again. Then he got up and banked the fire and turned out the lights. On his way out of the room, he stopped by the dwarf longcase and looked long and hard into her face. She was protected by glass, so he leaned his forehead against hers. Her touch was cool.

James went on up to bed. There was nothing else he could do that night. It would have to wait until the next day. Until after school, when Cooley came home.

James waited across the street from the high school. He wasn't sure if Cooley came to his house straight after school or if she stopped at home first, so he thought it best to nab her here. He knew she wanted to escape. He also knew how hard it was to leave.

The ache of that still stayed in his bones. It's amazing how long a person can stay hopeful, even when locked in a dog cage down in the root cellar. Or burned with cigarettes.

Eventually, students began to straggle out, so James figured a bell must have rung. Some moved faster than others, some in groups, some alone. He worried that he would miss Cooley and so he tried not to blink, not even once, as he stared at the front door, hoping she wouldn't exit any other way.

Which she must have, because somehow, she found James. There was a tap on his shoulder and he turned and there she was. Clutching her backpack, she said something and he figured he knew how to answer. The question was clear on her face.

"We're going to your house," James said. "I want to talk to your mother."

She stood completely still, her face blank, the smile that a moment ago was welcoming now stretched to fun house proportions. Then she flushed red and shook her head vigorously. She said something, her mouth moving so fast, her lips and teeth became a pink and white blur, and then she swung away from James. He grabbed her arm. "Listen," he said. "I want to get you out of there. I want you to come live with me."

She stopped and she snapped her arm, forcing him away. When she looked at James, he recognized the expression in her eyes. Ice-blue fear. She twitched and he knew her thoughts. What would her mother do? What would James be like to live with? What would the kids at school say?

What did he want from her?

James could answer the last one. He could answer to anyone who wondered about the situation, who came close to letting the phrase 'dirty old man' into their minds, into their gossip. He would even tell the mayor if it was necessary, if he thought about taking the key to the city back. "You'll have your own room, Cooley," James said. "There's a few you can pick from."

The ice-blue mellowed then and pooled. She blinked rapidly and turned away, walking down the sidewalk. When James touched her elbow, pointed toward his car, she resisted for just a moment more. She looked away, toward the line of houses that stood on the other side of the school. Then she dropped her backpack from her shoulder and threw it into his back seat.

Her house looked normal enough from the outside. It was just a plain ranch, white with black shutters, black metal mailbox with a fancy silver scroll spelling out Dander. James thought of his mother's house, the little cottage he grew up in. James drove out there once, a few years after his mother died. The new family gave it a new paint job, pale green with a bright red door, but otherwise, it was just the same. There was smoke curling up from the chimney and at the time, James thought, Quaint. It's quaint. It's quiet and cozy and quaint. He wondered what that family thought when they went down in the root cellar and found the dog cage, the leftover leashes and chains and collars.

"Look," the man probably said. "She must have kept a poor dog chained down here."

"How awful," the woman would say and they would both shiver in the dampness. Maybe they used it now to store potatoes and onions, the way it was supposed to be.

Cooley looked at James and he nodded. When they went up the steps, he thought he heard something. Tilting his head, he heard it again and he felt the vibration through his feet. Cooley's mother must have the stereo on. James felt and heard the thrum of the bass.

They went into the living room and he saw her, sprawled on the couch, one leg up, the other stretched to the floor. One arm was over her eyes and James thought she was asleep until he saw her mouth open and moving. She was singing along with whatever was on the stereo. There were several empty beer bottles carefully shaped into a triangle on the coffee table. They reminded James of pool balls, all racked up, and he couldn't help but notice how neat they were. They were the neatest thing in the room. Everything else needed a good scrubbing.

But James went cold when he saw the ashtray on the floor by the couch. Several cigarette butts were mashed there and one half-finished cigarette smoked steadily. As he watched, she reached down without opening her eyes, picked it up and took a long drag.

Cooley glanced at James, then crossed the room and switched off the stereo. The thrum left James' ears and it was silent again. His feet stopped buzzing. Cooley's mother hurled to a sitting position, her mouth moving wide, already yelling. Cooley motioned to James and her mother looked. She stopped talking and stood up. She crossed her arms and cocked one hip.

"Mrs. Dander, my name is James Elgin. I run the Home for Wayward Clocks, where Cooley's been working."

She nodded. James noticed Cooley slowly sinking herself into a corner of the room. When James spoke next, she slid down the wall and pulled her knees to her forehead, her arms, hidden in long black sleeves, curling tightly around. She wanted to disappear.

James squarely planted both his feet to make sure he wouldn't disappear with her and he hoped his voice sounded deep and strong.

"I know what you do to Cooley, Mrs. Dander. I'm taking her away. She's going to live with me now."

Mrs. Dander looked at Cooley and the smile she gave was closer to simply baring her teeth. She began to throw words at Cooley and James saw Cooley's grip tighten on her knees. Her head sunk even lower. When Mrs. Dander moved toward Cooley, James saw her mouth widen and he knew Mrs. Dander was shouting. Her hands moved rapidly and one of them still held her cigarette.

James stepped between them. "Stop it!" he yelled and out of nowhere, his voice broke through his ears and he heard "it," bitten off and sharp. But when he spoke again, his voice was gone. "You have a choice, Mrs. Dander. Plain and simple. Either Cooley comes to live with me, or I take her down to Social Services and show them this." James reached behind him, pulled Cooley to her feet and yanked her shirt sleeve back. Cooley leaned against James, her head pressed into his shoulder. But she held her arm out straight, like a bizarre third arm of his own sprouting from beneath his armpit, her palm up, the scars bare and violent in their color across her skin. James noticed a new one since the day before, a simple black hole burned into the bend in her elbow, the skin around it ringed in red. He thought of a bulls-eye.

Mrs. Dander stepped back. She looked at James and the venom made him shake. But he controlled his panic, stopped it as it rose from the floor toward his knees, and he shoved it down. He kept his face stiff and firm, his eyes steady. He wouldn't allow her to see him afraid, not even for a second. A moment of fear was all animals needed to move in for the kill. She turned and left the room.

James pulled Cooley from behind him, pushed her toward the stairs. "Go up to your room and pack everything you can. Even if you have to carry it down in armfuls. Put it in my car. Get everything, Cooley. I don't want to have to come back here."

She pulled her sleeve back down, flexed her fingers, then ran up the steps.

James stood in the entryway to the kitchen and watched Cooley's mother make herself a cup of coffee. With every motion, he saw how her hands shook. Finally, she sat down and wrapped her fingers around her mug. She didn't drink. She just sat there and stared. James wondered if she would cry, but there was nothing. He was glad. If she cried, it would be harder for him to hold firm. He remembered his own mother crying sometimes. He always wanted to make the tears stop. It didn't matter how many times she made James cry; for him, there was nothing worse than watching his mother sink to the floor, placing her face flat against the carpet, and hearing her racking, retching sounds as her hair went from blonde to mud-brown with her tears. James never knew what to do. On those days, he locked himself in the root cellar, volunteered himself to the dark and the damp. Away from the noise. Away from her face and wet hair.

"I'll take good care of Cooley," James said. "She's a good worker. She'll have her own room, she'll be well fed, she'll have a job to put away money for college. Whatever she can't handle, I will. You can come see her all you want. But for now, I don't want her coming here, unless someone is with her." He stopped for a moment, swallowed. "I need to make sure she's safe."

Mrs. Dander glanced up then, just a fast shifting of the eyes, and James saw more hate there than he'd seen in a long time. He remembered looks like that. If he walked by too loudly on his way to the bathroom or school or bed. If he cried when she put him down the root cellar or when she hit him. If he said anything while they ate supper at night. It got so James tiptoed everywhere and he clenched his teeth to keep from making any sound. But the looks were always there.

Now, James clenched his teeth again. It wouldn't work to have them chatter. He would lose Cooley.

He didn't know how many trips Cooley made, he never heard her going up and down the stairs. They just stayed there, the two of them, Mrs. Dander and James, her sitting, staring, not drinking, James leaning against the wall. He locked his knees to keep them from shaking and he tried very hard not to blink. He couldn't let Cooley's mother know how scared he was. That all she'd have to do is raise a hand and he might shrink away. He was so glad he couldn't hear her voice.

Eventually, Cooley came into the room. She looked at James and nodded. Her cheeks were flushed from exertion and he thought he saw a spark of excitement in her eyes. She stood at the opposite end of the table from her mother and said something. Mrs. Dander didn't answer and Cooley said something again, raising her hands up, holding them out. But then, she shrugged and turned, motioning with her head toward the door. The excitement James caught in her eyes was gone. There was nothing there now and he recognized that too. The curtain that comes down, the shield, blocking off everything. He tried to meet her glance, tried to smile, to bring some life back into those eyes.

And that was his mistake, pulling himself away from Mrs. Dander. James never saw her grip her coffee mug, draw back her arm and throw it as hard as she could at Cooley. It crashed into the side of Cooley's face, hot coffee spilling everywhere, and Cooley went down.

But she scrabbled to a corner, so James knew she would be all right, she was conscious. In a breath, he flung Cooley's mother out of her chair and up against the wall. She slid down, but he grabbed her by her shoulders and smacked her against the wall again. Then he drew back his own fist. The river inside was raging, the blood in his parallel veins roaring in his ears. He felt the blackness of pure and rich anger descend down, leaving no sound, leaving no sight, nothing but the feel of power in his fists and the delight and righteousness he would feel when he smashed her face. When he smashed her again. When he left her black and blue and with nothing left to do but howl at a useless moon that allowed the pain to continue and continue and continue.

But in that blackness, James froze. As the dark turned to gray, he saw that Mrs. Dander's eyes were closed, her face squinted shut. Her entire body was braced. A thin line of tears slid between her eyelids.

James was now the stronger one, the bigger one, bearing down on someone much smaller. Someone weaker. Someone he hated with the full force of his heart. All he wanted to do was hurt her. Make her scream in pain. Kill her. As his mother wanted to do with him. As Cooley's mother wanted to do with her.

And from the way Cooley's mother looked now, there was someone else who hated her this way too. Cooley's father? Her own mother?

And as the gray turned to the light of a late afternoon in a kitchen in the middle of nowhere, in the middle of What Cheer, Iowa, James stepped back. There was a choke collar wrapped around his heart, its links running through his blood and through Cooley's too. He knew he had to break it for them both. He had to get her out of there. And he had to leave Mrs. Dander unharmed.

"I changed my mind," James said and he felt his voice shake. Mrs. Dander's eyes flew open and Cooley suddenly appeared at his feet, grabbing onto his shirt, looking up at him, grief deeper than the bruise purpling her face. James shook his head at her and quickly pulled her up, hugging her close. "Not that, Cooley, not that. You're still coming with me." She went limp and James held her up. He turned back to her mother. "I meant I changed my mind about you being able to see her whenever you want. You can't. You can only see her when Cooley wants. It has to come from Cooley. Do you understand?"

Mrs. Dander slid back down the wall. It was her turn now to wrap her arms around her knees, hide her face. James half-carried, half-walked Cooley out to the car. It was loaded with her stuff, filling the trunk and the back seat and the floor. He settled her in the front, carefully buckling her seatbelt, and they took off for home. Their home.

Cooley cried the whole way. She lifted her face to the roof and she wailed. Sounds of it broke through James' ears. Not all of it. But some. And with each broken sound, James became more convinced that he'd done the right thing.

Doc came over to look at Cooley's face. James wanted to make sure that her cheekbone wasn't broken or that the gash from the coffee mug didn't require stitches. Doc settled Cooley in James' recliner and put a cold compress on her cheek. He said a few words to her and she nodded. Doc's voice came to James' ears like a crackle, a static he couldn't clear. Cooley just kept staring at the fire that

James built in the fireplace. She shook so when they got home that James thought she'd need some extra warmth. Ione bundled her in a blanket and gave her a glass of milk and a plate of cookies. The whole house smelled like cookies; James didn't even know Ione could bake.

"Show Doc your arms, Cooley," James said. When she didn't respond, he pulled back her sleeves himself, but carefully. She kept her arms limp.

Doc winced as he looked. He tugged her sleeves back down and patted her hands. She smiled, but just for a moment. Then he motioned for James to follow him to the kitchen. They sat at the table and Doc rested his face in his hands for a few moments before writing in the notebook.

"I'll send over some salve for her burns," he said. "I can't do anything about the scars. But she's out of harm's way now."

James nodded. Doc wrote some more.

"I'm going to bill the girl's parents. I've seen them before, they have insurance. Whatever that doesn't pay and whatever they don't pay, I'll cover."

"I can handle it," James said, but Doc held up his hand. Something in his face made James stop. Cooley was being looked after by a lot of people. There was a lot of good in that and James wasn't going to fight it.

Ione bustled into the kitchen and she happily displayed the empty plate and glass. James realized he'd been looked after by a lot of people too. Ione pulled more cookies out of the oven and set a steaming plateful on the table, along with two mugs of coffee, before she took some more to Cooley.

Cookies suddenly looked like the most wonderful thing on earth. James and Doc both dove in and ate like they were starving. Then Doc tapped James' elbow and pushed over another note. "Did she hurt you too?" he asked.

James shook his head. "No. She wanted to, but she didn't." He paused. "We came to an understanding, I guess, though I didn't talk to Cooley's father."

Doc rolled his eyes and waved his hand and James understood that he wouldn't be talking to the father. It made him wonder about fathers, about how they could just stand by and watch. Or leave and never come back. Even if their intentions were good, even if they didn't want a little boy to have to walk the miles necessary to escape. Even if what kept them away was death.

At least James' mother stayed.

For a moment, he wondered which was worse. To beat a boy, collar him, lock him up in a root cellar, or stand by and do nothing.

I know what happens, son.

James began to think that maybe he hated the wrong person. Or maybe he was just one short.

Imagine.

He felt a poke in his ear and realized that Doc was beside him, otoscope in hand. Holding still, James heard the echo of the instrument moving around and thought he heard Doc's breath. Doc sat down and nodded. All was well.

"Say something," James said.

Doc's mouth moved and James heard the static again, like someone flipping a tuner, looking for a radio station. "I'm hearing crackles," he said. "I can't make out words, but there's sound now."

Doc smiled and gave the A-OK sign. Then he shook James' hand. It felt like they accomplished something together.

To celebrate, James got them both more cookies. But he knew cookies couldn't heal anything.

Cooley chose the room the furthest down the hall from James'. He didn't blame her, this room was an old favorite. It was right above the living room and so it had a fireplace too and he quickly fell into the habit of building one for Cooley every night, even when the weather was warm. She settled her grandmother's acorn clock on the mantel. James just had extra pieces of furniture in there, an old couch, a chair, an end table, furniture that was too good to throw away, but not good enough to sell. He went to the furniture store in town and bought Cooley a bed, a double-sized number that had a bookshelf headboard. He bought her an easel too and some art supplies, but while they stood at the ready by the window, she hadn't touched them. James had the picture of the little girl learning to tell time on his dresser. Eventually, he wanted to have it framed. But for now, he liked picking it up and tracing Cooley's lines and feeling the weight of the paper and the way it rumpled and wrinkled under her pencil strokes.

Cooley spent a lot of time in her room. She helped out after school and had dinner with James, of course. While the Home was open, she busied herself following visitors around, looking like a visitor herself, and she was always right there if someone was about to do something they shouldn't. She was better than the security system. James began taking more breaks when she was around. He still sat in his office, watching people on the cameras, but he sipped coffee and reread the paper too.

Cooley always left her door open, even when she was sleeping, and so he looked in on her as he puttered around at night. She was usually in front of her computer or curled up in a chair, a book open on her lap, but he caught her quite often standing in front of the fire, looking at her clock. She always smiled when she stood there and it seemed like she wasn't even in the room. James could walk in, stand next to her and watch, and she'd never notice he was there.

She showed James around the internet on her computer. And she introduced him to eBay. It was like an online flea market and he just couldn't get over it. The first time she typed in "clocks" in what she told James was a search box, 70,886 items came up. Of course, they weren't all clocks, they were clock parts, clock puzzles, clock toys, but it didn't matter. There was a lot. He couldn't get over how many people were dumping clocks and dumping them like they didn't matter, to people they couldn't even see. The first night, James just kept looking and looking and eventually, Cooley stretched out on her bed and fell asleep. After a few more nights of this, they went out and bought James his own computer. She had to teach him how to work it, but all he really wanted it for was eBay. She kept showing James other stuff, but he didn't care. Clocks started arriving regularly in the mail. It felt wonderful to be able to reach beyond Iowa and rescue them. James even bought one from Africa.

So after a couple weeks, they settled into a routine of sitting in their separate rooms and staring at their separate computers. James knew this wasn't good, but he didn't know what else to do. His hearing was still sporadic and he knew they could talk through the notebook, but he just didn't know what to say anyway.

At night, James watched his mother's anniversary clock spin round and round, the dancers following their worn path. But he held Cooley's drawing. And he wished a thousand times or more that he'd had a different mother, a different father, so he would know what to do now. James hadn't worn a collar in years, but suddenly, he felt chained to his room every night. Cooley was out there, just down the hall, and he didn't know how to reach her, any more than he knew how to reach his mother.

Though James knew Cooley wouldn't hurt him. But it was like there was this wall, a physical wall, that kept him in, just in case. Just in case. Just in case she was dangerous too, just like the rest of the world. The wall was just too big. It was like James' mother managed to glue those locked cellar doors to his mind and he just couldn't get out.

CHAPTER TWENTY-FOUR:

FAT GIRL OUTSIDE
The Miniature Mantel Clock's Story

The Fat Girl kept her private world miniature because she was anything but. Every morning, she shuffled around her apartment and adjusted all of the rooms in a dozen large and fancy dollhouses, moving couches in the Victorian living room, then setting a table in the Colonial, then transforming a child's bedroom into an art studio, a dining room/living room combo into a ballroom. In her own kitchen, the Fat Girl maneuvered her collection of tiny tea sets, arranging and rearranging the cups so that hundreds of fairy guests would have their share of tea. In the living room, she looked in a minuscule mirror, filled with only her mouth as she put on lipstick. She turned over two tiny hourglasses, one brass, one wooden, and checked the time on her miniature mantel clock. Nine o'clock. All this before she left for work in the Large and Luscious Women's Apparel store in the mall.

The Fat Girl hated her job which she took because she thought she blended in which was why she hated it. Everything there was gigantic. Sizes 24, 36 and 48. XL, 2XL, 3XL, 4, 5, and 6XL until the idea of so many X's made her eyes cross. There were shirts that promised to button down, but always gapped open. Pants whose pleats claimed to hide baggy bellies, but cradled them like unborn babies. Underwear that could flap for surrender in the wind. And girdles that lured women in with the promise of never having to come to a store like this again. Her customers bought scores of these, then flew out with large pink plastic bags, secure in the promise that once the girdle slid over their soft thighs and hips and squeezed in their stomachs in an attempt to find a waistline, they could cross the hall and shop at the Petite Sophisticate. The Fat Girl never tried these on. She never bought one. She wasn't blind.

Even the Fat Girl herself glanced over at the Petite Sophisticate on her lunch breaks as she sat alone on the bench outside her store. She no longer ate in the food court; the tables were too small and the looks were too long. So she pulled things out of fast food bags one by one and chewed and thought about going from Luscious to Sophisticated. Luscious. She looked down at her body, spread like an unbaked loaf of bread on the bench. Luscious was only in the store name because it started with an L. Large and Lard-Ass Women's Apparel just wouldn't sell.

But at home, in her miniature world, the Fat Girl could be Sophisticated too. She looked in the dollhouse rooms and spoke out loud about the fairness of the weather, the social events for the evening, the latest promotion or beau or dalliance. Her voice was high and soft and the accent changed from house to house, just a hint of British or gentle southern belle or the lilt of French which she took years ago in high school. She spoke for the dolls in her bedroom too, each having a distinct and refined voice. She turned the hourglasses over every time she strolled by. And she tilted her head, wherever she was, to listen to the delicate sound of the miniature mantel clock chiming the hour.

And she did all this naked. Sophisticated People walked around their homes nude, she assumed. They came home from their high-power, business-suit, do-lunch-eat-salad jobs and they stripped, putting their clothes in wicker and brass laundry hampers, the dry-clean-onlies on padded and scented hangers in their closets. Sophisticated People sighed as the air returned to their exposed, slim, beautiful bodies, their skin reflecting gold in the evening light flickering in the garden window, or rosy pink in the warm glow from the brick and marble fireplace. Sophisticated Women stretched agile cat limbs on black leather sofas and they sipped martinis from crystal stemware. Sophisticated Men stood by the home bar, their sculpted genitals rock hard as they shook another martini for themselves. Sophisticated Women watched and desired.

The Fat Girl did this too, although she had to imagine the genitals. She sprawled naked on her brown corduroy sectional, trying and failing to keep both legs on the cushions at the same time. She drank a light beer and wondered what a martini tasted like. How could something wet be dry? She thought they might taste like Arizona air.

At home or at work, Sophisticated or not, the Fat Girl avoided mirrors, in the bathrooms or the dressing rooms, the front windows of the stores in the mall, or even the minuscule mirror that she used for lipstick. A few dollhouses had mirrors as well and she stood in such a way that no part of her ever reflected.

When it came to slimming down, the Fat Girl tried it all. Slimfast. Weight Watchers. Jenny Craig. Gyms and wraps and hypnosis. She liked the hypnosis, it made her very relaxed, but her hunger never went away. She came home from each appointment, stretched out on the couch, every bone and muscle loose, and ate a bucket of ice cream.

But she tried.

One afternoon, after lunch, she lumbered down the mall to All Things Remembered, a gift shop. She loved it there, although the close aisles and breakables made her very anxious. After many trips, she planned out the best path possible for someone of her girth and she followed it each time, until she ended up in front of a glass showcase filled with miniatures. This was payday and depending on the sales, she could pick out one or more.

She stood there and pondered, her arms pressed tightly against her sides. There was a blue china cabinet she liked, complete with tiny plates and saucers and cups hanging on hooks. It would go well in the Country Dollhouse's kitchen. There was also a clawfooted bathtub and a little toilet, complete with a tank hanging above it with a pull chain. Her Victorian Dollhouse didn't have a bathroom yet. She debated back and forth for a while, wondering which house was more important, which was closer to completion, and then she decided to splurge. It was payday, she had no plans for the weekend, what the hell.

She went to the cash register and told the clerk what she wanted. She watched the girl go through the curtain to the back room, where all the lovely things were kept boxed up. The Fat Girl noticed the snug-waisted dress, the slim legs, the ankles that looked oh so chic in strappy red slingbacks. She looked at her own brown loafers, soles worn down on the inside, giving her heels a tilted look, her body knock-knees. When the clerk returned, she handed over the boxes for inspection and the Fat Girl noticed a large diamond on the skinny left hand. The Fat Girl quickly peeked in the boxes and nodded. "These are fine," she said softly.

Back at Large and Luscious, the Fat Girl found all the other salesgirls in a huddle around several huge cardboard cartons. "Look at these!" one called and the Fat Girl joined in, lifting a long and narrow pink box. On the front was an undoubtedly large woman, but she was also curvaceous and sleek in a full and round way. Inside the box was a long, one-piece body shaper. When the Fat Girl held it up, it flowed from her neck to her ankles.

"It trims everything!" one of the other girls said.

"Get a display set up," said the manager. "Put one on a mannequin."

The Fat Girl went to deposit her things in the back room, then joined another girl by a large squat podium. The girl was quickly stacking the body shaper boxes, so the Fat Girl dressed the mannequin. While the mannequin was large, the Fat Girl always noticed how she wasn't *that* large. She wondered if customers really thought that a body shaper could change the way a mannequin looked. If they thought that a body shaper could change the way anybody looked.

And yet, by three o'clock, the Fat Girl lost count of how many pink boxes she put into pink bags. As the afternoon and evening wore on, she held each purchase a bit longer, looked at it more closely. With her employee discount, it would only cost her forty-nine dollars. Which was less than the miniatures, both of them, combined. If it worked. The Fat Girl doubted it, but she hesitated more and more as she looked into the eager eyes of her customers and listened to their excited chatter. By closing, the Fat Girl noticed not a single body shaper had been returned and so she moved a little slower, studying the curvaceous woman on the slim boxes as she bagged them for each of her co-workers. Everyone else bought one. Even the manager.

It was the Fat Girl's weekend off which meant she was the Friday night closer. She stayed after everyone else, balancing the cash register drawers, straightening up, locking the doors. She stopped and looked at what was left of the body shaper display. The delivery cartons were empty and collapsed in the back room and there were so few pink boxes left, the Fat Girl couldn't even make a pyramid. She formed what she thought was an artful display, the body shapers spinning in a domino row, just one touch would send them falling. She glanced through the front windows and saw that the mall was empty, the lights dimmed. The security guard wouldn't even know she was here. Carefully, her fingers poised, she snatched the front body shaper and took it to the dressing rooms.

Selecting number eight, a number she always thought was lucky and the size she secretly wanted to be, the Fat Girl shut the door firmly behind her. With her back to the mirror, she undressed, then pulled the body shaper from its box.

Stepping into it was like pulling on a spandex noose. The Fat Girl grunted as she pulled it over one thick calf and thigh, then the other. It went over her backside first, then she yanked it over her stomach and she gasped as she felt herself squeezed. She tucked one arm into a strap and pulled until her right breast was squashed, then the other strap came up and her lungs compressed.

Stiffly, her body encased in white elastic (why not pink, she wondered, to match the box?), she stepped back into her clothes. Her pants did feel looser, her blouse didn't gap. She allowed herself one moment to wonder. One moment to wish.

But when she held her breath and turned to look quickly in the mirror, she knew she still couldn't walk across the hall and browse through the racks. She still wasn't Sophisticated.

She turned her back again and pulled her clothes off. When she lowered the straps of the body shaper, her breasts heaved out and down like the waves of the ocean and she could breathe a little easier. She loosened her body, roll upon roll, peeling the shaper down. But as she stepped out of one leg, her ankle caught and she tripped. Twisting sideways, trying to catch herself, she rotated and braced herself on the mirror.

And there she was.

Bent over, elastic halfway up one leg and bunched around the ankle of the other. Breasts folded together and wobbling, backdropped by a pockmarked swaying stomach which was framed by two creased thighs. Her arms, flabby wings holding her body up, flapped.

The Fat Girl shuddered and her body rolled in a huge tidal wave of weight. She felt it pour from her shoulders to her toes and suddenly her legs were too heavy to lift. She felt cemented to the floor, standing there, looking in the mirror, the body shaper crumpled and useless at her feet. Body shaper, she thought. Something to shape this into a body. This mountain. Not mountain. This slag-heap.

She turned slowly and dressed. She kicked the body shaper into the corner, then sent the box spinning after. Grabbing her miniatures, she left. She glanced over at the darkened petite shop, its windows filled with mannequins with no heads, but slender exquisite bodies, clothes clinging, curves and hollows so delicate and lovely. She thought for a moment of putting her hands around those tiny waists, just to see what the sharp bone of ribs felt like, the gentle swelling out of hips and breasts, instead of following formless curves that went forever out and out and out.

She passed the security guard. She saw him glance at her and look away.

On the way home, she began to panic. The seat of her car was thrust all the way back, yet still the steering wheel dug into her stomach. She felt enclosed and she cracked the window to let in some air. She stopped at the grocery store and roamed the health and diet aisles, looking for something new, something untried, a clinically proven miracle, but there were none. She put Slimfast in her basket, then took it out. She put Metabolife in her basket, then took it out. She began to gasp. There was nothing new, nothing here at all. As fast as she could, she stumbled over to the produce section and threw grapefruit in the basket, lettuce, more grapefruit, bananas, then already sliced and peeled carrot sticks and celery.

But she'd already tried it all. She knew the lettuce would grow limp and brown, the grapefruit would turn soft and eventually the whole dripping, moldy mess would have to be scooped out of her refrigerator, and she would chide herself for spending wasted money, hate herself for failing. Tears became trapped in the folds around her eyes. Abandoning her basket, she left the store.

At home, she stripped and her body rolled out over itself, skin against skin, and she felt the relief of freedom. She skipped her beer and sat on the couch, putting the two new boxes of miniatures on her coffee table.

She looked around at her miniature world, so small, so neat. In the dollhouses, the tiny families sat on sofas in front of televisions or radios or nothing at all. Some slept in beds while others cooked in tiny kitchens. The wrists of these little people, the ankles and necks, so thin and fragile, they could be snapped with a bend of the Fat Girl's fingers. As she well knew, from many mishaps when her fingers were just too thick and clumsy for what she wanted to do.

Yet the dollhouse people were all so beautiful. Their delicacy was sharp and refined. Sophisticated.

The Fat Girl leaned forward and watched as her elbows sank into the soft padding of her thighs.

She looked in the kitchens of the dollhouses and she wondered what the tiny people were eating. If they ate lettuce and grapefruit. If they drank diet shakes and swallowed pills. Closing her eyes, she pictured herself newly thin, just as delicate, just as beautiful, in the dollhouse kitchens. But all she saw behind her eyelids was the dressing room mirror full of trembling flesh.

The miniature mantel clock chimed eleven. The sound reminded her that she hadn't eaten. In answer, her stomach rumbled.

The Fat Girl started for her own kitchen, but then she stopped and looked back. The miniature people were there, living out lives so tiny and perfect, the men handsome, the children smart, the women with snug-waisted dresses and diamonds on their fingers. She wondered. She reached for something she hadn't tried.

Opening one of the new boxes, she pulled out the new miniature china cabinet. She set it aside and found the little plates and cups and saucers, all individually wrapped in bubbles. One by one, she opened them, then placed each in her mouth. The sound was delicate between her teeth.

She moved to the dollhouses and began picking out the people, placing them limb by limb in her mouth. Arms and legs, heads and torsos. Each impossibly small, each too tiny to taste. She took them in and felt herself growing smaller.

She moved to her kitchen, picking out the tiniest of teacups and tasted rose petals and gold filigree, green leaves and silver scrolls. When the clock chimed eleven-thirty, she returned to the living room. Turning the clock around, she opened the back and looked in at the miniature workings. She carried the clock to the couch, sat down, and began to pick through and graze.

With each swallow, her body shrank. She could feel it happening. She chewed or swallowed whole until she couldn't anymore, her eyes closed, in her mind the image of herself stepping up to the dollhouses, stepping in, taking the place of the families at the radio, or soaking her tiny body in the new clawfooted tub. She saw herself sleeping in the pink canopied bed, her body lost in the silk sheets and soft pillows. In the morning, she would get up, slip soundlessly to the ground, and go to work, where she would hand in her resignation. They would all stand amazed and applaud as she crossed the hall of the mall to the other store. To the world of Sophistication, the world where waists nipped in and breasts curved out, yet hung proudly high.

Her stomach felt tight. The way it was supposed to feel, her skin snug against sharp hipbones and ribs. Slowly, she leaned to the right and wrapped her arms around herself as she fell into the embrace of the couch. Her breath came easier as she entered this new world, her body floating and impossibly light, and she smiled and felt the lift and stretch of her sharp and prominent new cheekbones. Her world shrank into one tiny black hole. Lifting her arms over her head, her new body poised and taut on the edge, the Fat Girl dove in.

CHAPTER TWENTY-FIVE:

JAMES

And so you wade through the days, the river's unpredictable flow always slipping within you. You hear its roar on a trip to the grocery store where a little boy an aisle over spends an entire half hour shrieking in a temper tantrum with no end. No and No and No and repeat and repeat and repeat, his octaves soaring higher and higher and laced with tears and screams and inhuman grunts and the blood begins to pound in your parallel veins. You try to distract yourself. You hum with the Muzak and you move impossibly fast, not even stopping your cart as you throw things in, cans and boxes flying and rolling like noodles caught in a colander.

Then you round a corner and there he is. You stare at the boy and his horrific mouth, his squeezed-shut eyes and angry skin, and as you listen to the jumble of sounds purged from his throat, you realize how badly you want to hurt him. You realize how good it would feel to bring both your fists, curved and knuckle-hard, against each of this boy's cheekbones, how tremendous it would feel to rip him out of the cart, thrust him over your head, and then power him straight down to the concrete floor. And again. And again. Until the sound stops and nothing is left but the peaceful and predictable rhythm of grocery store music.

Imagine.

But he's a *boy*.

Your entire body shakes with your desire and the boy's howls until you leave the store and burst into the cool air of a beautiful fall afternoon. You breathe deep and wonder. Is this the day it happens? Is this the day your mother rises from inside and forces you out of control? Every day scares you, every day you wonder, but there is something about the vividness of this day, this right-now desire, that makes you feel you're in danger.

Your mother's voice in your ear makes you want to do things that you really don't want to do. Things that you know are wrong. Things that will allow her to swallow you, that will make her leap from your veins into the world again and you so need to keep her buried.

Throughout the day, the river inside you rises and by evening, you are fighting a rapids. The image of that boy spread flat on the concrete grows and you tell yourself, remind yourself over and over, he is an *innocent*, he is a *child*, that's all he is. Yet you see your mother's stick-straight arm, her shaking finger, as she points the way to the root cellar when she declares that you walk too loud, sigh too loud, think too loud. That boy in the grocery store was loud, louder than you were ever allowed to be. Louder than you ever dared to be. How is that fair? You feel the rage roll through your body, and you don't know who it's for anymore, the boy who shrieked, your mother who punished, or yourself for so wanting to grab a child and thrust him to the ground. Is that really what you wanted? Are you sure?

Your mother's face, the day you punched her, once and only once, bobs in the rapids and is gone.

Grabbing your jacket, you go outside, walk quickly down the sidewalk, and hope the action, the movement and the cooling air, will calm you.

But you find yourself at a park. A playground, and since it's growing dark, there are only a few people. You hear a laugh and you see another woman, another young boy, and she pushes him on a swing. Carefully, you move closer. You sit on a bench and watch.

The boy's curls spark gold in the falling sunlight and his shrieks, while sharp, signal joy. The mother sings softly a nonsense song, with each forward and back motion, she sings, "Swing, swing, swing,

swing," the same up and down tune over and over again and it's soothing and monotonous and wonderful.

Desire sweeps down your parallel veins like a log in the river and you are saturated with warmth. In your mind, you swing alongside and the mother touches you in the gentlest of pushes and sings for you too. You hear her voice and her melody and you find yourself wanting to cry. When the mother swoops the child out of the swing and carries him piggyback toward home, you imagine you feel the lift and the gasp, the settle of your pudgy legs around strong, yet soft shoulders. The boy waves at you as they pass by.

Their shadows recede and you lean forward and vomit onto the paved playground surface. You gag and you vomit until you are empty.

So which do you want then? The power, the control, the ability to make the world silent around you when you wish it, to make voices stop, behaviors stop, the smallest of lives stop, just because you say so? Or do you want to be blanketed with a love so deep, so soft and warm, you want only to drape it over your shoulders, wrap it around your knees, and bask?

What will stop your trembling?

As the cold of an Iowa autumn night settles on your skin, you wish for spring. For the warmth of spring, when the deep white snows melt and flow over the ground and join the river, bringing cool crystalline waters to the banks. Cool and clear and pure, winter's ice blending into the heat of a new season.

James wished for spring. He wished for clarity. He imagined a life where the great river flowed, then slowed, then trickled, then stopped, sinking memory deep into the mud. He imagined stepping onto the riverbed, baked into firm and rosy brown clay in the warmth of spring sunshine, and standing there. Rage gone. Fear gone.

His mother. Gone.

Nothing left but to move into the day and spread his arms and breathe. Breathe it all in.

Imagine.

Cooley was with James for three weeks when her father showed up. James was sitting in the control room, reading the paper and half-watching the monitor when a single man walked up the front steps. That was unusual. Most men came with families. If anyone came alone, it was women. For reasons James was never able to figure out, clocks drew more women than men. But this man walked up the steps slowly, looking around and over his shoulder. When he came in the front hallway, James saw Cooley look up from where she stood in front of the dwarf longcase, giving her her once-a-month wind. And Cooley stopped, her hands on the chains, forcing the clock to hold its breath.

James wasn't sure which one he was thinking to save, Cooley or the dwarf longcase, but he was out of the room and down the stairs as fast as he could go. By the time he charged into the hallway, Cooley's father had her by the arm and was dragging her toward the door. Cooley didn't seem to be putting up much of a fight. She dug her heels in, but her mouth was tightly clamped shut and so were her eyes. She wasn't yelling, wasn't calling for James.

James yanked Cooley's arm out of her father's grasp. Putting himself between them, he yelled, "Leave her alone! She's staying here now!"

Cooley's father, like his daughter, didn't put up much of a fight. James' ears were registering more and more sounds, but not enough yet to put a whole sentence together. He heard, "…she…wife… never…home…now!" The "now" was the strongest spoken word, his voice raised, and he looked at James then. Only a fast glance, but enough for James to see the drawn-together eyebrows, the cheeks flushed red. Cooley's father balled his hands into fists, but then he quickly stuck them in his pockets.

"Look," James said. "Your wife hurt Cooley. You hurt Cooley too." Her father looked up again, his mouth open, and shook his head vigorously. His breath was strong enough to strip the veneer off the clocks. "Even if you only stood by, you hurt her. She's safe here." James pulled Cooley forward. "She wants to stay here. If you or your wife make any attempt to see her, to get her to come back, I will take her right down to Social Services and report what was done.

I had a doctor look at her, he'd report too. You'd be just as guilty as your wife."

Cooley's father turned away.

He was almost out the door when James heard the word, "Dad," come out of Cooley's mouth. It might have been Daddy, James' ears might have cut out, but he wasn't sure. The blank look was gone from her face and she stepped forward. When she did, her father opened his arms and they embraced.

James didn't know what to do. He wanted to smack her away, to tell her she was being stupid, to ask her why she hugged this man who allowed her to be hurt. But James felt a pang when he looked at them and he had to turn away. He knew it too well, the ability to love the one that didn't hurt, the one that stood by and watched. Or even left. There was just no way to turn the heart off, even if the mind said that this person was just as evil as the other.

So James left them there. He told himself that Cooley wouldn't leave, but the whole time he was in the kitchen, warming coffee, gathering some of Ione's latest baked cookies, his hands shook. When he finally turned to sit at the table, Cooley was there, leaning in the doorway. She said something and James caught the word, "gone." He nodded.

She sat down and opened the notebook. "It's OK," she wrote. "My dad isn't bad. But I'm not going back. I told him."

James could see the sadness in her eyes, in the set of her shoulders. He looked away.

She tapped him on the shoulder. "Come...show...done," he heard her say. She yanked at his arm, so James scooped up the cookies and coffee and followed her. They looked through the house as they went; they were alone. No tourists that afternoon.

Cooley sat in front of her computer. She pointed at the screen. James saw a graph in bright colors, showing the different months of the year. Cooley grabbed a piece of computer paper and wrote, "I'm keeping track of how many visitors we get. I checked thru the guestbook, but not every1 signs. This will help U 2 C what our busiest months R, and which 1s need help. C how the numbers jump once we reached May?" She pointed again at the screen.

Cooley was smart. James always kept track of this himself, by totaling the number in the guestbook at the end of each month. But he had to flip back and forth through the book to compare numbers. Now it was here in front of him, the whole year. "How did you do that?" he asked.

She shrugged. "Show U L8R," she wrote. Then she pointed to the screen again. Another window popped up, this time showing the amount of money taken in each month. She clicked again and it broke it down to each week, then to each day. James thought of the piles of ledgers he kept in the office. Cooley smiled. "I'll show U how 2 do it," she wrote. "But if U want, I can maintain it 4 U."

James nodded, then handed her a cookie. She laughed. They both went downstairs to finish their snack.

James wasn't sure how he felt about her tackling the business this way. The Home for Wayward Clocks was his and his alone, only he knew the numbers, knew how to juggle them to make things balance, to make his life work. After their snack, James told Cooley to do her homework and then he went through the house, visiting, touching the clocks, making sure that all was well. Some clocks he could hear, others still withheld their voices, making him lean against the wall to feel their vibration. James told himself the numbers didn't matter. The clocks mattered. They were still running, still alive. Cooley was just adding her own touches, helping to make things run smoother. But James was still the only one who knew how to repair a clock's broken heart, how to warm its hands and then set it on its path again. Even with Cooley learning from him, she would never know as much as he did. Her heart belonged to one clock. James' went out to many.

The clocks knew this. He could feel it, see it in their faces.

Later that night, after supper, James was downstairs, working on Diana's new body. It was tricky business, getting this movement from a ceramic clock to go inside a wooden one. It was glued before, its smooth side plastered and thick so it would stick to the inside curves and bumps of the flowerbasket, but James didn't want to glue it to the wood. That wasn't proper, it wasn't the way it was done. So he carefully attached little brackets to the movement, making sure they fit the right measurements for the existing screw holes in the miniature mantel clock. He didn't want to create new holes in the clock, causing more stress to the wood. It was painstaking work and a couple of times, James knocked things loose in the movement and had to stop to fix it. He was sweating like a surgeon when Cooley appeared at his elbow. She stood so close, he couldn't move his arms right, so he finally set the clock down and turned to her. "What is it?" he asked.

She opened the notebook. "I want 2 fix it," she wrote.

James shook his head. "Not this clock, Cooley," he said. "I told you, this one's special."

James saw her sigh and he heard, "ALL…special."

She was right. But this was Diana. "Look, just not this clock, okay, Cooley? You're not ready for this yet."

She turned and walked away, going to stare out the door into the back yard. He tried to ignore her, but her neck was strung tight and from time to time, she gave a shudder. Finally, James put the clock down again. "Wait here," he said.

Going through the house, James reached the room just past the living room. It was small, a sitting room of sorts, but he used it simply for displaying clocks. Shelves were the only furniture. In the furthest corner, on the lowest shelf, sat a beat-up odd-shaped mantel clock.

James picked it up. Instead of having the smooth camel's hump, it had a square frame encasing the face. Hidden behind the decorative scroll on the base was a line of electric plugs, like a power strip. It was a handmade job from a high school's shop class. James bought it from an old woman at a rummage sale a couple towns over. She said her son made it, but he moved away and didn't want it anymore. The clock was ugly, but James wondered how her son could give up someone he made with his own hands. At the rummage sale, James held the clock under a maple tree and stroked its rough corners. "Did it ever run?" he asked.

She nodded. "Oh, yes. It ran very well." She sat heavily on her front step. "He just stopped taking care of it." She shook her head. "You know kids."

James didn't, but he handed over two bucks and brought it home. James tried fixing it, but the boy did things to it that he couldn't quite imagine. What were the electric sockets for? There were four knobs placed around the clock face, at each of the quarter hours. They turned, but James had no idea why. Nothing happened when he turned them. There were misplaced parts throughout the whole movement. James just wasn't sure what the boy intended the clock to do. Not wanting to disturb the boy's original vision, not because it was good, but because it was now the clock's soul, James left it alone.

But it would be a good clock for Cooley to tinker with. She was young too. Maybe she could figure out the way that boy's mind worked and restore the clock to what it once was. James patted the clock, then tucked it under his arm for the trip downstairs.

Cooley sat hunched at the workbench, her hand twirling a tiny screwdriver at a frantic speed. Diana's movement, which was two screws away from being firmly attached to the miniature mantel when James went upstairs, now lay in pieces on the bench. James' eyes tunnel-visioned, swooping down onto the movement, the parts, the clock on its side. Anger seared his skin, he felt the heat of the river flooding his body. "What did you do?" he yelled, loud enough that he heard every word.

"Tried…help…just…" James heard faintly. But he didn't look at Cooley. He couldn't see anything but Diana, in pieces again on the table. Shoving Cooley aside, he was conscious of the weight of her as her body flew away. But it was the noise that made him look down.

He'd knocked over the stool that she was sitting on. She was sprawled on the floor, her head against the concrete, looking up at James with an open mouth. The screwdriver was still clenched in her hand.

Something in James recoiled at her wide-mouthed expression. Something in him knew the sound she was making, remembered it, could feel it as it echoed in his own lungs and throat, even if he didn't hear it. But there was Diana. There was the clock in pieces that he would have to once again put back together. Another delay before Diana's heart beat once again.

Kathie Giorgio

James bent down and twisted the screwdriver from Cooley's hand. "Get out!" he yelled. "Get out of here!" Again, each word came through, James felt them falling against his eardrums. His ears rang with the force.

James didn't know how long he worked on the movement before his back began to ache. He didn't know when Cooley left. But when he turned to pick up the stool so he could sit while he worked, she was gone. James glanced at the skeleton clock on the workbench and noted that it was ten o'clock. Cooley was probably in her room, getting ready for bed. James thought for a moment about going up to her, but Diana's clock was insistent so he went back to work.

It was after midnight when James was done. The movement was in one piece again. He only needed to attach it to the clock. But his eyes were so tired and his fingers so shaky, he didn't trust himself to do it right. Diana's heart would have to do without a body until the next day.

James turned out the lights and locked the doors as he went upstairs. Cooley's room was dark, but he looked inside. The first thing he noticed was the acorn clock missing from its place on the mantel. And then he saw the empty bed.

It didn't take long to figure out where she must have gone. There was only one other place she ever called home. James got in his car and drove across town.

Cooley's house was dark. He thought about checking the doors, seeing if they were locked, if he could get inside and climb quietly to her room. But then her parents could call the cops and he didn't want to have that happen. Cautiously, he walked to the back of the house.

The moonlight shone down on a ragtag yard. What was once a garden was now a clumped mass of weeds, though James could see a few daffodils and tulips poking up. A rotting wooden sandbox, filled with more mud than sand, squatted in a corner. There was a rusty swingset. And Cooley sat in the passenger swing, the acorn clock on the seat across from her. James couldn't see her face. He wondered if she was bruised, then he saw again her expression as she lay on the basement floor. Her face was turned toward him; it was the back of her head that hit. But there could be a lump. A bruise well-hidden beneath the purple hair.

James wondered what to say. His mother never said anything. And he knew now that there was never anything she could say to make it right. But James didn't know it then. He remembered wanting her to say something whenever she opened the root cellar doors, whenever she released him from his chain. Something that sounded like a mother. A mother who knew she'd done wrong and was sorry. But James' mother was always silent.

James didn't know how to sound like a father. He wasn't a father. But he had to say something.

When James picked up the acorn clock to sit down, Cooley lurched forward and snatched it from him. Even James could hear the squeak of the swing and he glanced toward the house, to see if any lights came on. "Shhh," he said. Then he sat. "I wasn't going to take the clock, Cooley. I came here to get you."

She wouldn't look at him.

"Look, I'm sorry. I lost my temper, I know I did. I shouldn't have shoved you, I didn't mean to. But I told you that clock was special and I told you to leave it alone. You didn't listen."

Her arms tightened on the acorn clock. James worried that if she squeezed it too tightly, he'd have to repair it again. Reaching out, he touched her hands, hoping she would let go. But she only clutched tighter.

"Cooley," he said. "Cooley, from living here…don't you ever find yourself wanting to hurt someone? Like it's there, under your skin, and it would feel so good to let it out through your fists?"

Cooley's eyes flickered up.

James thought again of the moment he shoved her. Of the anger moving so swiftly through his bloodstream, it washed him away down the river. James thought of that contact, the moment of pushing against her, feeling her body react, feeling her fly through the air, and for just that second, the incredible rightness of the way it felt. That feeling of punishing somebody for doing something wrong. The same way it felt when he hit the cat that scratched him. The boy that taunted him. Diana, once. His mother. Once.

The way his mother probably felt when she hit him.

"The difference is," James said slowly, then stopped to try and find the words. "The difference is that I should know better. And you too, you'll learn to know better too. Because we know how it feels. We know, don't we."

She kept looking at James, but he didn't know what else to say. He didn't want to give her the details, load her down with another painful life. It wasn't time for that. She was supposed to be healing. "Listen," James said. "I do know. Just differently."

He thought they'd have to sit there until morning before she nodded, but she finally did. She loosened her grip on the clock too, just a little, just enough to yank on her sleeves, making sure they were firmly down around her wrists.

"I guess I have to get used to you, Cooley," James said. "I'm not really used to living with someone. It's going to take me some time, okay? That clock...well, it's special, like I said. It belonged to the last person I lived with."

So he told her about Diana. It wasn't any easier to find those words. In a way, it helped that he could only hear a few of them. He had to feel the words, rather than hear them. And by the end, Cooley looked fully at him, her grandmother's clock sitting beside her.

James stood up carefully, making sure the swing didn't rock too much. "I've put clocks first for a long time," he said. "It's a tough habit to break. But I think you should come first now, Cooley."

Her eyes glistened in the moonlight, but then she looked away. She shrugged.

"Let's go home," he said and started to walk away. It felt like a miracle when she fell in beside him.

At home, James waited for a while, giving her time to scrub up, to brush her teeth and change into her pajamas. While he waited, he went downstairs to retrieve the shop clock. It was on the floor, underneath a chair. James must have dropped it in the middle of his anger. He picked the shop clock up, relieved that it seemed to still be all together. It wasn't working in the first place, of course, but he felt like he must have hurt it somehow, just dropping it like the trash. He wiped it off with a damp cloth before bringing it upstairs to Cooley.

She was in bed, but sitting up. The acorn clock was back in its place. James set the shop clock on her lap.

"This is for you. See what you can do with it."

She held it carefully, a frown puckering the skin above her nose. James knew what she was thinking. The same thing he thought when he first saw it. What the hell is it? "I bought it at a rummage sale," he said. "I've never been able to make it work. The lady told me her son made it in shop class at school. You're probably the same age he was when he made it. So I thought you might be able to figure it out."

She smiled.

"I'll set up some kind of table in the workshop for you tomorrow. You can use all my tools and parts, as long as you always put things away and keep things clean."

Cooley got up and set the shop clock next to the acorn. She stood there a minute, the firelight casting a glow on her face. She turned to James and said something so softly, he couldn't catch any of the words. He told her he wasn't able to hear it.

She crossed over to her desk and wrote on some computer paper. "I want 2 stay here 4-ever," she said. "I want 2 take care of the clocks. All of them, but these 2 are mine."

James swallowed and held the paper as she went back to stand in front of her clocks. It was what James wanted too, so many years ago, when he began bringing the clocks into the Home, filling it, the clocks' souls singing and chiming in every room, keeping him company, keeping him from being alone. And now he had someone who could take over for him, when he died, someone who loved the clocks as much as he did. Or almost as much; James didn't think anyone could love them as much as he did.

He didn't think anyone else should.

James blinked and looked at Cooley standing in front of her fireplace. Her lips were moving, but he knew she wasn't talking to him. She was talking to the clocks. It was like he wasn't even in the room anymore. He started to leave, but then stopped and studied her again. He tried to picture her ten years from now, twenty, fifty years. Standing here, in this place, talking with these two clocks. After a day of talking to all the others, scattered around the house.

Clocks James brought home. Clocks she brought home. He saw her spending just a little extra time with his mother's anniversary clock. Because he was no longer there.

She lived there alone. There was no one else in the house. Just the way James had for all those years before Diana and then after she left. He remembered again the warmth of Diana in his bed, the sight of her, still sleepy, as they had coffee in the morning, the way she would hand him keys as he wound different clocks.

All those years of a cold bed. And only a newspaper to share breakfast with. Cooley wasn't alone now, James was there, but in a few years, that could all change.

"No," he said and Cooley turned sharply, her hands wrapping around her own shoulders. Protectively. Keeping the world and James at bay. "Cooley," he said, and he heard his own voice break. "Sit down."

She went to the bed and pulled up her blankets. James sat at the foot. "You can live here forever," he said and he watched as she smiled, the bright smile that he knew held Amy Sue Dander, the real child, blonde hair a halo, blue eyes shining. The child she should have been all along. "But you've got to do other things too."

The smile dimmed and Cooley came back. "What things?" she said.

"I want you to go to college, maybe study art, if that's what you really want to do. Or study something else," James motioned toward her computer, "like business or computers. Whatever it is you want to do. When that's done, then you can come back here to live." James nodded. "Forever, if you want. But bring others too." He thought of Diana, laughing up at him as she bent over a box of clocks from a flea market. "Bring a husband. Have children."

There was a blush, a quiet pinking of her cheeks, a lowering of her eyelashes.

But then the blush went deeper, turning into a deep scarlet flush and James heard every word that Cooley shouted. "I don't want to get married! I don't want any man! I just want to be here with the clocks!"

James sat back. Cooley turned away, curled up by her pillow, hid her face. James thought all girls liked boys. He thought they all wanted to get married and settle down to a life with a husband and children. He knew Diana did. Before she left, they talked about getting married several times. James thought that was where they were headed, until she disappeared.

They were going to have four children. Two boys and two girls. James remembered thinking about that, about holding an infant in his arms, other children playing at his feet. Diana talked about having to raise all the clocks on high, to keep the children from playing with the small parts and pieces. She talked about keeping the children safe, but all James could think about was keeping his clocks safe. He wondered if the children could stay in just one room, a playroom, with their beds and all their things, leaving the rest of the house in peace. Picturing this infant and children, he tried to summon a sense of warmth, of love and fulfillment, but none came. James suggested the children's room to Diana. She turned away and they never talked about it again.

Thinking of that now, with the silent Cooley on her bed, James wondered which room would have been the children's room. And then he thought of the root cellar, the only place besides his bedroom and the bathroom where he was allowed in his own home. His mother's home. But this wasn't like that; the children's room would have had windows and toys and noise and fun. It wouldn't be dark all the time and silent, except for the tick of a Mickey Mouse watch and a Big Ben alarm clock and his own voice, humming quietly to keep himself company. The jingle of a collar.

But as he thought of the children's room, sequestered away in a back corner of the house, he shuddered.

James' mother didn't seem to want a husband and children either. He looked at Cooley, lying perfectly still, and he wondered if his mother ever shouted those words the way Cooley did, ever lay stiffly across her childhood bed like this. James wondered if anybody listened. "Cooley?" he said. He reached out and touched her shoulder.

And it was like she erupted. She swung at James then, talking in a shriek that broke through any remaining swelling in his ears. It was like she had the flu and she was throwing up all over him, retching out the words, and he was frozen, unable to move, unable to do anything but sit there and let her bury him.

She shook and shuddered as she told James about a boy she met on the internet. A boy who wrote her love poetry and who told her he loved her. And he began telling her what he wanted to do to her if they ever met and she listened to him, listened hard. She closed her eyes when she said this, coiled her fingers into fists, and then she stopped shaking and she rose up on her knees, her body as straight and stiff as a stopped pendulum. The rest of her words were aimed at the ceiling, her neck tense and locked, forcing her face up, yet still everything she said fell down on James. He raised his hands as if to ward off her words, but they wouldn't stop coming. So he closed his eyes too and let her story fall.

The boy came to meet her and he turned out to be a man. A large man who took her to a shed in the park and did all those things he said he would do. Even though she was only fourteen years old. Even though she said no. Even though she screamed it until she had no voice.

And like then, she fell silent and the silence tumbled over James like a blanket. A wool blanket, heavy and scratchy and not comfortable at all.

He held still for a moment, then opened his eyes. Cooley stared back at him. She was shaking again and she sank back down onto her heels. She wrapped her arms around herself and James thought about hugging her, about securing her in an embrace other than her own, but he didn't know if it was the right thing to do. So he let his hands hold each other, gripping the fingers until his knuckles popped.

"Cooley," James said and heard his voice break. He cleared his throat. "Cooley, all men aren't like that. They aren't. And…it just never should have happened." James shook his head and when he felt the tears build behind his eyes, he tried to get angry and will them away. But they wouldn't go. "It never should have happened. Not to you." James tried closing his eyes again, so she wouldn't see him cry, but he felt his chin tremble and knew his own body was betraying him. "Not to you, Cooley. Not to anybody."

James felt her hands on his and he looked at her. She was still shaking, a little, and she was crying too. In a soft voice, he heard her say, "You're not like that."

James could hear her and with that, it was all over. The sounds were fully back. He tilted his head and said, "Say that again."

She blinked. "You're not like that," she said.

"Whisper it."

She began to smile. She leaned forward, but he pulled away, wanting to keep the distance, wanting to see if he could still hear, without her being close. "You're not like that," she whispered. Then she said, "You're hearing me, aren't you?"

James nodded and began to shake some himself. "I hear you," he said. He reached out, carefully, not quite knowing what to do, and touched her purple hair. "I'm not like that," he said, trying the words out for himself, and he felt their truth. He tried to picture his mother, sitting at the foot of his bed like this, talking softly to him and touching his hair. He failed. Yet he sat there, in a way his mother never did. "I'm not like that," he said again. "You're right. But I'm not the only one."

She looked away then.

"Just…give it a shot, Cooley," James said. "Go to college."

She shrugged. "I have to pass high school first."

He stood up. "There's no question about that." She smirked. "Cooley, there is no question," he said, trying to sound firm. "You're living here now, under my roof. You will graduate. You will study and get good grades." She shrugged again, but smiled this time.

James stood there a moment longer, even though he felt it was time to go, time to leave Cooley to her own thoughts and return to his own. But he couldn't get the picture of Cooley with that man out of his mind. Cooley with that man and then…what? "Cooley," he said, "did you ever tell anyone this before? Did you tell your mom?" James knew the answer to that before he even got the words out. Cooley lowered her head and that confirmed it. "The police?"

"No. No one."

"So he's still out there." James looked at her computer, feeling watched suddenly, as if that man was on the other side of the gray monitor, his hands braced on the edges, preparing to climb out.

"I haven't seen him since," she said. She got off the bed and moved over to the computer. A touch of her finger and the screen bloomed to life. "I've blocked all his emails, his IMs. I changed my email address." She shrugged. "There's nothing else I can do." She glanced at James. "I'm always afraid he might come back. But he wouldn't know to look for me here."

James nodded. He thought how his home was suddenly not just a safe haven for broken clocks. Then Cooley faced her computer. "James, what about Diana? How long since you've seen her?"

James stopped and leaned against the doorframe, looking out into the hallway. "Forty years or so, I guess."

Cooley looked at him like that was a lifetime. "What was her whole name? Do you remember?"

As if it was possible to forget. "McFarren," James said. "Diana Joyce McFarren."

"Sit down," she said. Her fingers flew over the keyboard and he wondered how she ever learned to find her way through this internet thing. Ebay alone was overwhelming, but Cooley jumped from website to website like a frog on lilypads. He watched Diana's name get entered, over and over again. Different women came up, but their ages were always wrong.

But then Cooley hesitated and James read the newly opened window and he knew it was right. Cooley moved the mouse, preparing to delete the screen, but he put his hand over hers. He needed to read the whole thing. He needed to be sure.

It was an obituary from a Wisconsin newspaper. The Waukesha County Freeman. It was a back issue, from five years ago.

NELSON, DIANA J.

(Nee McFarren) Found peace on April 30, 2000. Age 63. Preceded in death by her husband, Frank and her beloved grandson, Paul. Dearly loved mother of Grace Thomas (Nicholas). Adored grandmother of Mary Elizabeth Thomas and Jeffrey John Thomas. A longtime Waukesha resident, Diana moved here from Dubuque,

Iowa in 1960 upon her marriage to Frank McFarren. The family wishes to thank the staffs of Waukesha Memorial Hospital and Faithful Hospice for their loving care in Diana's final days. Visitation Friday at Anderson & Miller Funeral Home from 4:00—8:00 p.m. Funeral service at First Baptist Church on Saturday at 10:00 a.m. Burial following at Prairie Home Cemetery. In lieu of flowers, memorials to the American Cancer Society are appreciated.

James sat back and didn't stop Cooley from deleting the screen. Diana was dead. Presumably from cancer, given the wishes for donations. He pictured her, her young body next to his, always laughing, always moving. Diana was a whirlwind. Even in sleep, she tossed. Her constant movement left him without the blankets on most nights. Yet the cancer would surely have wasted her away, slowed her down.

James was glad he didn't see it. But he wished he'd been there in between.

"I'm sorry, James," Cooley said. She began shutting the computer down. James watched her work, each click bringing the computer closer to that darkened screen, the static hush as the light died from the monitor.

"It's okay," James said slowly. "She's been gone a long time anyway." He patted Cooley on the back and told her to get to bed. Then he went off to his own room.

He was exhausted. But after an hour of staring at the ceiling, he knew he wouldn't sleep. Quietly, so he wouldn't wake Cooley, James headed downstairs to the workshop. He had to finish Diana's clock. It was even more important now to make sure that some part of her was still alive.

James knew from the obituary that Diana had a daughter and grandchildren. Her blood flowed through them in their own internal rivers, and possibly her laugh and her quick movements and long dark hair too. But that Diana wasn't the one James knew. That Diana grew into a wife who loved another man, someone named Frank, and she became a mother who loved a little girl named Grace. She had grandchildren. James pictured her for a moment, gray-haired, lightly wrinkled, still beautiful as she stood between her husband and daughter and watched the grandchildren tumbling through fall leaves on a Wisconsin lawn. He wondered if she owned clocks. The Diana James knew picked out that ugly flower basket clock at a dusty beside-the-road flea market. She lay nude beside him and he still thought of her every night, leaving room for her in his bed. The soul of that quick and bright Diana was in the movement of the ceramic clock and he had to get it resurrected again.

James stopped at the head of the basement stairs, surprised to find the light on. He knew he turned it off, he always turned it off. Carefully, he crept down the stairs and peered over the banister.

Cooley looked up from the bench. She was working on the shop class clock, its parts already spread out in a systematic mess. A mess James recognized; she learned it from him.

He didn't say anything, but settled down to work next to her.

It only took an hour or so and then James closed the little door on the back of the miniature mantel clock. Resting his hand on its smooth upward curve, he felt the steady ticking. The beat of Diana's heart.

James held his hand there for a minute and closed his eyes. He remembered the moments after lovemaking, the only time he could get Diana to hold still. She folded herself against him, her back to his chest, and he threw his arm over her and cupped her breast. He felt the life thrumming in her then and he felt her now. Warm. And alive. And right here beside him.

Tears threatened again, so James cleared his throat and looked over at Cooley. She sat quietly, her chin propped in her hand, as she studied all the parts in front of her. James felt sorry for the shop class clock, sitting there, gutted. "Rest the clock on some lamb's wool," he said. "Give it a safe place to be while you work on its insides."

Cooley rolled her eyes, but she got out a lamb's wool cloth and carefully settled the clock in it. James cradled the miniature mantel in his hand and started for the stairs. "I'm going to bed," he said. "Get there soon yourself."

She didn't say anything, but James knew she nodded. For the first time, he left the light on in the workroom when he went upstairs to bed. It felt odd, knowing someone was down there working, someone else besides him.

But it felt good too.

James set Diana's clock on his bedside table, in front of his mother's anniversary clock. After he turned out the light, he reached out and cupped the clock, feeling again the warmth of Diana's breast, the rhythm of her heart. It didn't take long to fall asleep.

CHAPTER TWENTY-SIX:

MATCHING
The Shop Clock's Story

It was a tough time to be named Ernesto Viagrasa. It started in kindergarten, where the teacher immediately shortened my name to Ernie and the freckled boy next to me heckled, "Hey, Ernie, where's Bert?" Thus began several years of gay Sesame Street jokes that we were too young to understand, but everyone laughed and repeated them anyway. Why do Ernie and Bert have it in their will that whomever dies first will be buried butt up? So that the one who is left can pop in for a cold one whenever he's up for it. What's Ernie and Bert's favorite part of playing pirates? Swabbing out the poop deck. Ernie and Bert are relaxing in the bathtub with Rubber Ducky. Suddenly, sperm floats to the top of the water. "Hey," Bert yells. "Stop farting, Ernie!"

I learned to walk with my head down. A sympathetic gym teacher called it counting my footsteps. He counted my footsteps into his office one day after school where he got too sympathetic, encouraging me to spill my guts about how hard it was to be Ernesto Viagrasa. When I did, sobbing until my body shook, it took me a few minutes to realize he was no longer patting my hand or rubbing my back. He was stroking my balls and I was already hard. It was scary, but it was the first bit of pleasure I got out of life and so I let him console me through the remaining six years of elementary school. His comfort went deeper and deeper.

Middle school was a two-year blur of being shut in lockers, once breaking my wrist when I tried to block the olive green metal door from slamming on my face. Ducking under the bleachers at the end of gym class and then dashing in at the last minute to change, so I wouldn't have to shower in front of the other boys. Being tailed all the way home as kids made their first attempts at alliteration: "Hey, faggot-fart! Hey, fairy-face! Hey, fag-fucker!"

It was with some relief that I made my way to high school. The school was bigger, it presumably had more places where I could hide. At the orientation at the end of eighth grade, I already tagged several spots: behind the stage in the auditorium, a back hallway with a door leading only to a janitor's room, a spot just outside the school at the top of a wooded hill. And in some distant part of me, that I barely listened to, I knew there was a hope that in a bigger school, there might be more like me. A Bert to my Ernie. Or at least a Rubber Ducky. Someone to just be friends with.

But on the first morning, as I sat in homeroom with all the other squirming freshmen, the teacher taking roll called out, "Ernesto Viagra…sa?"

The room fell into one long peal of laughter. A guy in the front row, a bigger, uglier, more freckled version of my kindergarten heckler, turned and yelled, "Hey, Viagra! What's up?"

I slumped lower in my chair and again recounted the number of hiding places as the teacher attempted to regain control. But she never did and I knew why. The whole time she demanded silence, for the kids to leave me alone, she was smiling.

That night at dinner, my mother asked me how my first day of high school was. I responded by asking her if I could change my name. She looked at me, her eyebrows bumping into each other above her nose. "Ernesto Viagrasa," she said, rolling the r's, filling my name with that fine virile feeling that only her deep voice could give it. I felt regal when she said it, proud, like a large man standing on the edge of a cliff, his hairy muscular arms crossed over his massive hairier chest. "It is a fine name," she said. "Why change it? What would you change Ernesto to? The kids, the teachers, are they calling you Ernie again?" After that first awful day at kindergarten, my mother went on an annual phone-calling campaign, notifying the teacher, the secretaries, the assistant principal, the principal, that her son's name was Ernesto, not Ernie. But she could do nothing about the kids on the playground. And even the teachers slipped, sending home progress notes that always began, "Ernie is having difficulty finishing his assignments on time," and sometimes calling me Ernie right in front of her at conferences. Though it was kind of a relief then; she would fly into such a rage that the bad grades would be forgotten.

"It's not just the Ernesto, Mom," I said. She looked at me, chewing, and she waved her hand, willing me to continue. "It's the Viagrasa."

"The Viagrasa? But why—"

"It sounds like Viagra, Mom," I said and blushed.

When she put down her pork chop, I knew the light bulb had gone off. "Oh, dear," she said. "It looks like another round of phone calls."

I sighed and covered my face with my hands. It was a pose that often got me what I wanted. I heard my mother push out of her chair and then she stood behind me, wrapping her arms around my shoulders, nesting her face in my hair.

"Changing your name isn't for me to decide, Ernesto," she said softly. "You would have to ask your father. It is his name."

My mother resumed her maiden name after she divorced my father. My name was indeed his and it was one small golden goose egg that she never insisted on sending the Junior in my name to school with me.

I helped with the clearing of the dishes, then went to the hall phone to call my father. Although his one-bedroom apartment was on the other side of the state, his voice was always so loud on the phone, it was like he was still there with us. I waited for the usual "how are you" and "how is your mother" to pass before I told him I wanted to change my name. Especially my last name.

He was silent for a moment, then said, "You don't wish to be related to me anymore?"

"No, Dad," I said. "It's not that. It's just …Viagrasa sounds a lot like Viagra. To high school kids, anyway."

He immediately launched into a speech about how the Viagrasa Men were the most manly of men, well-hung, fertile, producing millions of sperm each day and impregnating any woman the magic wand caught in its spell. Each and every time.

Even though he produced only one son. One child.

When the rant was done, I hung up the phone and disappeared into my room. It looked like, "Hey, Viagra, what's up?" was going to be tattooed to my ass for the next four years.

And then hell got hotter. About three weeks after school started, my guidance counselor called me in. She said that I wasn't really supposed to have three study halls, that through some fluke mistake, the two study halls I was to have per year, one each semester, got shoved into one semester, and then somehow a third study hall got thrown into the mix as well. Those study halls were my reprieve, my chance to hide in the boys' bathroom behind the music department, doing homework or reading or simply leaning against a stall with my eyes closed, in my mind hearing a deep voice say, "Ernesto" in a way that was a caress. I was horrified to learn that I was going to have only one study hall from that day on, even more horrified when she dumped me into a gym class, and completely undone when she said with a smile, "Oh, and a shop class too. You'll like that." My immediate tears must have clued her in that I wouldn't like it, not a bit, because she said, "Now, Ernie. All boys like shop class. You'll get to play with tools." And then she blushed a deep scarlet while I sobbed harder.

I tried to hide that afternoon in my stall in the restroom, but the counselor found me anyway. Apparently, she had experience finding kids who didn't want to be found. She walked me to the shop class, her voice a soft drone of nonsensical phrases. I heard things like, "work with your hands" and "be with other boys" and "develop some self-esteem." But I knew as soon as I walked into that room full of jocks and boneheads that nothing she said was true. She didn't even follow me inside; she just closed the door firmly behind me.

There was one table of geeks and the shop teacher led me there. That helped me to relax a little bit. At least I was with others who didn't know a hammer from a screwdriver. But even they laughed when from across the room, the Freckled Heckler yelled, "Hey, Viagra! What's up?"

I braced my knuckles on the old wooden workbench and before I knew it, my mouth opened and I hollered back, "Fuck you, asshole!" Then I froze and so did everyone in the room. Although this seemed the place for language like that, with the nicked wood and the power tools and the smell of carpenter's glue. But it was still school and in school, we only talked that way in the hallways, in crowds where we wouldn't be detected. I cast a glance at the shop teacher, a man who looked the way my mother pronounced my name, and he grinned at me and shook his head.

"Way to fucking fight back, Ernie," he said. Then he threw a book of wood patterns at me. "You missed the first project. Bookends. Now we're making clocks. You're about a week behind, so you'd better get to work."

Freckled Heckler glared at me. "See if you can fucking catch up, fag dildo," he said and I shook a bit. As I looked through the patterns, I planned how I would scoot out the door as fast as I could after class and then duck down less-traveled hallways from that moment forward. I debated whether I should fly home right after school, hoping to outrun Heckler and his gay-bashers, or if I should hang back, hide somewhere, until he'd given up and gone home.

Then the patterns for the clocks caught my attention and my concentration focused down. It was fascinating, really, a mathematical and artistic wonder, the way movements had to be made different ways to fit in different clocks, perform different functions.

The shop teacher stopped by and looked over my shoulder. He told me to pick the outside first, the type of clock I was going to make, then go for the inside. "Match the inside to the outside," he said. "It's easier that way."

Freckled Heckler came by, supposedly to borrow a screwdriver. He grunted at me, "You should make a fag cuckoo clock, Viagra. Have the bird go in the back door."

My entire table sighed and I looked away. We all knew what the jokes meant by now. We weren't kids anymore.

I chose a mantel clock, admiring its smooth lines and reasoning that the long curve like a camel's hump would be easier to do on a scroll saw than something with corners. Five lopsided attempts and one week later, I counted my fingers to make sure they were all still there, and then adapted the design. Straight lines were easier, even if it meant a corner, and so my mantel clock's humpback became square, its edges sharp. No longer a humpback at all, it was a box on a narrow shelf. It was a freak and Freckled Heckler said I probably could identify with it and I didn't fire back with what was now my trademark shop class, "Fuck you, asshole," answer. Because I did identify with the clock. And because it took Freckled Hecker those two weeks to come up with a trademark answer to my trademark retort. "I don't wanna fuck your asshole," he snarled, before I even had a chance to clip the K in fuck, tongue the L in asshole.

But I could lose the Freckled Heckler in the movement of the clock. I put things together, took them apart, played with them, figured out formulas and timing mechanisms and thought about the timbre of sound. The other geeks stood around me and watched, their own simple circle wall clocks finished, as I added more and more functions to my square. I placed four knobs at each of the quarter hours. At the top of the hour, when the clock chimed, I only had to touch that knob over and over and the clock told me what time it was not only in Iowa, but it sang out eastern time, pacific time, mountain time. The other three knobs were fakes, just for show, for balance, as a single-knobbed clock would look stupid. I put in a second hand, a millisecond hand, a nanosecond hand that wasn't very accurate, but it moved so quickly, you couldn't really see it and I knew it was there. Because of my mother, I gave the clock electric sockets, wired it so that when it was plugged in, it could provide power to other appliances. My mother was always swearing at the limited number of outlets in our house, bitching as she had to unplug lamps to run the vacuum or unplug the toaster to turn on the mixer. When she used the bread machine, it sent her into a snarl that could last for hours. My mother would never again have to unplug to plug in. My clock was a power strip that could tell time.

This clock could do it all. Even bring life to other things. I impressed myself by creating it and while the wood was cheap and wouldn't polish to a shine, I tried anyway. When I turned it in to the teacher, I was already a week and a half late and behind on the next project, dollhouses, which we were going to donate to the Salvation Army at Christmastime. The teacher marked me down to a C because I was late, but he put the clock in the showcase, just outside the classroom.

My mother continued her phone-calling campaign. It didn't help, it never did, but the guidance counselor brought me in, asked me to talk about my feelings. I told her no. I told her that as a guidance counselor, she ought to be able to figure out for herself what it felt like to hear Ernie and Bert gay jokes for ten years straight and what it did to a psyche or even a soul to be called Viagra at the tender age of fourteen. She gave me a couple pamphlets on adolescent depression. I threw them away. I didn't see what good it would do to read about something that I already knew intimately.

I told my mother that I was going to change my name and I was going to change it now and if she didn't let me, I would do it on my eighteenth birthday, without her blessing. She regarded me steadily through the steam from her coffee. "So what would you change your name to, Ernesto?" she said.

And I went mute. I never thought past the changing part before. After thinking for several minutes, I finally shrugged. "I don't know," I said. "Maybe John Smith. Even that's better than Ernesto Viagrasa."

She frowned. "You figure out who you are, Ernesto," she said. "When you have the name, tell me. Then I will talk to your father."

So I thought about it. I thought about it while I sanded the floors of my dollhouse, cut windows, added a chimney. I thought about it while I ducked during gym class volleyball, though Freckled Heckler's spiked balls always found my nose. I thought about it while running home after school, cries of "Hey, Viagra! What's up!" stabbing me in the back of the neck. And I thought about it when I snuck out of school during my one study hall and climbed the hill and sat and stared as the leaves changed colors, then fell, then were covered with snow.

But there just wasn't any other name. Trying to match the inside with the outside, all I came up with was Ernesto Viagrasa. But I could hear it spoken the way my mother said it, firmly, with solid volume and graceful R's. So I began to correct people. "It's Ernesto," I said to my teachers, whenever they said Ernie. "It's Ernesto," I said to the geeks at my table in shop class. "It's Viagrasa, asshole!" I shouted at Freckled Heckler and his pals as I stood on the porch to my house. I ducked in before the slew of snowballs hit their mark. If my mother heard me, she never said. But she started making me hot chocolate, meeting me just inside the door with a steaming mug loaded with whipped cream from an aerosol can.

I stayed after school one day to wire a doorbell into my dollhouse. I was behind again, plus I thought an extended stay in the shop on a cold snowy day would get Freckled Heckler to head on home without his daily fix of jibes. As I was getting ready to leave, my dollhouse now merrily singing Westminster chimes whenever the little red button by the little red door was pushed, the shop teacher came in, carrying my clock.

"You can take this home today, Ernie," he said. He set it on my table. "Too bad you didn't get it in on time. You would have gotten an A."

"It's Ernesto," I said and he nodded.

The clock wouldn't fit in my backpack, so I carefully cradled it as I began the walk home. It was getting late and everything was shaded that bluish-gray, the hallmark of evenings during Iowa winters. I felt invisible as I walked home, my shoes not making a sound on the shoveled sidewalks. The silence worked for me and I relished it, the invisibility and the bluish-gray too, grateful that the air wasn't purple with profanity.

So I was surprised when I was knocked forward. The clock left me, flying through the air to land with a soft whoosh in a snowbank. My arms were twisted behind my back and even before I heard the voice, I knew who it was. Freckled Heckler said, "No one calls me an asshole, especially a faggot like you." He and his friends pulled me off the sidewalk and back behind someone's garage.

I went numb before they had my clothes off. Before they packed my penis in snow. Before they kicked me and peed on me. Before Freckled Heckler jammed his dick in my mouth and told me to suck him off so I could taste a real man. I closed my eyes and I did it. They buried me in the snow, face down, so I would be, they said, like dead Ernie, waiting butt up in his grave for Bert to pop in for a cold one.

I couldn't breathe and I took it for as long as I could, until my head swam from the cold and the pain and the lack of oxygen. Then I slowly pushed up through the snow and shook it out of my hair. The bluish-gray was darker now, but with what light was left, I could see they were gone. I got up and dressed, my fingers too numb to push the buttons through the holes, zip up my zipper. I pulled on my jacket, found my backpack, washed my mouth out over and over with handfuls of snow. Then I went to look for my clock. It was almost buried in the snow too, but a corner of its square humpback poked through and I found it right away. It seemed fine, but I wouldn't know for sure until I got home and plugged it in. Walking was painful. Everything hurt.

I saw my mother looking out the window as I moved up the street. She met me at the door, hot chocolate in hand. Hot chocolate she dropped as I tried to climb the steps. The snow was stained brown. It smelled good. The steam looked warm.

"Ernesto!" she cried.

"Mom," I said and then I cried too.

After the emergency room, my mother insisted I eat a bowl of hot soup, drink some fresh hot chocolate, take a hot bath. She put me in bed, covered me to the chin with her own electric blanket and turned it on high. She left my door partway open, a way I hadn't slept in three years.

But as soon as she was out of my room, I got up and plugged in my clock. It worked and I sat and watched the hands go around, waiting for it to chime. In my room, it was ten o'clock central. I reached out and touched the knob. Eleven o'clock eastern. Eight o'clock pacific. Nine o'clock mountain. And I wished I was in any other time zone but here.

I returned to school a few weeks later, after it was all over. My broken ribs and frostbite healed and Freckled Heckler and his friends were sent away, but I learned quickly that it made no difference. Everyone knew. Even the geeks in shop class moved away from me, leaving me to sit alone at the corner of the table. The teacher, someone I hoped might say my name in that deep soft voice I heard in the boy's bathroom, stopped calling me anything at all.

All that mattered was that I was Ernesto Viagrasa, Ernie, Viagra What's-up, a boy who sucked off real men on demand. A boy who curled up and allowed himself to be kicked, to be humiliated. Ernesto Viagrasa was a boy who could disappear butt-up in the snow, waiting for someone to pop by for a cold one.

What mattered was that I matched the inside to the outside.

CHAPTER TWENTY-SEVEN:

JAMES

So what do you do with a ghost in your head, a ghost who drifts through your body in a silent but boiling river? A ghost who wants to come out, but you know with absolute certainty if she did, it would be your destruction. What do you do with a ghost that is your mother, a mother who haunted long before she died?

You decide to visit the graveyard. You've never seen it; when your mother died years ago, you did all the arrangements via the telephone. She was found, you were told, by the mailman who was concerned that so many days of mail were ignored, overflowing the small metal box just outside her front door. He peeked in the living room window and saw your mother, old, gray, tiny, in her favorite place: a sunny spot on the living room floor. You were assured that she died in her sleep.

There was no funeral. She didn't provide one for your father; you didn't provide one for her. She was placed next to him in the ground, under an identical stone, a stone you ordered without ever seeing, and you asked that only her name and dates be engraved. No "Mother." No "Wife." No "Beloved."

You're sure that there were some in the town who thought this was a disgrace. But there were also some, you figured, who just looked the other way, the way they always did. The way they always will.

So now you go back to that little town and for the first time in your life, you go behind the Catholic church and walk through the graveyard. It takes a while, but you find them. They are in the middle of a back row, their stones together, the grass mowed. They are unadorned, no flowers, nothing. You stand at their feet and read their names. Plain. Simple. They wouldn't mean anything to anybody.

Except to you. Imagine. What do they mean to you?

You look at them and you think Mother. Father. And as your eyes start to well, the internal river surges up in you and you stumble forward, lean on the stones, one hand on each. And you feel your connection. To them, to your mother and your father. And you feel the rage that threatens to bend you in half, force you to rip the stones out of the earth, and beat them against each other. Beat them until they are senseless. Beat them until they are no more. Just shattered chunks of stone scattered on the ground. Unintelligible. Unknowable.

But though your arms shake and your breath comes in shudders, you do nothing more than step back, release your touch. Release yourself. Breathe deep. And it is that easy. Like so many years ago, walking away from your mother as she lay bleeding on the ground, it is that easy.

They are here now. You can see them. Their names are plain as day, and their bodies are moldering in simple cheap caskets six feet underground. This is where they will stay. You, stepping back, can leave them behind. Can leave it all behind to decay here, in a small graveyard, under the snows of winter, the leaves of fall, the rich and splendid greens and yellows of spring and summer. It will all fall away to nothing.

But first, you cry.

Your tears flow from the river and as they fall faster, they form streams down both of your cheeks. You feel the heat of them washing your face, then falling away from you onto the ground as you kneel in the grass. As the river empties, you feel weak and alone, and yet, it's not a bad feeling. It's like that moment after a severe case of the flu when you are drained and empty, but know you will recover. Bracing yourself, you raise one knee, then the other, then slowly pull yourself to your full height. Looking around, you notice flowers and cards and plastic decorations on the other graves. You think for a moment about going to the little florist in town, buying some daisies, some carnations. A hint of baby's breath. And leaving the bouquet at the graves. Settled directly in the middle between the two of them.

Imagine.

But you don't. And you know, as you turn your back and walk away, that you never, ever will.

James knew that day that he needed to leave his rage where it belonged. Where they belonged. It all needed to stay there, in two simple and plain grave plots, under two simple and plain gravestones. Their bodies were there. Their sins were there. What better place to lay his rage to rest? Than with those who would understand it the most. Who would deserve it the most.

Imagine.

****

The next morning, Cooley wasn't at the breakfast table. James checked her room and found her bed rumpled from her confessions of the night before, but empty. He stood there for a moment before he made the connection and went downstairs to the workshop. She was there, asleep, her head cradled on her arms as she slumped at the bench.

"Cooley," he said and tapped her shoulder. There was no response. He tapped a little harder, called her name again. Then he touched her hair and was amazed that harsh purple could be so soft. Again, he saw it as blonde, grown out, falling down her back in corkscrew curls. Goldilocks, Shirley Temple. Cooley could be both, though never with the wide blue eyes of innocence. For both of them, innocence left before they even knew what it was, how to spell it. James touched her back, patted it, trying to find the right way to wake a sleeping child, and he felt the muscles tensed even in sleep. "Cooley," he said, a little louder.

She woke and sat straight up, looking around as she tried to place herself. When she saw James, she smiled.

"You must've fallen asleep down here, even though I told you to get to bed," he said. "You've got to hurry…it's almost time for school."

Her smile faded and she nodded. Quickly, she patted the shop class clock and then she ran upstairs. Before she left, she stopped in the kitchen to grab a day-old doughnut and a glass of milk and the few dollars James set out for her lunch. He watched as she ran through the door and down the road, her backpack bouncing against her hips. He tried to tell himself that there was a lilt to her step that showed happiness settling in.

And James wondered what kind of parent he was, if he was a parent at all. Letting a teenage girl stay up all night fixing an unfixable clock. Sending her off to school on a stale doughnut and with money she would use to buy junk.

But he just didn't know how to do it. James thought of the previous night, of shoving Cooley, watching her fall, feeling the blackness come over him that was his mother's shadow, and he shuddered. The anger that hit at times was so hard to control. It was more than anger, it was a rage that slid between his brain and his soul and possessed his whole body, his thoughts, his heart rate, his sight. It was so much more than seeing red; it was being Red with a capital R. But with Cooley, James had to find control. He couldn't do to her what had already been done. What had been done to him. It had to stop here.

James stood in the kitchen, not sure what to do next. What do you do when you know that the seeds of meanness, of cruelty, are already planted inside of you? How do you dig them out, how do you keep them from taking deeper root, from blooming into lush lilies of the valley or the darkest of nightshade? James leaned on the kitchen sink and looked outside. How could he become someone other than who he knew he really was, deep inside?

His mother's son.

James saw Ione coming around the side of the house and he wished for a moment, wished so hard that his fists clenched, that she was his mother. Even though it was physically impossible, James and Ione were close to the same age. And in the end, there was no wishing. There was no other mother for James than the one he had, the one who still flowed through his veins and was responsible for each beat of his heart.

James had to kill his mother. Even though she was already dead. He had to kill her from the inside out.

Ione walked in and set her bag of cleaning supplies on the table. Even when James bought them himself, stocked them in his own cupboards, she insisted on bringing her own. Hers, she said, were graced with her own special touch, her flavor, though she wouldn't tell James what it was. He'd given up trying to convince her to stay home, to clean her own little knick-knack clock store. He gave up because she was stubborn and there seemed to be no getting rid of her. And though he would never tell her, never say it out loud, James gave up because he liked her company.

"Did you have breakfast?" she asked, the first thing she said every morning.

James nodded, then poured another cup of coffee.

"Something other than doughnuts?" she said, waving the bag.

James sat at the table. He knew there was no fighting the eggs and bacon that would be ready in a moment.

While he waited, he pretended to read the paper. Ione prattled away and James thought about his mother, how breakfast was always silent in her house. Most of the time, she wasn't even awake while James got ready for school. He learned to eat things that made no noise, that involved the least amount of opening and closing of cupboards. No cereal, because that meant getting out the cereal, the bowl, opening a drawer for a spoon, taking the lid off the sugar bowl, opening the fridge for milk. He learned to open only one cupboard without a sound, taking out one thing, usually the packaged doughnuts his mother bought at the supermarket. He skipped milk or juice or even old Kool-Aid so that he wouldn't have to open the fridge, slice the kitchen with the interior light. By the time James reached junior high, he'd learned to leave the house early, while it was still dark, and walk into town, rather than waiting for the school bus. He had breakfast at a diner there, or sometimes the bakery.

But that was only on days that James wasn't tethered in the cellar. If he was there, he had to wait for her to release him. Those days, she usually forgot and he ended up not going to school at all.

Ione slid the plate under the newspaper. A mound of scrambled eggs, light, yellow, sprinkled just enough with salt so that James could see the shiny diamond flecks. Four strips of bacon. An English muffin, buttered and fully jellied. So much better than day-old doughnuts, than silent breakfasts, than sitting alone in a diner, the only kid among adults. James set the paper aside. "Thank you, Ione," he said and he felt like a fool when his voice caught.

She looked at him. "You haven't heard a word I said, have you?" she asked.

James shrugged and patted his ears. "Still a bit on the blink," he lied.

She smacked his shoulder. "I saw Cooley on her way to school, James," she said. "When were you going to tell me you can hear completely again?"

He grinned at her and she sighed, then hugged him. "See?" she said. "It's all over. Everything's back to normal. You're okay." She turned away, filling her bucket with her cleaning fluid.

James ate his breakfast and listened to her hum. He wondered if he was okay. He wondered exactly what normal was.

After breakfast, James left Ione scrubbing the floor and went upstairs to his room. Sitting on the edge of the bed, he studied the two clocks on his bedside table. His mother's anniversary clock, the dancers a golden blur in the morning light coming through the window. Diana's miniature mantel, her soul newly risen and warm, the curve of wood so soft and distinctly feminine, the grain shot through with red and orange.

He thought of his mother sitting next to her clock, long before it ever took up residence in James' room. Before he took it, she used to spend her mornings with the clock, sitting on her bed like James did now, watching the dancers spin left, then right, then left again, their feet pushing time steadily forward. She hummed as she watched, a song James never could name, but it was the clock's own song, its signature chime, and he could hear it still, the endless one-two-three of a waltz. When the time came that she stopped humming and spent most of her time going from one sunny spot in the house to the next, James took the clock, placed it on his desk, and admired it as it deserved whenever he was allowed in his room.

The longest time she ever forgot James down in the cellar was when he was ten years old and he had no idea how many days went by. There was no way to tell the passing of time, no windows to show the sun going up, becoming a flat golden quarter on the roof of the sky, then curling back down into the earth again. There were only the cellar doors with just a little bit of light shining through the crack between them. The collar on James' neck grew loose and he pulled as far as he could to the end of the tether to get to a corner to relieve himself, something he knew he'd be punished for later and so he cried. After a while, he didn't go to the corner. He didn't have to. There was no food and once his water bowl was empty, there was nothing to drink. His tongue grew heavy and thick and his arms and legs were stiff. James began to hear things, voices, his father. He thought he saw his father, the shadow tall and wide against the cellar doors, but when James ran toward him, the tether caught and he fell to the floor. James heard his teacher, calling his name. He thought he heard his mother, laughing.

James wasn't sure what made him finally remove the collar. He remembered the feel of it under his fingers, the cold metal of the buckle, the thickness of the leather as he tried to push the flap through, poke out the stem, and the cool breeze when the collar finally fell away. He made his way to the steps and he pushed the doors open. They weren't bolted. She must have forgotten. Just like she forgot James.

It was early morning and as he blinked in the rosy light, James wondered if he'd maybe only been down there one night. If he'd been sick, had a fever, something that made the night seem to stretch on for days. His eyes hurt and he could barely move his tongue. He stumbled into the house and stuck his face under the kitchen faucet. Water spilled over his cheeks and chin as he tried to take it all in. He choked as much as he swallowed. Then he went looking for his mother.

She was sitting in her room, looking at her clock. She saw James and she frowned, as if she didn't recognize him right away. Then her eyes narrowed. "Where have you been?" she asked. "I've been looking for you."

James' voice seemed stuck in his chest. He had to force a whisper. "In the cellar," he said. "You forgot to come get me. What day is it?"

"You should always come when you're called!" She stood up. "I've trained you that way. You know better! I called until my voice was hoarse!"

When she began to come toward him, James tried to run, but his body was still asleep, still hungry and thirsty. So he dropped to the floor. His stomach growled over the beating, which he barely felt. He just waited for it to be over. He heard her humming the clock's song as she stepped over him and walked away. James knew she was in search of the sun. It wouldn't be in the kitchen at that time of the morning, so he felt safe when he rolled himself back to his feet and went in search of food. He was too hungry to worry about the noise. He just ate. He glanced once into the living room. His mother was curled up on the rug like a cat. Her eyes were closed and in sleep, she was beautiful. Her hair was long and blonde and it fell over her shoulders and spread onto the floor. James thought of Rapunzel and he wondered if he could use her hair, climb it, get himself out of the root cellar. Though her eyes were closed, James knew they were the blue of swimming pools in the summertime. She was thin; her arms curled around her body and her elbows stuck out like chicken wings. For a moment, as he ate, James thought about running to her room, grabbing a blanket, tucking it around her. But that might wake her up and then all the beauty would fall away.

After eating all he could, James felt sick. He went to the bathroom and tried not to throw up, but he did anyway. He debated between flushing the toilet, taking a chance on waking her, or leaving the mess for her to find later. He flushed. She didn't move. He went to his room and shut the door.

With the radio on low, James learned it was Saturday. He'd been in the root cellar since Sunday night. He missed an entire week of school.

Kathie Giorgio

James still remembered lying on that bed, crying with dry eyes. There were no tears, he must have still been dehydrated. He stayed in his room the rest of the weekend, slipping out for food and drink only when he knew his mother was asleep. On Monday, when he returned to school, his teacher said she was glad he was better, that she'd called his mother mid-week and learned he had the flu. She let James stay in at recess for three days to catch up on his work.

Sitting on his bed now, James felt his mother beside him. He could feel her weight on the mattress. She was a beautiful woman and he remembered the way his father looked at her. Like she could break. Like she could shatter into a million golden pieces that he could never put together. But James knew she wasn't that fragile. Despite the blonde hair, the blue eyes, the body slim as a twig, her blows were heavy.

James had to kill her. He had to get her out of his life. She was within him, and he had to be purged.

The anniversary clock chimed then, ten o'clock. Then it began to sing and he heard the waltz, heard his mother's voice as she hummed, her head dipping in rhythm. James waited until the song was over, then grabbed the anniversary clock and tucked it under his arm. "Ione!" he called as he ran down the stairs.

She poked her head out of the kitchen.

"I'm going to be gone for a while, probably the rest of the day. Can you watch this place until Cooley gets home?"

"Sure," she said. "Where are you going?"

But James just waved as he hurried to his car, the anniversary clock cradled tightly to his chest.

His mother's house was a couple hours away. He didn't grab a box or newspaper before he left and so for the first few miles, he drove with one hand on the anniversary clock beside him on the passenger seat. He protected it from potholes, from lane changes and bumps, sudden stops and accelerations. But as he drove and the scenery turned into a blur of Iowa's golden cornfields and flowing green oceans of grass, his mind fogged and James began to see impossible photographs. His life, in black and white, never recorded, never preserved on film, but still there, stuck in the folds of his brain, suddenly unfolded and flashed before him like an old-fashioned slide show. Someone showing their vacation pictures. Or family memories.

A bedwetting incident, his mother shaking him, her face a bizarre twirl of cartoon fast motion as his head ricocheted on his neck. The feel of the wall as she threw him and he hit, and suddenly the room stopped spinning and she was there, tall, her mouth wide, words falling out like lit dynamite. His father rushing in then, cradling James, his mother flying out, never to return. Again. James and his father changing the sheets, his father dressing James in jeans and a t-shirt, telling him he had to stay dry, he had to stay clean, then Mommy would come back and James did and she did.

In the root cellar, James' face pressed against the bars of the cage, his fingers no longer small enough to curl in between. He couldn't stand, he could barely sit, the best thing to do was lay on his stomach. Watching her leave, climb the steps, then the slow lowering of the doors. The light growing dim, then dark, just the strip of light between the two doors where they didn't quite meet, then the slide and thunk of the bolt. Closing his eyes. Completing the darkness.

The collar that changed over time. Soft leather of a puppy collar, a bright red, a little bell that rang whenever James moved. It was a sound and he liked it and so he shook his head, reached up with his hands, swatted the bell to light up the dark with the chime. Then it was too tight and she took it away, replacing it with a blue collar, decorated with white bones, no bell, no sound, thicker and stiffer, made his neck sweat. And finally in high school, a black collar with pointed studs like metallic teeth, a fighting dog collar, a pit bull, though James never fought. If he grabbed at the collar, tried to scratch, the studs caught and cut his fingers. James thought about taking it off, daring sometimes, but the fear of her coming down and catching him collarless was too great. The cage, unused, pushed in a corner, James was too big, so the addition of a tether, the steel spoke spiraled into the dirt of the root cellar floor, the chain heavy and easily twisted. It made a sound, there was a sound again, and James ran in circles in the dark, to hear it jingle.

The rolled-up newspaper, the brush, the belt. The belt a special kind, she said, bought especially for James, thin and metallic like a watchband, stretchy, its links pinching as they stung. Yet she bought it for him and when she wasn't there, when she left him in the dark, he would feel for it, find it in its spot on the wall, and he would caress it, feel the coolness against his skin, not stinging, but just there and firm and real.

James' father leaving, his face dim that early morning. His voice so soft, a whisper, a promise to come back, to save. Then gone in the fog.

James' mother telling him of his father's death. James' hand drawing back and then connecting with her face, the elation of fist to cheek, the crunch of bone and the pain shooting up his arm, but in her face too. James saw the pain, watched it bloom in the O of her mouth, the deeper flush of her skin under the newly born bruise, the sound, a soft puppy-whimper from the back of her throat. The joy of the rage that sped through his body, that let James know that he could inflict pain too, that he could make her cry out, stumble back, fall down. The raw power as he stood over her, her angular body crumpled on the grass, her hair streaked with the blood from her nose, and tears that he knew she didn't want to shed on her cheeks. Her pulling herself together enough to stretch out one thin arm, her finger pointed, and she threw the tears away and got her voice to bellow, "In the cellar!" one last time before James brought his foot down hard and fast on her wrist, heard the bone snap, heard the bellow fall away, simmer back to the whimper of a pup.

Recognizing that he could kill her. That James could throw her in the root cellar, strap a collar around her neck, beat her with the belt until her flesh was streaked with the red of blood and the purple of bruise. Clip on the tether and leave her there, climb the steps into the light, and then slam the doors shut, draw the bolt, and go lay in the sun himself for a day, a week, a lifetime. The recognition, and then the turning away, leaving her on the grass.

James shook in the car, the steering wheel trembled under his hand and he had to pull over. The knowledge that he could have had revenge, that he could have killed his mother, and that it would have felt so good to do, fell over his shoulders like a shawl, but without the warmth. Just a cold that felt like fear.

James thought of Cooley, of shoving her aside the night before, his mother's rage boiling up inside from a place he never could find, he never could pinpoint, to dig out, to excise, to throw along the side of the road. Or bury forever. He could never let that happen to Cooley. Not by his hand. She'd already been there, and James had to learn to uncurl his fingers, release the fist, and leave his arm quietly at his side.

The rage was in Cooley too. It was in her mother. The smoldering cigarettes that burned the outside of Cooley's skin were under the surface now and if James was ever to put them out, he had to douse his own rage first.

James took his hand off the anniversary clock and turned back onto the highway. The first bump he hit sent the clock over on its side. James winced, but didn't reach out to stop it, to pick it back up. He left it there, let it be jarred the rest of the way.

James pulled into the wooded road that led to his mother's house, then parked the car some distance away. He wanted to walk through the woods, approach the house from the back, look to see if anyone was home. If the way was clear, he was going to take the anniversary clock down the root cellar and bury it. He was going to bury his mother. He was going to bury her voice, her heartbeat, forever.

James tucked the clock under his arm and grabbed the snow shovel from his trunk. Setting off, he followed the path he knew well from his few afternoons and evenings of freedom. James glanced at familiar trees, remembered climbing them, feeling a joy when he found a branch where he could stretch out and survey the woods, his kingdom, almost like a normal boy. He tripped once and the clock sang a note in protest, but James tried not to hear. It had to be done. It was like a dog that had to be put to sleep; his mother had to be put down. She had to be put out of his misery.

Coming out in the backyard, James stood by a tree and looked around. There were no cars in the driveway, the windows and doors were shut. The house looked well cared for, cheerful in the sunlight.

James moved slowly around it, glancing quickly in windows, but he saw no one. The new owners must be away at their jobs.

James approached the root cellar. He had to put the clock and the shovel on the ground to slide back the bolt, lift the doors. They creaked, then fell away, landing on the grass with a soft thump. The sunlight rolled in and James walked down the gray cement stairs, stippled here and there with the green of moss.

At the bottom, the smell of damp surrounded him and he stopped dead. It was all still there.

The dog cage. The collars, hung on nails on the wall. The tether, screwed into the ground, the chain knotted and red with rust. The brush, filled with dust and cobwebs, rested on a shelf. And the belt, on a special nail all its own, glinting from the sun, shone silver and thin. It was all the same, except for a neat row of garden tools leaning against the wall opposite the cage.

James stood there and felt the world grow dark. It shrank and he slipped away with it, growing smaller, turning into a small boy inside a cage. His fingers curled and he felt the bars cold against his knuckles. He felt the choke of the collar, the sting of the belt. His arms fell loose and the clock and shovel tumbled away.

Then he grew. James felt his life here roaring up from the soles of his feet, up his knees through his hips and torso, bursting out of his head like a white-hot flame. His body stretched and his limbs trembled and he grabbed for the closest tool. A hoe. A sharp-pointed hoe with a wooden handle. His own roar burst through his ears as he ran at the cage and swung, battled the walls, chopped at the collars and the belt, broke the brush, slaughtered the tether. It all flew around James, falling in pieces, collapsing, until he felt his lungs collapsing too and he fell to the ground and sobbed.

When the sun warmed his shoulders, James looked around. Everything was shattered now, bits of leather thrown in with plastic and metal. It was a jumble. Nothing was left. With the sun falling down the steps, he could see all the pieces, big and small, torn and shredded and broken. The air seemed clearer.

James got up and replaced the hoe where he found it. Then he took up a shovel and began to dig. The floor of the cellar was soft from the damp and it didn't take long to excavate a grave. Carefully, he pushed all the bits and pieces toward it. They clanked and clicked and James thought of his mother, of her soul, scattered in the dirt and the dust, and he knew she would soon be gone.

With the last bit of metal and leather and plastic in place, James straightened up and turned toward the anniversary clock. It lay on its side at the bottom of the steps. The replaced glass dome was off, rolled to the side, and the dancers were still, their faces in the dirt. The clock still glowed gold in the sun and though its movement was stilled, he could hear the chime, the soft music of a waltz. James could see the dancers picking themselves up, moving again to the music, but more slowly now, less frantic, their grace smooth as they swirled their way around their familiar path. They shook off the dirt and their feet were light.

Carefully, James set the clock upright. He gave the dancers a gentle spin, willed them to keep going, kicking dirt aside, but after a few rotations, they were still. The clock's heart was stopped.

He looked at the grave, filled with all that remained of his mother. The grave was filled with James too, with the leather that dug into his neck, the belt that sliced his skin.

But the clock was different. Reflected in the gold was the thick quilt of his mother's hair, the softness of her eyes, a smile that made her face gentle as she watched the dancers sway. And in the gold too was a young boy, head resting on his arms, hair blond like hers falling into his blue eyes. There was no anger in the clock, no hatred, just the steady soft beat of the dancers' feet, the passing of time sung out in a waltz.

The clock was innocent. And so was James. So was his mother, before she crossed some undrawn line that took her away from the simplest of loves. Before she moved away from the clock that kept her moving steadily forward and instead just followed the warm patches of sun and the heat of her own dreams.

James filled the grave, smoothing the dirt until nothing remained but a root cellar floor. Picking up the clock and his shovel, he climbed the steps into the afternoon light. His body ached with fatigue as he pulled the doors closed, drew the bolt.

The house was still silent. James felt the need to acknowledge it, to say goodbye, and so he nodded, gave a stiff bow. Then he cradled the clock against his chest and started the walk back through the woods to his car.

There was one stop left, before home. James had to go to the graveyard.

When James got home, Cooley was just walking down the stairs. She pointed at the clock. "What happened?" she said.

"It's a long story," James said. "I'll tell you later." She followed him down the basement to the workroom.

"Ione left supper," she said. "Meatloaf and baked potatoes. It's in the oven on warm." She watched as James set the clock on a fresh piece of lamb's wool and removed its dome. "You're all dirty," she said.

James looked down. His clothes were sweaty and caked with the dirt from the root cellar. His fingernails were black. He had to be clean before he started work on the clock. "You're right. I'd better shower. Then we can eat." As James turned away, Cooley settled at her stool in front of the shop class clock. She picked up a piece, set it down, picked up another. Then she reached for the cleaning solution, filled a small bowl.

"Cooley," James said. She looked up and he hesitated. Then he moved forward. "Cooley, what color is your hair really?"

She blinked, then reached up and touched the short purple strands. "It's blonde," she said. "Sorta like yours. But curly."

James nodded. She was there, he knew it, beneath that purple hair, the baggy clothes. Beneath the sad face. "Cooley, what would it take for you to be Amy Sue again?"

"Amy Sue?" She turned away, began setting the various clock pieces in the bowl. "No one ever calls me that anymore. Not even my mother."

"Ione does."

Cooley smiled. "I know. When she says it, it sounds real. Like that's who I am."

He nodded. "Okay. Then we'll start calling you that. All the time. Amy Sue, come to dinner. Amy Sue, do your homework. Amy Sue, you're doing a good job on that clock." The name sounded odd, felt odd, but every time James said it, Cooley, Amy Sue, seemed to settle deeper into her seat. Her shoulders relaxed. Her fingers plinked at the bowl, swirling around the clock pieces in their bath. Her face softened.

"Amy Sue, you're the most beautiful young girl I've ever seen," James said and watched her cheeks go pink. She ducked her head, but with pleasure, not fear. "I think you should be blonde again. I think it'll help."

She ran her fingers through her hair, bringing up the purple in spikes. "We could dye it, I guess. It'll take a while to grow out."

James agreed. It would take a while. But this house was full of time and they could take all they wanted.

After supper, Amy Sue and James went downtown to the drugstore. They looked at the boxes of dyes and played with the little swatches of colored hair hanging in neat rows until Amy Sue found what she thought was her natural color. It was like James', but shot through with just a hint of red, burnished, a strawberry blonde. The purple toned down, diluted, made pure again in the gold and red fall of curls.

At home, she hung her head over the kitchen sink and James watched while she applied the dye, restored Amy Sue, and when she was done, she combed it out, smoothed it, instead of sticking it up in spikes all over her head. Spikes like the sharp teeth of a fighting dog's collar.

Blonde, her hair fluffed, she suddenly looked years younger. James looked at the long sleeves covering her arms and he thought about the scars hidden there. He knew she was using the ointment Doc gave her, the tubes in the bathroom were steadily growing smaller and flatter. But he wondered what would happen if she exposed her arms to the fresh air. To the light. If the sun could tan her arms and smooth the evidence, make it just another extension of her skin, of her body. Of Amy Sue herself.

Tomorrow, then, James would take her shopping. See if he could coax her into short sleeves. At least around the house.

"It's time for you to go to bed, Amy Sue," he said as she sat at the table, the towel still draped over her shoulders. She was finishing off a snack of Ione's cookies.

"Oh," she said and drained her milk. "I was going to work on the clock a bit first."

"No," James said. He cleared his throat, mixed some firmness into his voice. "It's a school night. You need rest. To bed now."

Her face clouded a bit, but James didn't see storms there. He saw just the normal rankling of a teenage girl being told what to do, especially being told against her own wishes. The rage was at bay. Maybe slipping away.

She finally settled for rolling her eyes at James before going upstairs. Later, when he checked on her, her light was off and he could hear her breathing softly in the darkness. The glow from the hallway nightlight set off her blonde hair on her pillow, blonde shot through with red, reflected again on the sleep-warmed pink of her cheeks.

James wondered how anyone could ever hurt such a girl. Yet even as he wondered, he knew. James flexed his fingers, relieved to find them loose, not jammed into a fist.

Downstairs again, James moved through the house, locking the front door, turning off the lights. Around him, the clocks softly sang the hour of midnight and he listened to the chimes and the songs and all the individual voices as if they sang only to him. At that hour, they truly did sing just to James. But in the morning, they would sing to Amy Sue too. Eventually, they would sing only to Amy Sue and to whomever else she brought into this house. They would go on singing, long after James' own movement slowed and stopped.

But for now, the swinging pendulums and the sweeping second hands moved James forward. Each tick brought him further and further away from the past. Each chime pushed him more firmly into the present and on to the future.

James turned out the last light. The air was filled with the soft steady heartbeat of the clocks. A sound he could hear and always feel. Even in the dark, there was the constant passing of time. James closed his eyes, held his breath, then stepped into the flow.

THE END